Just Matata – Second Edition

BEYOND THE CAPE

SIN, SAINTS, SLAVES, AND SETTLERS

Dear Zohra,
Thank you for all the inspiration that you bring to NTN at every meeting
with love
Braz Menez
Dec 12, 2015

Braz Menezes

Matata Books Toronto

Cover: Design and art direction: Rudi Rodrigues, Avatar Inc. Toronto

Image: Rendering of Portuguese caravel by Rudi Rodrigues - inspired by 'The Storm' (acrylic 61cm x 76cm) by the Late Leonie Menezes.

Book design & layout: bookdesign.ca

Library and Archives Canada Cataloguing in Publication

Menezes, Braz

[Just matata]

    Beyond the Cape : sins, saints, slaves and settlers

/ Braz Menezes. -- Second edition.

(Book one of the Matata trilogy)

Previously published under title: Just matata.

Issued in print and electronic formats.

ISBN 978-0-9877963-4-9 (paperback).--ISBN 978-0-9877963-5-6

(epub).--ISBN 978-0-9877963-6-3 (mobi)

    I. Title. II. Title: Just matata. III. Series: Menezes, Braz.

Matata trilogy ; bk. 1.

PS8626 E55 J87 2015   C813'.6   C2015-908140-8

                                                 C2015-908265-X

Matata Books Toronto. Contact: matatabooks@gmail.com   web: matatabooks.com

Contents

Dedication

For my Readers

Who took a chance on my debut novel

Just Matata –Sin, Saints and Settlers

And then sent me such heart-warming letters and reviews.

Thank you

BRITAIN
London
PORTUGAL
Lisbon
MEDITERRANEAN SEA
PAKISTAN
Karachi
INDIA
EGYPT
Muscat
OMAN
Bombay
Goa
MAURITANIA
SUDAN
YEMEN
BAY OF
BENG
Aden
GUINEA
GHANA
ETHIOPIA
ARABIAN
SEA
UGANDA
SOMALIA
SRI LANKA
Kampala
Mogadishu
KENYA
EQUATOR
Nairobi
Mombasa
SEYCHELLES
TANZANIA
Zanzibar
Mahe
Luanda
Dar es Salaam
ANGOLA
Mozambique
Island
SOUTH
ATLANTIC
OCEAN
NAMIBIA
MADAGASCAR
INDIAN
OCEAN
MOZAMBIQUE
L. Marques
SOUTH
AFRICA
Durban
Cape Town
Mossel Bay

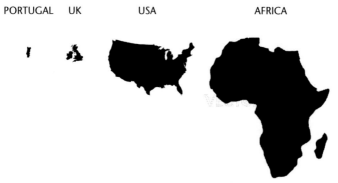

PORTUGAL   UK   USA   AFRICA

B r a z   M e n e z e s

Prologue

An unfinished sea voyage to India by Bartholomew Diaz, a Portuguese nobleman and mariner, changed the course of history for part of Asia and much of Africa.

In early 1488, Diaz's expedition had reached the dreaded Cape of Storms, later renamed the Cape of Good Hope. As the sun dropped low on the horizon, the crews fell to their knees on deck and prayed for divine guidance, seeking forgiveness for any unconfessed sins. At first light they sailed. Gale-force winds, high waves, and foamy spray lashed the fleet. Miraculously, the three ships were blown away from the destructive force of the tempest, as if the Almighty was allowing the angry Atlantic and Indian Oceans to negotiate a temporary peace.

On February 3, 1488, the ships inadvertently landed in a wide bay now known as Mossel Bay, about three hundred kilometres east of the Cape. Diaz and his men were ecstatic. They had managed to cross the southernmost tip of the African continent. For them it must have been equivalent to the moon landing in 1969.

Diaz's achievement hastened an explosion of seafaring expeditions and a land-grabbing competition among European nations, primarily Portugal, Spain, the Netherlands, France, and Britain.

Portugal captured Goa, forcibly rammed Catholicism into the local population with two hundred years of the Inquisition, and culturally transformed Goan society. (As further outlined in the Authors Note.)

In Africa, the arrival of Europeans in the Americas in the 1500s (occurring almost simultaneously with Portugal's arrival in Goa) led to the colonization of vast tracts of land, requiring labour. For the next two hundred and fifty years, enslaved Africans became "black gold" for the white man. The Portuguese took the first slaves to Brazil as early as 1575. Other countries followed to meet demand in the USA.

By the mid-nineteenth century, Africa was like a large pie surrounded by ants nibbling at its edges. The west coast was dotted with slave-trading centres often backed by small fortresses and ports for other merchandise. The east coast trading ports served Arab and Persian slave traders and Indian merchants of Asia-bound trade.

With the discovery of minerals, European attention turned to the forcible colonization of Africa and the carving up of the continent among themselves. The exception was the Cape, where the British had already vanquished the Dutch, forcing them northward into the interior during the Boer War.

The Berlin Conference hosted by Germany in 1884, brought more than a dozen European countries together in an attempt to bring order to the land grab. No Africans were represented.

By the time this party ended, Africa, with a land mass of approximately 11.61 million square miles (almost three times the size of the United States) had been divided into fifty territories. The boundaries were arbitrary and did not respect traditional, ethnic or cultural definitions. These were parcelled out to seven European colonial powers, of which Britain was a major player.

By the twentieth century, British rulers started to colonize East Africa with its own settlers. They needed administrators and accountants, bartenders and bakers, cooks and clerks, musicians and mechanics, engineers and tailors, doctors, and even domestics.

The people of Goa fit the bill perfectly, as they created no *matata* (trouble in Swahili), spoke English, wore Western attire, and drank Scotch whisky. They played card games and cricket. Although they gyrated to the *mando* and *dulpod*, they also danced the lancers, the waltz, and the foxtrot. They were Catholic and considered reliable to handle the public purse strings. Loyal to the point of being docile, they did what they were told. Above all, compared to the cost of British labour, they could be had cheap—very much cheaper indeed. They flocked to East Africa.

What follows is their story as told by an eleven-year-old Goan boy, Lando. It is based on real events as the twentieth century unfolded. This is the second edition of *Just Matata: Sin, Saints, and Settlers*, the first book of The Matata Trilogy, previously published in 2011.

1: My Day of Atonement

Lando," Mom calls out from the kitchen window, "have you and Simba been creating the usual *matata* for Mrs. Gelani?"

"Of course not, Mom," I reply. "Dogs will be dogs. Simba simply loves Mr. Gelani's pyjamas."

"It's not funny anymore," Mom says. "You promised you would train him, so try harder." I apologize.

Seeking absolution has be- come second nature since I live in a constant state of guilt. On my first Holy Communion at St. Francis Xavier's Church in Nairobi at age six, my older sister Linda had convinced me that World War II started because I was born in 1939.

Simba, a three-year-old Rhodesian ridgeback named for the tan colour of his fur, cocks his ears and trots to my side to express solidarity. *Simba* means "lion" in Swahili. I put my arm around his strong neck as he nuzzles me. He loves his daily runs when he chases after cats, dogs, birds—anything that moves. This after-noon, Mr. Gelani's saffron-and-avocado striped pyjamas on the clothesline proved irresistible, billowing in the breeze like twin windsocks. Simba leaped up to grab them, just as Mrs. Gelani glanced out her window and erupted into a frenzied, screaming, gesticulating fireball.

Simba pushes his big body closer to me. He always responds with blind affection, especially when he hears "matata." He seems to understand that I am in trouble again because of him. I hook his collar to a chain that slides along a galvanized wire in the garden. "I'd better sort out this problem, Simba." I give his neck a final rub and walk into the house.

Mom is chopping vegetables. She ignores my arrival and reaches out to stir a pot simmering on the wood-fired cast iron stove in its soot-covered alcove. I play with the kitchen door, swinging it to and fro, slowly, very slowly, to wring every possible creak from its rusty hinges. Then I rattle the latch to create a knocking sound.

"What is it, Lando?" Mom asks. "You're ten years old now, and you should know better!"

"Mom, it was an accident last Sunday."

"Even if it was, now you have to face the consequences. Just go to Confession as Daddy has asked you to, and learn from this experience."

I see tears in my mother's eyes. "Do you feel sorry for me?"

"No. I'm not crying for you," she says. "If you help me chop some more onions, you'll see they'll bring tears to your eyes, too. Now, please stop that noise and go outside and play. When will you give Simba his bath?"

I stomp out of the kitchen and slam the door.

In the bright sunshine, I feel empathy toward Simba, who is yelping. I too have been on a tight leash this past week. I have been placed under a curfew. I am not allowed out with my friends until after Confession on Saturday, a week away.

Simba and I drift aimlessly around the yard. An olive-green lizard with dark lengthwise stripes pops up on a wall of our neighbour's garage. Instinctively, I grab a rock and throw it. It misses. The lizard darts into nearby shrubs; the rock joins a pyramid below, a silent monument to the many lizards that have tempted fate. Simba leaps into the pile of stones, barking furiously.

"Your aim's getting worse," shouts Jeep, my best friend, who lives on the next street.

I cheer up. "Hey, Jeep, I have to go to Confession. Will you come with me?"

"More matata?"

"Yes. Big matata."

"Lando, I've nothing to confess. Not one little sin."

"Please make one up—then you don't have to do it later," I beg. "I just don't want to go alone. Please?"

After more pleading Jeep agrees.

Braz Menezes

It is a warm Saturday afternoon as Jeep and I set off for Confession dressed in short-sleeved cotton shirts, khaki shorts, and our rubber-soled canvas shoes; our leather shoes are reserved for Sunday Mass and weddings. The jacaranda and bougainvillea are in full bloom.

If we walk along Kikuyu and Forest, roads that mark the legal boundary between the European and Asian neighbourhoods, it will take us thirty-five minutes from my home in Plums Lane to the church. Instead, we take a shortcut. We turn off into Sports Avenue at the European Railway quarters, though it entails some risk of an attack by guard dogs. It will save us about fifteen minutes. We stop briefly by the elaborate brick and wood gateway to the Parklands Sports Club (1906) to gawk. Between the decorative palms, we can see workers repainting the white Mangalore-tiled clubhouse, with its painted green band under the roof.

"Look," I say to Jeep. "They've added a new sign. I wonder why they need a new one?" Below the old sign that reads, EUROPEANS ONLY, a new sign reads, MEMBERS ONLY.

"Dad has a Goan friend who works as an accounts clerk at the Muthaiga Club," Jeep tells me. "He told Dad it's very posh, and that Jews or even lower-class Englishmen can't be members."

"You mean they may have a caste system like Indians?" I say. "I'll ask Dad about that."

The lane is fragrant from overripe yellow berries in the thorny kai apple hedges, but I smell something foul and instinctively hold my nose: it is the smell of shit. The "honeywagon," into which buckets from each house are emptied at night, must have been overflowing. The lane is also used for garbage pickup, which makes it worse.

"I'm scared of these dogs," I say, as a cacophony of barking erupts around us.

"Me, too," Jeep replies. "Just be ready to scoot."

We count nineteen *Mbwa Kali* (BEWARE SAVAGE DOG) warning signs as we hurry past, hearts thumping, before we emerge at the crossing by the European Hospital Hill School. We stop here as we always do, to gape at the extensive green sports fields with its benches placed under shady trees. There is much activity around the swimming pool.

"Imagine if our school had a pool in this heat." Jeep says what I am also thinking. We both go to the Dr. Ribeiro Goan School, and we have nothing in comparison to this.

"At least we have a playing field with some grass," I point out. "I bet African schools have even less than we do."

Ten minutes later we enter our church. We dip our fingers in the holy water font and cross ourselves.

"Good, it's not busy," I say as Jeep dries his fingers on his shirt. I prefer my shorts.

I signal Jeep to follow me. "How about here?" We enter a pew halfway up the nearly empty nave. The first six pews are always reserved for European Catholics, who are mainly Irish.

Jeep kneels, bows his head, and seems to be almost instantly deep in prayer. I glance quickly around to see if I spot any neighbours. Nobody. Then I too kneel and shut my eyes tight to cut out distractions, while I replay in my head the chain of events that led to my curfew.

Suddenly Jeep nudges me.

"We must find out which priest is in which cubicle," he whispers frantically. "You know Father Patrick always asks your name and hands out a minimum penance of ten Hail Marys—there's no maximum." We have learned that priests do not assign penance uniformly, even for identical sins.

"Look for Father Joseph's lineup," I whisper back. "It always moves faster." Jeep looks at me as if he is expecting me to say more. So I tell him, "Your sin's smaller, you go first. "

He eases out of the pew.

I realize I am sweating profusely from the nervousness I always feel before Confession, and also from the church's heat and stuffiness. Even the windows high up are shut; a trapped sparrow flutters high above the altar, looking for a way out. I study the vault with its massive stone pillars, and the silver stars painted on a pale blue ceiling. Surely the night sky with stars should be black? Biblical scenes adorn the large stained glass windows, with the figures of God, the saints, and assorted angels all glowing pink. Inspiration strikes. I have cracked the riddle of our faith! I finally understand why the front pews are reserved for Europeans, why white people always live in nice houses with big gardens and have luxurious clubs, why their children have fancy schools with big swimming pools, why brown people sometimes do not have regular running water, and black people have even less. God is white! I look at the small black-framed oil paintings that mark the Stations of the Cross that are placed around the church at eye level. God and the saints are white there too! I study the paintings again. I look at the stained glass windows. They match the paintings. Everyone is white. I will have to ask Dad about this.

I look for Jeep just as he enters a confessional and pulls across the red velvet curtain. He has forgotten to signal me! I join the line behind a visibly anguished teenager who is furtively peering at notes on a paper tucked in his shirt. He urges me to jump ahead of him. At that moment Father Joseph emerges from the other confessional. Now only Father Patrick is hearing confessions! My heart starts thumping.

Soon it's my turn. I kneel, staring at a closed shutter behind a lattice screen. I hear a shutter close as my shutter slides open, and Father Patrick's deep voice mumbles a blessing in Latin. I inhale deeply.

"Father, I have committed the sin of adultery," I blurt out.

I realize I am so nervous, I have not recited the ritual preamble, so I quickly say, "Bless me, Father, for I have sinned...it's been two weeks since my last confession."

Up close Father Patrick's flushed pink face seems to glow. He slips his index and middle finger between the curtains and peeps at the length of the queue. I panic. This means my confession will be a long one. He pulls the curtain across again, sits back, and peers at me. I give him my name.

"Please tell me all about it…slowly…with all the details."

"It happened last Sunday. It was a big lunch. Senhor Almeida and his family were there. We were eight children in all. Because it was full of adults who wanted to talk to their friends, Dad told me to make sure we all stayed out of the living room; I was to play with the boys while my sister took care of the girls. First we all played hide-and-seek together, but then the girls went off on their own."

"Did you quarrel?"

"No, Father. They just went when my uncle Antonio came and taught us some card tricks. He's very good, and he does them very fast. Then we decided to go out into the backyard where Senhor Almeida parked his shooting brake."

"Shooting brake?"

"It is a Ford wagon with no doors and an empty gun rack behind the front seat. The car battery was almost dead, so it was parked on a slope facing the driveway. To start the engine again, Senhor Almeida just had to release the brake and the car would start to roll."

"Go on." Father Patrick's voice is stern.

"My cousin dared me to drive the car. We all climbed in. I released the handbrake like I had seen Senhor Almeida do, and the car started to roll down the slope. But then I couldn't stop it, Father. Even with my cousin squeezing the handbrake, we couldn't stop it." My throat is dry, and I want to cry. In fact, I want to die.

Father keeps staring straight ahead. "Go on, finish your story."

"He and I turned the steering wheel, pointing the car at an electric pole. I knew that if it bumped against the pole it would stop. It stopped, all right. There was a loud explosion. The wires tied to the pole got yanked away. All the houses around us lost power."

"What happened then?"

"Dad was very angry. Senhor Almeida said he would have to

specially import a new headlight from England, and it would take five months...then he just took his whole family and left, promising never to step into our house again. My dad spanked me and said I was not to go out all week until I confessed and showed I was truly sorry. Mom was sorry that everyone was angry. We had no lights that evening, so we ate porridge by candlelight."

"Why did you confess to the sin of adultery?" Father Patrick's voice seems gentler.

"I have studied the Ten Commandments. All week my parents have been reminding me children should not touch things that belong to adults. For a whole week, it has been adult this...and adult that...and adult this and that... that's how I knew it had to be adultery."

"Good. Now listen!" Father Patrick says. "Sunday was a lesson for you. What you did was wrong—very wrong. Your cousin led you into temptation. You must always resist temptation. You were boastful simply because he challenged you. It is a sin of pride. You wrongfully used property belonging to someone else without getting permission. This is like stealing. Further, you damaged property that does not belong to you. You must respect other people's property." Father Patrick squints through the latticed screen.

"For your penance I want you to recite the Hail Mary ten times and tell God you are truly sorry. Then from tonight and every night for five nights with your nightly prayers, you must recite the Hail Mary ten times. Who is your catechism teacher?"

"Miss Costa," I reply.

"Good. Now, listen! I want you to pay special attention to Miss Costa in class. I shall watch your progress. Now go in peace."

Father Patrick blesses me. I feel a burden has been lifted off my back. I return to the pew, quickly recite my penance and go outside where Jeep is waiting.

"Hey, Lando, what took you so long?" he says. "How much did you get?"

"Sixty Hail Marys! I may have broken a record."

"Sixty? Phew! What sin did you commit?"

"Original sin. Come on, let's celebrate. I'm free again."

We walk to Mombasa Ali's Fruit and Vegetable Stand, a wooden shack near the church and school. Ali's white teeth flash his happiness at our arrival. He selects two mangoes from a cane basket, gently rolling them in his hand, then slices them with two cuts lengthwise and then some crosscuts, before sprinkling salt and chilli powder mix from a perforated metal can.

Jeep and I sit on a thick plank placed across two logs. Surrounded by a deep purple carpet of fallen jacaranda blossoms, we bite into our masala mangoes: slightly unripe, their sweet, tart, bitter, pungent tastes all merging into one. We are already in Heaven.

———————

2: Chico

I have often wondered why Dad wants me to go to Confession so frequently. Besides the all-consuming hold that religion has on our community, perhaps it had to do with his own early life as an orphan in Goa, Portuguese India, and the circumstances that led him to take a trip to Mozambique in Portuguese Africa. He was following in the footsteps of his brother and instead landed in British-ruled Kenya. His subsequent lucky win in securing his future wife (my mom) during a game of poker in Goa, and the challenges both of them faced, surviving the complexities of life during the World War II years in Kenya, may have shaped his thinking.

My father Francisco (Chico) Menezes was born in the village of Raia in Goa early in the twentieth century. Both his parents died unexpectedly when he was just fifteen, and he was brought up by his aunt, *tia*, Filomena. Portugal's declining fortunes shaped his destiny, as they did for most of our people. Desperation and lack of good jobs, and sometimes a desire for adventure, pushed Goans abroad. With Goa's economy in shambles, Chico went to Bombay, the great city three hundred miles to the north in British-ruled India. Bombay was an irresistible magnet for job seekers, drifters, and dreamers. But his work there as a junior clerk left him unhappy, and he was soon back in Goa. By 1920, my father's oldest brother, Nicolau, took a boat to Mozambique and found employment in Lourenço Marques, the capital. Four years later a second brother, Orlando, joined him there. Gripped with wanderlust after having got that far, Orlando decided to trek westward across Africa to Angola, where he hoped to catch a boat to Brazil. Tragically, he died of fever on the way. Chico began dreaming of sailing to Africa, as his brothers had done before him.

"Why Africa?" I asked him once.

"Because it seemed so close," Dad had replied. "Whenever we could we would go down to the beach at sunset and watch the sun drop into the sea. Sometimes we'd see the ships sailing west, vanishing over the horizon. We knew that if we sailed in a straight line, we would bump into Africa."

"Was that why Uncle Nicolau and Uncle Orlando went there?"

"That is why I went there," my father said.

This is my father Chico's story.

In 1928, a lean, moustached Chico and his friends—all single, able young men in their twenties—were on the open upper deck of a steamer heading from Goa to Mozambique; they had signed contracts for well-paying government jobs in Mozambique's cap-ital, Lourenço Marques. Fernando, dark and handsome, was a trained accountant; Manuel (Manu), fair- skinned, rotund, and stocky, was a student of Islamic influences on Portuguese culture; and baby-faced Alfredo (Fredo) was obsessed with public service. Fredo loved bureaucracy so much that he just wanted to work for any government, anywhere.

An almost cloudless dome of blue sky was marred only by the grey smoke from the ship's funnel. Schools of flying fish dipped in and out of the ultramarine waters. Somewhere to the left, music leaked out through a half-open lounge window, while from the far side of the deck, children squealed at play under the watchful eyes of their mothers. The four newly acquainted friends exchanged family details and shared their anguish at leaving Goa. Almost three hours had passed. Ahead, the sun was about to disappear.

At the sound of the dinner gong, cheers went up. Chico held open the heavy door as they stepped over the raised threshold of the lounge and headed for the dining room. Everyone was grateful to the man who had got them their contracts, Senhor José de Milagres Fonseca, popularly known as "Joca," the entrepreneurial owner of the Empresa Fonseca on one of Panjim's main squares. Joca's reach as a recruiter extended from Bardez in North Goa to Salcete in the South.

"My father knows him," someone said. "Joca pays money to anybody in the administration or in a parish who helps him in his deals. He wears that little gold crucifix on his linen jacket as an insurance policy."

The well-groomed, big-bellied Joca had greasy black hair and sported a handlebar moustache; he was renowned for his addiction to money, booze, and voluptuous women. To pay for them, he had close ties, not only with the administration, but also with important Hindu traders and Christian dealmakers. He interposed himself in any negotiation where there was money to be made, and most often collected commissions from all sides.

When Joca first came to visit Chico and his aunt, he told them that Lisbon had contracted him to recruit suitable candidates for special duties in the Mozambique administration. He said he could offer Chico an excellent job and would give him time to think it over, but that he would like a quick response, as the recruits had to arrive in Lourenço Marques within ninety days. Chico was excited. Lourenço Marques! He would meet his brother Nicolau "Nico" there. It took him just seconds to agree.

Within two weeks, Joca had located the rest of his candidates by word of mouth. In Bardez and in Salcete, he raided Sunday

Mass congregations on both sides of the Zuari and Mandovi Rivers. Parish priests were particularly helpful, and he rewarded them well. After all, they had known the families and the young men from the time they were just altar boys. The priests also somehow knew which youths would be eager to leave Goa anyway and provided written references.

Chico remembered how Joca came back to Raia in a horse-drawn carriage, accompanied by a clerk, who stayed outside while Joca walked straight into the open hallway.

"Chico, I have very good news for you," he said. "Your papers are ready. You and the other passengers will travel to Lourenço Marques via Mombasa on the SS *Khandalla* on April 7—that's three weeks from now. That should give you enough time to prepare. The Office of Overseas Territories has issued all the necessary approvals."

He handed Chico a sealed envelope, embossed with the official green, red, and gold emblem of the Republic of Portugal. "Go ahead, open it. It's for you," Joca said. "I insisted that the administration offer you a written preliminary contract."

He watched Chico's eyes. "And look, for you I have negotiated a monthly salary equal to more than three times the advertised official Overseas Territories rate. Nowhere in Goa is such an offer available."

During his stint as a junior clerk in Bombay, Chico had been the one who prepared the red wax seals, but now he was going to break one for the very first time. Nervous and excited, he carefully pulled out the beige-coloured letter with the Republic's monogram. He read it quickly, not fully understanding the contents. The bottom of the fifth page carried a government stamp and a signature in blue ink. He wondered if it was the actual signature of the president of the Republic.

"Thank you, Senhor…Senhor José," he stammered. "This is good news. I was thinking that maybe it would never happen."

Joca wasted no time. "Please sign here," he said, pushing a red leather-covered notebook towards Chico. "I will meet you at the docks to make sure everything is all right." He held out his hand. "Please convey my special consideration and highest respects and esteem to my dear Dona Filomena. She is such a wonderful, lovely, and cultured lady. She is going to miss you so much." He wiped his brow with a silk handkerchief.

Chico walked Joca to the carriage, shook his hand, and rushed into the house to read the contract again. It seemed to cover every detail, including what would happen when the period of employment with the government in Mozambique ended.

"To Joca!" Someone was raising a toast. "Joca!" came the resounding cry from the bar.

Life on board the ship was fun in second class. (It was a whole different scene below). They could spend time in lounges playing cards or board games. On deck they played ping-pong and deck tennis. The steamer rolled from side to side on the open sea anyway, but on the fourth day even walking became impossible; the ship had sailed into a monsoon storm as it approached the Seychelles.

Every night they each dressed in the one formal suit they had packed, then met at the bar. After dinner, if they were in luck, some of the single girls travelling from Bombay to Mombasa (ostensibly to visit relatives, but known to be open to marriage proposals) would stay up to dance. One young woman who was travelling with her family had caught Fernando's eye. She was Clara Esmeralda Albuquerque, and it turned out that her parents, Professor Rodolfo and Dona Dulce, knew everyone there was to know in Lourenço Marques.

Dinner the night before they were to reach Mombasa was a scrumptious affair, with speeches and toasts to newborn friendships. Fernando and Manu dined with the Albuquerques.

"Fredo, let's wait for them in the lounge," Chico said when dinner was over. " They should be joining us soon."

"Do you really believe our Fernando's in love?" Fredo asked.

"I suspect the lovely Clara Esmeralda has set his heart aflutter," Chico said. "Or at least her mother must think so. She's the one who invited Fernando to dine with them, and also invited Manu to provide cover."

In the lounge, Bento Ferns and his Goan Melodies, commenced a medley of waltzes, and some couples took to the floor.

"I wish those two would hurry," Fredo said, "or we won't get our pick of partners."

But when Manu and Fernando joined their friends, Manu was almost frothing at the mouth. "*Puta, puta, filho de puta!* Son of a whore! Joca is a crook—he has cheated us all." He ordered a large brandy.

Fernando was calm but angry. He explained what he had learned at dinner. Professor Rodolfo and Dona Dulce said Joca had played this trick before: the job offers were false; the letters were made up, the signatures forged. There would have been no way of knowing this in Goa, but there were very few vacancies in the administration; the Portuguese economy was in ruins. In Mozambique they would have to bribe people to make appointments for "compulsory exams" for jobs they would find out later no longer existed. The salaries they were offered were absurd; they'd been promised much more than even the head of the government service in Lourenço Marques had received.

"Will the administration help us now that we are on our way?" Chico said.

Manu said he had asked Rodolfo that question, and the answer was a definite no, especially as this was the work of a private trickster. The government would have nothing to do with it. Some of Rodolfo's own friends had been stranded in Mozambique and had used up all their savings. The Portuguese government couldn't afford to get them back to Goa.

Joca and his accomplices in the Goa Administration created all the fake paperwork to raid the public treasury. Lisbon was too preoccupied to notice: it had a turnover of at least eleven presidents between 1910 and 1928 while the monarchists and the republicans struggled for power. The current president, General Oscar Carmona, was trying to restore order with the help of his finance minister, Antonio Salazar, but it was unlikely that they would give priority to scrutinizing Goa's accounts. As for Mozambique, it was bankrupt. For Joca and his collaborators, this was a great time to get rich quickly in Goa.

Chico and his three colleagues discussed their plight. With their anxious voices getting louder and shriller, other passengers in the lounge had started to stare. Chico said, "We can jump ship in Mombasa and find a way back to Goa."

They were interrupted by a PA announcement. "Attention, please! Attention, please! This is your purser speaking. This is a special announcement for those passengers who had been booked in Goa for onward travel to Lourenço Marques. We've been informed that the repairs to the ship *Vasco da Gama of Navegação Fluvial India Portuguesa* have not been completed. There will be a delay of about ten days. During this time the Portuguese consulate in Mombasa will make arrangements for your extended stay. Please report to the consular representative at the docks on disembarkation. For the honour of serving you on the *SS Khandalla*, thank you."

"Did you hear that?" Chico grabbed Fernando. "Ten days! Ten days to find a job!" Almost in unison, they bowed their heads and made the sign of the cross. "God has worked a miracle for us. Thank you, Lord," Chico said.

The party now began in earnest. They did not sleep much that night. Clara Esmeralda had retired early with her parents. The Bombay girls, however, dragged the four friends onto the dance floor. In the grey pre-dawn, they saw a silhouette of land emerge from the darkness. Africa!

Behind them the sun rose rapidly into a brilliant blue sky with a sprinkling of white clouds. As the ship steamed forward, the land seemed to rush toward them. Bright white beaches, lush coconut palms, a dark green jungle behind, and a few buildings tucked into pink coral cliffs came into view. They sailed past Old Harbour where dhows lay moored, and then into Likoni Channel. A pilot boat guided them into their dock. They set foot on Kenya's soil.

"Look at the difference between British and Portuguese discipline," Fredo exclaimed, his sharp brown eyes opened wide. "Have you ever seen such order in Goa?" He stood in awe, impressed by the sheer efficiency of the British bureaucracy. He was looking at the shed that handled large numbers of people. Uniformed officials sat behind a row of desks: the first class passengers went to a desk on the left, those from the second class were processed at three desks in the centre, and the deck class was diverted to desks at the back.

The Portuguese representative, Senhor Aires de Ornelas, had a chest full of medals. He told them the consul had been detained. He said they would each be given a temporary visa authorizing their stay in Mombasa for ten days, and consular staff would guide them to accommodation they had arranged at three rooming houses.

That evening two Goans arrived at their quarters to invite Chico and his friends to the Mombasa Goan Institute, known to the locals as the GI. One of them was a consulate clerk they had met in the customs shed.

"Hello, I'm Antonio Alvares," he said, "but here we have anglicized our names. I am known as Tony, and this is my colleague Theodore Noronha."

"Please call me Tito," the other man said. "Welcome to Africa."

They set off for the GI on Salim Road, behind the Catholic cathedral.

"This Aires Ornelas," Chico asked, "is he a famous hero with that chest full of medals?"

"He is a junior assistant at the consulate," Tony said. "His main responsibility is to greet Portuguese nationals at the docks. Nice man, but shy. They say he acquired those medals at an antiques dealer in Lisbon. People are impressed with a chest full of medals. They become nervous and don't ask questions, just like this morning."

That Friday night the bar at the institute was busy. Everyone greeted them warmly; they exchanged details of family names, villages, marital status, and any previous connections already in Africa. Drinks flowed abundantly. Their new friends all claimed to be homesick for Goa and saw their life in Africa as a short-term economic solution.

"How easy is it to find jobs?" Chico asked.

"You have to be lucky," a man called Eddy said. "You have to be flexible. You may be a Brahmin in Goa, but here the British don't care. If you can work hard, drink Scotch whisky, play cricket, and you do not create any matata for the *muzungu*, you're okay. I am the assistant chief clerk at customs and excise. My family and I are very happy here."

"What's matata?" Chico asked.

"Trouble…no trouble. Nobody wants any trouble here," Eddy said.

"And what's muzungu?"

"What a British or European man is called in Swahili…that's the local language. At first, the muzungus will try and boss you around, but then they settle down. Listen, all of you…here in Kenya our clerks and cashiers keep their government going. Our tailors and cooks keep folks well dressed and well fed…remember that and be proud as a Goan." He ordered another beer.

"Nothing works here…they say there are more jobs in Uganda," said a cigar smoker. "My brother-in-law has just started with Uganda Railways in Kampala, but I hear that Mozambique is good too. I wish I was going with you."

"In my opinion, this is the wrong time to come to Africa," said a man a few paces away, sliding his glass toward the barman for a refill. "Better to have stayed in Goa, if you ask me."

Tony whispered in Chico's ear, "This guy came here two years ago of his own will and hasn't stopped complaining since. In my view, he should just pack up and go somewhere else. Nobody owes him a living!"

"If you're adaptable, something will always come up," someone else offered. "It's by word of mouth: you'll first hear about jobs right here, in this bar." He glanced at his colleagues. "Come every day. We'll let you know if anything comes up."

Chico and his friends spent almost three days taking up numerous invitations to lunches and dinners at the homes of fellow countrymen nostalgic for news of the motherland. They were encouraged to stay on, and they wished they could. Mombasa's hot, humid climate, and its thick growth of mango, papaya, banana, coconut, and cashew trees made it feel like a home away from home. Even the hordes of mosquitoes seemed friendly and familiar.

By Wednesday, however, the job prospects looked bleak. Some of Joca's other recruits had also decided to look for work—four had secured jobs, but as low-paid clerks.

Chico, Manu, and Fredo were beginning to panic, while Fernando remained unperturbed. "If destiny wills it," he said, "I will sail on with my beautiful Clara Esmeralda."

That night two messages awaited them at their lodgings. One was from the Portuguese consulate: the SS *Vasco da Gama* would definitely sail on Monday. The other gave them a list of Goan-owned businesses they could try.

"We have just one working day and the weekend," Manu said. "What do we do now?"

"Pray," Chico said. "Tomorrow let's split and try that list and see what happens." But by sunset the next day, they had had no luck. As they left for the GI, Manu had an idea.

"Why don't we explore Kilindini Road? We have not seen much of Mombasa by night."

A few hundred feet away, they came upon a sign, OLD KILINDINI BAR—GOAN MANAGEMENT.

The small busy outer room served food. A barefooted African waiter, dressed in a vest and a shuka, a striped cloth wrapped from the waist, showed them a table on a rear terrace overlooking a treed garden. The oil lanterns on tree branches could not take away the beauty of the starry sky. The patrons seem to be mainly European men with a sprinkling of Indians.

"Where is the owner?" Fernando asked the waiter in English.

"It is him there, *bwana*, called John." The waiter pointed to a man serving behind the counter of a rustic bar framed in wattle poles and thatched with palm fronds. Soon the waiter was back with the first round of beers. The men drank them quickly.

Fernando stood. "I'll ask the manager to join us. At least we can introduce ourselves."

The waiter returned with beer. A young Englishman who had been watching them from his perch at the bar counter walked over, beer in hand. He dragged a heavy wooden chair over the red cement floor.

"May I join you?" He looked closely at Chico. "I have this feeling we've met somewhere before. I'm Robbie Craig. I used to be in Bombay until ten months ago with the National Bank of India." Chico stretched out his hand and studied Robbie's sun-burned young face. He did look familiar. Could it have been at the bank? But he had only been there a couple of times, during the few months he had been employed in Bombay, and that had been a couple of years ago.

"I'm based here now as the bank's local manager," Robbie said. "You wouldn't consider staying in Kenya and working with me, would you? I'm looking especially for Goan staff in our accounts and cashiers departments."

Chico thought Fernando looked unsure but could tell Manu and Fredo were interested. "I can offer you terms as if you had been recruited in Bombay or Goa," Robbie said. "So while the salary is not high, it includes paid home leave to Goa every five years and a pension. We can talk about the details on Monday."

"Our ship leaves for Mozambique on Monday," Chico said. "For us to change our plans, we must have something in hand by tomorrow."

"You're interested, then?" Robbie asked. "You too?" He looked at Fernando.

None of them could hide their relief. Robbie wrote out an address that was close to where they were. By Saturday afternoon, signed letters and temporary immigration papers were delivered to their lodgings.

Late afternoon on Monday, the four of them waited on the high ground overlooking Likoni Channel. A gentle breeze blew over them in the shade of a giant flamboyant red tree, its flowers in full bloom, periodically replenishing a carpet of vermillion, crimson, and pink petals.

"Here she comes," Manu shouted as he leaped to his feet. The SS Vasco da Gama, carrying the beautiful Clara Esmeralda and their erstwhile travelling companions, steamed into view on its journey to Lourenço Marques. The ship sounded its siren as it passed by, as if to say goodbye. Chico and Fredo put their arms around Fernando as his eyes filled with tears. They watched until the ship was well on its way and its passengers could no longer be seen, but Fernando kept watching until the tiny speck on the horizon disappeared from sight.

———•◆•———

3: Nairobi

It wasn't long before the temporary immigration permits were made permanent. Chico and Manu worked directly under Robbie—Chico as a cashier, while Manu, the historian, attempted to pull together statistics about Mombasa's population. He was surprised to learn that Arabs and Indians had traded along the coast, long before the Portuguese arrived. Fernando and Fredo took up positions in the accounting department of the company. They continued to meet weekly to drink beer.

Chico and his friends soon settled into the GI's social club routine: sports, card playing, bingo, socials, and fundraising for charity. As single men with secure, albeit modestly paying jobs, they were popular. Chico began learning Swahili and two months later he was transferred unexpectedly to the head office in Nairobi.

Having been warned that the baggage car was usually packed with commercial goods, Chico arrived early at the train station in Mombasa to make sure his black metal trunk from Goa, a present from his brother Orlando, would travel on the same train. He wandered around the platform and recalled Manu talking about this railway. It was planned to provide a link from the Indian Ocean to Lake Victoria. Their talk had to do with the discovery of Lake Victoria as the source of the Nile, and about two Goan cooks in the mid-nineteenth century, who, like Chico and his companions, had strayed far from their Goan homeland.

The two cooks had landed in Zanzibar, then became part of the 1862 expedition of the British explorer John Hanning Speke. They were with him when he discovered the exact spot near the village of Jinja where water from the lake cascaded into the River Nile. The railroad had been built because the British needed to move soldiers, munitions, and other supplies to ensure that the water flow to the White Nile was not interrupted by other European powers. The volume of water in the Nile was critical to the economic survival of Sudan and Egypt and British interests there.

Soon the platform bustled with passengers, porters, and peddlers. Chico wondered if some raucous Europeans milling around in the first class area were the upcountry muzungus he had heard about. During his stay in Mombasa, he'd had cordial relations with his European colleagues. He dutifully called them "sir" at work and used "Mr." in front of their first names if they met in a public bar. He walked past them. Non-whites were barred from travelling first class.

Chico boarded the second-class car and entered a four-berth compartment, which he shared with a young Sikh and two men from Gujarat. Like him, they were relative newcomers to the country, and apprehensive about what awaited them in Nairobi. Soon they were so busy talking that darkness enveloped the landscape before they were aware of it. Eventually, they settled down for the night. At first Chico couldn't help sitting upright at every station as the train pulled up to take on more water for its thirsty boilers. For him, rail travel was not a novelty. Everything seemed familiar: almost all personnel on Kenya-Uganda Railways, from the drivers to the stationmasters, were on contract from Indian Railways. Though thousands of Indian workers, as well as Goan engineers, surveyors, clerks, and cooks, had been brought over by ship to construct the railway, and many had stayed behind, the idea that so many would now be running it had never occurred to him. He had assumed Africans would be running it.

The next morning the train groaned and whistled as it climbed through vast swaths of barren land. An hour before the expected noon arrival in Nairobi at 5,450 feet above sea level, the landscape changed. Under almost clear blue skies, the panoramic expanse of the Athi Plains was filled with teeming herds of deer, antelope, giraffe, and zebra. In the distance he saw a range of blue-grey hills that had forced the railway builders to set up camp before tackling the arduous climb to the rim of the Rift Valley. Nairobi was snuggled in a swamp at the base of those hills, and it was packed with muzungus. He felt a slight trepidation.

"Chico, welcome to our beautiful town." Michael, a colleague at the National Bank of India's headquarters, had come to meet him at the station. They had previously met at the Mombasa GI. Michael, in his late twenties, was single and handsome. He told Chico that Nairobi was a great place to live in, but it did have one drawback: a shortage of marriageable Goan girls with a "good family background."

"I'll have to worry about that later," Chico said, laughing. "I have more urgent problems to think about right now—such as finding a place to stay."

"I managed to rent you a room with half board for a good rate," Michael told him. "But Mrs. Coutinho can only let you have it for two weeks while her current boarder is away."

Chico watched two porters heave his trunk onto a rickshaw. With Michael by his side, it was a short ride to Mrs. Coutinho's boarding house on Whitehouse Road behind the railway station.

That evening Chico was introduced to the Nairobi Goan Institute on nearby Campos-Ribeiro Avenue, just a block from the intersection with Government Road, Nairobi's main street. The clubhouse, painted grey, was a long corrugated iron building. It was raised off the ground as protection against white ants and termites, with a veranda that ran the length of it.

"You've got yourselves a fine location," Chico said. "The land alone must have cost a pretty penny.

"Have you heard of Dr. Rosendo Ribeiro?" Michael asked as they climbed the stairs. "He gifted us the land."

The famous Goan, Michael told him, had come to Nairobi around 1900 as a young doctor trained at the Goa Medical School. He ran a small clinic in the crowded Indian bazaar packed with dukas, shops in which each shopkeeper and his family lived in the back. In 1902, Dr. Ribeiro saw that bubonic plague had broken out and alerted the authorities. The muzungus panicked, fearing the disease would spread to their neighbourhood. The mayor gave in to political pressure and ordered the police to surround the bazaar and evacuate everyone. The authorities unceremoniously burned the bazaar to the ground—goods, grains, personal effects, rats, and all.

Hundreds of families lost everything; many went bankrupt. They lived in tents for months with minimal water and sanitation until they were relocated, mainly through fundraising from within their community. But the muzungus were happy, and Dr. Ribeiro was feted and credited with saving the people and the town. The government rewarded him with a big tract of land in the middle of town. He donated a small part of the land so the community could build a social club called the Nairobi Goan Institute and he became its first president. Over the years Dr. Ribeiro became a very wealthy doctor.

Michael pointed to where the doctor lived in another two-storey corrugated iron bungalow. "I must say, he is generous with his donations. Most older folk remember the years he used to make house calls riding a tame zebra."

That night Chico made many new friends. He also learned the lay of the land: whites lived in the higher land on the hill in houses built on large lots with many trees and savage dogs. The brown people, classed mainly as Indians and Goans, were crowded together in the bazaar area and by the railway station, in the zone east of Government Road stretching down to the Nairobi River, and also in the Ngara area, where many civil servants and railway workers lived. On the south side of Ngara, in the area surrounding the railway lands, were treeless, choking, cheek-by-jowl housing units allocated as "native housing" to the Africans.

The next day a nervous Chico, dressed in a light beige-coloured suit and tie, entered the bungalow-type corrugated iron building that was the Kenyan headquarters of the National Bank of India.

"We've been expecting you," Mr. Fawcett, his rotund new boss said, as he shook his hand. "You have an easy name. I'll call you

Chico. You can call me 'sir.'"

Mr. Fawcett quickly walked him by his new colleagues—Goans, Hindus, Muslims, Parsees, and Sikhs. He met two European supervisors. Chico was somewhat shocked that the African uniformed messengers were required to walk barefooted while in the office. A colleague said it was official policy from the top, but perhaps it was a way of ensuring the Africans never forgot their place in the hierarchy.

Chico soon relocated to a more permanent accommodation with five other bachelors who jointly leased a small bungalow. They split costs, including the wages of a houseboy who also served as a cook.

At the Goan Institute, inspired by one of Dr. Ribeiro's speeches, Chico transformed himself into a zealot fundraiser for a Goan school that was still in the planning stages. Up until then the only way for parents to provide a quality Catholic education for their children was to send them to school in faraway Goa or Indian cities like Bombay, Belgaum, and Poona, thus separating them from their parents and their siblings from as young as seven years of age. Upon arriving from Africa, these school-bound children were often greeted by relatives they were meeting for the first time. The fundraising effort bore fruit, and the Dr. Ribeiro Goan School opened its doors in 1932.

From the civil servants who frequented the GI, Chico learned why so many Goans had found jobs in Kenya. When the railway line through Kenya was finished, the colonial government needed to carry more goods and passengers to defray its running costs, so a program to aggressively attract new settlers was started. Large tracts of land were offered to white farmers, including Boers from South Africa. After World War I, cheap land was offered to British soldiers who wanted to stay on after defeating the Germans in Tanganyika. Hundreds of settlers arrived and, as a result, the administration had to get bigger. However, since the cost of bringing civil servants from England was prohibitive, the Western-educated Goans were a cheap, suitable, and efficient alternative.

Chico couldn't help thinking that, had he and his colleagues known this earlier, they could have come to Kenya directly and been spared the anguish of falling prey to Joca's trumped-up recruitment schemes.

———•—•———

4: Anja

Being a carefree bachelor suited Chico fine when he was surrounded by other single friends, but over time all his buddies found brides, some in Kenya itself, others on trips to Goa. As they began raising families, Chico felt lonely, relying for company on friends like Patrick and Leonor, who welcomed him into their home. But in a few years, they began raising a family.

"Uncle Chico, Uncle Cheek-oh, untel teeko," their toddlers cried as they ran to greet him and climb on to his back.

"Chico, you are so good with children, and you love playing with them," Leonor said. "Are you going to be an uncle all your life? Have you thought of marrying and becoming a father yourself?" Although she said it half in jest, Chico got the message.

That evening Chico took a hard look in the mirror, looking for bags under his eyes, pinching and pulling at his cheeks, imagining he had gained as much weight as his friends had after they got married. He added five years to his last birthday. His home leave was due in eighteen months; if he waited another five years to find a bride, he would be thirty-eight. He decided to go back to Goa and look for a wife this time around.

At the first whiff of his marital intentions, a network of matchmakers on both sides of the Indian Ocean swung into action, months ahead of his travel date. Wives of colleagues at work glowingly described the younger sisters and other female relatives they had left back home. By their accounts, all were beautiful, in the prime of their youth, and keen to make a life in Africa. He could not see the forest for all the Brahmin family trees that had been laid out for him to choose from. Meanwhile, his attributes, both real and imagined, had been enumerated in letters from match-makers—some of them posted, others hand-carried by departing passengers on every ship bound for Goa.

In 1935, after seven years away, Chico was headed home aboard a ship in which some of his fellow passengers were carrying letters recommending him as a matrimonial catch. In Goa young potential candidates were being prepared for the arrival of the ship carrying not only Chico but other single, bride-seeking men as well. Some of the more experienced matrons had taken it upon themselves to negotiate the best matches ahead of time.

On the day the SS *Nirvana* steamed into Mormugao Harbour, the docks were crowded with families to welcome homecomers. Chico, however, had no family, as Tia Filomena, his only surviving relative, had died three years earlier. So he was met at the dock by his one close friend, the distinguished-looking Lucas Figueiredo, who had served in the administration under his father in Margao.

"Stay with me for a few days before you face all these women," Lucas told him. "You need a cool head when it comes to thinking about marriage."

The very next day, Lucas suggested that Chico join him in a weekly poker evening.

"I play a little poker, but I'm not a gambling man," Chico demurred.

"Come anyway," Lucas insisted. "You'll enjoy meeting this family."

They would go to the home of Senhor Joachim, a well-estab-lished civil servant, and Lucas suggested that, to make a good first impression, they should arrive in a horse-drawn carriage, though the two houses were only a short distance apart.

The evening air was filled with the fragrance of dama de noite, the night-blooming jasmine. The house sat on a high plinth in the middle of a well-manicured garden dotted with guava and chiku trees, as well as abundant hibiscus and bougainvillea. A well-dressed, neatly coiffed lady welcomed them on the front porch.

"Dona Imelda," Lucas said, "allow me to introduce my friend Francisco Menezes—Chico—of Raia, just returned from Nairobi. You may have known his aunt Filomena?"

"Not just his aunt, but his parents as well," she said. She led them into the living room, where some of the card players were already seated. "Joachim," she said, stopping beside a lean elderly gentleman who was puffing at a cigar, "we have an unexpected treat. This is Lucas's friend Francisco Menezes of Raia, of whom we have been hearing so much recently."

Joachim embraced him. "I remember your parents. Your father was my colleague at work. When they passed away, one after the other like that, they left a void for all of us. But tell me…I believe you were stationed in Africa. Have you returned for good, or will you be going back to Nairobi?"

"I'll be going back."

"Then tonight you must stay for dinner. You too, Lucas. We have much to talk about. But before we get to that, you must meet our friends."

"Do you play poker, Francisco?" Dona Imelda asked. "Everybody who has been to Africa plays poker," her husband said. "What else is there to do over there, aside from hunting lions?" He laughed at his own joke.

Chico barely registered the names he heard and was further distracted by a young woman, struck by the fluidity of her movements as she came in and leaned gracefully against Senhor Joachim's chair. As the cards were dealt, he kept stealing glances at her fair skin, dark eyelashes, silken black hair, and her air of quiet calm. By the time they had played the first hand, Chico had made an assumption and reached a conclusion. The assumption was that the girl couldn't be more than seventeen years old. The conclusion was that she might be the bride he sought.

Chico appealed to his hostess. "Dona Imelda, won't you do me the favour of an introduction?"

"Oh my dear Francisco," she said, "how remiss of me! Allow me to introduce our daughter, Angela Alice…Anja is our eldest."

Anja blushed.

Despite being distracted by her presence, or perhaps because she was there, Chico played well that evening. He felt lucky deep in his bones. Senhor Joachim lost heavily, but it didn't seem to bother him.

As they were about to climb into their carriage for the homeward trip, Lucas waved back to Senhor Joachim and Dona Imelda, and so did Chico, but his eyes were gazing wistfully at a silhouette in the window of a dimly lit bedroom. Abruptly, he turned to Lucas. "Anja has everything I'm looking for in a wife. Although she does not speak a word of English, she can always learn that in Kenya. What's the point of looking further, Lucas? This is the very best hand life has ever dealt me!"

Lucas smiled. He knew that people regarded him as merely a quiet eccentric, but he also knew that he had just beaten a number of matchmaking matrons at their own game.

Within four months Chico was sailing to Africa with Anja. Senhor Joachim and Dona Imelda, Anja's sisters, Lucas, and Anja's close friends bid them farewell at the dock. Anja's emotions were churning. The speed of events had been overwhelming, and now she was leaving her family to go thousands of miles away to an unknown future with a man she had never set eyes on before her father's fateful poker evening. Yet there was all the excitement of starting a new life, away from the protective bondage of being born into a privileged middle-class family in a restrictive small Catholic community. For Chico too the pace of events over the past months had been hectic. First, during the pre-betrothal discussions, Chico told Anja's parents he did not want a dowry. They unexpectedly insisted she sign a *recindicao*, a document under Portuguese law in which a woman forfeited her right of inheritance to a share of her family's property when she married into another family. There followed the formal engagement and days of preparation for the wedding. Although her family organized almost everything through Senhor Joachim's extensive network, Anja insisted that she and Chico have a say in the details. She even persuaded Chico that his Nairobi-tailored suit was too English in style, even though it had been made by a Goan tailor. She wore a white dress of her own design with a silk embroidered bodice over a satin skirt with a train edged with silver lace, topped with a headpiece of silk flowers. Chico and Anja were pronounced husband and wife in the Holy Spirit Church in Margao.

The ship's horn blared. Chico felt Anja's hold tighten on his arm and instinctively hugged her close. They watched the waving crowd shrink as the steamer was freed of the dock and slowly pulled away. Anja could no longer contain herself. She sobbed uncontrollably as Chico led her to the deck chairs. Chico had never seen her unhappy even for an instant.

"I'm sorry, querido," Anja said. "I cannot help it."

"It's all right for you to cry, amorzinha. I'm close to tears, too."

Chico's calm, sympathetic voice reassured Anja. Soon the rhythm of the engine in the distance, coupled with the constant murmur of the ocean, lulled them to sleep on the deck chairs. Waking first, Chico planted a gentle kiss on Anja's cheek.

"Come, my love," he whispered in her ear. "Let's go inside. You will be cold here." He took her hand and helped her over the raised threshold into the main lounge, the Victoria Room.

One of the Goan bartenders in the Lord Nelson Bar told them that there were five other newlywed couples on board also bound for Mombasa. At the dance after dinner, Anja found out all about them. She told Chico that Beatrice, the fair-skinned one, had met her husband at a tea dance in Bombay. He had graduated from St. Xavier's College and had a job offer in Uganda, but her parents did not approve of the match because his family was considered lower class. She married him anyway.

"Leaving Goa was probably the best solution," Chico said.

"Olga, with the long black hair, was born in Panjim," Anja continued. She had married her first cousin, who had gone to Kenya five years earlier. He was sixteen years older than her, and the marriage had been negotiated by the mothers; their husbands had no say in the matter.

"Chicozinho, you must hear about this one." Anja was so enthusiastic about her sleuthing skills, she couldn't slow down. "Josephine was introduced to her husband through a matchmaker who brought two photo albums to their house. Her father-in-law had gone to Kenya from Karachi, on loan from Indian Railways. Her husband was born there and is in business and loves fishing, but he dreams of owning a pig farm. When the family came out for the wedding, his parents discovered that the couple were related, but they knew the village priest well, and he blessed them anyway."

"I saw you talking with Joyce," Chico said. "I know the family in Nairobi."

Joyce was born in Nairobi. Her father was a civil servant in the district office. She was sent to Goa to complete high school and had lived with her grandmother before going to college in Bombay. There she fell in love with a young lawyer, but her father would not approve of the match. He had already picked someone for her, an accounts clerk on his staff.

"So tell me, amorzinha," Chico said, "what story about us did you trade in exchange?"

"Oh, querido! I told them the whole truth," Anja said, her eyes twinkling. "I said you won me at a poker game within twenty-four hours of arriving in Goa and, because you own the National Bank of India, I would live like a princesa for the rest of my life—just like you promised."

Over the next two days, the northeast trade winds freshened on the Indian Ocean brought grey skies, colder temperatures, and green complexions to the ship's passengers. Anja was seasick, but calmer weather returned. On the fifth day, as dawn broke, Chico felt Anja's fingers tickle his cheek. He woke up, one eye at a time. "Guud mon-ning. Dis is uare kapitan speakin'. Pleese kan I hav uare attension pleese? You see, querido, I am already learning English."

"Amorzinha, you speak it so well," Chico said, and pulled Anja toward him.

Less than a week later, the steamer docked at Kilindini, and the following day they boarded a train for the fifteen-hour journey to Nairobi.

Patrick and Leonor were waiting at the Nairobi station as the packed train pulled in at noon. The jacaranda trees outside the station were in full bloom and at the height of their beauty, seemingly intended as a special welcome for the newlyweds.

"Anja, you are so exactly as Chico described you in his letter," Leonor said. "Welcome to Kenya. We are now your family away from home."

"Jambo. Karibu." Their taxi driver welcomed them as they set off together for the temporary home Patrick had arranged for them at Chico's request.

As the taxi rattled down potholed Government Road, Anja took in the sights and sounds. They passed a handful of cars driven by Europeans. Overloaded ox-drawn carts seemed stalled by the wayside, their turbaned drivers chatting loudly, while bell-ringing bicyclists swayed past, also bearing loads. Everything was so utterly different from what she had imagined.

"My love, look this way," Chico said. "The Goan Institute is just past here, and that's my office there." He pointed to the National Bank of India.

"The buildings are so different from ours in Goa," Anja said, as they passed the newer masonry buildings and the corrugated iron structures. "I would never have imagined it."

European men clad in khaki safari suits and high boots hitched their horses to rails outside stores; white women in long skirts and wide sun hats bustled about, many accompanied by big dogs;

Indian men wearing jackets over traditional Hindu kurtas, or even dhotis with boots, walked briskly, gesturing as they talked. A turbaned Sikh mounted a mud-splattered motorcycle. A gaggle of talkative Indian women in bright saris spilled out of Choitram's Silk Store. Indian clerks in European-style suits with stiff collars and ties walked awkwardly, as if they were wearing badly fitting shoes. Everywhere you looked, Africans stood by as if waiting for someone or something. They were mostly barefoot, in worn shirts and shorts. Some wore shukas, wraps tucked in at the waist.

Anja was suddenly filled with a sense of foreboding. "So many different people," she whispered to Chico, "and so many strange languages."

He squeezed her hand.

"It's easy once you have even a few Swahili words on your tongue," said Leonor, who had overheard Anja's comment. "I will drop by with a list of useful words and phrases. Please don't worry. Every newcomer adjusts, and you will probably adjust faster than most."

"Here on the left is the Indian bazaar," Chico said. "Anything you imagine, you will find there." The taxi made a sharp right turn just past the grey stone Khoja Mosque into Fort Hall Road and trundled down a steep slope and over a small bridge.

"Chico, look. They're growing bringelas and bendes," Anja cried, excited to see the familiar eggplant and okra growing on riverbanks. The taxi swerved to the left. They had arrived on Chambers Road in Ngara, behind the Lady Grigg Indian Maternity Hospital. They got out and stretched.

"Your new home." Patrick dangled a key at Chico, who unlocked the apartment door, letting Anja enter first. It was no more than a sparsely furnished room subdivided to create a tiny bathroom. Leonor had made it comfortable with fresh linen and a clutch of dahlias from her garden.

That night they dined together at Patrick's. Anja was a hit with the children.

"It won't be long before you have some little ones too," Patrick said.

As Chico and Anja were about to leave, Leonor passed along some basic survival tips.

"You should write a book called *Coping with Life Abroad for Goan Newlyweds*," Anja said as they left for their own home.

The loud chirping of birds outside their window and the incessant barking of dogs woke them at dawn. It was Chico's first day back at work. They rushed through a breakfast of bananas, fried eggs on toast, and tea. Chico put on his jacket.

"Amorzinha, Leonor will be here shortly to help you through the day. Here is some local money and the names of some shops for groceries and household items and some useful Swahili words. By the way, remember that all the *dukawallas* expect to bargain over everything, whether it's eggs or eggplants."

He kissed Anja, straightened his collar, and stepped into the street. Unexpectedly, the door slammed behind him.

To Anja it was the sound of an explosion, signalling the honeymoon was over. She paced around the room, concerned that there was no one to talk to. She sat on the stool by the dressing table, looking at herself in the mirror and thinking. *Chico will expect me to cook his meals, to attend to household duties and to his every demand; he'll say all the other Goan wives do that. I've learned some basic cooking, though I've seldom stepped into a kitchen. I learned embroidery, painting, and music. But Mama insisted these were rites of passage for young women, never intended as skills to be used in real life.*

Anja practiced her English and Swahili. "Jambo Karibu and Guud mon-ning. Dis is uare kapitan speakin'. Pleese kan I have uare atten-sion pleese? Dis is uare kapitan speakin'. Guud mon ning. Karibu."

She lay on the bed, staring at the shoddy lampshade dangling from the ceiling. Thinking. *For better or for worse, in sickness and in health, so help me God.* She had pledged that in church. There was no turning back.

Letters took two months each way to Goa and back. Anja was lonely, and not even the emigration to Kenya of her elder brother Antonio made things better. To add to her woes, in the first fifteen months of their marriage, she and Chico moved four times. Every day Anja wept quietly when he left for work. She knew he was working as hard as he could, but this was no consolation.

"You never told me it would be like this," Anja sobbed to him one night.

On the evening of February 13, 1936, Chico got back earlier than usual. In the privacy of their two square yards of stone-paved patio, amid potted geraniums, crotons, and begonias, he told her the news. "Sweetheart, the British banks in Nairobi are in serious trouble." Anja braced herself for what was coming next: Chico had lost his job just as they were expecting their first child.

"They have many unpaid loans owed by their European customers, perhaps because they rely on income or transfers from their investments or estates abroad. Economic conditions are still very bad in Britain and Europe after the 1929 collapse."

Anja just stared at him—that bank was ruining him. He was using big words that meant little to her. "So our banks have put many houses up for sale, but there are no buyers because of the residential colour bar."

That she understood. Non-whites could not live in European areas. "Also, the banks aren't permitted to make new loans, so the managers are putting their Asiatic staff on long-term contracts so they can take over the payments on these mortgages. This way the managers can save their banks first—and save themselves as well."

"Does 'Asiatics' include us Goans?"

"Yes, yes. When there are rules or restrictions on all brown-skinned people, such as who can buy land or grow some crops, we are labelled Asiatics too. Today I was told that I'm eligible to apply," Chico said.

"Don't we have to pay anything?"

"Yes. We must deposit five percent of the price of the property within ten days when we make an offer. In case new economic problems occur, the mortgages will be guaranteed by our pension schemes from the bank's Staff Provident Fund."

"So really it is not a special offer?"

"It is, amorzinha! Can't you see? It's a good deal for the bank. For us it's an opportunity that will not come back in a hundred years."

"But Chico, what about the colour bar?"

"The banks will push the mayor to make changes."

"What changes?"

"The new boundaries will run along Kikuyu Road starting by the museum, west up to Westlands, and everything north of Chiromo and St. Austin's property. This area will be rezoned to permit Asiatics to own houses there."

"But what about the houses and the European club?"

"The European railway quarters and the Parklands Sports Club as well as the European Hospital Hill School will remain restricted."

"But these are big houses with big plots." Anja could imagine the housework ahead, knowing they couldn't possibly employ a servant on Chico's salary.

"Yes, they are. At least four times the size of this place. I have been thinking about this. My plan is to borrow part of the deposit from friends. If we rent out two rooms with shared facilities, we can pay off the deposit loans in four years; the mortgage we can pay off over thirty years, and it will cost no more than the rent we are now paying. Perhaps we can even share the cost of a houseboy with the tenants."

"Oh, querido, you are so impulsive! I'm worried about how we will pay for everything on just your salary. The baby is due in November!"

"It's for the baby that I want us to be settled. God has answered our prayers, my love. We'll be alright."

"But Chico—"

"I am so glad you are asking these questions. I wanted to know how you feel about this whole idea. You can see I'm quite excited. In fact, I have already put our names down."

They moved into their new house in Plums Lane in September. Within a week one room was sublet to newlyweds recently arrived from Goa, and a week later the other was taken by an older couple relocating from Kampala.

In November, Anja gave birth to a baby girl at the Indian Maternity Home. As the midwife held up the newborn, Anja, still groggy, exclaimed, "Que linda!" And she was beautiful. Seven days later Linda Maria was baptized at St. Francis Xavier's Church. While with the arrival of the baby Linda became Anja's only priority, life for Chico in 1936 became more complicated both at work and in his volunteer duties.

The colony's economy worsened. Salaries were frozen while everyday prices soared in spite of government price controls, and his work increased. Club responsibilities became a burden too. Earlier that year, about fifty members of the Goan Institute had broken away and founded the Goan Gymkhana, intended "to promote social, sports, and literary activities" for the erstwhile disgruntled Institute members. Mr. Jos DeSouza, a wealthy and generous member of the breakaway group, offered temporary space at his home, already endowed with a tennis and badminton court. Very shortly thereafter, the government gave the club some land near the museum to build on, and Chico was on the fundraising committee for construction of the new permanent clubhouse. His time and fundraising skills were also in demand by the St. Vincent de Paul Society, which was desperate for money to help repatriate destitute individuals to Goa and help other families cope during hard economic times. The government was too broke to offer assistance to anyone. Chico firmly believed God would find him an answer.

Meanwhile, house prices in the Asian area skyrocketed.

In January 1939, a neighbour, the charming, resourceful, and persuasive Mr. Patel, approached Chico with a proposal. He said he had a client whose needs matched Chico's house.

"He needs the house in six months and is willing to pay now," Patel said. "My dear Chico, just think. With the profit you can pay off all your debts and own a plot directly overlooking your St. Francis Xavier's Church, on which you can build a self-contained separate flat on the ground floor for renting. Upstairs you will have a nice big flat for your whole family with a balcony overlooking the church. You will live there peacefully without any matata until you retire and one day return to Goa."

The momentary glint in Chico's eyes did not go unnoticed. "As a matter of fact, I have exactly the land for you," Mr. Patel continued. "I can negotiate a special price. The owner is a close friend of mine. Chico, now is the time. Believe me, you will never again find a better time to buy good vacant land."

Patel's firm hand on his shoulder was reassuring. For three long nights, Chico considered the options and the risks. Living next to a church was a dream Goans would die for. Moreover, Patel's vacant lot was next door to the Dr. Ribeiro Goan School and a mere ten minutes' walk from his daily card-playing session at the gymkhana. He might even make enough of a profit to donate something to the St. Vincent de Paul Society, and to the club's construction fund. He knew better than to question God's will.

But Anja believed it was the Devil at work. She sought her brother Antonio's help.

"Chico thinks he has died and gone to Heaven. I have tried to warn him against being too impulsive, but do you think he listens?" Anja threw up her hands.

Two weeks later the completed sale was followed by a private thanksgiving mass, at which Chico, Anja, and Linda, now aged three, beseeched St. Francis Xavier, the patron saint of Goa, for special blessings to be bestowed on Patel, a Hindu, and on his extended family.

As Europe hurtled toward war, the economy floundered. The government prohibited imports of building materials. Banks stopped lending completely. Some parts of Kenya were hit by a drought, and famine struck the northeast. In other rural areas, Africans restricted from entering urban townships managed with what they could grow on their land. Chico's dream of a new house had to be postponed.

Patel once again came to the rescue. It turned out that he now owned Chico's house in Plums Lane. "Okay, Chico, you can continue to live here with your family, but you must pay me the full market rental price, because I must also make ends meet. I give you permission to sublet so you can afford the rental price. They do this in Bombay."

Chico had little choice. St. Francis Xavier could not influence rents. Soon after, Chico's rent escalated further when prices rose again.

It was 1939, and Anja was preparing for the birth of their second child, expected in mid-July. The weather during July was perfect, hot but with no humidity and the gentlest of breezes. Now in week thirty-five, Anja could feel the movement and thumping getting strong.

"Querido, what are we going to do about getting to the hospital?" There were no taxis except in town, and Chico might be at work when Anja went into labour.

"Didn't Doctor Faiz say that in ninety percent of cases, the contractions start at night and the baby is usually born within six hours?" Chico asked. "Don't worry, my love, I'll make some arrangements. Still another week to go."

Three days later, at about ten in the morning, Anja felt mild contractions. She called out to the ayah, who had taken Linda to the ayahs' meeting place on the grounds of the Parklands Sports Club. Nita, one of the tenants at the Plums Lane house, heard Anja's cries and rushed to her room. She called for the gardener.

"Njoroge, do you know where bwana works? Please take this letter to him. Mara moja. It is very urgent. Memsahib will have a baby. Give it to him only."

"Ndio, memsahib." The ever-obliging Njoroge sped off.

"You'll be all right, Anja," Nita said, placing a blanket over her. "I'll be right back." She dashed across Plums Lane to Jaswinder Singh's home. The Singhs owned two vegetable stores and were the only people who had any form of transport in the neighbourhood. Fortunately, his wife Jaswinder Kaur was home nursing her three-month-old son.

"Kamau! Kamau!" she screamed for her driver. Within minutes they were on their way to the maternity home. Anja, in a housecoat and covered with a light blanket, lay in the back of the van on another blanket laid over some burlap while Nita tidied away cabbage leaves and vegetable matter from the van's floor.

"I suppose we can really call this a delivery van," Nita said. Anja rewarded her with a faint smile. Her pre-labour pangs were quickening.

By the time Chico arrived at the hospital, the baby boy was already three hours old and had weighed in at six pounds, twelve ounces. Two weeks later he was baptized Orlando Francisco, after his late uncle. The parents called him Pooch Pooch, Babush, and eventually settled on Lando for short.

———•—•———

5: The War Years

Baby Lando's arrival was of particular interest to the precocious Linda, who quickly assumed the role of protective older sister. She helped Anja with little tasks of baby care. She also nursed her favourite doll and cooed soothing lullabies. When Anja's friends visited, Linda showed off her new brother. During these visits, she picked up morsels of adult conversation that she did not always understand. On one occasion Mrs. Singh and Mrs. Shah were agitated to hear that hundreds of Indian troops had arrived in Egypt to protect British interests in the Suez Canal.

"It is funny, isn't it?" Mrs. Singh said to Mrs. Shah. "Our brothers in India are fighting for freedom from Britain, and at the same time our shameless sons of India are now going to fight to save their colonial masters."

"Come, we mustn't talk so loud near the cradle," Mrs. Shah said, holding her finger to her lips. "This baby chose a bad time to arrive."

"Did the war start because of Lando?" Linda asked. Nobody responded, so Linda took their silence as "Yes!"

For Chico, the start of World War II was much more perplexing, as the prospect of being laid off became a distinct possibility.

Even before bombs began to fall in Europe, the Colonial Office in London bombarded the Kenya administration with war bulletins, requests, instructions, and orders. In preparation for a long war, Kenya had to mobilize fighting men to defend its northeastern frontier, which bordered on Italian-occupied Abyssinia and Somaliland. Two regiments had to be ready for deployment in twelve weeks, and twenty thousand fighting men in total would be required within a year. Farm production had to be stepped up to ensure adequate food supplies to the troops. Security at ports and airports was a priority. Rules would be temporarily eased to permit Asians to assume more responsibility in the civil administration, provided prior security checks were satisfactory.

White farmers faced hardships and were refused loans by commercial banks; they had to resort to begging for extended credit from Indian shopkeepers. The dukawallahs, in turn, had to borrow heavily from Parsee moneylenders in Nairobi and Mombasa.

Although there were widespread layoffs at banks, Chico's job was spared, but his savings were tied up in a vacant lot on which he could not build. He sought advice. Mr. Patel could not have been more helpful, "Chico, by chance I have a good friend arriving from India, who will buy your vacant land." Chico sold his land at a big loss. More prayers were offered for the continued well-being of Patel and his family.

Anja had by now amassed a collection of words in Swahili,

Hindi, Punjabi, and English, besides her native Portuguese and Konkani, and could use them with neighbours, shopkeepers, and servants. "I had a long conversation with Njoroge today," she told Chico as he arrived from work. "He told me he has joined the King's African Rifles. It happened at a meeting in his church last night. He must leave us next week. He's very excited because he will get free cigarettes, food, uniforms, and boots."

"Has he been told what joining the KAR means?"

"He's been told he is going to fight Italians and Somalis," Anja said. "I suppose he thinks that's safer than his part-time houseboy job with us."

"One third of our messengers have left to join the KAR. I hear South Africa and Northern Rhodesia are sending some air squadrons and some ground troops. Everyone seems to be scared of the Italians."

A year passed. Italian troops crossed the border from Somalia and raided a security post in Kenya. There were casualties and counterattacks by Rhodesian troops supported by the KAR and a British regiment. Within a few months, many Italian soldiers were captured and taken south to detention camps in Gilgil, Naivaisha, and other centres. Under the headline Italian boots are on the run, a Nairobi newspaper ran a photograph of sparsely clad nomadic herdsmen, wearing Italian soldiers' boots and tending their cattle in the semi-arid landscape around Wajir. But anxiety in Nairobi ran high even then. Chico overheard his assistant manager, Jolly Tucker, tell a European customer, "I hear the Italians may return with air power to blast Nairobi."

"I'll bet not, old boy!" the man replied. "This raid at Wajir was just to remind their HQ in Rome to send some more troop rations. My guess is the Italians will just sit out the war in remote Africa and find other ways to spend la dolce vita. I know these chaps, old boy."

For Anja and Chico, while the war that raged in Europe and North Africa seemed distant, they knew its impact on Nairobi affected ordinary people in many ways. Earlier in 1939, the Admiralty in London had commandeered all ships of the merchant navy flying the Union Jack and placed these on a war footing; some were converted into troop carriers and hospital ships, severely reducing cargo space for imports from Britain and India into Mombasa.

Meanwhile, locally grown food was sent abroad to feed the troops, creating widespread shortages and even more severe rationing of basic items like rice, sugar, flour, salt, matches, and kerosene.

The Indian shopkeepers were accused of hoarding. Their friends envied Anja's lockable pantry in the previously European-owned house. She was increasingly desperate living under these conditions and was anxious to take the children to Goa. She longed to see her family there. "With reduced sailings, are you sure we will find a cabin on the ship for our home leave?" she asked.

Chico learned that the family would have to wait a minimum of eighteen months to obtain tickets for their return trip to Goa, so he made a reservation. It was the morale booster that Anja needed. She burst into frenetic activity. First there was Linda's first Holy Communion, which would be in two months, after which she would tackle the to-do list before the trip. The twin menaces of import rationing and price gouging hovered over their decision.

"They have no idea what the world outside Goa is like," Anja told Chico. "I have drawn up a list of names. If we don't take a present for each one, they will think I have married a bamto, a scoundrel, and feel sorry for me. People out there believe money falls off trees in Africa like their mangoes in May."

"I know, but we can't afford it," Chico says. "Everyone is having a tough time. You know we have the new clubhouse under construction? At last night's meeting, the treasurer reported that even with the two bazaars and two special fundraisers they had raised only enough money to pay for the doors. You wives will have to sell hundreds of homemade pickles and jams and dresses yet."

Braz Menezes

Chico and his family embarked for Goa in July 1942, along with their friends Mathias "Marc" Maciel, his young wife Effeginia, and their four children. Two older boys were already enrolled at St. Paul's boarding school in Belgaum, where the third son, Wilfred, was to join them. Both families had made reservations to sail back together on their return voyage in November.

The steamer was about three hundred nautical miles from the Kenyan coastline when monsoon winds whipped the sea, as if to tease and test the limits of its patience and get it to show its fury.

Giant waves lashed at the ship, causing it to pitch and roll, making almost all the passengers dreadfully seasick. It was a relief to mind and body when they made it into Mormugao Port eleven days later and were able to disembark. Chico's family then went south by taxi to their home in Salcete, and Marc's went north to Bardez.

Although the monsoon was in full swing, with lightning and torrential thunderstorms expected to continue for three consecutive months, nothing could dampen the welcome awaiting Anja and her family after an absence of seven long years. Senhor Joachim, a cheroot tightly gripped between his teeth, greeted Chico as he would the winner of a memorable poker game. Dona Imelda, Anja's brothers and sisters, and even their friends doted on Anja's two garotos lindos. Six-year-old Linda held forth on any topic she was asked about, and Lando basked in her reflected glory. The biggest surprise was reserved for Anja. Her younger sister by five years, Magdalena, known as Magda, would be married just ten days after Anja and Chico were due to board the SS Tilawa for their return journey. Everyone had assumed Anja and family would be staying over until after Christmas.

"Chico, you could go back as planned," Anja suggested. "Please let me stay behind with the children. It will mean so much for Magda. She wants Linda to be one of the flower girls and Lando the pageboy. What shall we do?"

"The war is on," he replied. "Nobody knows when it will end.

The mail service is erratic. Can you imagine what life will be like for both of us without any contact for weeks on end? Please leave it to me. You might as well go to the chapel first thing in the morning. With God's help we will find a later passage together."

The next day Chico took the bus to the port city of Vasco. He met with one official after another as his appeals were referred up the chain of command. Eventually, the Vasco office telegraphed the shipping line's agents in Bombay. It was past closing time when Chico left the office clutching a revised booking date for three weeks later.

It was late afternoon on November 23 when the bell at the main church of Margao began a death toll, a repeated pattern of one ring followed by two rings, that was echoed by the bell of the church in the village of Salvador do Mundo in Bardez, the ancestral home of Marc Maciel. Almost at once details came by word of mouth, spread from neighbour to neighbour. Three days after the SS *Tilawa* had set sail from Bombay, with the Maciel family and about nine hundred passengers and crew on board, the ship was torpedoed at least twice by a Japanese submarine. About six hundred persons were rescued and taken back to Bombay by a British ship. The sea had taken Marc, Effeginia, their two infant girls, and a three-month-old baby boy, leaving Wilfred, Mervyn, and Joseph orphaned in a boarding school in India.

Chico and Marc had been friends from the time of Chico's arrival in 1928. Anja remembered teaching Marc's young wife so many ways of coping with life abroad and had been by her side at the birth of each of their three younger children. Anja and Chico could only stay briefly at Magda's wedding and then had to leave early to continue grieving in private.

"What is it, my love?" Chico asked. Trembling, Anja had shaken him awake.

"Imagine if you had agreed to go back alone on that ship," she said. "I would have been a widow with two children. I am so frightened." Chico calmed her back to sleep.

But the next morning she was troubled again. "Chico, I feel insecure in Goa now," she complained. "It was never like this. I cannot bear the sounds of those church bells. Please, let's go back to Plums Lane."

"We will soon, dear heart."

"Funny, I now think of just us as my family. Just the four of us," Anja said.

Ten days later they set sail for Mombasa.

In January 1943, the new spacious gymkhana clubhouse was opened, and membership was growing. Chico and his colleagues began to raise funds for the next phase, to include a reading room, library, billiards room, and a separate bar.

"We must preserve our culture," he told the members when it was his turn to speak. "This club will nurture our future generations."

Anja's face glowed. He was talking about their children's generation. God would soon bless them with their third child, expected in five months. Anja was praying for a baby girl to keep Linda company.

A few months later at the Lady Grigg Indian Maternity Hospital, an Anglo-Indian midwife gently placed a freshly cleaned baby into Anja's arms. "Congratulations!" she said. "I haven't had such an easy one to deliver as this beauty. No trouble at all. Got a name for her yet?"

"Yes. We'll call her Fatima. Our Lady of Fatima made it such an easy pregnancy and a trouble-free delivery."

Chico had good news of his own. "My salary increase has been approved, amorzinha. We can employ Njeri as a full- time ayah now."

———•◦•———

6: Dogsbody

In November of that year, with the jacarandas in bloom and the weather perfect, a nervous Njeri returned from her daily outing with Fatima in her pram, Lando clinging to her and tears running down his cheeks. "The museum dogs attacked him, memsahib," she told her mistress. "He is very frightened."

Anja grabbed Lando and examined him. The dogs had not touched him. She cuddled him.

"It's those wild Dalmatians that Dr. Leakey at the museum keeps behind his wire fence," Chico said later. "Poor Lando! Can you imagine the terror for any four-year-old threatened by those snarling monsters, with their long sharp teeth?"

"What shall we do?" Anja asked. "Lando is now frightened of all dogs."

"Ask Njeri not to take him by Leakey's place again," Chico said. "Let's give him time to get over this."

Over the next few weeks, whenever Lando saw a dog—any dog—he panicked. This worried Chico, since he couldn't imagine a childhood sheltered from dogs, especially in Nairobi with its Mbwa Kali warnings on every street.

One Saturday morning Jolly Tucker, Chico's normally calm submanager, strode into the office. Red-faced and uncharacteristically dishevelled, he was closely followed by a barefoot boy carrying several puppies in a big wicker basket. Tucker paused at a clerk's desk. Santana Braganza, recruited barely a year earlier from Goa, nervously jumped to attention, managing to simultaneously salute and genuflect.

"Good…good morning, sir."

"Stan, look here, old chap!"

The day Santana had first reported for work, Tucker had said to him, "Let's keep it simple. I'll call you Stan. You're going to work as my dogsbody, old chap."

Stan had often wondered about the term "dogsbody," but had never thought of asking his colleagues what it meant. Now he knew. While he tried to listen to Tucker's instructions, he saw five squirming puppies watching him from their basket. Stan, even more nervous now, realized these five cute dog bodies were about to be dumped on his lap.

"Stan," Chico heard Tucker say, "Susan—my memsahib—and I would like to give away these purebred pups to any staff willing to take them. If you can't dispose of them today, we'll be forced to put them to sleep by Monday. So be a good chap, Stan, and deal with it, won't you?"

The boy placed the wicker basket squarely on Stan's desk. The pups were gazing at him with round pleading eyes. They seemed to know their future now rested in his hands.

Stan was shocked and disgusted, horrified that anyone, especially a sub-manager—and a British one at that—could consider putting helpless puppies to sleep. He suspected it was a trap. He was sure now that Tucker was exploring his initiative, checking on his problem-solving skills and his business acumen. Stan had previously worked for a tricky Indian boss who was always testing him. In his commerce course at the University of Poona two years earlier, he had heard about a new approach some American firms were using, where they used "skill-testing games" as a way to assess potential management candidates.

Within two hours Stan had come up with a solution to his dilemma of unwanted puppies. He appealed to his co-workers on behalf of their children. The pups would make wonderful family pets, and the money he raised from the sale would go into a charity that Susie Tucker managed. Five colleagues purchased a pup each, signed papers for payment of weekly installments over ten weeks, and carried home their puppies. Stan tried to not think about how his colleagues on meagre incomes could possibly feed an extra mouth on their stretched wages.

Chico was one of the buyers. "It's helping a charity," he explained to a wide-eyed Anja. " Sweetheart, I know the last thing we need right now is a dog, but it will help Lando get over his fear of Dr. Leakey's Dalmatians."

"What shall we call this jolly little fellow? Isn't Jolly your boss's name? That's it. Let's call him Jolly."

"I don't suppose he'll find out. Yes, Jolly it is," Chico agreed. That night, after Lando had helped tuck Jolly in his wicker basket and had gone to bed, Anja asked Chico why his boss would want to put the pups to sleep.

"We don't know yet," Chico replied. "But we'll find out."

Over the next few days, through the grapevine of houseboys, gardeners, drivers, messengers, and the rumour mill, Chico and his colleagues got scraps of information. They carefully reconstructed the events that led to the pups arriving on Stan's table.

In a suburb of Nairobi, years later renamed Karen (after author Karen Blixen of *Out of Africa* fame), the Tuckers bred pedigreed Labrador retrievers. These dogs when grown offered security and companionship to English memsahibs while their husbands ventured on safari or searched for business deals in a wilderness of black and brown people and red Masai tribesmen. The Tuckers needed the extra income they gained from dog breeding to support a large acreage of land and their comfortable home with the shaded veranda overlooking a vast garden. Its upkeep required a multitude of servants, albeit on meagre wages. Two totos, young boys, employed only to look after the dogs, were upset over their own low wages while the dogs enjoyed daily rations of expensive fresh meat and corn flour.

But the plump Memsahib Tucker had a ready answer. "We must all make sacrifices and tighten our belts while our troops fight to preserve our freedom," she told her thin underfed servants. "Hakuna pesa, hakuna chakula mingi. No money, and not much food, in these difficult times," she added when they asked her for higher wages. She waved them away.

Braz Menezes

To express their anger one weekend when the Tuckers were away, the totos allowed two of the neighbours' mongrels to frolic inside the carefully guarded enclosure where Brunhilda, their prize-winning bitch, was in heat.

"Bloody bastards!" Memsahib Tucker screamed some weeks later, when she took her first look at Brunhilda's newly delivered litter of puppies. With their semi-erect ears and blotchy fur, they would never pass for pedigreed Labrador retrievers. Their dog-breeding business would be ruined.

"Damn those bastards, bloody bastards!" the memsahib said, and she was not referring to the pups. The totos were dismissed, given fifteen minutes to collect their belongings, and told to "bugger off."

Jolly Tucker first suggested to his wife that the pups be put to sleep but then changed his mind. Perhaps the Asian staff could pay something for these mongrels. And that is the story of how Jolly the pup came to be Lando's pet and companion at the house on Plums Lane.

———•+•———

7: And Now My Story

It is September 1946. I am seven years old, and my best friend Jolly is three. We have been inseparable since the day Dad brought him home. I love my Jolly with his strong, firm body, his big black eyes, and his short stubby tail. If I pick up a stick, Jolly leaps to the chase even before I throw it. He loves fetching sticks, rocks, shoes, or anything that I throw for him.

Our house in Plums Lane is cramped because we share it with two other families who rent from us. Dad and Mom occupy the largest of three bedrooms, along with Linda and Fatima, who are ten and four and share a double bed; Baby Joachim, ten months old, has a cot. I sleep in the enclosed front porch, which I share with two wardrobes, a desk, and odds and ends. The other bedrooms are sublet to two families.

From my room, I can see and hear a lot. I know when Aunty Maria says goodbye to her husband each morning. If he thinks nobody is looking, he will kiss her lightly on her cheek and run to the bus stop at the end of Plums Lane. I don't know if Dad kisses Mom the same way in the morning, as he is on his way to work even before we are up. When he returns home tired, and if there has been a problem at home, I will usually be blamed and punished. "You are the eldest son," he says. "You set a good example, and the others will follow."

Our tenants share cooking facilities. A room that once served as the servants' quarters for the previous English owners has been converted into a second "outside" kitchen with space for two jikos charcoal burners, a worktop, and a sink. Our three families share one indoor bathroom, a separate toilet, and a large common sitting room, which has space for two sofas and a His Master's Voice gramophone. At the rear of the house, a veranda serves as our dining room. Before and after mealtimes, other Goan mothers often meet

Mom here and exchange news. At other times we children play games here.

A door off the veranda leads to our family's crowded indoor kitchen, which features a cast iron stove to heat a small indoor water tank along with the usual furniture. Hot water for our baths is heated by firewood in what used to be a large oil drum placed outdoors beside the kitchen. The three families take their baths on pre-agreed "bath days."

Our house, built with grey stone blocks, has a red-painted iron roof with other panels nailed below it to create a painted flat ceiling that stops the roof's heat from entering the rooms. A colony of bats lives rent-free in the space between roof and ceiling. The room that Mom's friends envy most is a separate lock-up pantry that's joined to the kitchen. Though the war ended a year ago, rationing is still in place and shortages continue, so Mom and our neighbours buy lots of items when they are available and lock them up in the pantry. But I also hear neighbours say this is now a dangerous thing to do, because gangs of thieves with machetes haunt our neighbourhood.

So, I hear people say, while robbers roam free, residents in the area live behind bars. Windows typically are burglar-proofed with steel bars set in the wood frames and a steel mesh over them, with only a small hole to allow windows to be opened and closed. However, there are constant break-ins and robberies.

In spite of this, Dad does not worry too much about our being robbed. "With a dozen people living in our house, robbers would think twice before trying to break in. And besides, we have Jolly to raise the alarm."

Goans love to party. Because a number of birthdays and two wedding anniversaries are coming up, the three families living in our house decide on a joint celebration.

"We can have a buffet lunch in the garden," Anja says. "We women will plan the menu, including desserts, and draw up a list of reliable helpers. Chico, you and the men can be in charge of the drinks and glasses."

"We have just three weeks left," Dona Maria points out. She and Jules, with their baby, live in one of the rented rooms.

As the days pass, I notice Dad is looking increasingly worried. For some weeks there have been rumours of a shortage of Scotch whisky in Nairobi. Dad is sure that to even suggest a party without whisky is absurd, and people will criticize him for life. So the hunt is on. Two days later Linda and I are in the veranda when in the distance we hear our Uncle Antonio's coughing, spluttering BSA motorbike approaching. We run out to greet him, and he brings good news.

"Francis at Jardins Wines has sent us word," he tells Dad. "A shipment of Johnny Walker Red Label is due in next week. But they won't do retail sales. They'll only sell by the case... twelve bottles."

"Twelve bottles? We can't afford that many. If we keep four bottles for the party, can we find some people to share the cost, say, by buying one or two bottles each? Also, will Jardins accept installment payments?"

"I'll talk to Francis," Uncle says, and rides off in a cloud of dust. He returns next day with news that Jardins Wines will accept installment payments, and that two friends will take two bottles each. Dad, meanwhile, has found two colleagues at work willing to take another two bottles each.

"I have asked Francis to deliver one case directly to Plums Lane," Uncle says. "Since it'll be here just two days before the party, there'll be no time to distribute the eight bottles before the weekend. So will you please store all twelve bottles in your pantry? It's the safest place."

"No matata," Dad says.

It is the Friday before the lunch. The ladies and their helpers have been working since Thursday, but my friend Jeep and I miss the fun of the party preparations, since we have school. Today we have a holiday, but it is not our lucky day.

"You two stay out of the way, please," Mom says. "Jeep, keep an eye on Lando. We don't need any last-minute surprises...now off you go and play." With that we are unceremoniously shooed out of the kitchen.

There is much activity in the dining area. The table is set out with the spices that Portuguese explorers and mariners had once risked their lives to acquire on journeys that had led them to Goa: red chilies and garlic, bay leaves and ginger, tamarind, turmeric, and cumin seeds, cloves, mustard seeds, pepper, and salt are all set out neatly. I can tell from experience that two dishes on the menu are my favourites: *xacuti* and *sorpotel*. Helpers are cutting, chopping, and trimming lamb, pork belly, pig's liver, and other ingredients that go into making both of those dishes spicy and delicious.

Mukiri, who replaced Njoroge when he joined the KAR, is our houseboy. One moment he is busy scrubbing pots and pans or stoking the wood-burning stove, the next moment he is picking fresh cilantro and hot green chilies from Mom's vegetable patch, or plucking limes from the tree in front of the kitchen window.

Late that afternoon, as Jeep and I are talking under the peach tree, a Jardins Wines van arrives, and Mukiri unloads the case of whisky. Later another van arrives with slabs of ice from the ice-making factory in Ngara. Mukiri takes two of the slabs, each covered in sawdust and wrapped in burlap, and places them in the enamelled iron bathtub.

Dad is home especially early. He opens the whisky case, makes up the four packages for the other buyers, carefully labels each one, makes sure they are stacked safely, and locks up the pantry for the night.

By late Saturday afternoon, Mom, Maria, Nita, and their helpers, are exhausted after three consecutive days of food preparation. The food is neatly stored in the pantry. Food that needs to stay cool is packed in small containers, which are then placed in larger containers filled with cold water. Mukiri breaks up the large slabs of ice into smaller pieces and places them in the water as well. I tell Linda they will melt quickly, but instead they sit there bobbing like icebergs.

Dad then personally locks up the pantry that night.

We have all been told of the next day's plan: High Mass as usual at St. Francis Xavier; guests have been invited for 1:00 p.m.; lunch will be served at 3:30 p.m.; and we hope the guests won't stay past 9:00 p.m., as the next day is a working day.

Everyone is looking forward to the party. That night I go to my room, but I lie awake too excited to sleep: this is the first big party of my life. Far away I hear the muffled clatter as Mukiri puts away the pots and dishes. "Good night, bwana," I hear him say to Dad as he leaves. He will be the first one to wake up in the morning to make our tea.

Mom is tired and is already asleep. I hear Dad lock the door to the corridor that leads to all the bedrooms, including mine. He pops his head in my door.

"Are you okay, son?" he asks. "Now go to sleep. You have a long day tomorrow." Dad smiles as he turns off my light at the switch by the door. I hear his footsteps fade as he goes to his room, and I eventually fall into a deep sleep.

It is about 4:00 a.m. when I hear Jolly's bark. I listen. In the next room, I hear Dad say something to Mom. But the barking stops abruptly. I listen again. When there are no further sounds, I fall again into a deep sleep.

At 6:30 on Sunday morning there is a heavy, urgent knocking on the door that separates the bedrooms from the kitchen and veranda.

"*Hodi, hodi, bwana, bwana…*Please come soon. It is very important, bwana."

"Who is it?"

"Bwana, it is I, Mukiri. Please come soon. It is very important." Dad recognizes the voice and grabs a robe. Mom, bleary-eyed, wraps herself in a housecoat. I rush out in my pyjamas. By this time the commotion has woken up everyone except Nita's baby.

We crowd into the veranda. The kitchen door has been forced open, the lock on the pantry door has been wrenched out, screws and all. The food for the party, neatly stacked the previous night, has disappeared; twelve expensive bottles of Johnny Walker have vanished. Our pantry has been cleaned out except for the plates, cutlery, and glassware.

Dad's face is pale. The adults are all nervous and frightened. No one imagined something like this, especially with so many people living in the same house. We children are scared too. Everyone is talking at once.

"Where's Jolly?" Dad asks.

"The dog didn't bark!" Dona Maria says.

"But he did, Dona Maria," I tell her. "I heard him and woke up. I think Dad heard him too because I heard him talking to Mom. But then everything went quiet, so I went back to sleep."

"Lando's right," Dad says. "I did hear Jolly bark a couple of times, but then he didn't bark again. I too thought it was a false alarm and went back to sleep."

"How can they have been so quiet?" Mom asks. She is trembling. "How did they know the pantry was full?" Nita asks.

"Where's Jolly?" Dad asks again, now taking control. "Mukiri, run to the police station and ask the inspector to come quickly. Mara moja—please hurry!"

"Ndio, bwana." Mukiri too seems very anxious and nervous. He moves quickly.

Dad speaks to the families crowded in the veranda. "I'll go and see if anything else is wrong. All of you had better get dressed. The police will be here soon. Please check if anything is missing in your kitchen as well," he says to Maria and Nita, who use the outside kitchen. Everyone is asking questions as if they are detectives; I run out of the house to look for Jolly.

I can't remember anything after that, but Mom tells me later, "You were screaming, Daddy, Mummy! You were just crying and screaming, 'Jolly's dead! The robbers have killed him! They've cut his neck!' Then everybody rushed to where you lay on the ground, and then they too started to scream."

For me those terrifying moments Mom talks about are a blur. Apparently, as I turned the corner of the house, I saw Jolly: he had been killed with a sharp blow of a panga machete to the side of his neck. Blood was all over the place, and a strange smell. I passed out.

Now I hear a babble of voices around me as I regain consciousness. I am lying on the bench in the veranda. Mom is fanning me gently, occasionally stroking my head. I stay in shock for hours, too afraid to venture from home on my own.

That is the day when Mwangi Macharia comes into our lives. Mwangi works as a day labourer at the Plums Hotel. He notices the commotion that morning as the police arrive. He comes over to gawk and stays on. He helps dig Jolly's grave as Mukiri is taken to the Parklands police station for further questioning. Later that afternoon, Dad and Mom take me to the grave Mwangi dug for Jolly by the peach tree in our garden, where Jeep and I would often sit and talk and Jolly would eavesdrop with his ears cocked.

Three days later, with the help of a shamba boy at a neighbour's house, Mwangi finds a big rock. They do not have a wheelbarrow. So the two of them place the rock on a sheet of corrugated iron, tie it with ropes, and pull it like a sled over the length of Plums Lane to the peach tree. About a month later, "Jolly" in white letters is painted on the rock.

We never really find out what happens to Mukiri. First the police keep him in jail, thinking he might have been involved in the burglary, then they release him. Perhaps he has decided to work somewhere else, just in case we too thought he had been one of the robbers. But Dad told the inspector that the theft could have been a coincidence. Maybe one of the gangs had already planned to break into our house on that day anyway.

On that Sunday we are all left feeling guilty. Dad and I feel guilty that we did not go out when we heard Jolly barking. Everyone feels guilty about missing Sunday Mass. Mom and Maria feel guilty about planning a party while rationing is still in place. Dad is upset, as eight of the twelve bottles belonged to others and his security has failed them all. I suspect the confessional will be packed next Saturday. It also seems everyone has lost his or her appetite. The lunch party is postponed indefinitely.

<hr />

8: Friends and Neighbours

I have never felt so desolate. I tell Jeep, "I can't stop thinking about Jolly. Even when I'm asleep, I see him so clearly that I think he is still alive. Then I wake up wanting to hug him and I remember he is buried under that rock. When I picture all the blood again, it makes me sick."

"I miss him too," Jeep says. "Jolly was so clever that he understood Portuguese words from your mother, Swahili from Mukiri, and English from the two of us. Do you think your dad will get you another dog?"

"Maybe. The whole family misses him too."

Jeep—short for his real name, José Emerico Ernesto Pinto—is my closest friend and constant companion. He lives on Blenheim Road, a short walk from us. Jeep has a mop of curly black hair on a round head, and he is plump while I am skinny. Our friends say we look as funny as Laurel and Hardy walking together. He looks older and wiser, but that's because he wears tortoiseshell glasses. His parents, Marco and Vicky Pinto, are Goans who were born, raised, and got married in Bombay, and he is their only son. Jeep says their only hobby seems to be pushing him to do his homework.

Jeep is with me when, three months after Jolly's death, Uncle Antonio comes over with a surprise. "I've brought you a new dog, Lando," he says as he lets a large, powerful dog glide out of the taxi. "He's a Rhodesian ridgeback, and dogs like him are trained to hunt lions. He's just a year old, not quite grown yet. Look how beautiful he is!"

"Uncle, he looks like a little lion," I say. "I'm going to call him Simba, for 'lion' in Swahili." I want to hug the dog right away, but I am afraid; standing on his hind paws, he would be much bigger than Jeep or me.

"Let him get to know you first," my uncle says. "Hold your hand with the palm facing up, so Simba knows you're not going to hit him. Now watch, he's going to smell your hand, to make sure you're a friend."

Simba's breath feels warm as he slowly sniffs my fingers. The next thing I know, he is licking them all. I laugh because it feels ticklish, and for the first time in months, I am happy again. "You can pet him now," Uncle says. I am overjoyed.

When Jeep puts his hand out, palm up, Simba sniffs it too. Soon, the three of us are playing like old friends while Uncle Antonio watches and tells us more about the breed. Then he shows me how to groom Simba.

"Now I've got to go," he says at last. He gives me a hug and shakes hands with Jeep. "Don't forget to exercise Simba," he says as he gets back inside the waiting taxi. "Run with him every day… remember, every day!"

Dad says I should take Simba out for a run at the same time every evening. Mom agrees but says that I must be home on time if I want dinner. So Jeep, Simba, and I walk daily to the museum and then run down to the river below Ainsworth Bridge. At home, though still a puppy, Simba is not left to run wild. Instead, he is chained to a long cable that allows him plenty of exercise—he can run along its length and also some distance away from it sideways. Simba grows quickly, and soon he can bark as angrily as any mbwa kali. He scares strangers, makes friends nervous, and frightens children when he bares his teeth, snarls, and strains at his leash, but I know he will not hurt anybody.

After the burglary my parents had not replaced Mukiri, since

Njeri, the ayah, had brought a friend who needed work. But about a month after I was given Simba, Mwangi Macharia turns up once again at our doorstep, this time with his wife Wangari and their two-month-old baby boy, Stephen. Mwangi flashes a big smile and shakes my hand. "Lando, is Bwana Chico in?" he asks.

I go inside and call Dad.

Mwangi tells us he has had no job almost from the time Jolly got killed; he needs work desperately to support his family. I hope Dad will give him a job because I like Mwangi, since he helped bury Jolly and also found the right stone for his grave. Dad gives him a job right away; he also pays him more than he paid Mukiri because Mwangi is older and has a family. Dad pays half his wage and the two tenants share the balance. They too like him.

Every morning it's the same; Mwangi waits in the front yard, raising his voice above the chorus of barking dogs to exchange greetings with a small procession of shamba boys, ayahs, house-boys, cooks, and street vendors who take a shortcut past our house.

At 7:30 a.m., Jeep comes to Plums Lane and then we walk with Mwangi to the Dr. Ribeiro Goan School. After school, Mwangi meets us at the gate and walks us home; the dogs go crazy when we take a shortcut through the European area because they are trained to bark louder at black people. Mom says that in another two years, when Jeep and I are both ten, we will be allowed to walk alone to school without Mwangi.

It is July 1947. Dad comes home in a shiny black Chevy sedan. Mom, frightened, rushes out of the kitchen, as she knows he will only pay for a taxi in an extreme emergency. Linda and I have been doing our homework at the dining table; we follow her out.

"I want you to meet Ahmad," Dad says, grinning as he climbs out of the car. "He's our new neighbour." Ahmad is a young Muslim mechanical engineer in his late twenties. Mom invites him to have a cup of tea. Ahmad tells us that Kenya-Uganda Railways recruited him as an engineer in Karachi but gave him junior jobs below his level of experience once he arrived in Nairobi. When he asked for a better salary, he was told he could not be paid according to European scales because he was an Indian.

"Ahmad decided to leave his job after three years and start his own business," Dad says. "I helped him get a loan so he could buy a taxi."

Ahmad tells us that he has recently been married in Karachi, but his new wife needs the British Consulate to issue her an entry visa to Kenya. In the meantime, he has sublet a room in Mrs. Gelani's house across the road.

Jeep and I instantly become Ahmad's fans. We love that he lets us help him wash and polish his black Chevy sedan every Saturday afternoon. He tells us stories of his adventures as a young man in Karachi and Peshawar on the border with Afghanistan, where he has an uncle who makes umbrellas that can shoot real bullets through the stem. He also tells us funny stories about Europeans in Nairobi who are so drunk when they enter his taxi outside the Norfolk Hotel that they do not remember where they live.

"I always take them to the Mayfair Hotel near Westlands," he says. "They sleep in the veranda with the *askaris*, the watchmen. In the morning the hotel gives them free coffee before kicking them out."

At midnight on August 14, India and Pakistan declare their independence from Britain, and Ahmad takes Jeep and me, and our dads into town the next day so we can see the Independence Day processions. I am carrying the new Indian flag Dad got from his Indian colleagues—it has orange, white, and green bands and a blue spinning wheel in the centre. Ahmad brings the Pakistani flag, which he hands to Jeep; it is green and white with a crescent in the centre. There is no official bank holiday to mark the historic occasion, but nearly all offices and banks are as good as closed.

"Too many chiefs and no Indians," Dad says. "All the Indian staff have taken the day off."

We stand outside the Khoja Mosque at the corner of Government and River roads. This is the best place to see the processions,"

Ahmad says. He seems to know all the details. We see one group come along River Road, joining with another coming down Government Road. Both processions then march up through the Indian bazaar on Biashara Street.

"*Hindustan Zindabad! Pakistan Zindabad!* Long live India! Long live Pakistan!" shout the participants. The Indians are dressed in white cotton kurtas and trousers, both made from homespun cloth, and little white caps. The Muslims are in green or white cotton tunics and trousers; many of them are wearing prayer caps. Everyone is united and happy. "Hindustan Zindabad! Pakistan Zindabad!" Ahmad shouts one more time, and Jeep and I do the same. Then we go to the Blue Room on Victoria Street for samosas and a mango faluda.

It is March 1948. We are outside Ahmad's flat at the Gelani house, helping him polish his taxi, when Jeep brings up what has been bothering him and me.

"I heard my father talking to his friends," Jeep says. "He says Muslims and Hindus are killing each other daily by the thousands in India and Pakistan."

"Yes. It is a very bad situation now," Ahmad says. "Nearly one million people have died so far. The Indian state of Punjab borders on Pakistan on the west side, so the Sikhs are also caught in this violence."

"But why did they start fighting?" I ask.

"Before granting independence to India, the leaders of the Muslims and the Hindus started to argue. Both groups protested that they didn't want to be ruled by the other. Each group met separately with their British rulers in London and said the other side would kill their people if there was not an official separation... then they started fighting anyway."

"What about the people in Goa?" I ask.

"They escaped because the Portuguese were not in the picture. Some people say that more than ten million people are on the move between India and Pakistan."

Ahmad's explanation helps us understand what has happened recently between two of our friends living on Plums Lane. Abdul is Muslim, and Hardev is a Sikh. We are all about the same age and have grown up together. Now that they are nine years old, they both help out in their parents' shops after school, even on holidays. They continue to be friends, but Abdul and Hardev have been told by their parents that they are not to enter each other's homes. However, the boys can come into my home or Jeep's home, and we can go to their homes. Despite these restrictions, whenever we can, we meet and have fun.

Plums Lane is a potholed cul-de-sac that comes to life twice a day as a shortcut for domestic servants travelling to and from work on foot. Bougainvillea and a few jacaranda and acacia trees soften the open, rocky-edged storm drains that line the street. Jeep, Hardev, Abdul, and I are standing below a beautiful monkey-nut tree. Its branches spread everywhere like an affectionate grandmother waiting to hug us. The temptation is overwhelming. I look up and down the lane. Nobody is watching. A quick race to the top is irresistible.

"Okay, let's see who can get up the highest and fastest," I say.

"But let's start from here," Jeep says, four paces behind me.

Within minutes we are in the branches with Hardev leading and Jeep closely behind. Abdul and I are catching up. Suddenly there is a yell as Jeep takes a misstep.

"Watch out!" I shout as he slips and crashes past me. He grabs a branch, which snaps under his weight. Whoosh, thud. He is on the ground. Abdul, Hardev, and I shimmy down to see Jeep lying white and motionless with blood oozing from his arm. I start to feel queasy at the sight of all that blood.

"Quick, Hardev! Get your mother," I shout. "Maybe Jeep has to be taken to hospital before he dies…" The monkey-nut tree starts to spin faster, and I pass out.

When I regain full consciousness, I find myself in Mrs. Singh's (Hardev's mother's) van, headed for the Indian hospital with

Hardev and his mother looking after Jeep and me, their driver Kamau at the wheel.

"Hardev came running into the house to say Jeep was dead, but when we arrived you looked more dead than Jeep," Mrs. Singh says grinning. Jeep is sitting up holding his arm.

The duty doctor in the emergency room is the Singhs' family doctor. He cleans and bandages the wound on Jeep's upper arm and the abrasion on his right leg. Jeep flinches as the doctor applies a touch of iodine. The doctor gives me a glass of cold water. I feel no pain but have begun to worry that my father will hear about the incident. He will assume correctly that I am the ringleader and reward me with a spanking. Perhaps I will be placed under a curfew and have to go to confession, again—Dad's favourite punishment for serious misdemeanours. The doctor gives us all sticky toffees from a jar on his desk.

A small crowd outside the Singhs house awaits our return. I look for Mom and Jeep's mother. Both are looking very worried. So I look over and wave at them to show them we are all right, and they hug each other, laughing and crying at the same time.

We discover later that emotions were running high at Abdul's house while we were at the hospital. Abdul's shamba boy had told Jeep's mother, Vicky, about her son's accident as she stepped off the bus while returning from her doctor. Vicky then rushed to my mom, who had already told Maria and Nita about the accident. Mom had heard the news from Mwangi, who had heard it first-hand from Abdul's shamba boy, who had said, "*Toto mkufa*," the child is dead. In response, the Goan ladies had started a daylight vigil outside the Singhs' house. The message had been beamed across the length and breadth of Plums Lane by a network of houseboys, ayahs, shamba boys, and casual day labourers until it finally reached the other homebound memsahibs of Plums Lane.

Kamau helps us climb out of the van. We cringe at all the hullabaloo our accident has generated. There is a moment of silence as the crowd looks at us, as if to make sure we are real...then everyone starts clapping and cheering. Mom hugs me, her eyes filled with tears. I see Jeep overwhelmed by his teary-eyed mom as she holds him tight against her ample bosom. Maria and Nita smile. Mrs. Singh receives special applause as she climbs out of the passenger seat. Hardev smiles proudly. His mother, his driver, and his van have saved the day.

"Thank you, Mrs. Singh. Thank you very much for what you have done," Mom says.

"Yes, thank you, Mrs. Singh," Jeep's mom says. "I always knew that my Jeep would be very safe in your care."

"It is my duty, we are like family," Mrs. Singh says. "Will you please all come in and have chai in my house?"

"Please, let's go home, Mom," I whisper, tugging at my mother's frock in embarrassment.

"Thank you, Mrs. Singh, but I must take Lando home," Mom says. "He's had a rough day. Maybe later you can bring your husband and come visit?"

"Yes, I will come. I will bring Avtar," Mrs. Singh says.

Just as the crowd breaks up, my sister Linda arrives back from school and instinctively holds me responsible.

"Dad's going to spank you," she says gleefully. "You know what he said: 'You're the eldest boy. If you're good, the younger ones will follow your example. But if you're bad and they follow you, then you will catch God's punishment.' Have you found my missing coloured pencils yet?"

Mom takes our hands and walks us home.

That evening the Singhs turn up with a gift basket of fresh fruit from their grocery store. Hardev's dad and mine discover they have a mutual friend called Johnny Walker. Mom and Mrs. Singh drink tea. Hardev and I talk in the garden, sitting on my favourite branch of the peach tree by Jolly's grave. We discuss the crowd that came to welcome us back. It has never occurred to us that in our little neighbourhood, where we all have the same skin colour, our families are still so different from each other in food, dress, religion, music, and social customs. Yet whenever there is a problem, everyone quickly comes together.

Dad does not say anything about the incident directly to me. Later that evening, however, I overhear my parents discussing me.

"Lando needs more discipline, amorzinha," Dad says. "We must consider sending him to boarding school in Goa. You are spoiling him. When will he become responsible at this rate?"

"Leave it to Him," Mom replies. I imagine her index finger pointing heavenward. "God knows what's good for us all. We must believe in destiny."

I pull the sheet over my head to shut out the whine of a mosquito. I can live with destiny. God's been good to me today, and I will thank Him personally at Sunday Mass.

9: The Man in the Big Hat

In 1948, I can walk to the ends of my world in just minutes. The gymkhana and the nearby Coryndon Memorial Museum are only a twenty-minute walk away from Plums Lane in one direction, while our school and the church are next to each other, and only about thirty-five minutes away in the opposite direction. Mom and Dad walk with us to church every Sunday, and they have agreed we must receive Communion every other week. On those Sundays, since the church says we must fast completely before receiving Communion, we go to the 7:00 a.m. Mass because Linda could never go without breakfast until the 8:30 a.m. Mass ended.

Today is a non-Communion Sunday, so we have eaten a quick breakfast, taken care to polish our shoes—Dad insists on it, he calls it our Sunday dress code—and we are finally on our way. Linda and I walk ahead with Dad, who tells us stories, while Fatima walks with Mom, who is pushing a mosquito net-covered Joachim in a pram with big wheels.

We are almost at St. Francis Xavier's. Ali's fruit and vegetable kiosk is open as usual. I cannot help looking longingly at the wicker basket of green mangoes on the counter as Ali gives me a big wave, his white teeth glinting. I wave back, but I dare not buy any fruit in Dad's presence. He insists open kiosks do not control flies, and I have failed to convince him that no fly can survive the chili powder and salt of a masala mango.

We arrive at the large piece of land with a small car park flanking the stone church and the gardens with hibiscus and poinsettias set in beds of marigolds, day lilies, and dahlias. Behind the church is the priest's residence, surrounded by its own grounds planted with fruit trees.

"Quiet, now," Dad says as we climb the steps of the porch and wait while Mom lifts Joachim from his pram. High Mass is due to begin in a few minutes.

"Who's this, Dad?"

A shiny big black American car drives up to the front steps a few feet from where I am standing. A chauffeur wearing a dark blue uniform with gold stripes steps out from the left. This amuses me since all British cars in Kenya have the steering wheel on the right side. He walks behind the car and opens the right rear door. A frail, fair-skinned elderly lady climbs out, leaning on his arm. She is wearing an overcoat, a fur stole, and a petite pillbox hat, with a black lace shawl hiding her face. The chauffeur escorts her up to the first step where an altar boy, dressed in a red gown and white tunic, waits to take her arm. The chauffeur walks back to the car and opens the left rear door. An old man climbs out slowly. He is dressed in a black suit and a big black hat with a wide brim. An altar boy takes his arm too. I realize the parish priest is waiting at the church entrance to greet the couple. Then the priest turns around and leads them to the front pew as the organ music sounds. Only now can Mass begin.

"That's Dr. Rosendo Ribeiro and his wife," Dad tells Linda and me. "About fifty years ago he used to make his house calls to patients on his tame zebra, and he rode to his surgery on the same animal."

"Oh please, Dad," I whisper. "Please can we get zebras too for the whole family to come to church every Sunday?" Mom signals us to hurry up.

We enter the church by a side door. The church is packed except for the first six pews, which are strictly reserved for Europeans. A man stands up and moves over into a space in the next pew so our whole family can squeeze in. I see Dr. Ribeiro and his wife have taken seats in the first pew; perhaps he does not know the first six rows are reserved for white people. The organ music stops. The doctor has removed his hat; it looks as if his head has suddenly begun to glow, as it is hit by a ray of sunshine coming through a high window hidden behind an arch.

Throughout Mass the old couple distracts me. I wonder why they are allowed to sit in the front pew. When the collection plate comes around, I wonder why the doctor puts an envelope in it when everyone else gives either paper money or coins. (Dad always gives each of us money to put in the plate. Linda and I like to see what other people give as well; we do not want to appear miserly, especially with Dad's money.) I keep thinking about the old couple all through Mass. Maybe instead of going to Confession like us, they have written a letter to God saying they are sorry for their sins and have placed it in the collection plate, and the priest will now send the letter on to the pope in Rome. Maybe it is just a doctor's certificate in that envelope to say they are very old, and must be allowed to sit in the pews reserved for whites. Maybe it is a note from the governor allowing them to sit in the front pew. Dad has told me more than once that the Church does what the government tells it to do.

The priest climbs the teakwood pulpit, carved in Goa and donated by a wealthy Goan businessman. As the congregation grows silent, he coughs and clears his throat. His sermon is about God's love for all persons irrespective of the colour of our skin, our gender, or where we come from, "We are all God's children, and God loves us all equally," Father Patrick insists. It's uncanny how he knows what Hardev and I were discussing.

I shut my eyes tight and pray: "Please God, first make my friends Abdul and Hardev and their families be friends with each other, in spite of the bad killings going on in India and Pakistan. Also, please can you ask the priests to change the rules so that Mwangi, who often walks to church with Linda and me, can also pray with us here at St. Francis Xavier's instead of having to go to St. Peter Clavers in his African neighbourhood? Also, please God, after Easter, can Goans also sit in the front pews, as they are always almost empty, while the rest of the church is crowded. And one last wish—please God, and this is very important, can Dad please not send me to a boarding school in Goa? That's all for now. Thank you, God."

I feel Linda nudge me, and I open my eyes. In the front pew, the doctor still glows brightly. I realize I forgot to ask God for six zebras as well, or perhaps three if we share, but there's no time now. The priest confers his last blessing. Mass is over. The congregation files out. Some parishioners gawk as Dr. Ribeiro and his wife get back into their car. I gawk too. Mom strolls ahead with Joachim, Linda, and Fatima. I walk with Dad.

"Dr. Ribeiro must be a very rich man," I say.

"Maybe one day you too can be a famous doctor like Dr. Ribeiro," he says. I pretend not to hear him. "Or maybe even a lawyer. You'll need to work hard at school when you're young if you expect to go to university one day. Every day I regret I did not have a chance to study more when I was young. Next year will be very important, especially if you go to Goa."

I am disappointed. Jeep and I want to travel in a dhow and go around the world, just as Abdul's grandfather did, and here Dad seems serious about sending me away to boarding school in Goa. Will he force me to be a doctor? Does he realize I faint every time I see blood?

Confirming my worst fears, he continues, "Lando, you'll really make Mummy and me very happy and proud if one day you graduate as a doctor or a lawyer. We'll still try to guide you, but you must have direction now. Don't depend on luck or this talk of destiny. The world is not what it used to be in our day. Education is the key to progress. I will help you while I am alive. My own life changed for the worse when my father died. I had to earn a living so I didn't have the luxury of continuing my studies. Please believe what I'm saying. Every parent does what he can for his children."

I don't reply. I am shocked that Dad will even consider sending me away. He always said it was not right to have to send children to Goa for their schooling, and that we should put pressure on the Church and the government to change the rules so that Goan children can attend the Catholic schools restricted to Europeans only. I know God will answer my prayers, and Dad's plans will then have to change.

——— ·•·———

10: A Job on the Horizon

Two weeks after seeing Dr. Ribeiro in church, Jeep and I visit the Coryndon Memorial Museum again, with Simba in tow.

"You have Dr. Leakey to thank for being able to get in," Dad tells me. "It's only after he was put in charge as the curator that the museum was opened to non-Europeans, with children being admitted free. You're better off there than roaming around and getting up to mischief."

Dad tells me that Dr. Leakey and his wife Mary are world-famous anthropologists. A short lane leads to the main entrance door. To our left is the Leakey residence, a newly built stone bungalow fenced off with barbed wire and wire mesh. The two signs on the gate read, LEAKEYS and the warning, MBWA KALI.

Those Dalmatians had scared me when I was about four, and I

have to admit I'm still nervous when I walk by that pack of snarling black-and-white spotted dogs.

"Let's cross over," Jeep says. The ayahs still meet as they did before, on the same patch of grass shaded by trees. They exchange neighbourhood news while keeping an eye on their toddlers. Little Richard Leakey, who I estimate is about five years old, is playing on the front porch. He sees us and waves a greeting, but the dogs ratchet up the barking and snarling until we are out of sight. Simba is not amused and snarls back. He seems willing to take on the whole pack single-handed.

We leave Simba by the front entrance, since everyone leaves him alone and walks around him at a safe distance. He will wait patiently for us to return and then go berserk for a few minutes with pure joy. Uncle says maybe Simba was abandoned as a pup before he came to us, and that explains why he might be anxious that it could happen again.

The museum's main collection is contained in a large stone building. The central hall has a high ceiling with tall windows, but most of these have screens to block out light, so as to protect the exhibits. Jeep and I know our way through the maze of small exhibit halls leading off from the main hall.

"Let's look at the new gerenuk display," Jeep says.

But I want to look at the zebras. I wonder which type Dr. Ribeiro used to ride. We decide to look at both so we skip "the big five": the elephant, rhino, lion, leopard, and cheetah, and proceed to a new window. The display features a rare klipspringer, the beisa oryx, and the gerenuk of Northern Kenya. Jeep reads out the printed label; all three are specially adapted to arid landscapes and able to go for long periods without rain, as their body temperatures rise during the day and cool at night, so they do not need to evaporate water (perspire) to stay cool.

"We could do with something like that during confessions," I tell him.

"Won't work," Jeep replies. "Hey, look at those eyes. It's all so realistic. I wonder how they stuff these animals?"

We step into another alcove that has three full-grown zebras and a little one. A European in his thirties is admiring his handiwork on an adjacent display under construction.

"Good afternoon," I say.

"Good afternoon," he replies. "You blokes interested in zebras?"

"Yes. How can we tell the difference between the two types of zebra?"

He points at the display. "That's a common zebra on the left, and so is the little one. On the right you can see the difference. They're both Grevy's Zebra. You will see a Grevy's is taller and has thinner stripes. Also look at the different ears and little fur tufts that look like a fringe."

"How do you make them look so real?" Jeep asks.

"That's the job of a taxidermist," the man replies. "Have you met one before?"

"No. Are these animals stuffed in England?" I ask.

"Not really. We do it right here. Come, let me show you. My name's Eric."

We follow Eric outside through a side door, then into a shed behind the museum. He explains the process as he takes us around. We see skins being tanned and stretched. All signs of fresh blood have been removed from them, but the smell of chemicals is sickening. He shows us the mannequins for birds, fish, and mammals, the fleshing machines, and the moulding and casting supplies.

"Come back here when you're finished with high school," Eric says. "We will train you. And by the way, if you have any talent or artistic skills, that's even better."

I look at Jeep to make sure he hears the man offering us jobs.

"Come over here," he says again, showing us the wooden moulds for mounting exhibits, sculpture and painting tools, airbrushes, and paints. As I look at the work in progress, I suddenly freeze. Hundreds of lifelike eyes follow me as I move, glass eyes and plastic eyes—just staring from their respective dishes. I move forward and then backward. The eyes follow me. It is unnerving. I realize that it is the eyes on those stuffed animals that make them look so real. It feels spooky now with just Eric and Jeep and all those eyes watching us. We thank Eric and leave.

When we go to fetch Simba, I think that God has answered my prayers. I will not have to go to boarding school after all. I will become a taxidermist instead and work at the museum and devote my life to stuffing birds and beasts. But this means I will first have to pass the Senior Cambridge Exam at Dr. Ribeiro Goan School, seven years from now—that is a long way away.

It is a month later and the end of the school year. The morning assembly seems like it does any other day, except the principal speaks longer than usual after morning prayers. He tells us he is proud of the school's performance and is sorry our classrooms are crowded, and he promises we will have extra classrooms within a year. Most of us do not listen to his every word since we have our own special worries. I worry about the future as I look at the teachers neatly lined up on either side of the principal. Some look tired and worn out. I wonder if they will make it to my graduation in seven years. Mrs. Jacques, for example, has been with the school since it opened in 1932. She welcomed me to the school way back in 1945. She is much respected by students and staff, though she is tough, and when she is upset, God help you. She is in charge of the cafeteria and is always very annoyed when she catches us sneaking out for a mango masala at Ali's kiosk.

We troop off to our classrooms, which look exactly alike, the lower three feet of wall painted a glossy dark jungle-green and the wall above painted a light cream colour. One side of each classroom, adjacent to the corridor, has space for display boards, with small windows opposite. Today class ends at noon. It is memorable because I receive my first award ever, a book. In my teacher's handwriting it says, "For an outstanding year in Catechism Class." I am delighted, as this should show Dad he can drop the Goa boarding school idea. I am doing just fine here.

The class is dismissed. We start our Christmas break of three weeks, when Santa competes for our attention with Baby Jesus.

11: The Christmas of 1948

Every Christmas season, Mom, along with almost every Goan mother, begins the ritual of preparing traditional Goan sweets. Like every mother, she will swear she is following her family's special recipes handed down through generations. For Jeep, who seems to live in our house during this preparation period, and for me, the waiting is an ordeal.

Linda is welcomed into the kitchen to help Mom, but we are not allowed to enter and are treated like predators: vultures that circle above a carcass, waiting for the right moment to strike.

Jeep and I hover near the kitchen door, sniffing and then deeply inhaling aromas of vanilla, cinnamon, nutmeg, cardamom, almonds, pistachios, cloves, ginger, and saffron. Our sense of smell is fine-tuned: we can even detect when roasted nuts, poppy seeds, sesame seeds, dried fruit, or caramel syrup are added to the potent mix. For weeks we sniff and suffer. Mom always hides the sweets after making them.

"Remember what happened to Abdul last year?" Mom taunts us. Of course we remember. Jeep, Hardev, and I overate and were sick, but Abdul suffered the most.

"For me, your Christmas is just like Eid al-Fitr after Ramadan," he had said, referring to the end of the fasting period for Muslims, when food is abundant and children are given money for presents. Abdul was ill for four days.

The pressure does not ease for the mothers trying to transfer cultural traditions from Goa to Kenya. Goan families visit each other bearing sweets, a tradition called a *consuada*. Hosts and visitors trade their homemade assortments, which carry Portuguese or

Konkani names such as *bathica, bebinca, bolinhas, cocada, kulkuls,* and *neureos.* For Jeep and me, these sweets are like currency or marbles and can be exchanged for favours or even our most prized toys. Jeep and I look forward to the Annual Children's Christmas Tree Party at the Goan Gymkhana on Sunday, December 19, which kicks off the holiday celebrations. They could not have chosen a more beautiful sunny day with an almost cloudless sky for the party; the red and white bougainvillea are in bloom and look like part of the Christmas decorations. We are excitedly waiting to welcome Santa.

"Hey look! It's exactly 3:30 p.m. Here he comes!" Jeep, appointed the lookout, shouts from his vantage point on the upper balcony. He takes this responsibility seriously and has borrowed his father's Omega watch for the purpose.

"He's riding a horse this time," I announce to the nearly twenty-five children assembled on the veranda. Santa arrives, as he does every year, from the direction of the museum on Ainsworth Hill. I clamber up the steps and perch myself next to Jeep and my other classmate, Gerson. A big plump white man clad in a bright red suit sits astride an elaborately decorated horse. The sacks bulging on either side are full of toys. Red and white balloons flutter and bounce around the overburdened pair.

"Lando, do you remember last year?" Jeep asks. "When Santa arrived riding a bicycle pulling that trailer loaded with toys and—"

We are interrupted by an announcement from Aunty Mabel; megaphone in hand, she is the tireless organizer of social events. She asks us to gather by the club gate immediately. Her volunteers, who herd and prod us like sheep, help her.

"Let's give Santa a really big welcome," Megaphone Mabel says. Jeep, Gerson, and I climb down and join the others milling by the main entrance to the grounds. Some older boys, ineligible to receive gifts, jeer and tease us.

"Hey, kiddo, hold Lando's hand," a boy called Dafty taunts us.

"Hey, Jeepy, stop sucking your thumb," another yells.

They all laugh. Santa arrives amid cheers and clapping and alights clumsily from his horse, as the bags of toys are in the way. Mabel's volunteers help untie the bags. Santa hauls one over his shoulder, and someone from Mabel's committee takes the other sack while an African servant takes the horse away. Santa leads his procession of little people up the steps into the clubhouse, and though he seems happy with the welcome, his vocabulary seems to be limited to saying, "Ho, ho, ho!"

"Lando, do you think Santa is a Goan?" Jeep says. "His face is so pink."

"Of course not," I reply. "If he was, we would know everything about him by now: the village he comes from, his family background, whether he is a Brahmin or not, and if he attends church regularly."

We watch Santa settle comfortably into his big chair. Mabel's committee has organized Christmas carols and welcome songs, followed by party games with prizes. After that the children sit down to ice cream, cake, and orange juice.

Finally, Santa hands out toys, shaking hands with each child and sometimes adding a little hug. A father lifts a toddler into Santa's lap as everyone cheers. The toddler looks up at Santa's face, then back at his father, then back at Santa. The child screams, then bawls, as the mother comes to the rescue.

"My mom says I cried like that when I was two," Jeep says.

"Me too," I reply. "I used to be very scared of Santa. Perhaps because we had never seen white humans before."

The gift-giving is over. Aunt Mabel expertly distracts the children for a few moments, announcing that a magician has arrived. There is a flash of light on the stage, and then the lights go out. Seconds later they come on again. In those few seconds of darkness, Santa has vanished. The party is over.

Jeep and I decide to enjoy ourselves in the clubhouse. We scurry down passageways.

"Look, Lando," he says, pointing to where a red suit and pointed cap, a facemask, and white gloves are lying in a bundle behind the bar. "Like that snake in the museum, Santa has shed his skin."

Back at home we prepare for Christmas. Linda and I are busy wrapping up presents. We have collected toys and hand-me-down clothes for Mwangi's little son, Stephen. Dad and Mom have also bought the boy a new shirt, shorts, and canvas shoes, along with a shirt for Mwangi and a frock for his wife. Four days later it is Christmas Eve.

"Mom, will we be going to midnight Mass? Linda says we won't be."

"Sadly, we won't be going this year," Mom says. "I can't find anyone to look after Fatima and Joachim. We will go to the service on Christmas morning."

Dressed in our best clothes, we attend Christmas Day Mass at St. Francis, receive Holy Communion, place extra money in the plate, and line up to look at the crib and kiss little Baby Jesus' feet. After Mass, we are eager to get home to open our presents.

When Linda was six, she received a picture book. It told of Santa arriving on a sleigh pulled by eight reindeer over a lot of snow and then creeping down a chimney. Of course, living a couple of hundred miles south of the Equator, neither Linda nor I could imagine what a sleigh, eight reindeer, and snow were like. I wanted to check the chimney, but Dad said I was too young to climb onto the roof, so Linda, helped up the ladder by Dad, went up to see if Santa would manage to deliver our toys. The only chimney we knew was connected to Mom's wood-fired oven. Still, Linda had thought he'd be able to do it. Santa had proved her right.

Back home, I get through the door first. That's how excited I am to unwrap presents.

"Look, Santa must have arrived while we were in church," I say. A big wicker basket has landed on our dining table but with no message attached. Linda takes charge of distributing the gifts. Joachim's eyes light up at the sight of the brightly painted tin drum, two red drumsticks, and the picture book about Jack and the beanstalk. Fatima gets a book, as well as a doll in a bright pink frock with big brown eyes and eyelids that open and shut.

"Lando, this is for you." Linda hands me two gifts. Inside are a mouth organ and a watercolour paintbox with two brushes. "And this is for you, Mom and Dad." Linda gives them the gifts "from Joachim, Fatima, Lando, and Linda" that we had left on the dining table last night. Santa must have added it to his basket.

I pick up the two packages for Linda. She unwraps them. They are books, as well as two thick wooden knitting needles and a ball of wool. She announces she will knit a sweater for her doll, Margaret, named after the young British princess who has just turned eighteen. My idea that we could entertain the family with Joachim's drum and my mouth organ turns out to be a mistake; within fifteen minutes we are banished to the garden.

For Christmas lunch in other years, Mom and Dad would invite someone who had just arrived from Goa, or unmarried friends without close family members in Nairobi, but this year there are no visitors. By the early evening, everyone is tired. Mom and Dad decide they will not attend the members' Christmas dance that evening at the Goan Gymkhana and save their energy for New Year's Eve.

The next day is the Goan Gymkhana's Annual Boxing Day and Sports Fair, in which members compete against those of the athletically superior Railway Goan Institute. Actually, the RGI is the best at athletics, but after 1936, when the RGI and GG separated, the two clubs have never competed with each other. All my friends and I love the day's fairground atmosphere. The sports field is rimmed by stalls made of lashed bamboo poles covered with burlap; we feel very important as we help at the prize stalls, lucky dips, air rifle shooting galleries, and hoopla stands. Dad is in charge of the fundraising this year—the money will go to the St. Vincent de Paul charity.

The RGI wins most of the competitions, but the GG takes the awards in novelty sports such as the wheelbarrow race, in which one partner runs on his hands while the other lifts him off the ground by the feet, and the three-legged races for men and women. The "mixed-married tug-of-war" teams are equally matched; the RGI kids win the egg-and-spoon race, but the GG kids are superior racing in gunny bags. We are exhausted by the time the last race is run.

At sunset everyone adjourns to the clubhouse. For Jeep and me, this day brings to an end the season's festivities, and I find myself starting to think of school again, a new year in a new class. I am determined to convince Dad I do not need to be sent to a far-off boarding school.

12: Dr. Leakey, I Presume

After Boxing Day there is nothing to look forward to. The Christmas sweets have all been eaten, the parties are over, and even Santa has returned to the North Pole somewhere in Canada.

"Lando, you and Jeep may be interested in this," Dad says, showing me a newspaper clipping he has brought home. A photograph shows Dr. Leakey standing by a large African rock python; the caption says it will be on display for two weeks as part of Dr. Leakey's plan to encourage return visits. The next day Jeep and I go to the museum. We leave Simba outside as usual and head straight for the snake house, where the python is lying curled up on the floor. It has beautiful buff-and-black markings but an ugly blunted arrow-like head, as if a pointed end has been chopped off.

"Hey, Lando, do you think it's alive?" Jeep asks me after the python has not moved for several minutes.

"Can't tell," I say. "Maybe it's just tired."

I lose interest and turn away, but Jeep grabs my arm and takes a step backward. "Hey, Lando, look!" he cries. "There's something moving inside it."

A big lump about a third of the way down the python's body seems to be pulsing in and out, like a heartbeat in slow motion. It's unsettling watching the snake's body move mysteriously in the eerie silence.

"It's probably lunch," I say. "A large rat or a chicken eaten whole going down?"

"Do you lads know anything about snakes?" says a voice right behind us, and we almost jump out of our skins. It is a muzungu about Dad's age, but muscular and much taller. From his thick eyebrows, strong nose, short moustache, and dark hair, I recognize him as Dr. Leakey. He is amused that he has scared us.

He asks us our names, then gestures to a young assistant and says, "Tell Lando and Jeep everything about this one, John," Then he walks away, grinning.

"Do you know who that was?" John asks.

"Leakey?" I say. He is pleased.

John knows a lot about snakes, and I have a question for him. "Is this python fully grown?"

"Oh, no. This baby is about nineteen feet long," John says. "A fully grown one can reach up to thirty feet and weigh more than 250 pounds." He sees the bulge on the snake. "They can also go for many months without eating."

"Is that something it's eaten that's moving?"

"Yes. It was fed about a week ago," John says. "Its mouth stretches like elastic to swallow any animal up to the size of a small goat. Special juices inside the stomach break down the bones and eventually all is absorbed." John looks around and points to another exhibit. "That one there is the Kenya sand boa."

That I did not need to know.

"Thank you," I say. "We just came in to look at this special exhibit but must leave now."

"I'm glad you got us out of that snake house," Jeep says, as John hurries off to rejoin his boss. "I have already heard more than I care to know about pythons."

We amble into the main hall, then out the door.

Simba is delighted to see us. We go down to the river under Ainsworth Bridge and disturb a few fish and tadpoles. Simba too joins in.

13: Safari

January 1949. My world already seems different. One of the tenant families sharing our home has moved out, allowing our family room to expand. Dad too has calmed down; he has not uttered the words "boarding school" recently. Even Simba has lost his enthusiasm for attacking Mr. Gelani's striped pyjamas on the clothesline. But by Easter I feel an undercurrent of unease: Dad has now begun launching into periodic monologues over dinner, talking longingly about his days at St. Joseph's High School in Arpora, Goa, and of the renowned skill of the Jesuits in transforming rock-hard brains into gemstones. I say nothing to him but resolve to work harder in school and trust in the Almighty.

Another term goes by, and soon we will have our holidays in late July.

On Saturday afternoons, Jeep and I continue to help Ahmad polish his taxicab. I love the big twin taillights and huge round headlamps that are mounted on the front wings and bulge like frogs' eyes. In return for our help, he hands us little treats that he keeps hidden in the many pockets of his embroidered Kashmiri waistcoat and entertains us with stories of his real-life adventures.

"This week I took two Americans from the National Geographic Society to Magadi," he tells us. "One's a journalist and the other's a photographer. They wanted to see the soda lake at the bottom of the Great Rift Valley. The heat is so intense there that the air shimmers all day. The journalist fainted at one point, but we were close to some fresh-water springs by the edge of the lake, so he stripped down to his underpants and sat in the water for twenty minutes."

"Dad said that in two weeks we are going to travel with you to Nakuru," I remind him.

"Yes, I have business there. Your family will continue by train to Kericho. Your father has many friends, but I must personally show you the magnificent Great Rift Valley."

"I wish I was going too," Jeep says.

"Jeep, next time it will be your turn," Ahmad says, placing his hand on Jeep's shoulder.

The day before our departure, I cannot contain my excitement about going on my first real safari. After dinner I check the items in my bag and leave it by my bed. Then I fall asleep, and it seems I wake up almost immediately, trembling.

In my nightmare I am swinging from vine to vine just out of reach of four trumpeting, evil-looking elephants who seem determined to drag me down and trample on me. I cannot see through a cloud of dust. Suddenly, the vine breaks, and I land in a clump of bushes, face to face with a giant monitor lizard. It is yellow ochre and chocolate in colour, and the size of a crocodile. It spits and snarls at me. Its scaly orange neck expands and contracts like a balloon with air being blown in and out of it. In the dusty haze, I see thousands of snakes sliding and slithering, and the hissing gets louder. I feel like a wild animal caught in a car's headlights. With more of a screech than a hiss, the lizard lunges at me; its long green tongue shoots out of its mouth, barely missing me. The lizard lunges again. I scream. It lunges again, and I scream again. I sit up, trembling and sweating.

"It's okay, Lando," Mom says, and soothes me until I fall asleep.

I wake up to Simba's barking—a car is being driven up the gravel track to the back of the house. I rush out in my pyjamas to find that Ahmad has already popped the trunk lid open and has the car ready for loading. He lights up a cigarette, tilts his head, and blows a puff upward.

"Good morning, Lando," he says. "Ready for your big safari?"

"Ahmad, I'm so ready for safari," I tell him, "I even had a scary dream about it."

"I blame Tarzan movies, Lando," Dad says. "Now hurry and get dressed. It will be a long day."

I shiver. It is a crisp Nairobi morning. Dewdrops glisten on the big leaves of the fig tree by the veranda. Ahmed starts loading parcels, carefully squeezing little ones into nooks so no space is wasted. Dad returns with two bulging suitcases. While Mom gets breakfast ready, Linda, who is thirteen, watches over Fatima, seven, and Joachim, three.

"Can I bring this in case we need it?" I show Ahmad the slingshot he helped me make from the Y branch of a guava tree, with rubber strips cut from an old bicycle inner tube.

"Good idea," he says. "But you'll have to hit the target right the very first time. There is no second chance in this hunting business."

Blue-grey smoke from our cast iron stove billows out of the kitchen chimney and hangs in the cold air. I can smell the fresh eucalyptus logs burning, the same strong aroma as when Jeep and I squish green eucalyptus leaves between our fingers; but now it is mingled with a sweet smell of fresh baked bread and fried bananas. I'm suddenly hungry, just as Mom summons us all for breakfast.

Soon we are off, with me sitting on the wide front seat of the Chevrolet between Dad on my right and Ahmad at the wheel. Mom, Linda, Fatima, and Joachim are crammed in the back seat with the snacks and drinks. The big wooden dashboard is full of gauges—big chrome rings around glass, which Ahmad says tell you the speed, the engine revolutions per minute, the amount of petrol in the tank, and even how hot the engine is running.

"Look here," he tells me. "This is the first American car with the gearshift behind the wheel." He moves the lever proudly. Soon we are on our way.

In a few minutes we reach Kabete, eight miles from Plums Lane.

"Lando, your friend Dr. Leakey was born here almost fifty years ago," Dad says, pointing to a church and a cluster of corrugated-iron structures glistening on a nearby hill. "Those buildings belong to the Church Missionary Society. His father was a preacher there. They say he speaks fluent Kikuyu."

"Yes, Jeep and I read about him at the museum," I say. "It's because his ayah was a Kikuyu, and his play friends were Kikuyu totos." Dad turns to look at Mom, and I can tell he is pleased that I know so much.

We travel slowly along the up-and-down winding road from Kabete to Limuru, past clusters of mud huts, some very close to the road, set amid groves of banana and plantain dotted with papaya and cassava. Some huts have iron roofs while others are mostly thatched with grass. I see smoke from open-air fires rising here and there; it seems everyone is cooking at this hour. Linda, Fatima, and I play a counting game. In one group of huts, we count five dogs, two goats, and a donkey but lose count of the many chickens grubbing for food. Laughing half-naked children run to see our car pass and shout greetings.

Ahmad reaches below his seat and hands me a crumpled map. "You can guide me, Lando," he says, pointing to where we are on the map and where we need to go while trying to keep an eye ahead. "We have to reach Nakuru, here."

I am nervous now since everything here is strange, but I realize there is little risk of getting lost, as there's only one road here and we are on it—narrow and winding, and it has been cut into the side of the Aberdare Hills high above the Rift Valley. A sheer wooded mountainside rises on one side, and a precipice drops steeply on the other. One false move will send our overloaded car hurtling down thousands of feet.

"This road was built by Italian prisoners of war," Ahmad explains as our Chevy bravely climbs a steep hill. At times a thick mist reduces visibility to about twenty yards—and we are still on the edge of the precipice. We arrive at the crest and start moving downhill again, leaving the mist behind. About three miles later, a small sign announces a scenic lookout. To the right is a little stone chapel overlooking the escarpment, and on our left, the panorama of the valley. The road narrows further. There is barely room for two cars.

Approaching a blind corner, Ahmad tenses, then edges the car over as far as he dares. Dad reaches out to grip the dashboard; I hold on to his arm. In the back seat, Mom holds Fatima and Joachim close, while Linda clutches Mom. Everyone is too scared to say anything in case it might distract Ahmad. Linda snuggles her head tightly into Mom's neck, then Fatima cuddles up to her too. Joachim pushes his two sisters away; he must feel suffocated. Ahmad eases the car into the overlook, then manoeuvres back and forth until he almost touches a low stonewall that is supposed to protect us from going over the edge.

"Please get out from the other side," Ahmad says. "But be careful. A car or lorry can come up from behind." He walks ahead to warn us of traffic coming around the corner.

Next to the chapel is a bell tower and turret with a steep roof. Dad and I enter the chapel first; it is small and octagonal, with a simple wooden cross hanging on a wall.

"During World War II," Dad tells us, "many Italian troops were taken prisoner by the British on the border with Somalia and Abyssinia. They were put to work building roads and bridges; this is one of the roads they built. Being good Catholics, they also built this chapel so they could pray."

"Come, Lando, come. Just look at this view!" Ahmad calls. I have never imagined anything like this. Dad and Mom also join us.

"Many people believe that what we are now looking at may once have been the Garden of Eden," Dad says. He points out herds of zebra, flocks of ostrich, groups of impala, giraffe, buffalo, and small herds of Masai-owned cattle grazing on the valley floor.

Ahmad, who has driven this way more than once, points to the Ngong Hills and the Kedong Valley, and to a place near Lake

Magadi where a young Dr. Leakey discovered prehistoric bones.

"So here it is at last, Lando," he says, "just as I promised you—the Great Rift Valley. And there, far away, is Mount Kilimanjaro, the highest mountain in Africa."

Cigarette dangling from his mouth, Ahmad walks along the wall and faces the sun. He takes a long piss. I have seen Simba mark his territory that way. I walk along the wall in the other direction, and I too mark my spot.

When I jump off the wall, Dad snaps, "Don't ever do that again." He is so annoyed that I stay out of his reach.

"Mom, when are we going to have lunch?" Linda asks as an overloaded lorry rattles by, leaving us in a smelly fog of diesel fumes.

"This is not a good spot. It's too dangerous to sit here," Dad says. "Perhaps Ahmad can find a safe area ahead where we can picnic away from the road?"

"I know a perfect spot," Ahmad says. We drive miles down from the rim and are almost on the floor of the valley.

Hot air whooshes through the open windows, coating everything and everyone in fine dust. Ahmad's right arm resting on the window is hairy, dusty, and sunburned. Outside, the soft green tangled grasses of the escarpment have given way to coarse, dry brown grassland with clumps of trees and shrubs drooping limp in the heat. To our left the grassy plateau of grazing land stretches as far as I can see, up to the blue-grey and green of what Ahmad says is the Mau Forest. Below us cattle stand in clusters in the shade of trees. Two men on horseback drive the herd in the distance.

"Linda, look, cowboys," I say. "How did they get here from America, Dad?"

"They're not American cowboys, Lando," Dad says, laughing. "You and Jeep really must stop going so often to the cinema. They're probably local dairy farmers."

The Chevy bumps along at what seems like breakneck speed, but the needle does not quiver past thirty-two miles per hour. Heat has caused the road's surface to buckle. I point at the dozens of rusted rectangular tin cans mounted on fence posts and ask Ahmad what they mean.

"They're called *debbes*," he tells me. "They're boundary markers for muzungu farms." Suddenly he is angry. "Do you know that each farm extends nearly five miles along this road? The Kikuyu closer to Nairobi have been complaining for years that the muzungu have stolen their tribal land. Here they have stolen some more also." He waves his hand. "All this land once belonged to the Masai. Now it is all in the hands of a few white people."

"I'm sure one day the Africans will want it back," Mom says, and changes the subject. "Ahmad, shall we stop for a picnic? The children are hungry. You too must be tired."

A short while later, Ahmad turns off on the gravel shoulder and onto grass. He parks some feet away from the fence posts, one of which is capped with a rusty debbe marker. We all get out. Ahmad stretches both arms, moves his neck up and down and sideways, then walks away to light a cigarette. Dad helps Mom unload the picnic items. She and Linda spread a thick red-and-white table-cloth as a ground mat, while Fatima and Joachim wait impatiently in the shade of an acacia tree.

"Look, Lando, these are bullet holes," Dad says, inspecting a fence post. "Someone must have been carrying out target practice here." I pick up two bullets from the ground.

"Show me those," he says. "I want to make sure they are really spent." He tells me they came from a .22 rifle. This is the first time I have seen real bullets; I slip them into my pocket, planning to trade one with Jeep for at least four of his new glass marbles with the flame design. We move back toward the shade: it is very hot and bright. Mom calls us to sit down for egg sandwiches and chicken, raw, peeled carrots, and bananas, which we cannot touch until we have finished lunch. She is pouring out the orange juice when suddenly we hear galloping horses and a bang. A bullet hits the debbe near the car and ricochets. Mom screams and leaps up. She grabs Joachim and drags Fatima behind the Chevy. Dad grabs

Linda by the hand and pulls her toward the car. I look in the direction of the shot. The two cowboys I had seen earlier are galloping toward us. Nearby, two giraffes stop grazing to watch.

"Quick, quick, this way—into the car, Lando."

Ahmad takes my hand. Another shot strikes the dirt, sending up a cloud of dust. Then another shot. Joachim starts crying, and Fatima screams. This time they have aimed near the car.

"Everyone inside!" Ahmad shouts. He and Dad grab the tablecloth with its contents and shove it into the car, leaving our wrapped sandwiches behind. Ahmad starts the engine. The two cowboys are urging their horses on and waving their rifles in the air. They scream abuse but not completely in English.

"Fook off, you Indiaans. *Vertrek*. Geet off my plaas. Geet off our land, Indiaans." The white men look like teenagers. They are up close, screaming at us from the other side of the fence. I can see their red faces. Mom clutches Fatima and Joachim and pushes their heads down. Linda is crouched on the floor.

"Fook off, you Indiaans. *Nee piekniek*. Go! *Vinnig!* We'll blow your fooking tires. *Vinnig*. Bugger off! *Mara, moja!*" They fire more shots in the air as Ahmad revs the engine. The Chevy lurches forward. Dad tries to pull me below the dashboard, but I want to see the cowboys. If I had a rifle, I would pick them off one by one; then we could finish our picnic.

"Kaburus! Bloody Afrikaners," Ahmad says, followed by something in Punjabi. He mutters in Punjabi and English. "*Madarchot! Kaburus!* They should go back to South Africa where they belong."

"Daddy, why did those cowboys want to kill us?" I ask at last, although now I am trembling.

"They just want us to picnic somewhere else. They have no right to do that. We are on public land. Don't worry. They are just uneducated boys with guns."

"Tell Lando the truth," Ahmad says harshly. "Those fellows hate us, hate all Indians, Arabs, Kikuyu, Masai—all people who are not white like them. Some other time I will tell you how they treat us Indians and Pakistanis. But now I've got to find a place where we can eat. Shall we continue to Nakuru or look for another picnic spot?"

"No, no, no, don't stop!" a chorus replies from the back seat. "Please drive fast."

"But I'm hungry," Fatima says.

Dad and Ahmad agree that we will keep on going and perhaps find a petrol station that sells snacks. Ahmad says he knows of a Sikh-owned petrol station at a turnoff. While we enjoy a snack there, he points to specks in the distance against the backdrop of the Menengai Crater. "That's Nakuru," he says. "Thanks be to God."

Ahmad's cheerful announcement brings relief all around. Our plans are to spend the weekend in Nakuru with Dad's friends and then go on to Kericho by train on Monday. Ahmad will return to Nairobi. After a quick cleanup of food strewn throughout the car, we drive on.

———•••———

14: Saboti

Finally we arrive, tired and relieved. Our hosts, Uncle Arthur and Aunty Philomena, are meeting Dad and Mom after eleven years. They have two daughters, Rosita, aged ten, and Lizette, seven, who are an instant success with Linda and Fatima; however, I will have no one to play with all weekend. As the four girls ignore me, I decide to play with the dog. But the terrier does not budge an inch, and I think he must be glued to the porch floor.

"Dad, that stupid terrier won't even fetch a stick," I whisper. "I'm bored."

"Too bad," Dad whispers back. "Go outside and explore the garden."

It is still light, so I skip over the dog and go into the backyard, which is empty and quiet except for the chirping of bulbuls, star-lings, and the yellow-and-black weaverbirds. I spy ripening fruit on a guava tree; as I walk toward it, I hear a girl's voice on the other side of a wooden fence. She is talking to someone. I peep through a gap in the planks and see a little girl about Fatima's age; she is alone, and she is talking to her doll.

"Hello," I call out, still peeking through the gap. "What's your name? I'm Orlando from Nairobi, but you can call me Lando."

She looks up. She has not seen me yet and does not answer. I say, "Hello, I'm here," and knock on the fence. "Wait." I step on a large rock so I can see and be seen over the top. She walks up and peers at me cautiously.

"Hello, Lando. My name is Saboti, but my sisters call me Boti," she says. "And this is Dusi. Say hello to Lando, Dusi." She straight-ens the doll's pink limbs and holds her upright so the bright blue eyes open wide and look straight at me. I don't want to look at the doll. I look at Saboti instead.

"Your hair is funny," I say. "It looks African, but it looks orange. Do you paint it?"

Saboti puts her hand to her hair, as if to see whether it is still there.

"I am not African," she says sharply. "I am Shelishely. I'm from the Seychelles. Do you know where that is? My Aunty Mena and Papa are also Shelishely."

"I know where the Seychelles is," I say. "It's where ships from Goa stop on the way to Mombasa. I know that because my dad came that way. He says there are pirates in the Seychelles. Do you know any pirates?"

"No," she says. "But maybe Papa knows some."

"Are you Catholic?" I point to a medal hanging around her neck. "Papa told me I had to become Catholic or the nuns wouldn't take me into their school. It's near Nairobi. Do you know my school?"

But I'm not interested in her school. "What's that?" I point to a mark below her right shoulder.

"Nothing." She pulls her dress over to cover the scar and turns away.

"Wait!" I say as she turns to go. "Look. These are real bullets!" I pull the two bullets from my pocket and hold them out to her.

"Where did you get them?"

"I can't tell you. Would you like one?"

She hesitates. "No. I'll get into trouble." Again she turns to leave.

"Can I have that stick?" I point to a knotted branch with mottled grey-and-brown bark leaning against a wall.

"Papa wants to carve that into a special walking stick." "Why special?"

"He calls it a ceremonial stick, but I can give you this instead." She gives me a ripe peach. "It just fell from that tree."

Suddenly I hear a woman's voice calling her. "Boti! Boti! Saboti! Dinner!"

Saboti takes a step backward. "That's my Aunty Mena," she says.

"Please wash your hands and come to the table immediately!" Aunty Mena calls again. "Dinner is ready."

"I must go." Saboti takes another step backwards. "I'll not be allowed out after supper. Shall we meet tomorrow?"

"Yes, except it all depends on my dad," I tell her. "We may not be here. We're going to do things all day, and we have planned to go on safari to Kericho. Now I hope I can stay here instead."

Saboti turns to her doll and waves its plastic hand. "Say good night to Lando, Dusi." She holds Dusi close, turns, and runs indoors. I feel as if someone has just snatched something from me. I sit on a bench, wipe the peach on my shorts, and relish its ripe sweetness. I think how sweet Saboti is. Linda will tease me no end if she finds out how I feel. I will not tell her about Saboti.

I go into the garden the next morning, hoping to meet Saboti again, but no one's out. Soon I'm called back in. Uncle Arthur has borrowed a Land Rover and is now ready to take us on a short safari around Lake Nakuru. We are six in all. Dad offers to sit behind with Linda and Uncle's daughter Rosita. Fatima and I share the front passenger seat. Lizette has decided to stay behind.

"Lando, your father tells me you have met Dr. Leakey," Uncle Arthur says. "His wife Mary is also an anthropologist. She did a lot of digging at Hyrax Hill near Nakuru."

"My friend Jeep and I saw the model at the museum," I say. "Her notes said thousands of hyraxes are living among the rocks. Do you think they are still there?"

"I think so. Unfortunately, it's in the other direction, and we'll be short of time on this trip. You must keep your voices down and be careful not to stick your heads or hands out of the window. Besides the birds, there are also lions, leopards, and rhinos around Lake Nakuru."

We are driving along a dirt track. From a distance the lake looks like a mirror laid flat, bordered by a bright white-and-pink edge. The pink is from the millions of flamingo feeding around its perimeter, and the white is from the reflected soda that covers the ground. The lake's mountainous rim is constantly changing colour with the movement of the clouds and the sun.

"If we are lucky, we'll see many animals," Uncle Arthur says. "They'll come for a drink at the springs by the lake."

"I hear the government wants to declare this area a wildlife sanctuary," Dad says.

"Yes, though a couple of big shots are trying to work it to their advantage so they can make money from it."

Linda, Rosita, and Fatima point excitedly at the wildlife they see as Uncle Arthur carefully manoeuvres the Land Rover through the woodland over wheel tracks sprinkled with quarry chips. The sound of the engine and the thuds as we bump along are broken by the sharp, shrill racket of starlings and weaverbirds, probably objecting to the invasion of their refuge.

We emerge into open savannah, but Uncle turns the wheel and plunges us again into a forest, skillfully following a trail until we emerge again into the open grassland.

"Look, giraffe!" Now everybody is excited.

"Look at those herds of zebra!" someone says.

"I see warthogs!" another says.

"Baboons! Oh look! A baby!" There's so much to see, we hardly know where to look.

As our Land Rover moves closer to the lake, passing clumps of woodland, we hear a constant, uniform buzz that slowly grows louder, and we detect a strong new smell.

"What's that smell?" I ask Uncle Arthur.

"The smell of bird droppings in alkaline water," Dad tells us. Before I can ask him a question about that, Uncle Arthur shushes us with a finger to his lips. He brings the jeep to a halt.

Only a few feet away on our left is a huge black rhino scratching itself against a tree trunk. We might have missed it altogether if the upper branches of the tree had not been swaying. The rhino turns to face us, looking at us with beady, unmoving small eyes; it twitches its hair-fringed ears from time to time and snorts.

"What do we do now, Uncle?" I whisper. My heart is pounding so loudly, I think everyone can hear it.

"We do nothing, Lando," he tells me quietly. "If I get the jeep moving too suddenly, it could upset the rhino, and then it might charge at us. We'll just sit here for a few minutes until the creature loses interest and turns its head to get back to scratching or just moves away."

Sure enough, the rhino goes back to scratching its hide, and Uncle once again puts the jeep in gear. As we near the water's edge, the background noise grows louder. Now we can barely hear ourselves talk. We look at each other, not sure what is happening. Uncle says, "That is the sound of millions of birds squawking, tweeting, quacking, honking, and cheeping."

"How many birds are there, Uncle?" I ask.

"The experts say there may be as many as four hundred different resident species alone. The most common are flamingos, pelicans, and cormorants, as well as ducks, terns, and eagles, among others—must be nearly two million."

Uncle Arthur looks at his watch. He turns off the track into open ground and finds a spot well away from wildlife. We get out, stretch, and walk around. I'm not nervous anymore.

Dad looks at his watch too. "We'd better be turning back," he tells us kids. "Uncle Arthur and Auntie have more visitors coming around tonight."

Uncle Arthur takes us back by a different route, staying closer to the lake. Skeins of flamingos, pelicans, cormorants, and other birds rise and swirl, flutter a little distance into the air, and then gracefully alight, creating a continuous wave of colour and movement. When we get back, Saboti is still not home.

On Sunday, after Mass at a nearby Catholic church, we go for lunch to the Goan Institute, where many of Dad's old colleagues are happy to see him again, and return to Uncle Arthur's home in the late afternoon. I wait until everyone is busy and then sneak out into the garden. I'm in luck. Saboti is there.

"I missed talking to you yesterday," I tell her.

"Papa took us to Rongai to see his friend," she answers. "Are you leaving tomorrow?"

"Yes, but I want to see you again."

"Please come and see me in my school," Saboti says. "It's near Nairobi, and all my friends have visitors on Saturday afternoon and Sunday, but I seldom have any."

"I'll come. Tell me the name."

"Saboti! Boti! Where are you?" It is her Aunty Mena calling her again.

"I must go in now," Saboti says. She grabs her doll's arm again and waves it. "Dusi, say kwaheri to Lando now. Kwaheri, Lando!" She runs toward the house, pauses on the step, waves, and then she is gone.

I go back into Uncle's house. The girls are busy elsewhere, and the adults are talking in the lounge. I hoist myself onto the porch swing and pump with my feet to get it going. I change the angle at which I'm swinging so that now my feet sweep just inches above the dog's head and snout, and still the terrier does not move. I think of Saboti. She never told me about her family and I should have asked her about that scar. Perhaps I will find a way of visiting her school near Nairobi, if I ever find out what it's called.

• • •

15: Jimmy

Uncle and Aunty and the two girls, Rosita and Lizette, come to say goodbye at the station. Rosita will not let go of Linda's hand. Lizette is nice to talk to, but I think she is shy of talking to boys. The daily mail train from Mombasa to Kisumu is only fifteen minutes late, but Uncle says it will leave on time, as there were not as many passengers waiting to get on. We say goodbye on the platform and continue our goodbyes through the open windows of the coach. A final whistle, and the train pulls out of the station. They wave, and we wave back. I wish Saboti was also here. On second thought, no, since Linda could end up a better friend of hers than I.

Our journey will take us to Lumbwa Station, where we will travel by car to Kericho with Uncle Fernando, who came out to Kenya on the same boat with Dad in 1928.

Linda and I seize places by the large picture window. The glass and insect-proof screens can slide out of sight. If we kneel on the bench on either side, we can get good views.

"Lando, please keep your head in," Dad warns me. "It can be dangerous."

Linda and I decide to explore the train. We are travelling second class and our carriage is next to the dining car, which is all set for the next meal. Each carriage is divided into compartments with two cushioned bench seats that can be converted into sleeping berths. The one first class carriage is almost empty. The rest of the compartments in our carriage and the next are occupied by Indians, and the rear ones by Africans. The two third class carriages have wooden bench seats and are packed with Africans only. When we return, Dad is telling Mom about Uncle Fernando.

"Fernando and Clara Esmeralda will be very happy to see us," he says.

"Was theirs an arranged marriage?" Mom asks. "Yes, I suppose, only it was Clara who arranged it."

Dad explains how she and Fernando got together. They'd met on the steamer when Fernando and Dad first came to Africa. Fernando spent most of his time on board, charming all the ladies, especially Clara Esmeralda, who Dad said was the most beautiful of them all with her fair skin, dark hair and eyelashes, and deep brown eyes. She was the daughter of one of the boas familias, good families, travelling to Mozambique. The fresh sea breeze, the dancing every night, and the time spent together on deck gazing at the full moon shimmering over the Indian Ocean worked magic on them both. But Fernando, like his friends, got nervous about going on to Lourenço Marques and stayed behind in Mombasa.

He started work with the National Bank and rose quickly in the ranks. Meanwhile, Clara, badly missing him, used the Goan social network in Mozambique and Kenya to locate him. Having found out that he was still single, she arranged for them to get married by proxy. With a new passport as Clara Esmeralda Albuquerque, née Fernandes, she travelled by steamer to Mombasa, and they got formally married.

Afterwards, though, Clara got ill, apparently because of the hot, humid climate, and Fernando took a job upcountry with a tea plantation. They started a family and sent their first son to boarding school in Goa. Their two girls and a little son were younger than Linda and me.

"We will meet them in a few hours," Dad says.

The scenery scrolls by our windows. Linda and I stick our heads out quickly as the train rounds a curve so that we can see both the engine and the tail end.

"Ouch!" Linda yanks her head back. A hot cinder from the wood-fired boiler has just hit her. Dad says nothing, but his glare plainly says, "I told you so." We retreat from the window.

It is only forty miles from Nakuru to the railhead at Lumbwa, but it seems to take forever.

Dad points at a framed photograph. "Here's the next station if we were to go north, but our train will go west to Kisumu," he says. A sign reads, TIMBOROA 9,150 FEET—the Highest Mainline Station in the British Commonwealth. It's a small quaint building in corrugated iron, with a wide porch all around.

"Will we be stopping there?" I ask.

"No. This station is lose to here."

"Lando, count the chug, chug, chug," Linda says. "You can feel the train is struggling to climb up these endless hills."

"Funny, I'm listening to different sounds," I say. "The puff, puff, and hiss of the steam."

We can feel the engine's exhaustion when it's climbing and its excitement and joy when it hurtles downhill, as if the driver has lost control. The train whistles on its way and blows thick black smoke through deep gorges and ravines. We travel through giant cuttings in the hills, partially open landscape, and thick forest. Sometimes the sloping banks are the red colour of the earth; sometimes they have been cut into solid black rock.

Suddenly, our train enters a tunnel. Everything goes pitch-dark. Linda and I find that a bit scary, as the noise is deafening and choking smoke comes into the compartment. By the time the train bursts out of the tunnel, our faces and clothes are covered in soot.

"Look how beautiful it is!" Mom says. We are looking down along hillsides and over open countryside that seems to stretch forever, merging with the sky. In the distance the hills are purple and blue. As we approach Lumbwa, we see glimpses of silvery-white Lake Victoria. In small townships people stand and wave.

It is afternoon when we arrive. The air is moist. As the train slowly rolls into the tiny township, people wave. Half-naked children gleefully run along the track, shouting greetings. We wave back. The platform is small, but the station is important to the farmers. Africans with handcarts wait to put their produce on the train; the women are dressed in sunflower yellow and shades of red, orange, and black. Two Europeans are talking to the African stationmaster. An Indian couple, the woman wrapped in a green and deep blue sari, stand to one side.

Dad recognizes Fernando standing near a group of people on the platform.

I instantly decide I like Uncle Fernando. His face is one big smile, and his wrinkles are exactly where they need to be to laugh often. He has a full head of black hair and neatly trimmed sideburns. His deep brown eyes look directly into mine when he talks to me. First he and Dad hug each other for long seconds. Dad wipes away a tear as Uncle Fernando gropes for a handkerchief under his hand-knitted sweater.

"Fernando, this is my family: Anja, Linda, Lando, Fatima, and Joachim."

"Encantado. Enchanted, Anja! At last we are meeting in person," Fernando says to Mom. "We have waited years for this day." He kisses her on both cheeks and Linda on one as Fatima holds Mom's hand and shyly hides behind her skirt. Joachim stares curiously at him.

"Hello," I mumble, offering to shake hands. I've never much liked kissing, and I'm not starting now.

"My boss's son, Jimmy, is looking forward to meeting you, Lando." Fernando returns a firm handshake. "Jimmy goes to boarding school in Eldoret, and he's home for the holidays. He's your age and knows you are coming. You'll have a great time together."

"That's great news, Uncle," I say. Linda had told me I would have to spend a whole week playing with two little girls and a five-year-old boy. We arrive at the car park. I wonder what Saboti is doing at this moment in Nakuru.

"Lando, you sit in front with your father and me," Uncle Fernando says, interrupting my thoughts. "You may have to take over the steering wheel if we get stuck in mud; Dad and I will have to push from the back."

"Okay, Uncle," I say. This is my first ride ever in a Morris Eight, and everything is different from Ahmad's Chevy. I climb into my seat.

"This is one of our company cars," Uncle Fernando says. "That's why it's painted green and black. Like the colours of tea."

As he drives, he says, "It's been raining almost non-stop over the past three days. Some stretches of the road are in a very bad state."

I watch as he jiggles the steering wheel left and right, avoiding red-brown potholes filled with water yet maintaining a constant speed. We overtake two Africans sitting atop an ox-drawn cart piled high with bamboo cages full of live chickens. Going in the opposite direction, a cart drawn by seven pairs of oxen is also piled high.

"It's called a Scotch cart," Uncle says.

In the driver's seat a white man with a red beard and a floppy hat wields a very long whip. A stout woman in a big hat sits beside him; their two children sit behind them on top of the goods. A man and a woman follow them on horseback, while another horse-man brings up the rear.

"Kaburus," Uncle says. "They are Afrikaans settlers, perhaps moving to the Uasin Gishu basin. Many of them have settled around here." He turns to Dad. "They say that the British wanted to settle European Jews here permanently, but it didn't work out."

Suddenly, a herd of bush pigs dashes out of the undergrowth, taking a suicidal leap onto the road; luckily Uncle slams on the brakes. Flocks of guinea fowl, sandgrouse, and yellownecks feeding by the side of the road take wing and disappear as our car passes. Finally, we turn into Anglo Kericho Tea Plantations and meander past the offices, factory, and other outbuildings to the staff quarters. Two Sikhs fundis, perched on top of some scaffolding, wave at us.

"The company is building a hotel," Uncle says.

We hear them first before we see them. A Labrador, an Alsatian, and a dachshund bark loudly as they race out to greet us. Aunty Clara, in a white blouse and a frilly long pink skirt, follows them with the children. Once the mushy greetings are over, we all sit down on a large veranda overlooking the plantation. A houseboy brings a tray laden with tea, fresh cheese and coriander chutney sandwiches, and a freshly baked cake. I stake out the best seat to do justice to the food. The adults chat. Linda and Fatima go with the girls to their room, with Paulo and Joachim trailing.

Suddenly, the dachshund resting at my feet leaps up and the Labrador's ears cock forward, then the Alsatian's. All dash off barking. I stand up to investigate.

"Ah, Jimmy!" Uncle greets him and waves his hand toward me. "Lando."

Jimmy pauses, as if taking in the scene, then walks straight to me and shakes my hand. My mind is racing. I had not even thought about it before, but Jimmy is a European. I have never talked to a European boy before, although I have seen them out with their dogs as I walk to school and to Sunday Mass in Nairobi.

"Hello, Lando," he says. "Fernando told me all about you. Do you like fishing?"

"Yes, I like it very much," I reply. "But I haven't been in really big rivers or lakes. Just at the Nairobi River by the museum and once near the Fourteen Falls at Thika."

"You shoot?" Jimmy asks. "I can shoot a green pigeon at thirty feet. What about you?"

"I don't have a gun. But my Uncle Antonio showed me once how to clean his rifle and also how to aim and shoot. He has a .22 rifle and a twelve-bore double-barrelled gun."

"I'm talking air guns," Jimmy says. "Don't worry, I'll show you how."

"Jimmy, I brought my slingshot," I say. "I can hit a can of sardines from twenty feet away."

"No sardines here, but I'm going fishing," Jimmy says. "Would you like to come?"

Uncle Fernando tells Jimmy to make sure we are back in good time for dinner. We go fishing in a nearby pond. He shows me where to look for bait worms, how to insert the hook, how to feel the line pull, and how to unhook my one single fish, the product of my ninety-minute first lesson. After all the effort, I decide to throw it back into the water anyway and return to Uncle's before dark.

The next day Jimmy arrives at the veranda at sunrise as we had agreed.

"Have you seen the prisoners?"

"What prisoners?" I ask.

"Let's wait here. You'll see."

The morning is crisp and cold. It is green everywhere you look, every imaginable shade of green, like a patchwork quilt. The bright green growth of new tea plants is almost luminous. The low early-morning sun casts a soft pink glow.

"Good morning." Clara in her housecoat has brought us enamel mugs with warm milk, a banana, and a slice of bread each. She leaves us alone.

"Here they come," Jimmy says as the dogs begin barking. A few minutes later, the prisoners from the local jail, in white shorts and marked tunics, walk past in single file.

"They have come to pick tea leaves for the factory," Jimmy says. "The armed askaris escort the prisoners; one walks in the front, leading the group. Another two askaris walk behind. If anyone tries to escape, the askaris can shoot him."

That evening, I ask Uncle and Dad about this.

"The company cannot find enough local men to work for the wages," Uncle says. "They prefer to seek work in Kisumu or go on to Nairobi. The company has had to use prisoners, since the women are not allowed to work. According to their custom, they

Braz Menezes

have to stay home to look after their families."

Jimmy has lots to show me, and there are so many things he has planned for us to do. We go to his house, where his huge bedroom is filled with interesting things. He says he has everything he needs, sometimes two of each. He has piles of comics and books, including my favourite Just William stories by Richmal Crompton; puzzles; magic sets and instructions on how to make stink bombs; playing cards and board games like ludo and Snakes and Ladders; and the biggest marble collection I have seen. He even has a metal slingshot imported from England and two air rifles. And more.

"Tomorrow we will go hunting," Jimmy says.

The next day we set off soon after breakfast to a woodland area on the edge of the tea plantation. Jimmy shows me how to use one of his two air rifles. In just over an hour, we bag two green pigeons and a yellowneck. We go back to his house where Mpishi, the cook, shows me how to pluck the feathers and pull out the insides, using only my index finger.

We hold the birds under a running tap. Then, we walk to a little barbecue area by a tree near the main house. It is paved with stone slabs and has a giant grill made from a forty-gallon oil drum, sliced lengthwise.

"No, no, Mister Jimmy," Mpishi says. "*Kubwa sana*. Too big, we will use this one."

He lights the small charcoal *jiko* instead and leaves us alone. Jimmy and I shove skewers made of old bicycle spokes into the birds and cook them over coals; we sprinkle a bit of salt over the charred remains and devour them. Hunger can deaden the most discerning taste buds.

Every day is different. Jimmy has some toys that are not really toys, like his radios.

"Lando, come and see this." We are in his bedroom. He opens a small box. "This is my old one. My grandfather has sent me another one from England, and it is much better, but I haven't tested it yet."

He sets out the old one. It has a small wooden base on which is mounted a crystal about the size of a large kernel of corn. It has a thin wire contact attached to a spool of very fine copper wire.

"This crystal, called galena, can pick up sound waves," Jimmy tells me. "It must have a very long antenna attached like this. And you need these earphones to amplify the sound. Go ahead, put them on."

I listen first. Then we take turns to listen to scratches, squeaks, broken voices, and melodies from around the world.

"I can listen to the BBC in England," He says. "It's best at nighttime, though."

I can't get enough of Jimmy. At Uncle's place, Linda jokes that I am in love with him since they hardly see me at home. His mother invites me for a sleepover, and Jimmy and I talk nearly all night long. He shows me his photos taken at the Hill School in Eldoret; in the first he is in his uniform of blue shirt and grey shorts in front of the water tower; another shows him in the quadrangle; in a third he is with his friends Roby and Jack. He tells me many stories about his school.

"Do you like boarding school?" I ask him.

"I love it there," he says. "Really, I hate coming home here for the holidays. Normally, there is no one to play with. I wish I had brothers or even a sister. In school I have many friends. I think parents even forget how to talk to kids after they send them off to boarding school."

"My dad wants to send me to boarding school."

"Really? Can you please come to the Hill School?"

"No, I will be sent to Goa. My parents like religion, and priests run this boarding school."

"So when will you go? I think boarding school is a great life."

"Dunno yet. Actually it may not even happen. But my dad thinks I need discipline."

"You haven't been caught smoking, have you?" Jimmy sounds alarmed. "Two of our boys were caught trying their first smoke, and they had no end of problems. Our teachers are crazy for this punishment thing because if word gets out that the students do this at school, they will not receive any new boarders."

"Jimmy, will your dad bring you to Nairobi? Before I go to Goa, that is? I was thinking we could go to see Saboti by bus…I told you about her."

"When are you going back to Nairobi?"

"On Sunday. Tomorrow is our last day. Dad says we can't stay longer on this trip."

That Sunday at noon, Jimmy brings me a gift.

It is his old crystal radio. Of all his hundreds of toys, books, marbles, gizmos, and guns, this is the one thing I would have asked for. How did he know?

I say, "I will be right back."

The most precious things I can think of to give to Jimmy are the two bullets I picked up at the picnic spot where the cowboys tried to kill us. They are inside an empty matchbox on a bed of cotton, like the jewels I'd seen displayed in a store in Nairobi.

Back on the veranda, I give him the gift. "Come and see me in Nairobi. We can go to the museum. You will meet my friends Jeep and Simba."

Jimmy opens the matchbox slowly, like a girl might if she is hoping for an engagement ring. From his face I can tell he is pleased. "Mr. Fernando, will there be room for me to go to Lumbwa?"

"I'm very sorry, Jimmy," Uncle says. "You can see what a tight fit it is."

Jimmy and I exchange addresses. Late that afternoon, the Kisumu train to Nairobi pulls out of Lumbwa Station.

In the distance Lake Victoria is framed by rolling hills in various shades of green and brown. The sun streaming through cloud breaks creates spotlights of bright lemon on darker tones of green. Overhead, black and grey clouds mill around each other slowly, a few edged in silver and white, as if choosing dance partners for the daily late-afternoon downpour. In the far distance, bright sun filters through as if the whole picture is lit from behind. I close my eyes and imagine I am listening to my crystal radio. I like Jimmy very much; I must ask Dad if I can go to the Hill School in Eldoret, instead of Goa.

———•—•———

16: Dark Clouds Gather

Back home in Nairobi, I cannot wait to get Jimmy's crystal radio working. The most complicated task is to fix an antenna as high as possible above the roof, then run the wire down through the attic and into my bedroom. Jeep and Ahmad are very excited about the radio as well. Jeep cannot believe that a tiny crystal, smaller than a chickpea, can actually pick up sound waves—he bets half his new glass marble collection that I can't prove it works. Ahmad offers to help set it up. He sees it as a chance to get news of Karachi and his bride, Serena, who is stranded without proper travel papers in the violent aftermath following the Indiaand Pakistan partition.

Ahmad walks straight to the back of the house, carrying a bag of tools and a metal grid, which he says must be secured to the chimney.

"It works like a spider's web," he says. "Invisible and inaudible sound waves travelling uninterrupted through space, fly into the grid, and whoop!" He makes a sucking sound. "They are caught and sent down the wire to the crystal, which converts them into sounds that you will hear on the earphone."

"It's like our prayers," Jeep says. "They move silently and unseen through the air. When we pray, we do not have to shout. We can ask God for things, and He hears everything and talks back to us."

I really hadn't thought about how God sends messages. "Ahmad, do you think that's how it works? Does this mean we might hear God directly if His messages are trapped in our spider web?"

"Yes, if you're lucky you may."

"Jambo, Mwangi," Ahmad says to the houseboy, and asks if we have a ladder. Mwangi, as excited as everyone else, goes off to fetch one from behind the garage. Ahmad gestures for us to come closer as he grabs a stick and sketches a cross-section of the house and roof in the dirt.

"Lando, you must go into the attic. I will climb up on the roof and attach this to the chimney here." He holds up a metal grid. "At this spot, where the sloping roof meets the wall in the attic, you will see light coming through the vents. When I give you the signal, you take one end of this wire and send it outside to me, and I will grab it and pull it out slowly and fix one end to the antenna. Let's see where you want to set up the radio in your room."

Ahmad suggests we install the radio by my bedside. "Just here." He drills a small hole through the asbestos board ceiling and takes one end of the thin wire and pushes it though the opening. "Lando, you will have to crawl to the edge to reach the wire. It may be dark up there, so carry a flashlight. Maybe Jeep should go up as well."

We go out to the rear veranda where Mwangi is waiting. He carefully carries the wooden ladder into the house and leans it into the trap door opening.

"Remember to put your foot only on the wood frame," Ahmad warns. "Do not put any weight on the ceiling board, as it will break and you will come crashing down."

Jeep follows me up the ladder.

Notwithstanding the ventilation, the space under the iron-sheeted roof is sweltering. The musty air smells of decayed fruit, chicken shit, and dust. Jeep flashes his light, and moves closer to me. I grab his arm in terror. The underside of the roof is covered with hundreds of fuzzy tiny grey bodies clinging to the trusses and beams.

"Bats," Jeep whispers. "Look at those droppings all over. No wonder it smells up here."

"We always knew there were bats up here, but I never imagined there would be so many."

"Do you ever hear them flying about at night?"

"Some nights I do. They squeak together as if they are having a party," I say. "Dad says they're good to have around because they feed on insects as well as fruit, and that's why we don't have many mosquitoes in the house."

Mwangi has taken the ladder outside for Ahmad to climb up on the roof. "Lando, will they attack us, you think?" Jeep's whisper has a touch of panic. "How will we escape?"

"Let's be very quiet. We have to get that radio working." I try not to show I am scared. "If we are attacked, we can hold on to the edges of the trap door and jump. It can't be worse than falling off the monkey-nut tree."

Ahmad calls to say he's waiting.

I creep over the beams, crouching low to reach the wire poking out of the hole in the ceiling. I cannot hold onto the beams for support because they are covered with bats. I think Jeep has stopped breathing, but as long as he does not drop the flashlight and plunge us in darkness, I won't worry. I creep, pulling the wire slowly, very slowly, until it's exactly at the spot where Ahmad will get hold of it, while Jeep holds the light with one hand and slowly pulls the wire through the hole in the ceiling from its spindle in my bedroom. We watch out for any movement by the bats and hardly dare breathe in case we wake up the crepuscular creatures.

Mwangi has returned with the ladder and now jams it into the trap door. "Aaahh, ouch!" The sudden noise makes Jeep spin around, anticipating a full-scale bat attack, and he ends up scratching himself on a protruding nail. Dripping in sweat, we descend quickly, leaving the bats to their own devices.

Back in the bedroom, we watch Ahmad as he connects the wires to the earpiece of an old dismantled telephone. He moves the wire connectors, gently trying to find the best signal. Crackles, screeches, and whistles struggle out of the earpiece along with intermittent clear signals.

Braz Menezes

"Okay, ready, Lando!" Ahmad announces. "You must now listen for good news from Karachi and tell me immediately. I must get back to work in my taxi now."

Jeep's amazement shows all over his face. He thinks it is worth the sacrifice of half his marble collection. He starts to receive the clearest English-language broadcasts: "This is the Overseas Service of the BBC coming to you on shortwave radio." Although the sounds are coming from London, I feel I am still connected to Jimmy in boarding school in Eldoret. I wonder if he too could be listening to the BBC right now. I cannot understand the magic that makes this tiny crystal pick up sound, out of the air, but I hear questions and answers from European settlers across the Commonwealth exchanging news with London. Night after night I filter the crackles and voices coming from the blackness beyond the stars for some good news to pass on to Ahmad. The BBC reports instead about unhappiness among members of something called the North Atlantic Treaty Alliance—NATO —formed only about six months earlier in April 1949 by twelve countries including Britain and Portugal. Sleep overtakes me.

The radio becomes an addiction. Every night there is some news, most of which I do not understand, but it helps to divert me from dwelling on my immediate future. Despite giving the impression that he discarded the idea of my going away to India for boarding school, Dad has recently displayed a renewed excitement about this. Apparently, his card-playing colleagues at the club have refuelled his enthusiasm, having sent their boys to Belgaum, Bombay, Poona, or Goa.

"FX was at our table," Dad tells us over dinner. "His son Paul has been in boarding school since he was quite young. He has been doing very well, it seems, and is now entering medical school."

I refrain from any comment and go to my room.

Invariably, as I put the earphone down each night, I think of Jimmy and what he had to say about boarding school. He is happy at the Hill School in Eldoret, but the more I think of it, the more I realize how different my own circumstances are. For a start, I'm not an only child, and I know I will miss Linda, Fatima, and Joachim. I will miss Jeep, Mwangi, Simba, and my pals at school. I keep hoping Dad will change his mind.

As I arrive home one evening in November, Uncle Antonio's BSA motorbike is in the front yard. He does not normally drop in at this time. I wonder if something is wrong. I secure Simba to his leash and walk indoors by the veranda, where Linda, Fatima, and Joachim are eating dinner. Linda gestures for me to be quiet. I hear Dad's voice. He is not usually home on Wednesday evenings—it's his card-playing day. Now I feel certain that something is wrong. I slide along the corridor and edge myself toward the sitting room to listen. I can hear Uncle's voice and Mom's…and I realize they are discussing me.

"Anja, we will all travel to Goa in January," Dad says. "I'll be on long leave. We will all be on holiday together, so it really won't be an abrupt separation for Lando."

"But he's only ten," Mom pleads. "Let's wait a year until he finishes primary school at the Goan school. Who knows, he may change his mind about boarding school."

"But Anja, listen to Chico," Uncle Antonio says. "It will be expensive to make a separate journey later if you don't combine it with Chico's passage-paid home leave. You know it's not unusual for Goan families to send their children to Catholic schools in Goa."

"But I still think he's too young," Mom says.

"Sometimes the mother stays in Goa for a few years while the father returns to Africa," Uncle says. "Then when the children reach high school age, they're placed in boarding schools run by Jesuits or in convents run by nuns."

"Exactly, Antonio! Anja, we are lucky that Lando had at least some primary school years here with us," Dad says. "Even now, many Goans working in the districts still send their children abroad for secondary school. We must think of the future."

Shocked to hear my favourite uncle supporting my father's

argument, I barge into the room. I realize Dad has asked him over to help persuade Mom. Dad, Mom, and Uncle Antonio look up, startled. Guilty looks are engraved on their faces.

"I will not go! I do not want to go to boarding school!" I shout. "I have nothing to do with Goa. This is my country. All my school friends are here…Jeep, Savio, Gerson, and—"

"You'll make many new friends," Dad says. "I know you'll have a wonderful time. Jimmy told you how much he liked it. Boarding school can be great fun."

"But I want to study, not have fun," I say piously, not really expecting anyone to believe me.

"The world will be in your hands," says Dad, sounding as if the issue has already been settled. "With God's grace, Mom and I will make sacrifices to help you. If you work hard, new opportunities will come to you. If you waste this chance, you'll have only yourself to blame." He glances at Mom.

"Of course we'll miss you terribly," Mom says. "But it'll be good for your future."

"Remember, Lando, the Jesuits have been training scholars for centuries," Dad adds.

"St. Joseph's in Arpora is a well-known school," Uncle Antonio says.

"Just be careful. They'll try and turn you into a Jesuit too, like they did to your uncle," Mom says, but Dad cuts her short.

"You'll be the first in our family to go to university," he says. "If your grandfather had not died so young, I would have gone to university, instead of counting rice grains and coconuts in Goa, or bookkeeping in Bombay."

"And ending up a slave in a suit for the National Bank of India in Africa," Mom says.

I stomp out. Mwangi is in the kitchen and hands me a plate. I am tempted to go hungry and show Mom how upset I am but change my mind. I did that once before and spent the night hungry, with the refrain of Mom's "Think of the starving children in India or in China…" buzzing in my brain. I eat quickly and go to my room. I must wait two hours before the clearest broadcasts of the BBC come through about midnight. I turn off the light and lie on my back, staring up at a dark ceiling.

I realize my life is about to change completely. I know Mom is against the idea of sending me away, but she will not openly oppose Dad over this decision, especially as he has Uncle Antonio on his side.

"Perhaps after high school," Dad had said, "you'll want to continue in medicine or law in Bombay, or we may be able to save enough to afford further studies in England if you wish."

That will mean another ten years away. I am just over ten now, so I will have to spend the equivalent of my whole lifetime away. I cannot understand it. Suddenly, even my bed feels uncomfortable. I hear Dad's footsteps approaching. There is a knock on the door.

"Lando, are you awake?" I remain quiet. "Are you asleep, Lando?"

I hear Dad walk away, and I start breathing normally again. I want him to know I am not about to forgive him for messing up my whole life. Above me I hear the bats in the attic having a party.

Maybe they're sending me away to make room in the house for the others? But maybe I am imagining the worst. Jimmy seems happy with his school in Eldoret. Perhaps the Jesuits will be okay after all. They had trained Dad for two years in his youth, and surely no father would want to send his son to a place that was bad? Dad had said that at the end of our holiday together I would be left in the custody of the Jesuits, who would "mould" me as though I was a lump of clay and guide me through the next five years up to the Senior Cambridge Exam.

I turn to the BBC for comfort. In China, Mao Zedong, who led the Red Army on a long march and defeated the rulers after a twenty-year-long war, says he will end starvation in China. I switch off the radio. I think Mom will have to change her script about the starving children in China…I fall asleep and dream of Christmas.

17: The New Year's Eve of 1949

The weeks seem to rush by. Suddenly, it's December.

"Lando, I won't be here for Christmas," Jeep says as we walk home from school. "My folks are planning a trip to Zanzibar."

"So you'll miss your last Christmas tree party before you are over-age?"

"Yeah, I guess. This will really be your last Christmas too. Lando, aren't you scared or something? Going to Goa, I mean?"

"Yes, definitely something. I heard from Linda that Mom and Dad said I will be going to the New Year's Eve dance, since I will not get a chance till I return when I am twenty years old. So that'll be different."

"No kidding! Is that how long you are going to be away?"

"At least that."

"Gosh, I may be married by then. Bye. See you at Mass on Sunday."

The holiday season arrives. I attend the Christmas tree and Boxing Day events, but now for some reason they seem routine. Perhaps it's because Jeep is away, or it's the anxiety of what awaits me in Goa, or the thought of losing all the connections I've made. The big dance on New Year's Eve, however, begins to attract me.

Everyone will attend at one club or another, the only night in the year when everyone seems to celebrate. I will attend my first gala ball at the Goan Gymkhana.

The club's Anniversary Dance and the New Year's Eve dance are the only two occasions when formal wear is mandatory. It is no big deal for the men to wear pukka dinner jackets and black trousers with a silk stripe down each trouser leg, and white starched shirts with black silk bow ties; it is the same every year. However, for women and girls, the lead-up to the dance is frenetic. I know my older sister Linda and her close friends discuss the colour and style of their dresses secretly, almost obsessively. They pore over a colour catalogue of *Evening Fashions for Young Adults*, purchased at Choitram's Silk Store on Government Road, the only store that sells the packets, which include dress pattern cut-outs on flimsy paper. All the dressmaker has to do is to place the pattern on the fabric and then run the scissors along the dotted lines and sew the bits together. It looks so easy.

"Please, nobody choose pink," I overhear Evelyn saying. "I chose it first."

"I'm wearing a bright red," Linda announces. "I don't care what anybody thinks."

Clarice has decided on a turquoise-green silk outfit; her sister Ivy has selected the muted purple of a jacaranda blossom; Jean will wear a black gown, but her cousin Shirley hasn't made up her mind yet.

Then begins the complex part of making the dresses. Most Goan women have learned to sew, since dressmaking and the basic elements of cooking are prerequisites for girls contemplating marriage. Mom cuts and sews her own gown and helps Linda and two of her friends with theirs. They make frequent visits to various dukas in the Indian bazaar. These are where the best deals can be found by the yard: bargain-priced remnants of silks and satins; organdy, chiffon, and velvet; printed cotton with fast dyes; and the latest postwar sensation, printed polyester from Britain. The final visit is to a duka in the bazaar for the trimmings: braiding, grosgrain, velvet and satin ribbon, lace, sequins, and beads. That store also carries more buttons than there are stars in a Nairobi sky. With barely two days left, one girl wants changes made. Mom works into the night to help her.

"I hope we will balance the books on time," Dad says as he leaves for work on the morning of New Year's Eve. "I will come to the dance straight from work."

The British commercial banks like the National Bank of India, Barclays, and the Standard have a policy that all books must be balanced by year-end, down to the last cent. The numbers must be reconciled with handwritten entries made each trading day of the year in large green linen-bound ledgers, and any shortfall of shillings and cents will have to be contributed jointly, in cash, by the clerical and accounting staff.

"So will the club hall just be full of ladies?" Mom asks.

"Amorzinha, you know this happens every year." Dad tries to calm her. "We will be there well before midnight. Most of our members are civil servants. They will not be affected and will be happy to have so many extra ladies to dance with."

Uncle Antonio gives us a lift in his Austin A40. That includes Mom, Linda, me, and our neighbour Anita, whose husband Luis is also working late.

While Uncle parks the car, I walk proudly up the steps of the gymkhana, escorting three lovely ladies. I feel very grown up. A smartly dressed couple warmly greets us. I recognize the man as Mr. Lobo and assume he must be the president. His beautiful wife, Alina looks stunning in a figure-hugging tomato-red *choli* and a jungle-green silk sari trimmed with gold and red.

I suddenly feel self-conscious. I am not wearing black. But it is my only suit, which is the same shade of light grey colour as an African grey parrot. This year marks the first occasion when my suit is actually a comfortable fit. Three years ago, when imports were restarted after the war ended in Europe, Dad had my first suit made by Casmiro Coutinho, who owns a busy tailoring business in Reata Road near his bank.

"Boys grow very fast at this age," Mr. Coutinho had said to Dad. "If you ask me, better I make your sonny boy's suit on the big side, for the same small cost."

Dad couldn't argue with that. My double-breasted suit arrived, large and baggy, complete with a buttonhole in the lapel, and short pants with appropriate hooks for braces to hold them up. Special accessories were the long grey socks from the Woolworths store on Delamere Avenue.

We enter the hall, decorated with twisted streamers, buntings, and balloons. Many chairs around the perimeter of the hall have already been taken. Many others appear to be reserved seats for absentee husbands balancing the books somewhere. Dona Pulchera and Dona Linda wave to catch Mom's eye. Dona Lenore has reserved a seat for Mom.

"The hall will soon be packed," she says to Mom. "You know how some families will always arrive fashionably late." As if on cue, the large families start to arrive as the band plays a foxtrot, but nobody is dancing yet. It is time to see and be seen.

Senhor Olivet Almeida, the owner of the bruised headlight that cost me sixty Hail Marys, and his family troop in. There is an audible buzz as the five daughters, each young lady in a beautiful gown, dutifully follow their parents into the hall, with the three brothers bringing up the rear. A past president, Norbert Menezes and his wife Annie, accompanied by daughter Milly and son Neves, are next.

J.M. Nazareth, Q.C., and his wife and two others walk in just ahead of the two Albuquerque boys, Olinto and Ayres. I see Dr. Manu, nephew of the zebra-riding Dr. Ribeiro, accompanied by Dona Angela Ribeiro and her sister Dona Eslinda Rocha, who walks in with her two daughters, Ally and Cecilia, followed by Arthur Da Costa and the third Ribeiro sister, Roselia. Andrew Ribeiro is holding the hand of Arthur's sister Juracy. My classmate, Gerson, walks in with his parents and his two sisters, Angela and Grignon. Nearby, Rom is handing his mother Bridget a drink. Anselm comes into the hall holding Servita Martryes's hand. Alex Fonseca's family walks in.

The Merry Melodists are playing today, and Bobby on the saxophone is the bandleader. The band looks very sharp in white tuxedo jackets, black trousers, black bow ties, and red rosebuds in their buttonholes. I follow Gerson and join two other classmates, Edgar and Savio, by the stage. We love watching the band from close up. On special occasions Alec Pereira, Rom's dad, sometimes plays the drums instead of Bobby's regular, Luiz Da Costa. Some months earlier at a daytime dance, he had shown Savio and me how to assemble the bass drum and the snares and how to position the tom-toms, conga drums, and cymbals. He even showed us how to hold the drumsticks and the brushes and play different strokes. I wave at Mr. Pereira. He smiles and nods but keeps on drumming.

"You blokes want to learn some basic steps?" Jean asks. She, Linda, Milly, and friends are beginning to dance with each other nearby. Jean grabs my hand. "Come, Lando, I'll teach you to dance."

"What? Me, dance?"

"Yes, but you hold the girl like this." She puts her left hand over my shoulder, grabs my left hand with her right and raises it, and pulls me close toward her.

"Let's get outta here," I hear Gerson say. Edgar and Savio follow him.

"No thank you," I say, pulling myself away from her grip as quickly as possible. I too am horror-struck at the thought of even touching a girl let alone wanting to dance with one.

Since it is our first New Year's dance, we explore other areas of the club. Every nook and cranny is packed. The two bars are doing a roaring business. We think we might sneak in a game of pool while the adults are busy, only to discover six babies asleep on the pool table. The billiards room has been temporarily transformed into a crèche. The high spectator benches with the tall backs have been placed to enclose three sides of the table, over which a rubber sheet has been laid on the green baize surface. Layers of Nakuru-brand blankets covered by a sheet have been arranged to fully cover the table surface. The two ayahs on duty unceremoniously shoo us out since they are also trying to get some sleep.

Ninety minutes later, I see Mom and the other husbandless wives look worried. Will their men balance the books on time?

The MC announces the buffet dinner is open in the library.

We line up, fill our plates, collect a soft drink, and make ourselves comfortable in the only space available—the steps of the club entrance. Suddenly, a fleet of taxis arrives, each packed with men in black suits: bookkeepers and clerks, accountants and cashiers. Their books balanced, they can now enjoy themselves. We eavesdrop on Dad and Uncle Patrick, listening to their stories. Their tales differ from the other men's only in the minor details.

All the muzungu management staff had gathered in the GM's office from about 6:30 p.m. They had to wait until the balance sheet could be signed off. Working downstairs under great pressure, the Goan and other Indian cashiers and accounting staff could hear them talking, laughing, and drinking. They imagined the uniformed waiters in white gloves serving canapés to the management while the staff was toiling away. The smell of whisky was killing them. The outside doors were locked. Nobody was allowed to leave the premises until the GM gave the okay.

By 9:30 p.m. they thought they had finished. The chief accountant, puffing on a cigar and whisky in hand, came down. He spoke briefly with the assistant chief accountant and signed off the accounts. He thanked them and authorized them to leave. At that moment, the GM walked in. Already in his tuxedo and well oiled, he wanted to party. He started telling jokes. Patrick and Dad were trapped and couldn't leave. Finally, they agreed to meet outside; they crept out one by one, as if going to the toilet, and just left. They would not have made it otherwise.

"Shush!" Savio says. The MC makes an announcement. It is just past 11:30 p.m. We return to our vantage spot by the stage. There seems to be a new tension in the air.

The MC is working up the crowd. Everyone scrambles to get their partners for the "midnight special" to bring in the New Year. The minutes tick away as the dance couples join arms and sing "Auld Lang Syne". Husbands and wives, fiancés and fiancées, wannabe marrieds, and confirmed spinsters and bachelors all drift onto the dance floor.

The minutes and seconds tick away, the MC starts the count-down, and the revellers join in: 4...3...2...1...0. The lights go out. *Boom! Boom! Boom!* Fireworks erupt on the tennis courts. The lights come on. Balloons come floating down from the ceiling. A chorus of people shouting "Happy new year" rings through the hall amid kisses, hugs, more shouts of "Happy new years," more hugs, and fewer kisses, until the jubilation eventually dies down. Men light cigars. Ladies head off in groups to re-powder their noses and whatever else needs touching up.

It is now 1950. A short, stout man walks onto the stage. The band plays a few chords of their signature tune and a drum roll. The MC is at the microphone.

"Ladies and gentlemen, I give you your president, Mr. Jos Pinto." Bobby's drummer produces another drum roll.

Mr. Pinto makes a short speech. He seems overcome at the sight of so many families coming together on this special night every year. He talks with emotion about his family not being here to share this moment. He mentions his wife Gladys and his chil-dren, who had been sent to Poona for their primary and secondary schooling. On behalf of his absent family, Mr. Pinto wishes us all a very happy 1950. He finishes up optimistically: "...and I know the Goan Gymkhana will still be here fifty, seventy-five, and even a hundred years from now. Thank you, and God bless you all."

Loud applause follows. I realize that as long as the children cannot have access to higher-level education in Kenya, which are reserved for Europeans only, we will be forced to go abroad.

Bobby and his boys play regularly at British clubs and hotels, so they know the latest tunes and the classic oldies. The band strikes up their well-rehearsed medley of dances. Short sets follow, one after the other: waltzes, foxtrots, quick steps, polkas, tangos, rumbas, and the Charleston, followed by a medley of Goan mandos, dulpods, and deknes. There is a break.

The MC asks the partygoers to form groups for the lancers. Suddenly, there is a renewed burst of energy. Dad and Mom; A.P.

and Dona Esmeralda; Alvaro, famous for his gold Rolex and patent leather shoes, and Dina; and Jules and Dona Maria Fernandes form a group. Next to them, Sylvia and Fred, Angelo and Annie, and Fidelis and Ida form another. Members of the Almeidas, Andrades, Alburquerques, Cordeiros, Costas, Dantas, De Cruzes, Da Gamas, D'Souzas, Fernandes, Fonsecas, Gomes, Menezes, Nazareth, Noronhas, Pereiras, Rebelos, Ribeiro, Rochas, Sequeiras, Toscanos, Torcados and more mix and mingle. They manoeuvre to avoid collisions. Soon the whole hall is whirling away.

"Do you think one day we will be like these folks?" Gerson asks Savio and me.

"Most definitely," Savio says.

"I will probably never dance ever by the time the Jesuits finish with me in Goa," I reply.

It is nearly three in the morning, and everyone is full of energy. That night, Savio, Gerson, and I witness almost biblical scenes of miraculous cures. We see friends of our parents, who we assumed were year-round cripples, jump and jitterbug in gay abandon. We conclude that they have probably overdosed on one of the world's most effective painkillers—Johnny Walker Scotch whisky.

Tired, we adjourn to the library where the caterers have largely cleared up. We curl up in a corner and fall asleep.

"Wake up, boys." Linda has been searching for us. "The dance is over. It's time to go home." Revellers shout farewells to one another.

"*Boa noite!* Good night! Happy new year! See you soon! *Kwa heri na tuonane!*"

It is 5:30 a.m. when we arrive home. I am very tired.

"Why all this fuss over New Year's Day?" I ask Dad. "Is it a Catholic feast day?"

"It marks the last day of the Christian Gregorian calendar, so almost all Christian cultures celebrate it," he says. "We Goans inherited it along with our religion from the Portuguese."

In the few minutes before I fall into a deep sleep, I cannot help thinking of the gymkhana president's sadness as he talked about his absent family. I wonder whether my parents will miss me and regret their decision. But I am now also reconciled to going away.

18: The Black Tin Trunk

Within a week the excitement leading to the New Year's Eve dance and the event itself is last year's news. A letter arrives from Jimmy, who is home in Kericho for the holidays. He has had a good term at boarding school and an uncle has given him the latest model air rifle for Christmas—he now has three rifles in all. He will start high school next year and may come down to Nairobi in August to visit me. He wants to know if I managed to see Saboti again. He writes that boys his age at the Hill School in Eldoret are starting to pair up with their girlfriends. He adds that the Christmas holidays are the best time to be home from boarding school, since everybody else is home then too, so he always has lots of company.

I fold Jimmy's letter and take it to my room. I will give him all the news; perhaps he missed the letter in which I told him I would definitely be going away. Funny he should mention Saboti. I have been thinking of her red-brown hair, her smile, and those intense deep brown eyes that stare right into your own but don't give away anything. This reminds me that she never told me how she got that scar just below the shoulder.

"Lando, are you there?" Mom's voice interrupts my thoughts. "Please keep an eye on Fatima and Joachim. Linda and I are going into town for about two hours. And by the way, I think Simba needs a bath."

The relatively slow pace of our lives has been ratcheted up a few notches in preparation for the forthcoming voyage to Goa, now barely three weeks away. Dad must work until the day before we leave, so Mom has to bear all the burden of preparation, and she is getting anxious—no matter what the economic conditions elsewhere, family and friends will expect gifts, even if they deny it.

Mom says the most difficult task is picking gifts for eleven family members whom she hasn't seen for seven years. "The women in my family keep changing shape and size," she tells her friends. "I can't even imagine what to buy them. The men are easy."

I can understand her plight just from glancing at her family photograph taken in 1935, the year of her wedding. According to Mom, Avozinho, as Granddad Joachim is called, is the only one who is still the same—tall and always elegantly dressed in a suit and tie; his position at work and in local society requires it, so he is like that at home too.

My grandma, Avozinha, on the other hand, is always changing to keep up with the times. She recently moved with all the younger siblings to their family home in the village of Loutolim to shelter them from the bustle of city life in Margao, but even though she has neglected her physique and gained much weight she has not given up her taste in fashion. On a previous visit home in 1942, Grandma had specifically asked Mom to bring her only one dress, but it had to be in the current Portuguese style with the poufy long sleeves and high collar trimmed with handmade lace. Now in 1950, no dukawalla in Nairobi's Indian bazaar is likely to stock such an item, as those dresses are already out of fashion.

"What about Aunt Lucia?" I ask. "Linda says she is now married and lives in Bombay."

"Your dear Aunt Lucia?" Mom rolls her eyes heavenwards. "Look at that photo. She was only a chubby little flower girl when I sailed away to Africa with your father in 1935. During our last visit to Goa, she was a teenager just waiting to discard any trace of discipline or decorum. She hated everything about the Catholic school uniforms, from the long dresses, to the long sleeves, to the high collars, and even all the ridiculous buttons, belts, and buckles that the nuns had diligently incorporated into them. God only knows how fashionably she dresses now, after all these years living in Bombay's high society with that handsome and wealthy Rodrigues boy she married."

That evening, Dad brings the latest news of our trip.

"Smith Mackenzie Shipping has delivered our tickets. We'll take the train to Mombasa, where we will have a two-day stop. The SS *Karanja* sails on the 29. Our journey will include a day's stop in the Seychelles."

"Seychelles?" I say excitedly. "That's where Saboti's from."

"So she's your girlfriend now?" Linda teases. I kick her under the dining table, but my leg doesn't quite reach. Only Mom notices my vain attempt to hush her up.

"Lando," Dad says, "your clothes, books, and any other stuff for boarding school, as well as Mom's gifts, will be packed in the black metal trunk. Will you please help me empty it this weekend?"

The trunk with an unlocked padlock in place has lain in the main bedroom, untouched for almost ten years. Dad opens it carefully, as if expecting something to jump out at him. I lean forward to look inside. He picks up a newspaper, slightly browned with age, glances at it, and places it carefully to one side. It is a copy of *O Heraldo*; he tells me it's a Portuguese-language daily printed in Goa, dated March 1928 on the eve of his departure twenty-two years ago.

"Your late uncle Orlando gave me this trunk in 1924. He bought it in a shop near Victoria Terminus, the main railway station in Bombay. He had planned to travel to Lisbon, but he suddenly changed his mind and decided to go to Brazil instead. He knew it would involve an overland trek across Africa." I see Dad's eyes turn moist. It's not like him to be sentimental.

"What happened?"

"It's a sad story," Dad says. "When both our parents passed away in 1917 within three months of each other, we suddenly became orphans. We were placed in the legal care of my father's only sibling, our aunt Tia Filomena, a spinster. She could not raise four children on her own, so we were separated. Our sister, Maria Theresa, the youngest, was only twelve years old; she was placed in a convent run by nuns in Margao. Later she was moved to another convent in Bangalore, and we never saw her again. Uncle Orlando was the second-born. His happiness was sacrificed for the good of the Church as well. He was placed in a seminary in Rachol, near our village of Raia, to be educated and raised by the clergy. Uncle Nico, my oldest brother, got a job in Mozambique and went to Africa."

I feel a deep sadness in hearing this story. I cannot imagine what it is like to lose both parents and then be separated from my brother and sisters. "Why? Couldn't they have tried to keep your brothers and your sister together?

"The tradition in Goa," Dad says, "is that the oldest son will look after the family property, and the second-born will be sacrificed to the Church and join the priesthood. Maria Theresa was so young that she needed full-time care, so they felt the convent was the best place for her."

I do not like what I am hearing. I am disturbed by what this might mean for me. In our catechism class, I remember seeing a picture of Abraham in the Old Testament with a big knife in his right hand, standing over his son Isaac and looking up at the sky toward God. Above him the dark grey clouds were parted to let in bright rays of sunlight. The boy was kneeling on a rock beside a pile of firewood. His head was bowed low to the ground. He looked frightened.

"Dad, am I being sacrificed to the Church on this trip?" I ask. "I am the second-born after Linda." I watch his face. "Or do they mean the second-born son, which means Joachim? But he's still only three years old."

"This custom is less common in Goa now, and it's certainly not done at all in Kenya." Dad senses my anxiety and smiles. "In any case, with the matata you get up to, no seminary is likely to want you, let alone keep you."

I feel an instant sense of relief. "So what happened to your brother?"

"Orlando studied hard. The more he read, the more convinced he was that he must abandon the seminary, which he did, one year before his ordination," Dad says. "Soon after, he decided to start a new life in Brazil, so he left Goa and boarded a ship to Mozambique where he was going to break his journey, before heading off to Brazil." Dad's eyes are tearing up again. I pretend I haven't noticed.

"About three months later, we received some news through Uncle Nico, confirming that Orlando had arrived safely. But apparently he didn't like Beira or Lourenço Marques. He made arrangements to join a foot caravan and travel overland to Luanda, the Angolan capital. He thought he would find a boat there that would take him across the Atlantic to Salvador de Bahia in Brazil."

"How far is that?"

"Let me show you," Dad says. He goes into the next room and returns with an old revolving globe. "Look, Lando." He points to a spot on the globe. "This little speck here is Goa; all this is India. Here is Africa. We're here in Kenya. Mozambique is down there. Uncle Orlando took a ship from Goa to there, and then he was going to cross Africa from east to west here. At Luanda he planned to get on a boat to take him all the way to here," he says, pointing to Brazil.

"That's more than halfway around the world!" I say in disbelief.

Uncle Orlando was just twenty years old at the time. I am over half his age but have done nothing in my lifetime, except that trip to Kericho with my family. "What was it like when Uncle reached Brazil?"

"He didn't. Back in Goa, we had no news for almost a year. Then one day a letter arrived from Uncle Nico. He told us that Orlando had joined a caravan and trekked for more than five months through grasslands and dense forests and jungles full of wild animals. He had crossed rivers and streams, setting up camp every night with his travelling companions and porters. However, he died of malaria when the group was just six days away from Luanda, and was buried in the bush. The few things he had were brought back to Uncle Nico. Tia Filomena and I were broken-hearted. Our ignorant villagers in Raia said it was God's punishment for Orlando's having left the seminary. But we knew better. Years later both Uncle Nico and I each named our first-born sons after Orlando. That's how you got your name."

Dad leaves the room for a few minutes. I feel a lump in my throat about being named after this brave uncle and make up my mind that one day I will travel to Brazil and achieve his dream in his memory. Yes, I will complete his journey. Dad returns and answers my unasked question.

"I brought this trunk to Africa, since it's all I have to remind me of Orlando," he says. "I came out with almost nothing: a brown linen suit, bought at a half-price sale in Bombay, to be worn on my first job interview in Mozambique; two cotton shirts; two replacement collars; two pairs of socks; an extra pair of shoes; some underwear; and one necktie."

Dad leans over into the trunk and picks up a folded, heavily creased Portuguese flag and a carved teakwood tray. I pick up two wood-framed sepia portraits.

"Who are these people?"

"My father and mother. If they were still alive, you would be meeting them in a few weeks for the first time. They would have been so happy to see all my children."

Both dead grandparents stare at me; they have peaceful, contented faces as they gaze directly into the camera lens. Dad picks up the final items at the bottom of the trunk: a Holy Bible, a rosary, and a wooden crucifix. "These are my last gifts from Tia Filomena. She died a year before I returned to Goa to marry Mom. That's why I have treasured them for all these years."

"But all this is very little for such a big trunk."

"Yes, you're right," Dad says. "In fact, every inch of remaining space was crammed with little packages, all of them gifts that family, neighbours, and acquaintances asked me to bring over from Goa for their friends and relatives in Africa."

In those days, he explains, most people had no idea of the distances to be travelled, or how difficult it was to send parcels from one country to another. It took months to dispose of everything, through onward travellers from here to Uganda, Tanganyika, Zanzibar, and even Mozambique. There were gift packages of Bombay duck, a dried salted fish; homemade Goan sausages; dried mango slices; roasted cashew nuts; lots of spices; dried solans; and pickled bimblims. He had added a week's supply of Goan newspapers in case any Goans in Mozambique were homesick because that's where he was headed when he sailed out of Goa.

"Now that you've emptied all your things from the trunk," I ask, "will we pack everything for Goa in just one trunk?"

"We will take two smaller ones as well," Dad says. "This trunk will carry presents for the family, your clothes, books, and any special items you want to include. Mom will add some gifts that close friends will be sending through us to their relatives in Goa. It will soon fill up."

The next few days rush by. The black trunk is placed in my room, and items are packed as they arrive. That night I sit down and write a note to Jimmy, explaining that a decision has been made, and that most probably I will be away for at least ten years. I thank him again for his kindness and the gift of the crystal radio, which I will take to Goa with me.

Meanwhile, Mom and Dad cope with a stream of visitors bearing gifts for their relatives. Linda has her own list and helps Fatima with her packing; little Joachim alone appears not to notice the matata that has touched the family.

————•—•——

19: Lunch with Abbajaan

The highlight of my final week before departing for boarding school in Goa is the wonderful lunch cooked by Abdul's mother. It will be the first time in more than two years that Hardev's family, who are Sikhs, have agreed to let him enter our Muslim friend, Abdul's home. Jeep is there of course. Abdul's mother has cooked us our favourite Hyderabad mutton biryani. Even as Jeep, Hardev, and I walk along Plums Lane, we can catch the aroma wafting through the windows of Abdul's kitchen. We instinctively hesitate by the monkey-nut tree outside his gate. The last time the four of us were together, Jeep and I had returned from hospital after being treated for minor injuries, only to be greeted by the whole neighbourhood mistakenly gathered in a daytime vigil praying for Jeep's soul to travel safely into the afterlife.

I am about to knock on the door, but it opens instantly. Abdul has been waiting eagerly.

"Come, come, all of you. Please wash your hands and come to the table," Abdul's mother calls from the kitchen. Like most mothers, she does not need eye contact to know what is going on around the house. The air inside the house is filled with the smells of various foods. Jeep and I automatically compete to guess the ingredients from the aromas.

"Roasted cloves, cardamom, onions."

"Ginger, cumin, garlic, cilantro."

"Mint."

We once saw her make the biryani. After marinating the mutton in a special yogurt mix, the cooked meat and basmati rice were added to a deep pot in alternating layers. Then the fragrant mix was baked for thirty minutes and served with a garnish of freshly chopped mint and cilantro. I never realized I was so hungry until I sat in the kitchen savouring the flavourful aromas as they melded together in the oven.

"Abba wants to talk to you, Lando, after lunch," Abdul's mother tells me. Abba is short for Abbajaan, Abdul's grandfather.

"Me?" I ask, concerned. Abba is a nice man, but like most old men with white beards, he is slightly scary as he shuffles about, feeling his way on the potholed gravel of Plums Lane. I know Abdul is frightened of Abba, since his grandfather had tried to instill discipline from an early age. The meal arrives, and any thoughts of Abba are instantly erased.

As we near the end our meal, Abba shuffles into the room, scraping one sandal with a broken strap on the floor. According to Abdul, Abba grew up in hard times and believes in saving for a rainy day. He glances at us and walks to Jeep, taking him by the arm that was grazed during the tree fall some months earlier.

"Jeep! You are a very brave boy, but I must tell you about real courage. Lando, you are going to Goa? You all come to my sitting room when you finish."

This is the first time ever that we are allowed or invited in there. I walk in closely behind Jeep; Hardev follows me. Abdul seems nervous about entering, perhaps because of having been forbidden entry ever since he was a toddler. Abba's private sitting room is nothing any of us could have imagined.

Persian rugs, Afghan and Turkish kilims, and hand-woven Indian silk carpets compete for floor and wall space. Beautifully crafted scale models of Arab dhows, a Portuguese caravel, and two British clipper ships adorn every shelf and windowsill.

On one side of the room, exquisitely sculpted ivory and wooden horses, and camels parade on top of a large coffee table, itself ornately carved in Burmese teak. On another low table, about a hundred miniature horses in shining moulded brass, on top of brilliant red silk fabric are ready for war against the horses and camels on the higher table.

"Look, it seems as if the army on this lower table is ready to fight those horses and camels on the higher table," I say.

Abba smiles. "History is made up of the poor revolting against the rich and powerful."

Muted sunlight struggles through louvred wooden shutters, which keep out the intense glare of the afternoon sun. Highly polished perforated brass lamps, some with inserts of coloured glass, reflect a multitude of white and coloured beams in every direction, making the already intricate patterns and colours of the rugs infinitely richer.

Abba sits on a well-used cushion, wearing his traditional white cotton tunic and white pants and fingering his prayer beads like a rosary. A disused hookah is parked to one side of a camel stool.

"Jeep, I see the scars on your face and your arm have gone. I remember the many times my father and my grandfather would have even worse wounds. We came in dangerous boats from an undivided India." I realize he wants to tell us the tale of his travels as a younger man. He turns toward me.

"Lando, so your father is finally taking you to Goa? Good! You must know where you came from and who you are." He glances around the room. "You must see Goa for yourself. You are Catholics now, but many Goans are descendants from Muslims...you ask your father. When the Portuguese arrived in India in 1492, Muslim rulers and Muslim traders occupied Goa. Turkish, Egyptian, Palestinian, and Arab dealers transported the finest racehorses and other supplies through the old city of Goa, to the mughals, maharajahs, and princes of India. They took back jewels and spices to Europe." He looks at Jeep.

"And you, Jeep. Ask your father if he knows about travel in the old days. We came in wooden dhows from India. Your father sells life insurance—we never heard of life insurance. We took life as it came, knowing we could lose everything, and sometimes we did."

Abba stands and touches one of his model dhows. "Look here. We traders would sail all over in these ships. We went from Muscat and Oman to Surat and Bombay and Cochin and back. Then sometimes we would sail from Aden to Zanzibar. The boats would carry food and wood and cooking pots and all sorts of goods. From India the boats would sail to Karachi and to the Gulf ports and Aden. Many goods would be taken off the boats at Aden, and then carried by camel to Alexandria in Egypt, and from there by ship to Tangiers and to Venice in Italy."

"Abba, what about pirates? Did you meet pirates?" I ask.

"Yes, sometimes, but we in dhows would travel together. The pirates would also travel in dhows. If our dhows were attacked and even one person were to escape alive, he would report the attack. When the pirates returned to their port, they would be hunted and instantly killed by relatives of the dead. The British navy was based in Aden. Trade was important for all, so pirates were hunted and killed on the spot."

"And Abba, did you come to Kenya in a dhow?" Hardev asks.

We all call him Abba even though he isn't really our grandfather.

"Yes, Hardev. I was eleven years only. My family had been living in Oman. On my first sea voyage, we sailed from Aden, where we left port bound for Kismayu and Mogadishu in Somalia, then headed to Malindi, Mombasa, and all the way to Mozambique. There was no other way to travel such distances except by dhows." Abba sits down. I notice that his eyes sparkle when he recounts his stories.

"Abba, when did you come to Nairobi?" I ask.

"I arrived first as a boy of eleven years in 1888 in Zanzibar, after twenty-nine days on a dhow. Our whole family travelled together, twelve people in all. There were two other big families from our village near Karachi. Later I came to Mombasa in 1902, and afterwards to Nairobi in 1912 with my parents, two brothers, and an uncle. I returned twice by dhow to Karachi and Surat and back. Now I am old and cannot travel."

"Were you frightened?" I ask. "On the boat, I mean."

"Very frightened. Yes, sometimes, definitely. We did not know if we would arrive alive. Many dhows would sink, and all the passengers would drown. When the weather was bad, very large waves would hit the sides of the boat, shaking it from side to side and up and down, like this." Abba made hand movements to demonstrate. "All the passengers would become sick and vomit. There was very little water to drink. The captain locked up the water tanks and would allow this water to be used only for cooking, and for drinking, this much." He indicates the quantities with his index finger and thumb. "About one cup per person."

"What about baths?" I ask.

"All bathing was with salt water from the sea, even for the women."

"Did women go in the same boat?" Hardev asks.

"Yes. Yes. Women and little children would stay below in here." He stands up again, pointing to the model. "Men and women would sleep in separate areas on bedrolls on the floor. When we had bad weather, the water would even splash below. We had to always keep emptying it out."

"What about the toilet?" Jeep asks.

"This is the toilet here, this box." Abba points to a box set a bit lower on the back of the ship. I see how a hole is cut in the base, and there is a metal pail with a rope attached to bring up seawater to wash up. I can see that Jeep and I are thinking the same thing: What about some privacy? But Abba has moved on.

"We also had to eat during the journey. All food was given to us by the captain in small rations. He was like a god, and we would have to obey his orders. The captain had to guess every day how long the voyage would last. On one trip the journey took nine days longer than was planned because of changing winds. We ran out of food; we did not even have enough atta, flour, to make chapatis, so we ate only the dried nuts and dried fruit that was being transported on the dhow to Africa. The captain let us break into this shipment because of the emergency." He turns to me.

"Lando, you must enjoy your voyage! I was young like you and very excited. It is wonderful to travel and stop everywhere. My own abba was already living in Zanzibar for fifteen years before

I came out the first time. I have been to Lourenço Marques in Mozambique and even Mauritius." Abba's voice fades, almost as if recollecting the past is sending him into a trance.

"Dad says we have an uncle and cousins in Mozambique, but we cannot visit them yet," I say. There is no response; Abba has closed his eyes. Abdul signals for us to exit the room quietly; it is Abba's nap time.

Jeep, Hardev, and I leave the room quietly; we say our thanks and leave. Almost at once the three of us start discussing what we had not learned.

"Abba didn't say what the traders carried back from Mombasa and Zanzibar," I say. "And also did the Hindus and Muslims and the Catholics travel together?"

"I remember my father saying his father came by dhow," Hardev says. "But I did not imagine it like Abba said it was."

"Another thing," I say. "How could they all eat together on the ship if Muslims don't eat pork but Goans eat it, and Hindus don't eat beef but Muslims do—"

Hardev interrupts me. His technical brain has been at work. "I wonder why the toilet couldn't be designed to catch rainwater from the sails so that the women did not have to pull up water from the sea."

"I like Abba's model ships," I say.

"Did you notice the difference in the ships' sails?" Jeep asks. "Yes. British clipper ships had long, tall masts and about seven sails each. The Portuguese Caravellas had a number of short square sails mounted in three banks on masts, and the dhows had a very big sail and a little one at the front." It's not often I know more than Jeep.

"Lando, are you going to Goa by dhow?" Hardev asks.

"Of course not. Dad says we are going by a steamer."

Hardev leaves us, and Jeep and I talk a little longer. We are sitting on our favourite branch of a peach tree, swinging our legs a short distance from where my dog, Jolly, was buried almost four years earlier. Simba sits quietly nearby. Jeep and I take time to dream of how one day we will sail in our own dhow to those distant places that Abba had talked about, like we always planned since we were just kids, listening to Abdul's stories about his abba. We will cross Arabia overland, riding the best racehorses and camels across the desert to Oman; we will pick up a dhow and sail from Muscat to Goa, where we will spend many months getting to know about our forbears and the country's history. From there we will sail down the coastline of India, across to the Seychelles, and back to Zanzibar. Only then will we come home, or perhaps keep sailing around the Cape of Good Hope and cross to Brazil, like Uncle Orlando had set out to do, and never return!

With everything now decided, Jeep goes home. I linger to spend time with Simba. He seems to sense something is afoot. This past week his exuberant bark has been conspicuously silent. Perhaps he already knows my train leaves for Mombasa in three days.

20: Train to Mombasa

On departure day Ahmad drives us to the Nairobi railway station for the overnight passenger train journey to Mombasa.

It seems the whole town is leaving for somewhere else; well-wishers seem to outnumber travellers. Accompanied by his mom and dad, Jeep comes to bid us goodbye.

Ever since returning from Nakuru and Kericho and meeting Saboti and Jimmy, I have been more aware of the separation between the races and how difficult it is in the course of my daily life in Nairobi to meet others my age who are not brown-skinned like me. All of a sudden, it feels as if a social gathering of all races is underway at the railway station. Unlike in some public areas and buildings and all residential areas in the rest of the town, there are no physical barriers or rules to separate people on the platform.

Though the first class passengers have the least distance to walk to their coaches, all of us start out our journey and say goodbye on the same level and on the same platform.

"Please stay with Ahmad," Dad tells Linda and me. "I will get everything arranged in the compartment." He instructs the porters to follow him while Mom drags Fatima and Joachim after them. It is a colourful sight under the familiar Mangalore-tiled steel-framed roof of the platform. The wrought iron columns have just been repainted with oil paint in cream above and dark green below; Jeep and I spot at least two people who did not see or could not read the warning notices. A plump Englishman has got two dark green stripes across his rear; another man in his group has caught the paint on his sleeve, but they seem unconcerned in the excitement of the moment.

European men are generally dressed in khaki or white cotton. Some sport pith helmets, others felt hats. They smoke and chat. Their ladies in frocks, skirts, and hats say goodbye to civil servants still in their stiff collars and light-coloured suits. Indian women in saris jangle around in their arm and ankle bracelets. Sikhs in turbans of white, black, pink, and orange talk loudly among themselves, occasionally slapping each other to loud guffaws. Hindu men in white cotton *dhotis* or skin-tight pants and white *kurtas* under black woollen jackets talk earnestly and loudly, perhaps concluding some last-minute bazaar transactions. African women in brightly coloured *kangas* move baskets and bundles balanced effortlessly on their heads. Porters and safari bearers scurry around madly like disturbed ants; vendors of snacks and cigarettes do a brisk trade.

Everybody's destination is different, but they share the same train. Their ship-bound onward journeys will carry them to India, Europe, South Africa, and countries in the Middle East. Perhaps some of the passengers will just sprawl on some beach near Mombasa during the day and drink to their heart's content until it is time to head upcountry again.

"Come, Lando, Jeep. Let's look at the engine," Ahmad says. An enormous locomotive is building up the steam pressure to start its overnight journey. As we walk, Ahmad puts his hand on my shoulder.

"Lando, you must study hard at school," he says. "Then later you must go to university and become a doctor or a lawyer… for your parents."

"Okay," I reply without resistance.

Moments later, a man with a megaphone walks the train's length along the platform announcing the departure. He returns a few minutes later with a second reminder. A loud whistle sounds. In a few minutes, everyone is aboard. Ahmad and Jeep give me big hugs. I feel a lump in my throat. I don't know when I will see them next, but Jeep and I will probably be grown men when we meet again.

The whistle sounds once more. The train pulls out of the station with a jerk as the wagons bump and goad each other into action. Farewells are shouted; some mouth their farewells with moist eyes; others just wave. Hands stretch and reach out of windows to touch other hands, some perhaps for the last time.

Linda and I are excited to be on the train again. We have window seats. Slowly, like a giant reptile, the train twists and turns its way out of Nairobi, past the African labour quarters, built by the railways almost fifty years earlier. Little children run along the tracks, laughing and waving. On the outskirts of the city, we pass shacks built of wood planks with shiny corrugated iron roofs, and others topped with flattened kerosene debbes. We see rubbish lying uncollected. The air is heavy with the stench of raw sewage in open drains. I wonder if there are honey wagons that empty the toilets at night in African neighbourhoods.

The train suddenly picks up speed, as if it too desperately seeks the fresh air of the Athi Plains.

"Look, Linda," I say, pointing to herds of zebra, deer, and gazelle.

"No, you look here…and over there," she says, pointing to

giraffes grazing nearby.

The herds of wild game seem undisturbed by this noisy, smoke-puffing beast encroaching on their home. In the west silhouetted against the setting sun, a solitary rhino looks up briefly and returns to grazing.

"Look, Lando." Linda points to three clouds of dust racing against the train. Then we see the cars that are racing along the compacted murram road, as the laterite soil is called. The cars are all driven by young muzungus. The Nairobi-Mombasa Road runs parallel to the train tracks. The motors will get to Athi River Station, about twenty miles out of Nairobi, ahead of the train. Their drivers will exchange more fond farewells with their departing friends.

Dad and Mom, relaxing with Fatima and Joachim, ignore us. Dusk descends quickly, and Linda and I settle back. It will be a long night ahead. Mom serves home-prepared snacks for our dinner. Dad has ordered tea and hot milk delivered by a polite cabin attendant. Dad tells us the food in the dining car is tasteless, bland, and expensive, and we have to believe him. Linda and I make a quick exploratory visit down the passageway. While the starched white tablecloths and the fine silver and glassware, every article of crockery and cutlery individually monogrammed with EAR&H intrigue her, I suddenly become aware that this will be my last trip on this train for a long time. I glance at the small note on each table: Fine Wines are Served. Linda and I decide the dining car is only affordable to first-class passengers. I wonder if one day Dad will earn enough to take Mom on a long holiday and drink fine wines.

"I'm heading back to our compartment," Linda says, bending briefly to catch a view of the scenery before darkness sets in. I follow her.

The sun drops quickly on the equator, and since we can't see outside, any movement along the corridor becomes our only source of entertainment. There is a knock on the door. An attendant delivers the bedding for each berth with a promise to return to lay it out.

Moments later a Goan man in a chef's uniform walks by, pauses, recognizes Dad, and stops to chat. They speak for a few minutes in their native Konkani, which Dad rarely speaks at home but clearly remembers; then the man turns to us and speaks English. "Have a good trip. Enjoy Goa. It is paradise." We are caught unawares. We mumble and smile and shake hands. He goes away.

"This is Pereira's last year with the railways," Dad says. "He is so happy to return home. He came out in 1918, almost thirty years ago, recruited from Indian Railways. Now he is retiring and returning to Goa in June, having trained all his African staff."

Some African waiters in crisp white starched tunics pass our cabin on their way to the restaurant car. They are very friendly and happy, with big smiles for us and other passengers. A dinner gong announces the second sitting in the dining car. We are still waiting for the bedding man to return. Mom is talking softly to Joachim, and Dad has his arms around Fatima.

"Lando, I will miss you when you stay behind in Goa," Linda leans over and whispers to me.

Her comment takes me by surprise, as she'd always bullied me; I suppose I'll really miss her too once I'm away. The bedding man arrives, and with a few quick movements the beds are ready; the crisp, freshly laundered sheets are inviting. Within minutes we are ready to sleep. Mom and Joachim share a lower berth, and Linda and Fatima the other. Dad and I take the upper bunks. Outside, the night sky is ink black, and I can see sparks escaping from the locomotive's furnace.

For me sleep is erratic since the train makes frequent stops to replenish the water supply for its thirsty steam boilers. I wonder why Ahmad did not mention engineer, as well as doctor or lawyer—perhaps he does not want me to end up driving a taxi like him. I change my position to see if sleep comes. The small overhead fan above the washbasin with the hinged varnished mahogany lid is droning away, distributing the hot air equally around the tiny compartment. Thoughts drift through my mind. I wonder why Dad insisted on sending me away to boarding school when my class-mates will remain behind.

Anyway, I am on my way. It is going to be fun; perhaps if the family was not travelling at the same time, I might have been frightened of going on my own. I wonder if I will be lonely with-out my friends and family. I won't have my crystal radio because Uncle Antonio convinced me not to take it. At the last minute, he told me he had heard that the Salazar government in Portugal was becoming paranoid about subversive political activity; there have been rumours since India's independence that troublemakers are plotting to gain independence for Goa as well. The secret police could mistake the use of a crystal radio. At best they would con-fiscate it and destroy it, or, as Uncle says, "they may just lock you in prison somewhere, and throw away the key. The police can be quite stupid."

I asked Dad about it. He just said that it might be difficult to receive clear signals from the BBC in Goa.

As the train rattles through the night, the frequent stops to take on water are accompanied by a cacophony of hissing steam jets under pressure, the clanging and clatter of wagons, the shout-ing and chatter of station attendants, and the barking of dogs. It is about three the next morning when I am woken up again by station noises. I peer out through the gaps in the wooden slatted shutters. A white concrete sign with black letters reads tsavo. Dad stirs. He is awake too.

"Dad, what does T-S-A-V-O stand for?" I ask.

"That's the name of the river nearby," he says. "It's pronounced 'Saa-voo'. It was made famous by lions." I sit up. "When they were building this railway from Mombasa to Uganda, about fifty years ago, they had problems with man-eating lions around this area while the bridge was being constructed. Hundreds of Indian and African construction workers were killed. Every few nights the beasts would pounce on the camp and drag their screaming victims away into the pitch-black darkness."

"But couldn't they trap them or kill them?"

"They tried everything. After each incident, as dawn broke, armed search parties would follow the trail of blood and drag marks in the soil, but these nearly always led nowhere. The remains of the victims were never found. Then finally, after the searchers had laid many traps, two lions were shot dead. An English engineer with Uganda Railways, Colonel Paterson, claims to have shot them. He later wrote a book about it. The first Goan engineer for Uganda Railways, as it was known, was Cajetan Francis Xavier D'Souza. He told his family in his letters home that when the lions attacked, the Indian and African workers screamed and ran in every direction."

"Were any Goans attacked?" I ask, though I know what his answer will be. By my tenth birthday, I was convinced that the all-powerful His Majesty the King in London would protect us at any cost, and that's why we sang "God Save the King" in school. From the stories I had heard, most Goans were working for the government; without them the government could not function. Surely no man-eating lion, however desperate, would risk angering His Majesty by dining on a few scrawny Goans.

"None," Dad says. "There were many Goans working as accountants, cooks, clerks, and mechanics for the railways. Cajetan D'Souza claimed it was our Catholic religion that saved the Goan employees from a similar fate. God was there for them."

Our train jerks back into motion.

"Now, Lando, go back to sleep," Dad says. "You don't want to be tired when you arrive in Mombasa. Good night."

But how can I possibly sleep after a story like that? Suppose those man-eating beasts had sired offspring before they were shot? And those offspring had carried dormant man-eating genes, produced another generation, transferring those genes again? Suppose these genes have awakened from their slumber, and their lion hosts are now about to launch another wave of terror in honour of their forbears? I spend the rest of the night peering out into the darkness for lions. For good measure I silently recite the rosary, using my fingers for prayer beads.

"Lando! Lazy bones! Wake up!" It's Linda. Our train is clattering noisily over the iron viaduct at Makupa linking the mainland to Mombasa Island, which is covered in palms and mango trees. The salty air is thickly scented after a brisk morning shower.

"That's Kilindini Port," Dad says, pointing to a cluster of cranes and sheds in the distance. "That's where I first landed on African soil in 1928. We will embark from there on Thursday."

On arrival in Mombasa, we all miss Ahmad and his big American Chevy that could swallow our luggage and all of us without a burp. Here we are obliged to take two taxis. Dad, Linda, and Fatima squeeze into one; Mom, Joachim, and I climb into a second taxi, with the luggage split between the two cars. We head for a Goan-owned guesthouse where Dad has made reservations.

After we venture out for a bit of sightseeing, we are soon back, gasping for somewhere cool to take refuge, tongues hanging out. Unlike Nairobi, Mombasa at midday is hot and humid. The sweat glues my clothes to my body. Mrs. Fernandes, the landlady, ushers us into the dining room for a simple Goan lunch: rice and fish curry with two vegetable side dishes.

"Here everyone takes a short rest after lunch." Mrs. Fernandes turns to face Dad. "You remember siesta time in Goa? Here life is the same—*sossegade*—relaxed. From two in the afternoon to tea-time at four, everything is shut, shops and all. Later they unclose by five; shops and business open late. Very nice and cool then."

"So nothing has changed since my days here," Dad says. He turns to Linda and me. "Let's make a list of what we must see, and then we can choose. We have even less time now."

21: Mombasa Old Town

Mom says she's exhausted and the children will be too tired to go out, so Dad, Linda, and I set off at 4:30 p.m. We take a taxi to the top end of Old Town Mombasa and the historic dhow harbour where, Dad tells us, Indians and Arabs have been trading for centuries. Only the previous week, Abba had told us how he came to Africa by dhow. I am excited to be following in his footsteps in some small way.

We look to the right; a short distance away is Fort Jesus, built by the Portuguese in the sixteenth century. Dad says it is used as a prison now. We walk along a narrow street with room for only pedestrians, bicycles, donkey-pulled carts, and handcarts. Three-storied buildings line the street; their upper windows are shuttered with wooden slats against the sun. One or two shutters are open: the sun is low in the sky.

"Lando, look—these people are living above their shop." Linda points to an open window where a woman in a *buibui*, a hijab, is laying out a garment to dry on the windowsill. Each building has a short lean-to, corrugated iron canopy to throw off the rain; these projecting roofs make a nice zigzag pattern as they stagger down the narrow street, paved with stone slabs. The street leads down to Old Harbour. Even as we walk, more stores open, or as Mrs. Fernandes had said, "unclose," their solid tall wooden entrance doors folded back against intricate carved wooden frames.

The doors to a rug warehouse are flung open; they are beautifully carved and embellished with heavy brass: polished hinges, big studs, and doorknobs. We stop to admire them as the owner, more likely the son of the owner, says, "Here in Old Town is a mixture of Indian and Muslim art and architecture."

I can see Dad is surprised, since the man does not look as if he speaks English.

The young man smiles. "I am visiting my grandfather; my family has lived here for two generations, but I am now studying architecture in Bombay."

"We are from Nairobi; we are on our way to Goa," Dad says.

"I know Goa. Portuguese people are there. Everything is different. Even the buildings."

We continue our walk. A coffee vendor clicks brass mugs together and points to a large cone-shaped brass coffeepot strapped to his trolley. Another vendor beckons us to his fruit store, which is nothing more than a long concrete shelf about waist height on which are arranged a few papayas, bunches of bananas, mangoes, and green vegetables. We follow the road around a sharp bend, and it seems we have left the persistent odour of open drains behind us. Next to the rug warehouse is another shop with stocks of building materials for export to the Gulf States, including mangrove poles, cement, lime, steel rods, and burlap. We pass vendors with trolleys plying all sorts of goods: roasted cashew nuts and peanuts sold in little newspaper cones, sweetmeats, jewellery, and trinkets. A man on a bicycle offers a special price on fresh-picked madafu, a green tender coconut. Some men seem to have no particular occupation but just stand around gawking or chatting, while nearby, donkeys snort and stamp in frustration as the flies bother them.

At the very end of the street, we arrive at the Old Harbour with its fishy smells. It is a naturally sheltered, cove that has served as a refuge for dhows over many centuries.

"Look, Lando," Linda says, pointing to men unloading cargo from three dhows that are moored side by side at the pier. They cross over gangplanks placed across other dhows to get to the docks. At dockside they and other workers load goods onto donkey carts while other handcarts wait their turn. Linda raises her hand, her finger on her lips for silence, and points to a cat silently creeping along a parapet wall. It appears about to pounce on a pile of unattended fish freshly unloaded from a Swahili fishing boat, which is a canoe dug out of a tree trunk.

We walk to Dad, who has stopped to talk to someone sitting at the dockside. The old man, dressed in a long white kaftan, an embroidered waistcoat, and an embroidered prayer cap, has a kind, wizened face, distinguishable despite his full beard. The crow's feet around his eyes are just as deep as the wrinkles cutting across his forehead. He seems happy to talk.

"And when did you first arrive?" Dad is asking him.

"In 1893." I quickly calculate that is six times my whole lifetime ago.

"I was seven years only when I first come to Africa. My family, they go from Karachi to Oman. Then we leave port for Aden, Kismayu, and Mogadishu…you know, in Somalia? After that to Malindi, Mombasa, and all the way to Pemba."

"All by dhow?" Dad asks.

"Yes, yes! Only by dhow. No other way except by dhow."

"Did you see pirates?" I ask. "Did any pirates attack you?" I was thinking of Abba's story, as he took almost the same route except for a stop at Pemba.

"Yes, yes, pirates, sometimes; but they will be killed by relatives of dead passengers of dhows when they come back," he says. "It is a question of family honour. Also in Aden…British navy is there; they kill bad pirates and sink dhows. They protect us boats. Trading is very important for everyone."

Linda pulls at Dad's sleeve; she is hot and bored. I, on the other hand, am intrigued.

"You want go inside and see my dhow?" The old man can read my mind. "Come tomorrow morning; now unloading. Very busy."

I look at Dad. He nods in the typical Indian up-and-down and side-to-side manner that can mean yes or no, so I don't know which it is. Dad thanks him, and we move across the dockside to a sweets vendor. Dad buys us small square pieces of sticky halva. Linda is smiling at me. We know how he has always warned us against buying foodstuff from kiosks, especially from Ali's kiosk by St. Francis Xavier Church. Perhaps travel is changing Dad. I will miss Ali's masala mangoes in Goa. Yummy. I can smell roasted nuts, along with other delectable scents wafting through the air from the outdoor food stands nearby.

Another vendor calls out to us. A dhow fully laden with cargo has just arrived from India. On the dock a stack of slatted wooden crates is piled high, awaiting transport. I can see through the openings between the slats. Each crate contains two debbes, exactly like the rusty debbe fence markers we saw on safari at the European farms. Other crates contain cashew nuts. As if to announce their arrival, a vendor is selling freshly roasted cashew nuts. The smell is tempting and intoxicating. He offers Linda and me a handful. Dad buys five pounds to take back to the guest house.

The next morning we are up early. Dad has cut a deal with a taxi owner called Ismail, who has a car big enough to hold all of us and our luggage too. He will stay with us while we indulge Dad and his familiar retelling of his early memories. I can almost recite Dad's stories by heart, as we have all heard them so many times.

"This is the Mombasa headquarters of the National Bank of India," he says. "I walked in through that door for my first day wearing the only suit I had…my first job in Africa. We knew nothing of what we would find here when we left Goa."

Ismail makes another turn onto Salim Road. "That's the Goan club on Salim Road, where members opened their welcoming arms and their homes to new arrivals, and still do. Despite coming to this country alone, we were so lucky that there was already an established Goan community to receive us and help us settle into our new homes. Their kindness made such a difference to us."

We see the Roman Catholic cathedral and drive around the government offices set in large spaces neatly laid out with paved roads, their edges marked by whitewashed stone curbs lined with exotic flowering flamboyant trees, tamarind, and coconut palms. Dad recites their names like a school principal announcing prize-winners: treasury, post office, customs and excise, among many others.

"All these offices depend on their Goan mid-level staff to keep running," he says proudly. I realize how much this means to him.

By mid-morning we are all bored except Dad, and we're hot and sticky. We stop for refreshments on a patio opposite Edward St. Rose, Chemists. Dad continues his history lesson. "That pharmacy, the first one in Kenya, was founded by a Goan in 1902. I knew a colleague who worked there once."

"Chico! Chico!" a man shouts from the street. Incredible! Dad had just mentioned a colleague—it really is a small world. Mr. Hippolito strides over. Solidly built, and with long sideburns and hair slightly greased, he rushes into the patio like a fireman putting out a fire. He embraces Dad, gives Mom a hug, and would clearly like to do the same to each of us. I lead the resistance. He retreats. Then without so much as a "May I join you?" he pulls up a chair and orders refreshments for all, including a plateful of samosas and pakoras.

Linda leans over and whispers in my ear. "He's okay!"

I nod in approval, anticipating the treats we are to be served.

Dad and Hippolito reminisce. They were on the same boat in 1928. After moving around "just surviving," for about five years, Hippolito finally landed a junior position at another pharmacy owned by an Indian and is now a partner. His wife and two children are in Goa.

When he leaves he insists that Dad visit the Indian bazaar. "Chico, ask for Biashara Street. It's like a small township in India—you won't believe it. It's not Africa. The whole area is a bustling bazaar at any time of the day or night." He is ecstatic. "Please don't let the children miss this experience."

Back at the guesthouse, Mrs. Fernandes continues to spoil us royally. "I miss my own children so much. They are just like you."

She explains that they have been left behind in Bombay to be brought up by grandparents, since they will go to university in Poona after high school. I realize how many parents of that generation send their children abroad. Linda and the rest of our family will be spared that, but I have been sacrificed for the sake of a better future.

Dad must have tipped Ismail well, as he insists on driving us during our last evening. We drive along a narrow road towards the bazaar until the car is almost as wide as the street. Ismail suggests we continue on foot through the narrow lanes and he'll find us when we're ready to go home.

We climb out and wind our way toward the Indian bazaar. The smells of food are familiar: the aromas could just as well be coming out of Abdul's or Hardev's mother's kitchen. Suddenly, we are all hungry again. There is nothing more scrumptious than the smell and taste of freshly roasted corn over a charcoal jiko, brushed with hot ghee and sprinkled with salt and red chili pepper. We all savour some corn.

The market area is lit by naked bulbs hanging from electric wires that criss-cross overhead in a giant spider web. Linda and I play a game to list what each of the stores is selling. We see silk saris, cloth, shoes, and sandals; aluminum, tin, and stainless steel cooking pots; jute rope, wire, nails, sacking cloth, and hand tools; gold and silver jewellery, and gemstones; bicycles; coir brushes and doormats; sweetmeats, groceries, fruit, and vegetables, paan, and tobacco.

Linda stops outside a shop window. The store seems to be the sole importer of Hindu images for worship. An adjacent shop stocks only Indian baby clothes, and at first it appears that a plump, life-sized pink plastic European baby is being strangled to death by its hand-embroidered Indian-sized dress.

Linda disapproves. "They should know European babies are bigger than Indian ones."

We nibble foods at different stalls. Mom buys a parting gift for Mrs. Fernandes as Dad starts to fret about finding Ismail in this crowd. He need not have worried. He has been trailing our every movement, discreetly invisible. He helps with most of the parcels we have acquired.

"Now everyone get straight to bed. No talking please," Mom says. "Ismail will be here tomorrow morning at nine sharp. Sweet dreams."

Sweet dreams indeed! I can't believe how much I have seen and learned since I left school the previous week. It seems I have been travelling for weeks, but it's been only two days. I think of that nice old man by the docks who invited me to look around his dhow. That would have been a dream come true. Jeep would have loved it too. Now here I am, already on my way to Goa, and I have left Jeep behind. I feel bad about that, but so much is happening to me, and so fast.

Suddenly for the first time, I am excited about going to boarding school. I wonder what it will be like travelling on a steamship instead of a dhow. I guess I will soon find out. I wish Linda could get interested in dhows, too, so I'd have someone to enjoy them with.

I close my eyes and wait for sleep to come like a giant wave and take me down into the sea of my dreams.

22: Steaming Eastward

We are at Kilindini Docks, and so it seems is the rest of the town. Rows of taxis, lorries, trailers, and handcarts crowd into part of the main dock area. Two horse-drawn carriages are parked under the shade of a tamarind tree, flanked by clusters of moving people. Travellers and well-wishers greet and say goodbye while parents try valiantly to keep their children from straying too far. Indian traders in kurtas, long white cotton shirts over ankle-hugging trousers, mingle with Muslim and Swahili men in simplified kaftans called kanzus. Bare-chested and barefooted African porters carry bedrolls, large packages, and cabin trunks out of the customs shed up the gangplank onto the ship; their sweaty black skin sparkles in the mid-morning sun.

My oversensitive nose picks up smells oozing from fruit and fresh food vendors: roasted corn and peanuts; the distinctive sweet smell of mandazis; ripe mangoes, bananas and tamarind; and freshly made samosas.

"Jambo. Here, totos," a vendor calls to us. "Very good, only ten cents, boys."

Along the length of the dock, cranes that look like metallic skeletons of giant prehistoric storks slowly transfer their loads onto the cargo holds of ships in harbour.

"When I first arrived in 1928," Dad says, pointing to a line of sheds, "these port facilities were only just being constructed. Only two berths had been completed. Just look at it now." He looks around and smiles. "It seems those two supervisors haven't moved. If only my old friend Fredo were here to see this. I remember his delight at seeing such order in a government office—so different from our backward Portuguese bureaucracy."

A short distance away, two European port officials dressed in white shirts, shorts, and stockings chat in the shade of an almond tree, ostensibly supervising operations. A uniformed Goan official apparently on an urgent mission walks toward us, recognizes Dad, has a brief chat, then hurries away again to his destination.

Soon it is our turn to go up the steeply sloping gangplank to the ship, where the purser welcomes us. Ushers direct us to our cabin boy, who leads us to our accommodations. Linda and I gasp as we step on deck. Just yesterday we were on the Old Harbour looking at wooden dhows, which now seem so fragile compared to our solid iron boat. Those adventurous men really lived life on the edge. I too would like to follow in Abba's and Uncle Orlando's footsteps and see the world, yet I feel anxiety growing within me. I take hold of Linda's hand.

"Linda, do you think we'll be safe?"

She seems to understand. "Yes, of course, silly! The war is over now. That attack on the ship happened during the war. Nothing like that is going to happen again."

"Then why did you tell me about it at home?"

"Because you were a baby when it happened," Linda says, "and the family were friends of Mom and Dad."

"Come along, you two," Dad calls out. Mom, Fatima, and Joachim are ahead, following the cabin boy. Even before we can look inside the cabin, Mom asks Dad to take us out on deck while she gets things sorted out. He takes Fatima's hand.

"The cabin space is small, and it will be congested," he says. "It will be ten days, but we will only use the cabin at night. Come, let's go and look around."

Linda and I lead the way out past the smell of Brasso. The brass stair rails are polished to a gleam that reminds me of gold, and the gilt-framed mirrors on almost every blank wall reflect more gilt, glass, and red mahogany. Everywhere there are smells of the wax floor polish that keeps the wood floors gleaming. It's all luxurious, at least for us, especially after our overcrowded house on Plums Lane.

We join the many passengers standing at the railings, still waving to friends and family who have come to see them off at the docks. The smell of salt air mingles with diesel fumes. Dark smoke billows out of the wide sloping chimney, which on either side shows the BI emblem of British India Steam Navigation. A short while later, the last load is lowered into the hold of our ship, and the crane on the dock slowly swings away as if in a ritual goodbye.

Crewmembers hitch the gangplank to two hoists on the ship, a slow, careful manoeuvre. Soon the gangplank is removed, collapsed, and secured to the side of the ship. A horn sounds from a pilot boat that has moved into position to guide us out of the long narrow Likoni channel. After three loud blasts from our ship's horn comes the rattling of chains and the clanging of metal on metal as the anchor is pulled up. The tie ropes loosen from moorings, pulled into the ship by turning winches. Dad has picked a deck chair, nearby since the slight movement of the ship makes Fatima afraid

Braz Menezes

to look at the water.

"We're moving!" Linda shouts. I see the seawall begin to float away from us, slowly at first. It is taking the well-wishers and dock cranes away with it. The people get smaller and smaller.

Dad leaves Fatima on the chair and joins Linda and me for a few moments.

"Look, those are the pink coral cliffs of Mombasa Island. Those were the escape points for the Portuguese troops." He explains that the secret tunnel openings connected from the steep face of the channel all the way to Fort Jesus. If the Portuguese garrison was overpowered by enemies and had to escape, they would find safety in the waiting gunships protecting the channel entrance. I linger at the railing.

On the channel side away from the cliffs, a wide strip of sugary beach separates the dark green of coconut palms from the turquoise-green and deep blue of the water. I feel a lump in my throat as I realize I may be away from Kenya and my family for a lifetime. Maybe something will happen to me, and I will never return. I feel my eyes well with tears, and an arm around me. Mom has joined us now; she draws me close as if reading my thoughts. I let the tears run down my cheeks.

Dad, with Fatima, Linda, and Joachim, are sitting on the deck chairs. He beckons us. Perhaps he has noticed I am crying.

"Lando, Linda says you still remember our last trip to Goa in 1942, when the Japanese torpedoed a ship on which our friend Marc Maciel and his whole family were killed."

"Yes," I reply, happy at a ready-made excuse for my tears. How can I possibly explain why I am tearful? "I felt a bit frightened."

"There is nothing to worry about now. The war is over, there is absolutely no danger."

"I don't actually remember anything from that trip, but Linda told me about it in Nairobi when we were packing."

"I remember everything," Linda says. "I remember hiding under the bed as the captain shouted at Mom."

"Linda told me your friends were all drowned when the ship sank." I want to check on her story.

"Yes, Marc and Effeginia and the younger children drowned," Dad says. "Thank God the three older boys were safe. They were left behind in boarding school in Goa, so they were not on the boat."

"Very nice boys. Wilfred, Mervyn, and Joseph," Mom says.

"So why was Linda hiding under the bed?" I ask.

"That was a month later as we were returning," Mom replies. "We were not allowed to turn on any lights at night, but I had to turn on a light for just a few seconds. The captain, passing along the passage, saw a glow under the door. He banged on the door and shouted as if he was crazy. Poor Linda was so frightened."

Something was still upsetting me. I needed to ask about it. "So if we had been on that Tilawa ship as planned, we might not have been alive today?"

"Yes. We too could have all gone down," Dad says. "Remember, God has a plan for each one of us," Mom says, giving me a hug.

I can't resist going back to the railing, drawn to the sight of the limitless horizon stretching ahead of us. The Indian Ocean completely surrounds us. The recent memory of the multitude of smells on the streets of Mombasa, a mix of diesel fumes, dust, odoriferous open drains, and charcoal-roasted fresh corn, is replaced by the pure smell and taste of salt air. However, in the dining room and the lounges, where every nook and corner is spic and span and highly polished, the fragrant salt air is constantly fighting with the odour of brass polish and floor wax. We settle down to the rules and routine of a sea journey.

In my upper bunk that night, I lie awake to the gentle roll of the ship and the distant sound of the engine room. I wonder why Dad hesitated before telling me those three boys survived only because they were in boarding school. My thoughts drift. I suddenly realize that there are no European passengers on board. Dad had mentioned something about it in a conversation with

Mom; perhaps I wasn't listening. Could it be something to do with India's Independence, when all the British left India? Didn't any Europeans stay behind? I will ask Dad about that in the morning. For that matter, why are there no African passengers on the ship either?

By the second day on board, Linda already has a friend, and I am left to fend for myself. I go to the games room. Ramnik and Kishore are twin brothers about my age. A better player, Ramnik has thrashed his brother at ping-pong; I offer to play the winner (actually I let him win just to be nice). Like me, my new friends are surprised at the dearth of boys; there appear to be few boys our age on the deck. Dad had guessed the previous day that there may be more than two thousand people on board, so where are they hiding? As travellers in second class, we have unrestricted access to almost everywhere, except the first-class section and the crew's quarters. By the end of day two, my friends and I have explored every nook and corner of our lounges, the dining rooms, the games rooms, and the library. We go out on deck.

"Look! More flying fish!" Kishore shouts as we exit through the heavy doors. Shoals of fish dart out of the ocean at great speed; they seem to skim, glide, and fly above the water for a hundred yards or more before the whole shoal dives back in unison, leaving only the shimmering glare on the water like a mirage. We talk about life in Nakuru and Nairobi. I tell them about my friend Saboti and my trip to Kericho and about Jimmy. "You mean you talk to African girls?" Kishore asks, surprised.

It is day three.

"We have a cousin in deck class," Ramnik says. "He's not allowed upstairs. Let's go downstairs."

Past the heavy storm doors, we descend one of the many staircases past a set of double doors. Deck class announces itself before we arrive by a buzz of voices in the air, as everyone seems to be chatting at the same time. Occasionally, a baby cries.

"Look for Arun," Ramnik says to Kishore, and turns to me.

"He's the cousin I told you about."

"What do you think I'm doing?" Kishore asks.

Deck class seems very crowded, and I feel my nose recoil. The whole space reeks of cigarette smoke, stale spicy foods, and stale cooking oil originating in the kitchen—and more.

"Do you smell goat manure?" I ask. I recognize its distinctive smell from a recent visit to a farm near Nairobi. Sometimes I wish my nose wasn't so sensitive, but of course I realize it is the result of years of training, sitting around a stove and watching my mother mix her aromatic spices as she prepared our favourite dishes, especially those before Christmas, when Linda, Jeep, and I inhaled the irresistible aromas of Goan sweets wafting from Mom's kitchen.

A group of boys our age approach us. Another group watches us from a distance. Arun walks toward Ramnik and rattles off the names of his Gujarati friends who drift past.

"We have come to see where you live," I say. Arun swells with pride like a new homeowner showing off his lovingly decorated abode.

"It's quite packed here," he says. "One thousand, eight hundred passengers. That's what my father said. Come." He walks us to where his family has literally parked themselves.

Each family has been allocated a "bay," marked off by painted white lines and personal baggage on the battleship-grey floor, and reserved with a bedroll for each one. Muslims and Hindus are separated across the deck. I ask whether it is because of all the trouble after Indian independence that Ahmad has talked about so often to Jeep and me.

"No. It is because we Gujaratis are strict vegetarians," Ramnik says. "It is about the distribution of food. Only two choices: vegetarian for us Hindus; non-vegetarian for Muslims and others."

Arun's father squats cross-legged in one of many groups gambling at cards. He smiles at us but concentrates on his game. Some men are smoking hand-rolled bidis. Many women, whether in saris or the *salwar kameez*, are squatting and talking. Others are finishing their daily duties of rolling up the bedrolls, sweeping and tidying up their bays, and tending to the children. Groups of older children play games, running around the deck between the bays and between the adults.

I detect the simultaneous stench of vomit and disinfectant. The washrooms, separated by gender, are in two blocks, labelled EUROPEAN STYLE and ASIAN STYLE to distinguish the modern porcelain toilets from the squat WCs.

"Come and look here," Arun calls out. At the rear of the kitchen are supplies for the journey packed in shelves from floor to ceiling, secured to keep them from moving around. We follow Arun down a passageway. On one side is an enclosure with a thick layer of straw on the floor. This is a special area for live goats, fresh meat for the Muslims.

"They kill these goats in a special halal ritual," Arun explains. "The blood must be fully drained."

I can see from the look on their faces that Ramnik and Kishore are uncomfortable here and want to return to the upper floor, so Arun and I follow. By the doorway to the staircase, Arun leaves to join his friends. The boys we had seen earlier are now by the door. The leader of the small group of boys stares at Ramnik.

"Next time," he says menacingly, "you must bring something for us, or don't come."

"Okay," Ramnik says. Safely up the stairs, he turns to me. "They're not Hindus."

"One of my best friends in Nairobi is a Muslim," I tell him. "He's an engineer and drives a black Chevy taxi."

Later that evening I tell Dad about the goats and the two gangs of boys. "Do you think they will start fighting on the ship?"

"No. Kenya is not like India. Even if we are different, we all live peacefully together. They're probably just boys who are bored with having nothing to do. Just stay up on this level if you feel uncomfortable."

23: Coco de Mer

Dinner on board comes in two sittings. The first sitting is made up of families with young children; the second sitting is about two hours later. Our family dines together at the earlier session.

It is almost at the end of dinner on the fourth night when the PA system interrupts all conversation: "Attention, please! Children too! This is your purser speaking. I wish to inform all passengers that our ship will be arriving at the Port of Victoria, on Mahe Island, Seychelles, at dawn tomorrow, at 0630 local time, to be precise. We will be in port for about ten hours. Those passengers who wish to go sightseeing ashore should present themselves at the first sitting for breakfast in Dining Room A no later than 6:00 a.m. That's 0600. Each passenger going ashore must collect a temporary disembarkation pass that will permit re-entry to the ship. Passports are not necessary. You are advised not to carry any valuables, personal documents, or an excessive amount of money. Please note that gentlemen passengers may have to wade to shore and back again from the ferry boats; however, ladies and children will be carried to shore by handsome Seychellois men, courtesy of the Department of Tourism. Thank you for your attention, and good night. Children, thank you for your attention!"

"Lando, you might meet your girlfriend again," Linda teases me, but I ignore her.

"I will stay behind with the younger ones," Mom says. "You can tell me all about it."

"Okay. Early to bed then," Dad says. "You must be on deck early to watch our ship coming into the Port of Victoria."

Of course I am too excited to really sleep. Linda and I are up and dressed by 5:30 a.m. There is a very gentle, cool breeze blowing. In that darkness of first light, we see the horizon start to light up without a visible source of light. At first just a few dark shapes appear on the grey eastern horizon. As dawn breaks the sun emerges, its rays shining squarely into our eyes. The purple and blue-grey shapes slowly merge to look like a single landmass, then separate again into the distinct islands as the steamer changes course toward the harbour. The bright sun quickly burns off the morning mist as the islands evolve into tones of light grey and green; minutes later the closest islands turn to shades of darker green. Finally, as we get really close to it, the island mass of Mahe explodes in all its splendour. Gigantic outcrops of granite, surrounded by lush forests, rise steeply into the blue sky from an emerald-coloured sea. The scale of the trees and bushes seem magnified, dwarfing the tiny wooden shacks sprinkled along the shoreline.

We hear the ship's engines being turned down, as we get closer. Some houses are thatched with woven palm; others are covered in rusted corrugated iron sheets. A church steeple emerges in the middle of a cluster of buildings. Several small boats are moored to wooden piers perched on floating empty oil drums. The steamer's engines finally cut off. Even before the anchor is fully lowered, flotillas of little canoes surround our ship. They seem a long way down from where we are on deck. The men and women in the boats wave enthusiastically and hold up handicrafts and curios. They shout out special bargains.

A PA announcement requests all day-trippers to go to the breakfast room immediately. Linda, Dad, and I gulp down our rations; we hug Mom, Fatima, and Joachim, who have joined us, and rush to the disembarkation point.

"Dad, why will they not allow the ship to dock in the harbour?" I ask.

"This ship is too big," he explains. "Mahe does not yet have a deep harbour berth. The water needs to be deep for such a large boat to dock."

A ladder has been lowered over the side and secured, and two men in uniform climb on board. Dad says they are from customs and immigration. They shake hands with the captain and the purser and exchange a sheaf of papers. Another man boards the ship. He presents the captain with a big basket made of woven palm leaves, full of fruit. Dad says it is probably a gift from the tourism department. That fruit basket signals the clearance for the day-trippers to descend into the five ferries waiting to row us ashore. We are each issued a large postcard-sized temporary ID card, numbered individually.

We descend first into the ferry, as priority is given to passengers with children. I am a bit scared since we have to climb down a swaying rope ladder with wooden treads.

"Slowly, slowly there. Don't look down." A crewman takes my arm. The sailors from our ship help us climb down into the ferry, which rises and falls and swings with every wave. It is scary, but I am better once we are seated. I decide that I would not be a good pirate.

We are now surrounded by the trading canoes, the men and women clamouring to sell their wares to the passengers still on board. There are lots of what Dad calls bric-a-brac, some of it made from shells of giant tortoises, others still from mother-of-pearl, others from the husks of coconuts. Other vendors have fresh fruit and flowers. Our rowboat heads for land but has to stop before it quite reaches the shore. The men jump out and reach for their children or women. More Seychellois men wade in from the shore to help carry the women and children onto the beach, including me. Linda gets a piggyback ride from Dad, who has rolled up his pants and carries his sandals in his hand. On the beach we have to wait for the rest of our group to arrive. Many local people have come to gawk at us. I grab Linda's arm and point to three girls who look as though they could be Saboti's relatives. Even Linda can recognize Saboti's beautiful smile on those girls. As they move closer, we see they are much older and speak a language that neither Linda nor I have heard before. Dad leans across and whispers to Linda, "They're speaking Creole, but they also speak English and French here."

"Hello. Welcome to paradise," a gentle voice says in English. "My name is Dominique. I will answer your questions. First I will tell you about my country and our people."

I turn around to see a woman wearing a brightly patterned dress, a big floppy hat made of freshly woven green palm leaves, and a beautiful smile. She is in charge of our group.

I have just one burning question: Are there pirates on the island? The scenery reminds me of a film Jeep and I saw together called Treasure Island—it was all about pirates—but I am too nervous to ask. To my relief, someone else does.

"Yes, yes!" she says. "We have always had pirates. We have many beautiful secret coves for pirates to hide away for months. We have had French, English, Dutch, and all sorts of pirates here since the eighteenth century. Before that there were no people at all on these islands. You will see a pirate boat later. I will show you."

"What about snakes?" a man asks. "The Bible tells us there were snakes in paradise."

"Yes, yes! Snakes." Dominique smiles. "First we had no snakes at all. But then, when the pirates came with their treasure chests and stolen goods, they brought rats in with their cargo. When the crates were opened, these rats escaped on the island and multiplied. It became a curse. Then the colonial government imported snakes from Kenya and South Africa and let them loose all over Mahe to hunt the rats."

I try to remember the types of snakes at the Nairobi museum that might have been sent to the Seychelles. I wonder if Saboti knows this; perhaps her family may have fled from the islands to escape the rats and the snakes.

"Now they are saying we must import mongooses from India to hunt the snakes." Dominique puts her hands together. "Okay, we walk now, yes?"

We start our short walking tour. We are shown the residence of the British governor-general set in lush gardens with flaming red and brilliant yellow flowering shrubs and climbers, and the

Cathedral of Our Lady of the Immaculate Conception, which, Dominique explains, is the mother church for the Catholic diocese of Seychelles. A short distance away is the wreckage of an old pirate schooner that ran aground in 1796 and the earliest wooden shacks built by pirates, but we cannot enter them. A rough wooden plank sign, bleached by sun and sea mist, warns of unspecified dangers. Dominique does not hesitate on her mission as tour guide.

She stops under a big overhead sign, ORIGINAL GARDEN OF EDEN, painted in gold letters. "You will not see this anywhere else in the world." She picks up what looks like a double coconut. "This is the *coco de mer* (coconut of the sea)."

Linda pinches me. We both look at Dad, who seems engrossed. Dominique is holding up a large dark wooden object that looks like the bum and pubis of a woman, as if her torso has been cut just above the waist and at the thighs. Dominique lifts it higher. Some people titter.

"This is the largest nut in the world," she says. "You can see that a coco de mer is like a double coconut joined together. It has a husk on the outside just like a coconut and inside a kernel of white meat."

"Does it grow on trees?" someone asks.

"Yes. Palm trees of course," Dominique replies. "But only on one island among all these called Praslin. The trees grow to a height of thirty or even thirty-four metres tall…sorry, in English…more than one hundred feet tall."

She points to another sample. "When the outer husk is removed, it looks like this." The shopkeeper is holding a polished double-nut kernel. Some are formed into fruit baskets and others into serving trays.

"This nut is beautiful because it is from a female tree," Dominique explains with a smile. "Chan, show me a male picture, please."

With raised hand she is waiting for Chan, the shopkeeper, to bring a large black-and-white photo of a male tree. It shows a detail of the palm top with large fan-shaped leaves, and in its midst hangs a long protruding sausage-like growth, about three feet in length and the diameter of a grown man's arm. The sausage is covered with hundreds of flowers. There is a buzz among the audience.

"Just like a man's thing," someone says, as Dad takes Linda away by the hand and she tugs at me. We drift through the store. Dad and some other passengers buy the nuts as souvenirs.

Dominique leads us to an open patio where she says goodbye. As the afternoon light shines on the side of her face, I realize how much her beautiful smile is like Saboti's. I wonder whether Saboti may even be her relative, and if she will look like Dominique when she is grown up. Linda tugs at my shirt again. We move around the food stalls, sampling steamed meat that had been freshly drawn from conch shells and flavoured with Indian spices. We are given a drink of fresh coconut water.

By the time we return to the ship in the afternoon, Linda and I are tired but happy. Once again the sailors give us a hand up the rope ladder hanging down the side of the boat. Many of the small boats seem to have left. Our temporary passes are collected and counted. Nobody has been left behind.

"All aboard!" the man collecting the passes shouts. The ship's horn sounds three short blasts and then a long, slow, sad wail. The anchor is hauled in. The steamer turns slowly around and picks up speed, and its bow once again points northeast. Soon a familiar rocking motion tells us we are making waves in the Arabian Sea. Mahe and the smaller islands shrink in the distance, and Linda and I watch them fade into nothingness. I imagine the sun setting over Mombasa, as the western sky is now a mottled backdrop of brilliant orange with streaks of grey, purple, and magenta. It surpasses in beauty the view over Lake Victoria when we returned from Kericho less than a year ago. Our next port of call will be Goa.

24: Within Reach of the Homeland

Over the past few days, Dad has been sounding more emotional, just as he did when we emptied the black tin trunk in Nairobi. He constantly refers to returning to "our homeland" as we talk at mealtimes, and he and Mom drip-feed us details of family members we will meet in a few days' time. Mom is also excited.

Four days after casting off at the Port of Victoria, we approach a coastline; beaches of glistening white sand punctuated by coconut trees give way to the broad mouth of a river. As our ship glides between two promontories, it enters the turquoise waters of Mormugao Harbour, leaving behind the deep ultramarine of the open sea. Whitewashed churches pop up amid the dark green of vegetation. We have finally arrived in Goa.

Suddenly, an inner voice is whispering to me that I will be left behind here when Dad returns to Kenya with the family, that this is my new "home." I pretend it isn't happening. Maybe it will go away. As we descend the gangplank and enter the disembarkation shed, Dad clutches our documents, and Mom grabs hold of Fatima and Joachim, leaving Linda and me to hold each other's hands. Except for me, the whole family is travelling on my father's Portuguese passport; mine includes a special document from the Portuguese Consulate in Nairobi, authorizing me, as a minor, for an indefinite stay until my studies end. This has such a note of finality to it that I start to become concerned.

"If this is our homeland," I say to Dad, "why must I have special permission to stay?"

"Because President Salazar in Lisbon says so," he answers curtly.

I know my questions sometimes irritate Dad, just as his answers sometimes confuse me. In any case I remind myself that he is always nervous when facing immigration officers and customs officials. Dad shows the documents to an official who nods approval and waves us on. He shows all the same documents separately to several other officials as well, explaining to me in a whisper that these double and triple checks of all our papers are how the government creates jobs for people who would otherwise go hungry.

Prior to leaving Nairobi, we were offered a choice of vaccinations including yellow fever, smallpox, typhoid, tetanus, meningitis, and cholera. Dad had decided our little skinny arms would not take all that abuse, so we were inoculated only against yellow fever and smallpox. On the advice of Dr. Manu Ribeiro, our family doctor, Dad also carries a five-month supply of quinine tablets in case of malaria. Now on the Mormugao docks, a health official adjusts his spectacles and fishes for earwax, wiggling his little finger deep inside his right ear while he slowly and carefully inspects our health documents over and over again.

"What about cholera?" he asks. "You should have had a shot for cholera. Has cholera in Kenya been eradicated?"

"There has been no cholera in Kenya for at least thirty years," Dad replies. He is certain of his facts: he used to tell us that the best way to deal with government servants is to know a bit more than they do. The official waves us on.

"He's just trying to show that he is single-handedly protecting the population of all of Goa," I hear Dad mumble to Mom. "They're probably still dying of malaria in the streets outside. Come, customs clearance is next." We troop into the customs area in the same congested hall.

Our trunks and bags have been collected and grouped together, as Dad's name is painted on every item. Two cheerful-looking bag boys in ragged uniforms hover nearby, awaiting an inevitable tip. The customs official, hair and moustache trimmed and greased to perfection, beams a welcoming smile. He is pleased with the detailed handwritten list of contents that Dad has presented, saving him the effort of asking endless questions. He shakes Dad's hand, wishes us a good holiday, and waves us on with a big toothy smile. Two of our uncles, Mom's brothers Dominic and Rafael, are waiting at the doorway of the shed. They greet us with hugs and kisses, though they seem confused about whether to speak to us in Portuguese or in English. Linda and I answer in English. The hint works.

While Dominic leads us out into the bright sunshine, Rafael takes charge of managing the two boys as they carry our baggage outside.

Suddenly, all our senses are under attack; the cacophony seems deafening after the relative quiet of the sea voyage. Drivers in a line of waiting buses, their engines running and their roof racks packed, are shouting out their destinations in Portuguese and Konkani: "Margao, Panjim, Moddgoam, Ponnje!" Ghadis, which are small bullock-drawn two-wheeled carriages, handcarts, and bicycles, crowd into the area, all determined to ignore a lone policeman's efforts to organize the traffic.

"It seems that all the crows in Goa are here to greet us," Linda says. I have to agree. They are everywhere: on ridges, parapets, and the roof racks of buses, and in the trees. They hop sideways, cawing loudly, and occasionally flutter off in a frenzy into nearby trees, as if in a well-rehearsed modern dance routine. Linda and Fatima clasp their hands over their ears to shut out the din. Joachim mimics them.

"It does seem much noisier than ever," Mom says. "I don't re-member it ever being so noisy."

Linda and I stare at each other. Everything seems so different from Kenya, and yet on the face of it, here on the docks there are many similarities.

Uncle Dominic signals to a couple of prearranged taxis that are waiting for us, and the boys quickly load our luggage in them. Dad gives them a tip that sets them off as if they are coin-operated, which in a way they are: they bow, smile, and salaam with their hands in gratitude.

Soon we are on our way. Uncle Rafael is riding with Mom, Fatima, and Joachim in one taxi; Uncle Dominic, Dad, Linda, and

I are in another. After the comfort of Ahmad's taxi, which I will use as a yardstick for the rest of my life, I find our car's interior coarse and every detail very basic. It certainly is not dust-proof—the window controls are broken.

"We're going to stay at Avozinha's house in Loutolim," Uncle Dominic tells us. He adds that the neighbourhood where our grandmother lives will be nice and quiet.

We leave Mormugao Port and travel toward the main Panjim-Margao road, following the banks of the wide Zuari River. Clusters of egrets adorn trees along the bank, while other species of birds circle and glide overhead. The many hours that Jeep and I spent with the bird collection in the Nairobi Museum now come in handy. I call the names out loud as they come into view: herons, egrets, river gulls, kingfishers…

"Oh, stop showing off," Linda says. I ignore her, happy for once to be the one with all the answers.

The landscape changes, as does the type of road surface. We travel past paddy fields in near silence except for the distinct rattle of the diesel motor as the taxi driver keeps rolling along parallel concrete strips embedded in compacted red dirt. There is almost no other motorized traffic, though the road is filled with handcarts, bicycles, and women carrying produce on their heads to the nearest village market.

We swerve off the concrete strips as a bigger vehicle heads toward us—our driver has to give it the right of way.

When we approach a village, it seems to trigger an uncontrollable reaction from the driver; from this point on, he sounds his horn continuously. Now vehicle size seems to establish the hierarchy: trucks have absolute right-of-way then buses; ghadis, taxis, handcarts, and bicycles. Pedestrians scramble, often making the sign of the cross as they scurry to the other side of the road. Drivers exchange shouted and prolonged greetings, even while overtaking another car.

"What are they saying, Uncle?"

"They're giving each other the latest news in the village." I sit back. Everyone seems to know each other. Even though they are all gesticulating wildly at each other and are always calling out in raised voices, nobody ever gets angry, or so it seems.

The landscape changes as the river gives way to paddy fields again, separated by built-up embankments and rows of coconut trees. We are now entering Loutolim village.

"Go past the chapel," Uncle tells the driver. "Please turn left after the Hindu shrine…by the jackfruit tree is best."

Avozinho and Avozinha, my maternal grandparents, along with Mom's remaining siblings in Goa, as well as two maidservants, a handyman, and three dogs are waiting to greet us on the big front porch. Mom's is a typical large Goan Catholic family, abundantly showered with God's blessings as measured by the number of surviving siblings (ten in all). Linda and I can quickly identify relatives from an old family photograph we had in Nairobi, even though they are all older and some of them have changed shape and size. Even as we are doing that, amid barking and yapping, we are ambushed. Grandparents, uncles, and aunts repeatedly hug us and kiss us. They wipe away tears. They insist on speaking Portuguese, which is already a problem for Linda and me. About five years earlier, Mom had wanted us to learn English faster in Kenya, so she started speaking English at home instead of Portuguese, so now, though we still understand Portuguese well, we have lost our fluency.

The greetings over, the maidservants slip away to their chores, and the dogs return outdoors to stretch and luxuriate in the sun. A couple of pigs that had watched our arrival snort their approval and rummage through the undergrowth. I am glad we have arrived at our destination, as it had been a long hot trip in the car. However, even before being given a tour around the house, we are shown directly to our rooms and given about thirty minutes to refresh ourselves, as my granddad is waiting.

"Avozinho likes everything to be on time," Mom explains. "He always told us as children that people who are late cannot possibly respect other people, or they would not keep them waiting."

Everyone files into the dining room. Avozinho presides at the head of a long dining table; he looks exactly like his photo taken fifteen years earlier: a handsome tall lean man with high cheekbones and a firm, well-shaped chin. He is formally dressed in jacket and tie.

Four of Mom's brothers are seated at the table: Uncle Thomaz (a priest), Uncle Dominic, Uncle Rafael, and Uncle Armando, who is only two years older than Linda and at sixteen is our youngest uncle. Mom's only sister present is Aunt Lucia, who, wearing a cheerful coloured dress from one of the famous fashion houses in Bombay, stands out from the rest, who are wearing brown and grey attire. With her long dangling jewelled earrings, a necklace and ring to match, and her shocking pink lipstick, she looks strangely incongruous in this village house. We have been told that she was recently married off to a young businessman in Bombay and has come down to Goa especially to meet us. In spite of her bold style of dressing, she is the only one who seems completely comfortable in my grandpa's austere presence.

Avozinha, our stocky grandmother at the other end of the table, smiles happily. I study her while we wait. She seems pleased that Mom is raising a brood of grandchildren for her. I can bet that the dress Mom bought her as a gift is going to be a very tight fit, but I can't share that thought with Linda or anyone else. This lunch is going to be a very solemn event, with no room for the good-humoured banter around the table that normally accompanies our mealtimes at Plums Lane.

Avozinho clears his throat. All eyes are now on him. I see him sitting upright; he glances quickly around the room, makes eye contact with Aunt Lucia, and nods. We bow our heads as she recites a short grace before meals.

From across the table, Avozinha says something in Portuguese to Avozinho. There is a pin-drop silence before he bursts into a welcome speech in Portuguese, looking directly in turn at Linda,

Fatima, and me as he speaks our names. Joachim, is not at the table as he has been whisked away by a maidservant. We nod and smile; then everyone drinks from their glasses and applauds.

After we have nibbled nervously at our food for a short while, my grandpa abruptly announces, "The children can now leave the table." We do not resist but leave quietly, although it has taken us by surprise. I am not used to being shut out of adult company and shudder to think that this will be my family home for perhaps the next ten or twelve years. Mom later tells Linda and me that our being whisked away from the table was not a reflection on our table manners but rather the normal attitude of her father's generation: children were seldom seen or heard at the table with adults.

Everyone has a short siesta in the afternoon, and when we wake up we spend a little time unpacking some items we need immediately before we are sent for our first baths. The hot water is boiled in big wood-heated cauldrons and then mixed in smaller buckets with cold water from the well. Following bath time, we say the rosary as a family and then share a simple evening meal, after which we are once again abruptly banished to our bedroom at the end of the meal. It all happens so fast that there is almost no time to react, and Avozinho's strict coldness evokes a sense of cruel and unusual discipline.

Our first night in Goa turns out to be very scary. There is no electricity yet in the village. Avozinha's house is lit mainly with small oil lanterns that shed a dim light. However, a bright pressure lamp called a Petromax is used when the adults gather during dinner or in the living room. We four children sleep in one room on two wooden beds; Linda shares one with Fatima, and I share mine with Joachim, who howls from the start, so he is taken to Mom's room.

Because this is our first night sleeping in a strange room, a small oil lamp has been left on for reassurance. Its flame is set so low that all it does is prevent total darkness. After Fatima falls asleep, Linda and I tiptoe to the window and peer onto the porch, from where

Braz Menezes

we hear voices. Seconds later we hear footsteps approaching in the corridor. We scurry back and jump into our respective beds in case it is Avozinho checking up on us. There is a knock on the door. We remain absolutely silent. Then there is another knock.

"Who is it?" I ask cautiously.

"Armando, Uncle Armando," he says, and enters. He sits on the edge of my bed, facing Linda and Fatima, who are now both wide awake, and tells us he has been banished from the adult conversation in the dining room to tell us bedtime stories to help us fall asleep.

Uncle Armando tells us stories, alright—stories that make us scared to stay in bed, and even more terrified to get out of bed. For added effect, he moves his hands as he speaks, shakes his mop of jet-black hair, sticks his beak-like nose right in our faces, and brings his bushy eyebrows together even as he rolls his eyes this way and that. He tells us about the ghosts that visit Avozinha's house regularly: some, he says, are dead relatives who are angry with someone in the family; others are ghosts from the village that come visiting at night. He also tells us about creatures that growl like panthers and tigers but are really humans who were changed into animals after they died. From deep inside his throat, he produces such sounds that, even though I can see him right there in front of us, make me ready to believe a real beast is prowling out there in the night, coming to get us.

He tells us that snakes originally lived happily in the Garden of Eden but are annoyed that they too were thrown out of Paradise because they were wrongly linked with Adam and Eve all those thousands of years ago, and they are still looking for victims on whom they can take their revenge.

"By the way," Uncle Armando tells us, "remember that in Goa you must always kill a snake by smashing its head first. Otherwise the head will travel separately from the body and come and get you." I feel a chill down my spine. Linda and Fatima cling to each other, petrified.

"Also, if you see a cobra, it will follow you home," Uncle continues. "Remember, if you kill a snake anywhere in the village, its mate will come and hunt you down. So you must kill both snakes. That means if the mates are not together when you kill one of them, you will have to look for its mate so you can kill it before it kills you."

I look at Linda and Fatima; they have closed their eyes, pretending to have fallen asleep so he will stop, but I can tell by the way they're still clutching each other's hands that they're wide awake and just as frightened as I am. I too close my eyelids tightly, hoping Uncle will go away before we all faint or the girls start screaming in terror. There is a brief silence, and we all hold our breath, hoping he'll leave.

"Okay, good night now. You must all be tired," Uncle Armando says. "Tomorrow I can tell you some really scary stories if you are interested."

He walks to the oil lamp and turns the wick down even lower until the flame just flickers; then he leaves the room, shutting the door quickly behind him. Within seconds Linda and Fatima have both relocated to my bed. I'd never admit it, but I'm so glad they did, because whatever is out there can't possibly get all of us if we stick together. Fatima clutches Linda tightly and eventually falls into a sound sleep.

"Lando, look up there." Linda is seeing what I have been staring at for the past several minutes.

The bedroom has no ceiling, so we can see the underside of the roof, hundreds of curved tiles set on rafters. Thanks to Uncle Armando, the flickering oil lamp has given birth to thousands of black shadow snakes writhing over us. We don't know whether to keep looking so we can see them coming or to turn away. We stay frozen with fear in our bed.

"Lando, I wish we were back in Nairobi," Linda whispers.

"Me too," I say. "But I am the one who will have to live here when you all go back. I don't know what will happen now. I can't imagine what it will be like being here all alone. Dad says we may have to visit my new school as early as next week."

From sheer exhaustion, we eventually drift into sleep.

At breakfast Avozinha smiles as we relate Uncle Armando's stories to Mom. Uncle Armando is very amused. "If you like, I'll tell you scarier ones tonight," he promises.

Trying to be polite, we tell him we'd like that very much, but we secretly hope he'll forget all about it by tonight. We can't take another night of excruciating terror. I'm sure some of those shadows really were snakes—I could swear I saw them moving this morning in the grey early-morning light.

25: Father Mendonça and Dona Paula

Four days later we are on our way to my boarding school to meet the principal for the first time, even though I won't be enrolling until the Easter term, still two months away. I am torn between curiosity and resignation at what might lie ahead.

On a beautiful February day under a blue sky with few clouds, Dad, Mom, and I travel by bus from Loutolim to Margao, and then change buses to get to Panjim. There, a ferry takes us across the Mandovi River to Betim, where we finally take a taxi to Arpora. I am exhausted; it has been almost five hours since we left Avozinha's in the pre-dawn.

St. Joseph's was the first English-language high school to be established in Goa. The main entrance to the two-storey building has the school's coat of arms and its motto engraved in thick letters: CIBARIA NECESSARIA SUMITE ET ABITE.

"What's that mean, Dad?"

"Take the necessary food and depart, if my Latin serves me well.

It looks as if you will be well fed."

Mom seems relieved because I am a bit on the skinny side. "It's bigger than I expected," she says.

"Some buildings have been added," Dad replies. "Otherwise it is pretty much as I remember it. Come, we must hurry—we're already late."

We get to a door that says, FATHER FILIPE NERI MENDONÇA – PRINCIPAL. A clerk answers the knock and ushers us into the office. The room is neat and well furnished.

"Very formal," Mom remarks to Dad just as Father Mendonça walks through the doorway.

"It helps parents feel that they have picked the right school for their son," Father Mendonça replies with a hint of a smile. He gestures for us to sit down. "Excuse me." He attends to a letter that his clerk has brought to him, clearly requiring his urgent attention. "Excuse me," he says again as he walks out with the clerk to the outer office.

On opposite walls, the portraits of President Salazar of Portugal and His Holiness Pope Pius XII stare sternly at each other while we sit and wait. In contrast, His Grace the Archbishop of Goa and William Robert Lyons, founder of St. Joseph's, appear to smile at each other across the room. A glazed trophy cupboard encloses dozens of cups, as well as gold, silver, and bronze medals that the school has won over the years while competing against its archrivals, St. Britto's of Mapusa and Mater Dei of Saligao. The cabinet also holds a framed papal blessing bestowed on Father Mendonça in 1946 and a photograph of him taken with the Archbishop of Bombay. Many more trophies, cups, and chalices are crowded onto the space above the cabinet. From where I sit, I can see Father Mendonça still giving the clerk instructions. From the way he stands and moves, I feel that he could have been a good sportsman in his youth. Perhaps he even won some of the cups and medals being displayed in the cupboards. Nowadays, his fame as a strict, competent educator has reached even Africa.

The principal returns. "I'm sorry," he says as he shakes hands with Mom, Dad, and me. "I'll make sure we are not interrupted again." He closes the door.

He and Dad first chat briefly as Dad hands over the various papers, testimonials, and financial documents that the school requested prior to our departure from Kenya. He looks at them carefully but quickly and sets them aside. From that point the interview with my parents and me is a simple and brief formality. He turns to me.

"Welcome to St. Joseph's, Lando," Father Mendonça says. "I know you'll enjoy your stay here and that you will contribute a lot to the school."

I know already he is in for a big disappointment because I have limited talent in sports. I know my Dad likes this school, and I don't want to hurt his feelings, so I tell a barefaced lie. "Thank you, Father. I'm looking forward to it." I remind myself that for this fib I will have to go to Confession later.

"By the way," Father Mendonça continues, "do you know the name Menezes is very famous in Goa's history?" He looks at Dad and smiles as if they share a secret.

After a knock on the door, the harassed-looking clerk announces the principal's next appointment. Father Mendonça stands and excuses himself again. "Lando, in two months you will be part of our family. I look forward to welcoming you personally on your first day." He shakes our hands warmly.

"Why is our name famous in Goa's history?" I ask Mom, as we get into our taxi for the trip back.

"Ask your father," she says. "It's only my name by marriage."

Dad laughs. He seems very relieved the interview is over. "Dom Duarte de Meneses was one of the earliest governors of Goa. He was in office for only two years from 1522, but he was a very bad man. The Portuguese king had him arrested and sent back to Lisbon in chains. He died in prison there."

"What bad things did he do?" I ask.

"Oh…all manner of evil things. He liked bad women, he also stole public funds for his own personal use and for his friends."

"Tell Lando about that other woman as well," Mom says. I realize she is enjoying seeing Dad answer difficult questions because he is usually the one who teases her.

"Which woman?" Dad looks confused.

"You know the one near Panjim? Dona Paula."

"Oh yes. That's one of the more famous ghost stories," Dad says. "Dona Paula was the daughter of a Viceroy Meneses—there were a few of them. The story goes that she was tied up and pushed to her death over the cliffs near Panjim by the jealous wife of a wealthy Portuguese gentleman who was her lover. Many people still claim to see her playing in the bay, but only when a full moon is out."

"So people in Goa believe in ghosts?" I ask. "I heard it is a sin for Catholics to believe in ghosts. Aren't we supposed to believe in ghosts only after they are declared saints by the Pope?"

"Saints are not ghosts," Dad says. "I hope that's not what you learned at Dr. Ribeiro's school."

"Are these dead Menezes our relatives, then?"

"No, no. At least I don't think so. And they all spelled their name with an s, not a z."

The taxi pulls into the Betim wharf, and we see a ferry taking on passengers. We rush to it as the last passengers are getting on board. As we cross the river, Dad points to the left.

"Old Goa is upriver over there, and we will visit it soon," he says. "There are just a few magnificent churches left there now, so it's hard to believe that in the sixteenth century it was a city as big and as important as London and Antwerp."

Many thoughts go through my mind as we journey back on the buses. I remember Abba, Abdul's grandfather, telling us about Goa's importance as a trading city during its occupation by Muslim rulers. I wonder if Abba even imagines where I am now. I have seen so much already in just a few weeks. I think about Dona Paula. Did Dad speak to me as an adult about women and lovers so that when he leaves me behind, I will feel grown up and he won't feel guilty about sending me thousands of miles away?

Back in Loutolim, Linda and I discover almost by accident that Avozinho actually lives in Margao during the workweek and only comes home on Friday evenings to spend the weekends with Avozinha and the family. Uncle Dominic and Uncle Rafael return to their own lodgings in Panjim and Benaulim.

We quickly settle back into Avozinha's daily routine, which Dad says seems engraved in stone. Every evening at about seven, the family squeezes into a small alcove off the living room in which there is a small altar—really a big arched niche in the wall. Squeezed into it are a painted wood-carved statue of the Blessed Virgin Mary holding Baby Jesus, and a big picture of the Sacred Heart. There's also standing room for four saints who have made it past Avozinha's private filter: St. Francis Xavier, St. Theresa of the Roses, St. Filomena, and St. Anthony, the patron saint of rain.

When we are all assembled, Uncle Armando lights a candle. Avozinha glances quickly around to make sure everyone holds a rosary in his or her hand, and then she leads the prayers. We recite endless Hail Marys, moving the beads along. When my uncles mumble the words, Avozinha pauses and glares to shame them, reminding them that we, their young nieces and nephews, will learn by example. Sometimes she interrupts the prayers to make sure the young maid has not carelessly left food to burn on the wood stove in the kitchen. In ending she always recites a long list of the names of people who need our prayers. Within days Linda and I know all their names, though we will never meet most of them.

On the Friday a week after our arrival, a beautifully painted statue of the Blessed Virgin Mary enclosed in a glass case is brought from the chapel to the house in a small procession led by our uncle priest, Father Thomaz. A makeshift altar is set up in the great hall, and the statue stays there for two nights. Many neighbours and friends turn up on the first night for a traditional singing of the litany. We begin first by saying the rosary, after which a violinist accompanies the singing of a hymn. The full ladainha, or litany, is recited, and another hymn sung. After just over an hour, everyone is served homemade sweets and soft drinks.

"Remember to greet everyone politely and smile," I hear Mom whisper to Linda. I realize that the ladainha is being held because it is a special occasion for friends of our Goan relatives to meet us. Linda, Fatima, Joachim, and I are on display as "newly arrived from Africa." The visitors, who will certainly be comparing notes the next morning when they meet at the village market, dutifully inspect us. After most of them leave, some of the male attendees congregate in the balcão with Avozinho and Dad and sample a potent local liquor called feni that's been distilled from Avozinha's most recent cashew harvest.

Back in our beds that night, we discover a miracle appears to have taken place. For a little over a week, we have spent every night talking about the reflected shadow images on the ceiling. Uncle Armando is no help, as he enjoys seeing us frightened by his unending stories of ghosts and gremlins and snakes.

Our uncle priest Father Thomaz, on the other hand, has come to our rescue. "Look, if I move the light from here to there," he says, "the shadows are not so bad."

By the night of the ladainha, the snakes have disappeared. We see the shadows as shadows and nothing more. We fall asleep to the sound of familiar voices coming from the balcão late into the night.

"You are finally settling down to village life in Goa," Mom says when we tell her about it. "It has been like that for centuries. Now please finish your breakfast so Consu can clean up and get on with her busy day." Uncle Armando is not ready to surrender his power over our imagination. He warns us that ghosts really do exist, and we ignore them at our own peril.

"It's not like life in the towns," he says. "Here in our villages, ghosts are the ones who control everything. Especially at night.

Especially when the house is quiet and the grown-ups have gone to sleep."

———•◦•———

26: Goa

Linda and I are talking in the balcão as Mom walks in. "We miss Nairobi," Linda says.

"Everything here in Avozinha's home is so slow," I add.

"It's because you're on holiday and this is a village," Mom interrupts. "By the way, Lando, it has made Dad so happy that you like your new school."

"It's his old boarding school, remember?" I say. "I'm only doing it for him. But how can I ever be a doctor when I faint at the sight of blood?"

"Well, there are other choices," Mom says. "We would also be happy if you studied law."

"Lawyers also deal with blood, Mom," I reply. "Didn't Uncle Antonio tell Dad his lawyer is a big bloodsucker? Remember? You were there in the room."

"Ah, here's Dad," she says as he enters the front yard with Father Thomaz.

"Thomaz and I have been to the parish church in Raia, where I was baptized in 1902," Dad says. "It's a lovely church. We met with the parish priest, who has promised to make a handwritten copy of my birth certificate."

"Doesn't the prefeitura, the municipality, keep those civil documents?" Mom asks.

"They are supposed to. However, the church has kept detailed and meticulous handwritten records of every child born and baptized since the priests first arrived in Goa in the sixteenth century. Just for that, it is worth having a copy." Dad turns to us. "Tomorrow, we will go to Margao. That's where I first set eyes on Mom, and we will say hello to Avozinho at work."

The next day, leaving Fatima and Joachim with my grandma, we go to Margao. The bus ride is a joy: the lush green landscape of mango, cashew, banana, jackfruit, papaya, and citrus trees is the backdrop for rows and clusters of coconut palms on the edge of paddy fields. Egrets and storks suddenly flutter away from one spot and alight at another, as if they are hired helpers to animate the bucolic scene.

We arrive at the big city where Avozinho works. From the bus stop, a short walk takes us to the treasury offices, where Avozinho proudly shows us off to his friends. "From Africa," he boasts. I glance at Linda. She and I look like everyone else: how does the Africa label make us different, I wonder?

Avozinho explains to Dad why he will not be able to prolong his welcome. I glean from the exchange that a crisis is about to spin out of control, a problem of the type only career bureaucrats can unravel and that is, says Avozinho, "too complex to explain, and too confidential to attempt to."

We leave the *fazenda* and walk directly across the street, past the magnificent town hall, surrounded by an arched colonnade. The air is filled with diesel and gasoline fumes and the smell of ripe fruit and fish set up for market day. But the smells cannot compete with the sounds; cars honk and bicyclists ring bells, trying to outdo the shouting of fisherwomen and sweetmeat vendors. "Watch out, Lando!" Linda shouts as a horse-drawn carriage hurtles from a lane, the driver flailing his whip and shouting obscenities.

We hurry past the cacophony and walk across the Municipal Gardens and down a quiet residential street with two-storied bungalows, before turning into a tree-lined parallel street. Peace at last, though not quite that of Loutolim.

"That's where Lucas Figueiredo lived," Dad says. "That's where I stayed the night I met Mom. He was my very best friend since childhood. 'Lulu' that's what we called him."

"Has he moved somewhere else?" I ask.

"Sadly, he died last year," Dad says. "He would have been so happy to see you all."

A few short streets away, we arrive at Mom's old home, in the middle of a well-manicured garden dotted with guava and chiku trees. Mom takes a step back; then she recognizes a lady on the balcão, walks up the short path, and explains why we are staring at the house. The lady lets out a little cry of delight; with arms outspread, she welcomes us in and hugs Mom. In an instant the story of Dad's and Mom's fairytale romance comes alive. Linda and I have heard it so often that we can probably recount it better than Dad. How Dad had been a lonely bachelor in Kenya. How, getting wind of this, matchmakers back in Goa had set to work. How, when he'd gone to Goa on leave, his old friend Lulu had taken him to the home of the Albuquerque family, where one of Senhor Joachim's regular poker games was in progress. How Senhor Joachim's daughter Anja came into the room. How Chico suddenly forgot about poker. How Lulu had known that that would happen, and how for Chico, Anja was the best card life ever dealt him.

"Is this the room where you played cards, Dad?" Linda asks.

"Yes," he says as Mom blushes.

"So little has changed," Mom says. We walk through the rooms and return to the sitting room. She turns to Dad. "You were sitting there when I came in and stood by Papa."

"Yes. Then your mother called you over to my side and introduced us. You were so sure of yourself." He turns to the lady of the house. "You must excuse me. I got carried away by my memories. Have you been living here a long time?"

"We moved in when Senhor Joachim took his family to Loutolim," the lady explains. "My husband Osvaldo passed away two years ago. Now it is only my mother and my unmarried sister who live here with me, and our two maidservants. Our two children have both gone to Africa. I can't blame them. They went to improve their lives; the situation here, as you know, is so bad."

"You must miss your sons!" Mom says as she puts her arm

around my shoulders. "I know we will miss this one terribly. We will leave him behind at St. Joseph's in Arpora." I can feel my stomach churn, but I repress my emotions. I am too proud to share my feelings.

"What a shame," the lady says. "You Africanders"—that's what East African Goans are called—"have good jobs and earn more money but have no schools, and we have very good schools and teachers, doctors, hospitals, and plenty of beautiful churches but no jobs and no money."

On the street he puts his arm around Mom's waist. "It was so nice that we could show the children this house." He smiles. "Any regrets, amorzinha?"

"None whatsoever," Mom says. "You have given me four beautiful children." She hugs Linda and me and turns to glance back one last time at the house. From the corner of my eye, I see her wipe away a tear.

As the weeks pass, we adjust to the daily routine at home in Loutolim. I do not admit it to anyone, but I feel more at ease with my life in Goa—or maybe I am so upset that I am pretending it doesn't matter anymore. I'm really not sure what I think about all that's happening. I stop reacting to the idea of being abandoned in boarding school. Whenever anybody asks me how I feel about starting it soon, I say that I am looking forward to it. I've said it so many times that I'm starting to believe it's actually how I feel now.

I follow the rhythm of the household. A doorway from the dining room leads out into an internal courtyard, which is overlooked by windows from the kitchen and some bedrooms. Each morning starts with a peep from the kitchen window into the deep well that was dug just outside it. The well is our source of water for everyday needs. Fermina, the slightly infirm maid, or the younger Consu, who is more fun to watch, draws from it often during the day. Consu will stand by the kitchen window, adjust the noose of a rope tightly around the neck of a copper pot, and then go into a little ritual before actually dropping the pot into the water. She first leans over and studies the water's surface, adjusts her blouse and her hair, and looks in again. Only then does she drop the pot in, and flip the rope so that the water goes gurgling in.

"Why does Consu do that?" I ask Uncle Armando. "Do what?"

"You know…look in the water first."

"Snakes!" he says. "Just weeks before you arrived, I had to fish out one that was almost this long out of the well." He gestures with his hands. "It had fallen in, probably while looking for frogs. I was standing here. Consu was drawing water, and she screamed when she saw the snake fall in. I didn't see it happen, but I heard the splash."

"So how did you fish it out?" I ask.

"I fixed a basket to a long bamboo pole, and slowly, little by little, I trapped it. From that day Consu started to peek into the well before drawing water. She doesn't want to be caught holding that heavy pot full of water while a snake is swimming in it."

"And I thought she was using the water in the well as a mirror because she always adjusts her blouse and her hair after peeking in," I say.

The story of the well doesn't end there. I too start looking in the well for snakes, but I don't do this from the kitchen window; I open the door to the courtyard, and walk up to the well's parapet. One morning, two weeks after I am told the snake story, I hear little Joachim clatter his way out of Mom's bedroom, dragging a toy behind him. Mom follows him out. I too get out of bed, open the doors to the courtyard, and go look in the well. There are no snakes this morning.

Suddenly, there is a commotion at the front door. The two dogs are barking at the local baker, which is unusual since he has been bringing poi bread to the house for years. It turns out that he's a substitute and this is his first day. He lowers his basket slowly. I bend to choose some puffed flat bread when Mom lets out a screech. "Joachim! Where's Joachim?"

She rushes back into the house. There is no sign of him. He

did not follow us to the front door. Suddenly we see him on top of the parapet wall. He must have crept out into the patio, somehow heaved himself up onto the low wall around the well, and started peering into it. Walking slowly, I get to him and put my arm around him, pointing to Mom so he stays distracted, and pray that someone stronger will help me rescue him in case he puts up a struggle. But he doesn't; he just leans into my arms, and I get him off the wall.

Mom's scream has not gone unheard. The whole household is now awake. Avozinha imposes new rules over locking those doors, and I get rewarded an extra poi for my quick thinking. I share a piece with Joachim, who hasn't a clue about the heart attacks he nearly caused.

Two papaya trees grow in the courtyard, and the freshly picked ripe papaya seems to dissolve in the mouth while the sweetness lingers on. Many others of various species share this view. My uncles and a pack of marauding monkeys regularly fight over the papayas. The monkeys creep along tree branches, jump onto the neighbour's wall, sometimes two or three at a time, their heads low. Often, a baby will ride piggyback on its mother or clutch her underbelly as she climbs or runs along. Both my uncles and the monkeys want the fruit. It is a battle of wits. More often than not, despite periodic blasts of blank cartridges, the monkeys win.

"Why do you use only blanks?" I ask, although I really don't want to see the monkeys hurt. I think they deserve the fruit more than my uncles, who can eat other food.

"It is out of respect for the Hindus. People will not kill a monkey."

"Why?" I ask.

"Because Lord Hanuman the monkey god helped Lord Rama to fight evil," he says. "Surely you learned this in school?"

"We are taught by Irish priests in Kenya. They don't talk about other religions, but I have a friend Hardev, who is a Sikh, and Abdul, who is a Muslim. They sometimes tell me about their customs."

As I await sleep that night, my thoughts wander. I think about my uncles' comments and my Dad's views over whether the Portuguese or the British are better rulers. They are on opposite sides of the argument. It's all so confusing for me. Goa is absolutely beautiful. Almost everywhere the roads are dotted with small shrines, both Catholic and Hindu, often within a few yards of each other and sometimes facing each other across the street. People live happily side-by-side. I haven't seen the university and hospitals that Uncle Dominic talked about.

Maybe Dad is right. He claims the British have done more in five decades in Kenya than the Portuguese have done in Goa in more than four centuries. Look at the roads. The streets in Goa outside the town centres are usually just two narrow parallel strips of cement for wheel tracks, and that is for two-way traffic. In Kenya, on the other hand, we can drive from Nairobi more than two hundred miles all the way to the shores of Lake Victoria on a paved road. But since that is so, why is Dad so madly in love with this place? It must have to do with being born here. But where will I live when I'm older? Can this be my homeland if I was born elsewhere?

I miss my peach tree in Plums Lane, as I think Kenya is my home, but I remember now that in Nairobi Mom always talked about missing her sharp-tasting bimblims from her youth in Goa. She was so happy to see her beloved bimblim tree in Avozinha's garden. I expect bimblims will jump out of curries from now on and introduce themselves to me. I toss and turn. In just three weeks, I will go into my boarding school. Maybe they'll serve bimblims for breakfast there. Maybe we'll get rice and bimblim curry day and night. Maybe we share the roots with our favourite trees; my ties to Nairobi are as strong as my parents' ties to Goa. Sleep overcomes me.

The weeks pass rapidly. I keep thinking of Jeep and Jimmy back in Nairobi. They would love to do the things I am doing, but they're at school and I'm roaming free. In two months, I have learned what has taken Uncle Armando almost twice my lifetime. He has taught me so much already. He and I each fish with a single bamboo rod and hook in the small streams, and with multiple rods in big rivers. We have only egrets, cormorants, and crows for company, especially in the early morning or at dusk. We trawl for prawns—shrimp, they're sometimes called—with nets and baskets as we wade in knee-high water, pursuing them back to their hide-aways in brackish marshes. Sometimes Uncle and I fish by moon-light, in silence, with only an oil lantern in a narrow canoe. Even in the total silence, the fish won't bite. Most times we give up, since we are hungrier than the fish. But I've become quite patient over these past weeks. I have also come to appreciate the silence and the slow pace of these simple village pastimes, and I don't mind anymore if we come home empty-handed.

Dad drags us out sightseeing. After all, it is our vacation, and he also wants to prepare me to see Goa as my homeland. If left to him, I would be an expert in Goan archaeology and botany and Portuguese history, a world-class anthropologist specializing in the merging and morphing of Hindu and Catholic Goan culture, and a doctor or lawyer to boot. But I get distracted too easily.

In the two months since we arrived in Goa, the fragrance in the air seems to have intensified in Loutolim. Although various *bhatkars* (landowners) hold parcels of land on the hillside behind Avozinha's house, nature has no boundaries. The hillside is abundant with cashew trees in bloom. I claim one tree as my own. Although it is not the tallest, it is a wide shade tree and almost as nice as the peach tree by my dog Jolly's grave at home, where Jeep and I used to sit and dream about the good life.

Its trunk twists grotesquely out of the ground and sends out low, twisted, long branches, creating a leafy umbrella of khaki and olive green. It is an easy tree to climb compared to the monkey-nut tree that Jeep fell off in Plums Lane. Over the next few weeks, I watch my cashew tree change. The blossoms start on a red-brown coloured stub that bursts out into tiny white flowers, which shrivel almost immediately, as if they had picked the wrong date for their coming-out party. And then the most extraordinary thing happens. A tiny seed starts to form on the end of each stub. I am mesmerized. Most fruits surround their seed with their flesh to protect it and ensure safe propagation—even the gigantic coco de mer is cocooned in a thick husk. The cashew is a blatant exhibitionist and throws caution to the wind. The seed grows outside the fruit into a plump kidney-shaped dark-green nut, about an inch and a half long.

"This is how you hold both sticks," Uncle Armando says. He is demonstrating to Linda and me how to pry open the outer layer of the nut with two small twigs.

"It is important to avoid getting any of the sap on your fingers and skin," he says. "It will itch and even stain your skin."

"Please, can I try?" I ask. I do it two or three times before I get it right. The prize inside is a soft, tasty version of a dried cashew nut.

But as the days pass, I notice more changes. Each stub, which at first looks like a stem attached to the thicker end of the kidney-shaped nut, gradually swells and takes on colour. Some turn a bright red, others a deep yellow, while others have a bit of both. The stubs are now converting themselves into a fleshy fruit. They grow to the size of a pear until the fruit dwarfs the nuts still attached to them. The fruits start to take different shapes—some remain slender, while others obese. Some are the shape and size of apples, others take on the contours of a pear. Then the nuts become thick-skinned and hard. The once gentle aroma is now very powerful and growing stronger by the day.

"They are sweet when ripe," Uncle says. "But be careful. It is an unpleasant taste when unripe; the sticky sap will irritate the inside of your mouth." He picks a fruit just fallen to the ground and holds it up. "It's time to harvest. These nuts are where the money is."

———•·•———

27: A Live Shark and a Dead Drunk

Later that week we receive a visitor. He is Andrew, a nephew of F.X. Fernandes, a colleague of Dad's in Nairobi, also on holiday in Goa with his family. We arrange to go to Colva Beach on the weekend. Dad will meet his fellow Africanders. The adults will sit in the simple palm-thatched beachside huts, strip each other of news and gossip, and finally exchange tales of olden times. The toddlers will sit or roll on mats under the supervision of gossiping mothers, and young children will build sandcastles, demolish them, and make frequent trips to coconut trees to relieve themselves. Linda and I will have to amuse ourselves as best we can.

We arrive in the late afternoon. A strong sea breeze brings us a powerful smell of salted fish set out to dry. Linda and I look at each other; we have figured it out—if we get to the water's edge, the smell will be behind us. Then we see people running toward the shore where three long narrow fishing boats are coming in. With the tide going out, the fishermen have to row strongly to make headway. Outriggers lashed to the sides prevent them from tipping over as they ride the waves.

Two new friends rush toward us. They are Johnny and Xavier, Andrew's sons. "They've caught a shark!" Johnny shouts from a distance. "They say it's over ten feet long."

"No, it's over twelve feet," Xavier says. "The fisherman who brought the news told me so; he saw it with his own eyes."

No one really knows the details, except that two fishermen brought their boat back in ahead of the others to get extra help to pull the shark in.

"Is it alive?" I ask. "How will they get close enough?" I need to know this if I'm expected to help. Dad will surely be very disappointed if, after all the trouble he took to get me into boarding school, I am devoured by a shark before school even starts, especially since he has already paid part of the fees in advance.

The crowds swell. Cheers erupt as the boats ride the last waves to shore. Men have waded out to meet them, and now drop logs in front of each prow so the boats can be pulled to shore without getting stuck in the sand. Even as the boats are being heaved up the beach to dry sand, other men seize ropes that are attached to the fishing nets; one of the fisher folk starts a chant, and they all join in, pulling on the ropes in rhythm. I tense my muscles, and Linda and I join the middle line, the one we think is pulling in the shark. Nobody objects. We also join in the singing, though we do not know the words.

A fisherman comes up, points at the nets that are still in shallow water, and says something quickly to me in Konkani. I look at him helplessly. Linda and I have picked up a few Konkani words, but not enough for me to understand what he is saying. He grabs me and gestures for me to climb on his shoulders. I know then that he is going to take me to see the shark. I get on to his shoulders and he gallops into the water like one of the three musketeers doing battle. Hanging onto my sea horse, I see the trapped shark. Johnny and Xavier run behind me, and Linda splashes behind them.

The man lifts his arms, picks me off his shoulders, and holds me as if he is about to throw me to the shark, now only about four feet away. For the first time, I realize he has been drinking. The powerful smell of cashew liquor hits me, and I can see he is delighted by the terror on my face. I am trapped between a live dead-drunk fisherman and a dead shark, and I don't know which is worse.

In that instant the shark struggles to get free. It is still alive! I see its pointed nose lurch upward. Its mouth opens to expose sharp white teeth that glisten in the sun against the red inside of its mouth. Blood oozes from just below one fin. The fishermen nearest to us shout a warning and scramble. My feni-man stands his ground, laughing as if this is the funniest thing that ever happened to him. I leap out of his clutches and splash toward where my friends are standing with Linda. She is very nervous.

"I was that close to it," I tell Linda, waving my arms. "It is the biggest fish I have ever seen. Did you see the gash on its side?"

Johnny is eagerly following the stories of the fishermen who have arrived with the boat and translates them to Linda and me. When the first fishing boat was lurching wildly with the trapped shark struggling to get free, a nearby boat had rushed to the rescue. One of the men snagged the shark with an anchor. With a second net over the shark, they still needed a third boat to haul it to shore. Dragged clear of the waterline, the shark now looks very dead.

That big lurch must have been its dying gasp. The crowd pushes forward to admire it, and then stands back in awe, astounded at its size and unsure as to what will happen next.

The fisherwomen instantly sort out the lesser catch and grade it by type, weight, and size. A background of shouting and laughter goes with this; sometimes a make-believe fight breaks out between men or women.

A man with a short iron bar walks cautiously to the shark, still wrapped in two layers of fishing net. He delivers a heavy blow to its head. I detect a sudden jerk of the tail, or perhaps I imagine it. Then all is still. Everybody claps. Someone shouts an instruction. The women fall on their knees, the men stand with heads bowed. A man leads the prayers. When they're done, the women chant a thanksgiving hymn.

"It's only about eight feet long," I tell Johnny.

"In Goa we always make everything look bigger," he says.

Soon the shark is cut up, first in slabs, then in smaller segments, then in chunks. Finally, there is nothing left. The ever-present crows hovering nearby move in; they are nature's efficient waste removal service. In a few hours the incoming tide will wash away the last traces of blood. The ocean too does its part.

But first the just-returned fishermen spread the nets out high up on shore to survey the damage. They will return at dawn, squat on the sand, repair the holes, and replace any missing floats of cork or dried coconuts. The nets will then be re-rolled so they can be cast easily and smoothly on the sea. The next trip is never more than a few hours away.

"Lando, look at that beautiful sunset," Linda says. We walk back into the water to let the receding tide wash the sand off our feet. Tiny particles of crushed shells move ever so slightly. Little crabs scurry.

"Let's sit here and watch the sun drop into the sea," I say when we are back to where the adults have gathered around talking. The big orange ball on the horizon seems ready to plunge. "Do you remember Dad's answer when I once asked him after dinner at Plums Lane, why he chose to go to Africa?"

"Yes," Linda replies. "He said when he was a young man they would sit here watching the sun set on this beach at Colva, probably on this very spot. They knew if they sailed straight into the sunset, they would bump into Africa. Isn't that incredible how brave they were in those days?"

The orange ball turns into a deep red and hangs just above the ocean's rim just hangs there and then drops out of sight, leaving only a warm dark pink-and-purple glow in the sky.

"What are you thinking about, Lando?" Linda asks. "That your holiday is over, that next week you'll be entering boarding school?"

"Yes, of course," I tell her. "But also how little time it took for that big shark to be cut up, how the crows and the tide will totally wipe out any trace that it ever existed."

28: Boarding School

When it's finally time for me to join St. Joseph's for the orientation term, Dad and Mom take me on the bus and ferry journey. My small new pale blue tin trunk is packed with clothes and basics as set out in the school's Boarding Instructions.

"We'll be back every weekend," Dad says as they leave, "and then we'll still have a month together before we return to Kenya."

"It will be a short term," Mom reassures me. I know she is fighting back tears.

I hug Mom and shake hands with Dad. I am suddenly aware of many pairs of eyes on me from the dormitory windows. It is as if I'm a lone camper among a herd of zebras in the African night, their eyes shining like bright dots in a sea of blackness. I am choked up too. I swallow my tears, hoping it will not show. I instinctively know from Dr. Ribeiro's school that any boy showing emotion will be labelled a sissy from the start and bullied or teased for life.

I am shown to my dormitory with the other new arrivals. They all seem excited about our new adventure. I wonder if they are also pretending this transformation is not happening.

We are quickly given the layout of the various buildings: chapel, dining room, classrooms, sickroom, and the chief meeting and assembly points. The grounds have lots of trees and coconut palms. The main school buildings overlook a slightly sunken large sports field, as if many rice paddy fields have been incorporated into one. I return to my dormitory, a two-storey block with arched windows that can hold thirty students in fifteen bunk beds. I have been assigned a bottom bunk. The bunks have metal frames with a wooden plank base over which my coconut husk mattress is laid. When I sit on it, I realize that, since it is an old mattress, the coconut fibre inside it has lumped. I imagine it will feel like sleeping on a sheet laid over small rocks. I will know for sure tonight.

Braz Menezes

At dinnertime, Father Mendonça makes an appearance and delivers a special speech.

"Welcome to St. Joseph's High School," he says, "the first and the best English-language school in Goa. In 1887, our founder, Mr. William Robert Lyons, a fine scholar, could not in his wildest dreams have ever imagined that in fifty years, our students would come from across India and all over the globe to study in our fine school.

"Last year was our sixtieth year, and we continue to reign supreme in academic achievement, dominate our rivals on the sports field, and excel in extracurricular activities. Over the years our institution has been the cradle for distinguished priests and professors, doctors, lawyers, and engineers. Today it is my pleasure to welcome our latest batch of Lyon cubs, spelled l-y-o-n, from across the globe to their introductory term. They come from our Goan diaspora as far afield as Yemen, Aden, Kuwait, Kenya, Uganda, and Tanganyika. Please give them all the support they will need to settle in and be part of our pride of proud Lyons."

I feel proud of my status as a "little Lyon", and grateful to Dad that at least he has chosen the best school for me. It makes me think of my own little lion, Simba, who's so far away. I wonder how he's doing without me.

It is the beginning of March, and the normal term will end in about three weeks. This mini-term for the newly admitted boarders from abroad gives us a chance to adjust to the school and to start a crash course in elementary written Portuguese, Latin, and Hindi, so that we don't lag too far behind in the term that follows. Classes for the overseas students start tomorrow. The experience of starting school as a small group brings us together. That evening I make my first three friends at the school, Peter, Ben, and Musso. Though we have come from different places, we are about the same age, have a Goan Catholic background, and have just been evicted from our protective family nests.

Peter comes from Kampala, so as a fellow Africander he greets me first in Swahili before switching to English. "*Jambo, habari gani?* Hello, what's new?" He tells me he is an only son but has three sisters. "Dad wants me to train as a doctor. Our family is from Saligao, right near here." His short clipped sentences sound like lines from a telegram.

"I'm Lando," I reply. "I was born in Nairobi, but my family is from Raia, Salcete. Dad works at the National Bank of India in Nairobi. He thinks the Jesuits here will teach me discipline and perhaps one day make me into a lawyer or doctor. Same thinking as your dad, really."

"You happy here?" Peter asks.

"It feels as if we have been sent to jail," I say. "Doesn't it?"

"They say you get used to it." Peter says. "This suits me fine. I was always changing schools. My father is with Cable and Wireless. Now they want him and the family to move to Aden, somewhere near the Suez Canal. Mummy does not want to go there."

Ben was born in the Gulf. His father, who works for Burma Oil in Kuwait, sent him to Goa at age eight, and for the past three years his grandparents have raised him. Ben finally begged his father to send him to Arpora, since his grandparents are very strict and he cannot even play with his school friends near the church in his village because they are "not suitable" for his family.

"Dad wants to make money in the Gulf," he tells Peter and me, "so he can fix our family home near Calangute Beach and make it bigger."

"Are your mom and dad returning to live in Goa?" I ask. "I think my dad would like to do that."

"No. He wants to build beach cabins for Goans on home leave who don't have relatives here," Ben says, "but he and Mum can't agree. My mum just says, 'Wot to do? Wot to do?' It drives me crazy."

Musso's father works for Tanganyika Packers, a meat-processing plant outside Dar es Salaam. We become instant friends when he turns to me the first evening in chapel and says, "You look like a saint." I do not respond, as he says it during the most solemn part of the service. We meet again after chapel, and I instantly love his dark sense of humour.

"Is Musso a saint's name?" I ask. By tradition, Goan children are named after dead saints or wealthy living relatives.

Musso laughs. "Not yet, but it will be after I die," he says confidently. "My mom chose that name, but it was more complicated than that. According to Dad, theirs was an arranged marriage. Mom was studying at St. Xavier's in Bombay. She was still in her final year at college, and Dad was working in Tanganyika. Some relatives arranged the match, but Dad could not travel in time to arrive for their church wedding, so they were married by proxy. My dad's brother stood in for him at the ceremony, and soon after that she went on a ship bound for Africa to meet up with my father."

"So what about the name?"

"According to my mom, she thought that if they named me after a tough leader, then I too might develop strong leadership qualities. Mussolini in Italy was a good leader in my mother's opinion, strong and decisive."

"So you can be our leader," I say.

"No, no, no! I hate making decisions," Musso says. "I think I'm a lot like my dad. He's good at math, sports, and parties, but he lets Mom make all the decisions."

We quickly settle into our new school routine: wake-up bell, cold showers, chapel, breakfast, classes, break, more classes, lunch, more classes, sports, dinner, chapel, exhaustion, and bed. My friends and I have become very close, but Ben, Musso, and Peter give no hint that they miss their families. I don't show them I miss mine. The fast-paced semester requires a consistent effort from us, and though we have lost our freedom we grin and bear it. Math is the toughest subject for Peter and me, but Musso is brilliant at it and coaches us. He also helps us complete special work assignments, as he skipped a year when he joined the school and so is ahead of us academically.

Our orientation term soon ends, and since the school break will last for two months, ending in May, Dad comes to take me back to Loutolim.

"Summer is the peak season for fruit," he says. "Avozinha and your uncles will need your help and mine."

"Will I be able to help them with harvesting the fruit too?"

"Yes. But the fruit has to be picked and stored in a certain way. All boys in Goa learn this from a young age. You will have to learn how it is done. It's part of your heritage."

The next day I am already working. I help my uncles get baskets of fruit from their small plots of land: cashews, coconuts, lemons, and chikus. Some lemons will be pickled or made into chutney, the rest of the harvest will be sent to market or stored at home to await buyers from the village. Everything is stored in a large room at the back of my grandma's house. This room is used as a granary for the storage of rice and also houses the rats that come to partake of the feast after a good crop, not to mention the ubiquitous snakes that come to feast on the rodents.

Dad wants to make the most of the month before they return to Kenya. We squeeze in visits to more historical sites. Prominent village doctors and at least two Margao lawyers invite us to visit. I know Dad is trying to help me find a career direction before he goes and probably hopes I'll be inspired by meeting some of his successful friends.

But after being away for just a month at boarding school, some simple pleasures I used to enjoy are no longer as much fun. Before entering boarding school, I was dreading leaving my family and couldn't wait to be back at home again after the first term ended. Now that I'm back, though, the joy I used to feel just strolling along the beach with Linda and other kids, looking for empty bottles that might contain a message from pirates, picking shells and pieces of driftwood, and—most exciting of all—sending sand crabs rushing into their sanctuaries on the beach just don't seem like fun anymore. For the first time, I suddenly feel more grown-up.

The family holiday is coming to a close, and I feel a deep sense of foreboding, of uneasiness.

The eve of my family's departure for Kenya arrives. Linda has admitted that my staying in Goa is going to change her life too. Mom used to send me to accompany Linda to parties, now she is not sure who will go with her or if our parents will even allow her to go out on her own if nobody's there to take care of her.

Avozinho throws a big farewell lunch to which the whole clan is invited; the event is full of cheerful talk and laughter and remembering memorable holiday events. I pretend all this is not happening, and I feel angry at the thought of being left behind. I hear them talking, yet I am not able to follow the conversation. It has become background buzz, white noise.

I am brought back to the moment when Mom leans forward, placing her hand on my arm. She quietly whispers, "Please do not join the priesthood without first talking to us."

After lunch, she comes to me again. "Lando, keep this." She hands me an ample supply of pre-stamped envelopes and writing paper. I promise to write at least once a month and more often during holidays.

The next day at the docks, Mom says, "Promise me you will not touch cigarettes or alcohol. And keep away from the wrong kinds of people, even in school. The priests don't see everything that is going on."

We say our goodbyes. I cry. Everybody else does too.

My uncles and I wait until the ship is completely out of sight and even the black smoke from its chimney begins to disperse. Once in the taxi, emotional colour blindness overtakes me. The greens of the rice fields, the multicoloured bougainvillea, and the red hibiscus, dahlias, and roses have all turned grey. Where once snow-white egrets and orange-and-blue kingfishers flew, there are just blackbirds and crows—plenty of crows...cawing, cawing, cawing. The sky and its clouds have morphed into endless shades of grey. These same beautiful sights that made my heart soar in wonder at nature's bounty only a few months ago now seem drab and uninteresting.

That night in bed, for the first time in my life, I believe that I am truly on my own. I will turn eleven in a month's time. I have been left behind to fend for myself. I move my hand over my stomach, trying to find the knot I feel somewhere inside. There is a strange tightness in my throat.

It is unusual waking up with no immediate family around me, no little Joachim walking from room to room in the pre-dawn telling everyone it is nearly morning, yawning and stretching as he waits for someone to come play with him while everyone else is still in bed. The cock crows as usual, but the pack of monkeys has disappeared. Consu has not turned up for work, and the frail Fermina is in a dour mood, so I give up my ritual peep into the well.

"Lando, we are waiting for you," Uncle Armando says. As usual he is bursting with energy. Today is the day of the big cashew harvest.

<hr />

29: Dik-Dik

Because the first term was an introduction, I imagine that things will be different when we start the regular year in July.

But my friends and I are glad to be back in each other's company. We meet as often as we can. "Matata" is our code word, and we use Swahili words to confuse "the enemy," fellow students we want to poke fun at. We endure the crack-of-dawn cold showers, morning chapel, miserable breakfasts, tasteless lunches, and insipid dinners. We are desperately hungry all the time because the food is served in small portions, forcing us to forage for fruit and berries near the school grounds and putting us in direct competition with the birds, squirrels, and other small animals for their only food source.

Before I left Loutolim to return to Arpora, Avozinha had baked a special cake for my eleventh birthday, and I promised I would wait until the actual day to eat it. I keep my word, and on the day before my birthday I leave a note for my friends. "The Matata Four will meet at our usual place at 4:30 p.m. tomorrow." Our secret meeting place for my birthday party is the fallen coconut tree on the far side of the playing fields, well screened from prying eyes. We sit on the springy trunk, our legs dangling off the ground. Monsoon winds and rain the previous year must have blown the tall palm over, though part of its root ball is still in the ground, making it the perfect perch for lazy tree climbers like us. It is the monsoon season again, and the air is humid and heavy. Around us freshly sown sunken rice paddy fields are sprouting growth. Egrets cling to low shrubs and trees like snowy cotton puffs. Slender grey paddy herons stalk frogs, insects, flies, and anything that moves. Silhouettes of dark green palms define the horizon in every direction. Sunset is about two hours away. The heat of the afternoon has eased. Soon a calm, cool breeze will usher in the darkness of the night to a chorus of crickets and frogs chirping.

"Here, Lando, you have a slice first," Musso says. "I have worked out a 25 percent share for each." With mathematical precision, he has cut up the cake into four identical segments with mathematical precision. The home-baked fruitcake is scrumptious, albeit a bit dry from sitting in my room for more than a week while I waited for my birthday to arrive. But after the dreadful boarding school fare we've had to endure, we devour the cake heartily and don't complain a bit.

"Happy birthday, Lando," Musso says. "Have you changed your mind about boarding school?" He flexes his knees back and forth, the movement gently rocking our tree trunk perch.

"No! Definitely no. I'm planning to run away," I say. "Anyone want to join me?"

There is no response. It is too early to plan an escape. Yet, the loneliness has become intolerable. In all these weeks, I have received only one telegram from Dad, confirming that they arrived safely and miss me. I console myself that Mom had warned me that letters could take up to six weeks to arrive, since surface mail depends on unpredictable shipping schedules.

Fortunately for me, I find the love of my life, and it eases the loneliness.

Peter and I, trying to ease our hunger, routinely roam through a grove of trees behind the school. Sometimes we are lucky and find a mango or two, or wild berries in a thorny bush to tide us over between meals. But at the end of the season, the trees and shrubs have been plucked bare. We step cautiously, listening for the slither of a snake in the fallen leaves, but hear instead only the songs of birds, the rustle of leaves, and the crackling of small twigs underfoot.

Suddenly, Peter freezes in his tracks, signalling me to stop.

"Listen," he whispers, "can you hear something?"

I hear a gentle, squeaky whimper. We inch forward. I see it first: a baby squirrel in a nest of leaves, tucked into the crevice of a cashew tree. In Nairobi my friend Jeep and I often picked pick up fluffy chicks, baby pigeons, squirrels, and the like. Now I instinctively reach out, squeezing my palm through the opening and cupping it to scoop the tiny squirrel out. Its big round eyes are frightened.

"Snake! Snake!" Peter shouts, and I nearly drop my prize. He is jumping in a panic. "Snake! Lando! My heart is beating so fast—feel it. It was that thick," he says, holding up his index finger and thumb. "Orange-brown with black marks."

The three-foot-long snake had been on the tree trunk, stalking the squirrel, just as I was putting my hand into the nest. Peter's shouts sent it sliding away.

"You scared us both," I say, holding the squirrel cowering in my hand. "I bet its little heart is going *boom, boom, boom*." I hold the squirrel to my ear to hear its rapid heartbeat. "Feel its fur—see how soft it is."

"By the way, it's not an 'it' but a 'he,'" Peter announces. "So what are you going to call him?"

"It's the colour of a *dik-dik* in Kenya. I'll call him Dik-dik."

"I've never heard of a dik-dik. Is that a bird or something?"

"It's like a small deer," I tell him as I carefully place Dik-dik in the side pocket of my shorts. The squirrel seems instantly at home and stays content as we walk back to our dormitory.

"Lando," Peter says, "do you think it's cruel to take babies away from their nest?"

"Haven't we also been taken from our nests and stuck here?"

"I don't mean us taking Dik-dik away, but the snake," Peter says. "You are going to feed it, but the snake would have taken it from the nest and eaten it."

I agree, that would have been cruel.

Some of my classmates already have pet squirrels of their own and help me learn the basics of parenting them. Dik-dik responds quickly to my affection and to his training. He makes no big demands: all he wants is just a few crumbs of food daily and a cuddle. He is just like one of us.

Within three weeks Dik-dik can run all the way across my outstretched hands. He can move himself around the back of my neck and crawl down my back. Within a month or so, I can walk around the school campus with Dik-dik on my shoulder, just like Long John Silver and his parrot in Treasure Island. Dik-dik is beautiful at three months. His body is about four inches long with dark streaks along his tan sides; he has a big bushy tail and big black eyes. Little do I suspect those innocent eyes will create some matata for me.

Finally, some letters start arriving from home. They all miss me—Simba, too. He must miss the long walks down to Ainsworth Bridge. Mom writes that Jeep is very sad, pestering his dad to send him to boarding school. I think that is because he is an only son, like Jimmy in Kericho, and now he has no one to play with. Linda says there's no one to go with her to parties.

I write back, but I don't tell them what it is really like in boarding school. I don't want to worry them. What can they do from that distance anyway? It might have been easier if I could return to Avozinha's on weekends, but it is too far. Then I realize there is one way they could help.

"Please ask Dad to write to the school about increasing our food servings," I write again and again in my letters home. "Even a full extra poi at breakfast will make such a difference."

Meanwhile, I continue to send out my Matata Four notes to Peter, Ben, and Musso: "We meet at our secret location on…" And we now have an agenda for each meeting: to discuss my plan to make a getaway.

"But Lando, have you really got a plan?" Ben asks.

"Yes, I have. I'll follow my Uncle Orlando's itinerary when he left the seminary. It's serious. I'm not just talking about cutting class, I'm talking about leaving boarding school for good so I can start really living like my uncle did."

"Then I don't mind coming too," Musso says. "We'll probably have to put on fake beards and act older. Maybe use grown-up clothes. We can go to a big city like Bombay, and then to Aden or Singapore by ship." Musso always thinks out the operational details.

"My uncle was on his way to Brazil when he died," I tell him. "I will go to Rio de Janeiro. I will complete his trip for him. Maybe Uncle will even help us from Heaven."

"I would come too," Ben says. "Trouble is, Father Mendonça knows my family personally. My uncle studied with him at the seminary."

"I'm eleven now," I say. "I'm old enough to work and make decisions. My friends Abdul and Hardev in Kenya are both my age, and they already work in their fathers' shops."

"But who'll give us jobs?" Musso asks.

"I'll find a way," I say. "My folks have no idea how we suffer. I've been telling them how little food they give us here, and they haven't even tried to do anything about it yet."

We agree that the best time to disappear is when we are

returning from holidays after the next break. We will be stocked up with supplies. The school will think we are on our way back, our families will think we have plunged straight into work schoolwork, and that they have not heard from us because we're just too busy to write home. The four of us agree that we will do our best at our studies now so that the authorities do not suspect our plan. But what will I do about Dik-dik if we carry it out?

For me Dik-dik makes St. Joseph's bearable, but one day he gets me into deep matata. No pets are permitted in the classrooms, but those of us who have squirrels as pets feel we cannot keep them in their boxes in the dormitory all day. So every morning at breakfast, each owner puts aside a few crumbs of bread in an envelope to take into class. We have individual wooden desks with hinged lids that are our work surface when they are lowered. Under the lids we place our books, pens, pencils, erasers, pet squirrels, and bread-crumbs. The desks have a little hole about an inch and a half in diameter that is plugged when the ceramic inkwell is in place, thus preventing any squirrel escapes.

One morning I place Dik-dik into the desk as usual, spread the breadcrumbs, and add an extra treat: half a cashew nut crushed into tiny pieces. Dik-dik's big dark eyes radiate affection. I put the desk lid down just as Father Damien, our Latin teacher, walks into the room.

Latin is one of our most boring subjects. The older boys joke that Father Damien is celibate in both mind and body. Neither sports nor other extra-curricular activities seem to interest him. He lives for and loves only Latin.

"Good morning, class," he says as he gazes over his wire-rimmed spectacles. "Today we will continue with Latin grammar and syntax. We will review the four verb conjugations and five noun declensions, and then we can spend time on the irregular verbs."

The class gives a collective groan, which   he characteristi-cally ignores. Ben is summoned first to the blackboard. As the class drags on, I open the desk lid just a little. Dik-dik perks up. I quickly shut the lid. It makes a gentle thud.

"Lando, let's see what you remember from last week," Father Damien says. His keen ears have picked up the sound of my lid closing. I walk to the blackboard.

"Please write down the present indicative, active singular, and plural for the verb to love, amare," he says. I visualize a simple table I had prepared the previous day and start scribbling with the short piece of white chalk that he hands me: *amo, amas, amat, amamus, amatis, amant*....Then pandemonium breaks out!

When a class gets unbearably boring, which often happens, someone will quietly remove the ceramic inkwell if a squirrel is in residence. Then events usually take their own course. On this occasion it is my inkwell that's removed. Dik-dik, sitting on a pile of books, finds the chance of escape and freedom irresistible. In a flash, he is out. A hand reaches out to grab him; Dik-dik leaps across two desks and then to a desk in the row behind. My inkwell crashes to the floor, splattering ink. The class is enjoying it. Somebody removes another inkwell. Everyone is yelling and laughing. Eddie's inkwell is removed, and within seconds, Armando's too. Now there are four squirrels chasing each other and being chased around the room. We scramble to catch our own pets, or any squirrel for that matter. Boys who do not own pets do all they can to escalate the level of chaos.

Father Damien has learned early that the best way to resolve this kind of petty anarchy is to leave the room. He can always return later to exact a toll from the class. Experience had taught him that conjugating Latin verbs ad nauseam as punishment can tame the wildest spirits. He quietly slips away, closing the door behind him to contain the noise.

Eventually, the squirrels exhaust themselves and surrender; one by one they creep back into their respective desks. The broken pieces of ceramic are swept away, and the spilt ink from two shattered inkwells is mopped up. We wait silently for the classroom door to creak open again. When Father Damien reappears, retribution is not as severe as we feared. The class pays a collective price, staying late to complete the work, but considers the penalty worth it. For some months after, I harbour a suspicion that sooner or later retribution from Father Damien will still come my way. I am on my best behavior, and even Dik-dik cooperates.

In the meantime, as if my family senses my growing unease, the frequency of letters from home is on the rise.

30: A World Away

I am reorganizing my filing cabinet, a tin with a painted lid reading THE PEEK FREAN AND CO. BISCUIT WORKS. Founded 1866. Sometimes I am so hungry, I open it not for the letters but to sniff the sweet smell of the biscuits that once lived there briefly. It now holds letters from Mom and Dad—mainly from Mom. Dad usually only scribbles a few lines at the end of each of Mom's letters, and occasionally Linda will add her pearls of wisdom, most of which need figuring out because she is telling me about friends of hers at school whom I don't know at all, so I can never make head or tail of her stories.

When my family wished me goodbye before sailing back to Kenya in May 1950, Mom whispered a litany of don'ts quietly in my ear as she thrust a thick stack of stamped envelopes and writing paper at me. "Babush"—she still uses my baby name in times of stress—"Do not forget your family. Please write regularly." She was trying to hide her pain. Only then, for the very first time, did the reality strike home. I would soon be on my own, an ocean away from her. I could hardly speak, so I just nodded in agreement.

I recall the weeks passing by rapidly and a succession of letters from Mom filled with news of the family's return to Kenya and adjustments to life without me. Even Simba it seemed was behaving differently. My replies were brief. The novelty of boarding school combined with a rigorous program did not permit time for reflection or self-pity. Now as the extreme pre-monsoon heat singes its way into our bodies, I feel anger and frustration setting in. I resolve to start telling my family frankly what it is really like in boarding school.

Arpora, 23 June 1950

Dear Mom,

First, please do not call me Babush anymore! I am old enough now, and I would like everyone to call me Lando. I'm sorry I have not written for two weeks. I feel like a prisoner in Dad's old school. I miss you all and also Jeep, Mwangi, Ahmad, and my other friends. Does Jeep have a new friend? How's Simba? Who walks him?

Two weeks ago in chapel, we prayed to San Antonio for rain, and these prayers really worked. You may not believe me, but it was like a miracle. The monsoon rains started the next day, and they are terrible. They say this season of wet and sticky days and nights will be long. The fragrance of cashew, mango, and jackfruit that filled the air during your visit has gone. I smell only my wet socks and my damp clothes. Nothing dries with this rain. The rice paddy fields are flooded, but our rations at mealtimes are tiny. I am now always hungry. Please send food parcels if you can. Please share my news with Dad and Linda and the others. Please give a big hug to Fatima and Joachim.

> *Love to all,*
> *Your loving son, Lando*

Within two weeks another letter arrives from Mom. It seems our letters have crossed.

Plums Lane, 27 June 1950

Dear Lando,

Everyone here misses you. Are you eating well and keeping your clothes tidy? Jeep was around here yesterday. He seems really lost without your company. Don't be surprised if his dad sends him to Arpora too, although since he is an only son, I heard his mom say it will only be over her dead body. I know exactly how she feels, but of course I kept my mouth shut in front of Dad, who is working as hard as usual. Linda especially misses you, as she cannot go out to parties on her own. You were such good company for her. Fatima's birthday party was a happy occasion, except Joachim fell during one of the games and bruised his arm. He is already learning that games with little girls can be dangerous. Please write with your news, as we love hearing of everything that happens in your life. It must be great fun. You have not answered my questions in my last letter. Please write soon.

　　　Your loving mom, Anja

　　Guilt haunts me. I owe Mom at least two letters, although there is not much real news of interest to anyone in Nairobi, which now seems so far away.

Arpora, 21 July 1950

Dear Mom,
Sorry for this delay in replying to your two letters. We are very busy and always hungry at school. If I had remained at Dr. Ribeiro Goan School in Nairobi with my friends, one day I would have completed my Senior Cambridge Exam and trained as a taxidermist at the museum. I would then be able to support my self, stuffing birds and beasts for the rest of my life, and I would at least be happy.
I have already written to you about Dik-dik getting me into a little trouble, but he didn't mean to. Without him life here would be unbearable. Does Simba still have his regular weekend baths? We heard today that we will not have a holiday to celebrate India's Independence Day on August 15 because President Antonio Salazar in Portugal won't let us.

Dad, did you remember to write to Father Mendonça about increas-
ing our food rations? If you did, thank you. But if you forgot, please
write as soon as you can.

> *Love to you all,*
> *Your loving son, Lando*

Meanwhile, for our group of friends, school life continues to be hectic, with the added burden of the special classes in Portuguese, Latin, and Hindi still being required for students from abroad, like us. There are extracurricular activities and meetings of the Matata Four, and our Musso wins a place in the school junior football team.

Mom writes back to sympathize but encourages me to be pos-itive; she says time will fly and one day when I look back at my past I will find that these were the most enjoyable years of my life. She thinks Dad has already sent a note to Father Mendonça about adding another poi for breakfast. As I lie awake one night, I imagine my letters are like the ghosts of wronged souls that have come back to haunt Mom and Dad. I want them to know that boarding school life is not the paradise Dad remembers from his days in Arpora, nor does it resemble Jimmy's glowing description of his boarding school in Eldoret.

Arpora, 29 August 1950

Dear Mom and Dad,
I am enjoying classes more and learning new things, but I am not
sleeping much, as the coir mattress is lumpy, and it feels as if I am
lying on top of a tray of small rocks. We are issued two rough cotton
sheets per week and one towel. We have bedbugs in our dormitory.
Now the rains have brought hordes of mosquitoes, but we have no
mosquito nets. We have eleven cases of malaria in our sickroom.
The rest of us are dosed daily with bitter quinine tablets, which
make some boys vomit. Mr. Dias, our science teacher, said that,
all together, more people have died of malaria in these past hun-
dred years of Portuguese rule in Goa than during all the wars put

together since Vasco Da Gama first set foot in India in 1498. I asked Uncle Dominic about this when he came for a surprise visit last weekend. He said that the city of Old Goa was moved to Panjim because sanitation was so lax that garbage accumulated in and around the city. There were so many rats, it resulted in a fatal outbreak of bubonic plague. He had heard that after the move to Panjim, the government did not seal the open wells in Old Goa, and these have now become permanent breeding grounds for mosquitoes. Please tell Jeep and Ahmad about my life here, and please ask Linda to write soon. I miss everyone.

Your loving son, Lando

For the first time, Mom, who always replies immediately to my letters, takes some time in writing back. When her letter finally arrives, she appears to be increasingly upset at my news.

Plums Lane, 30 September 1950

My dear son Lando,

I am praying that you are well. Waiting for your letters is already so difficult, but reading your news and what you are trying to say between the lines is an even bigger torment. Dona Maria is also praying that God grants you the spiritual and emotional strength to cope. We sit in the veranda and analyze each of your letters. We imagine we are like the volunteers during the Second World War in Europe, when people would go into secret rooms and decode secret messages. So you see how your letters have changed our lives. My days seem to zigzag one way or another, depending on your news and on the choice of your words. I can even read between the lines, and of course as your mother I will always worry and imagine the worst. Sometimes what you don't say is even more painful than what you do say. Your dad may appear strict and insensitive, but he too misses you. It's just that he's so busy at work that he doesn't have enough time to write back to you. He only wants you to have a better life than he had. Please don't give up, as we love you and *are praying hard for you. Linda has promised to write soon. She is studying hard for some mock exams. You won't forget her birthday, will you?*

Jeep brought Simba an imitation bone for his sixth birthday! He is so sweet to remember these things. Please be careful, dear son. I worry about you so much.

With much love from us all, Your loving mom, Anja

Mom's letter takes me by surprise. Why does she haveto read between the lines?

What does she mean? I resolve to write more explicitly. I am beginning to feel a renewed anger toward Dad, anger that I cannot adequately repress, as Father Mendonça has do ne nothing about increasing our food rations and I am still hungry all the time. I decide I must be more explicit about our conditions in school.

Arpora, 20 November 1950

Dearest Mom and Dad,

I am sorry for not writing sooner. I am happy everyone is well in Nairobi. You asked for details about our meals. At lunch and din-ner, we are fed rice with part of the husk still on the grain. It is served with a watery mix of curry powder and ground fresh coco-nut, except on Sundays when the cook will add a large spoonful of fried onions in turmeric and cumin seeds mixed with soggy peas, okra, or spinach. I weigh less now than when I first arrived here. Mom, I remember you often begged Linda and me not to waste food and to think of the starving children in India. Finally, I know what it means. Now I am one of those starving children in Goa. Not just me; my friends are also hungry.

Last week there was an outbreak of amoebic dysentery at the school. Father Mendonça personally spoke about it at a full school assem-bly. He told us about the need to wash our hands every two hours. He said it's a very contagious disease, accompanied by severe stom-achache, diarrhea, fever, and blood or mucus in the stools, and we should immediately report to a staff member if we have these symptoms. I am okay, but my friend Peter is ill with continuous stomach pains. But it is not dysentery, so they will not admit him to the sickroom in case he spreads what he has to others who are already in there with other illnesses. His grandfather will come to take him home to their village doctor. I miss you all.

>With much love,
>Your loving son, Lando

The feast of Saint Francis Xavier is a four-day long holiday celebration throughout Goa and initiates the month of Christmas. I imagine what my friends in Nairobi will be doing over the holidays. It seems years since my first New Year's Eve dance. I can't imagine wearing my funny grey wool suit with the short trousers and braces in Goa. I will look like a clown who's arrived too early for carnival in February. I scribble a letter home for Christmas.

Arpora, 10 December 1950

Dear Mom and Dad,

I am writing early to wish you and Linda, Fatima, Joachim, Mwangi, Stephen, and Jeep, a beautiful Christmas and a very happy new year. Of course I will miss not being there.

By the way, please do not worry about me. Just pray that I will not catch anything. If for some reason I die while in boarding school, then ask Jeep to keep my crystal radio as a remembrance of our friendship—I will not need it in Heaven. You will find it in a Bata shoebox on the bottom shelf of the large wardrobe. Jimmy hasn't written yet as he had promised to do. I am sure he will most likely not want it back. Should I die at school, I wish to be buried in Loutolim by the chapel near Avozinha's house so she at least can visit my grave.

>*Your loving son, Lando*

It is late January. I am in the dormitory tidying the area around my bunk, a regular part of our Saturday morning routine, when Musso rushes in.

"Lando, there's a letter for you at the office," he says and falls into his bed, exhausted. I rush down one flight of stairs and race down the corridor, and I'm in the office within ninety seconds. I recognize Linda's writing on the envelope, and my heart beats faster. The letter is thicker than usual, and I sense it will be newsy. I want to be somewhere quiet and private so I can enjoy it all to myself. I walk through the arcade of the main school building, past the white marble bust of founder Robert Lyons, and out toward the sports field. In the filtered shade of a tamarind tree with only the ubiquitous crows for company, I open the letter. I have to smile at Linda's doodles and sketches around the edges. I realize how close the two of us were growing up and wish we had spent more time together.

Nairobi, 3 January 1951

Dear Lando,

It appears bedbugs have got inside your brain. How could you have forgotten my birthday in November? Can you believe I am now fourteen? Had I been less busy with exams, you would have heard from me earlier. But let me tell you, this was the worst Christmas we have had, and all because of you. Mom and Dad are worried about you. They decided to return home from the New Year's Eve dance at 2:30 a.m. instead of dancing until five in the morning. Of course I had to come home with them. It's your letters. Can't you write some good news, even if the stories are all fibs? Ever since we returned to Kenya from Goa, there has been tension in our house. Mom has become more agitated, and Dad is less calm. I think your letters are the problem. Mom recently heard from Aunty Leonore. Even she knows exactly when your letter arrives and what happens, because Uncle Patrick tells her everything. Dad first asks Uncle Patrick to cover for him at the cashier's counter, and then he sneaks off to the toilet to read your letter. When he returns he places the letter safely inside his jacket to bring to Mom, but as always he stops on his way home to buy her a gift. And I know this is true.

One night Dad brought home a bunch of fresh flowers, which he had not done before. Mom became suspicious and asked whether a letter from you had arrived. I remember she grabbed the letter, glanced at a few lines, and burst into tears. Within weeks another of your letters arrived. This time Dad came home with a box of imported chocolates. Mom burst into tears and left for the bedroom to read your letter. That night Dad ate a cold dinner. Fortunately, Fatima, Joachim, and I had already eaten dinner earlier. Mom knows that Dad's gifts are intended to calm her after bad news: the costlier the gift, the worse the news. Sometimes she will burst into tears at the sight of the gift even before reading your letter, only to reappear later with puffy eyes from crying. So what I want to ask of you, Lando, is this: please can you send only good news? We all love you and miss you, but I want you to understand that you are destroying the happiness in our home with your letters. Simba is sad, and I know if he could write, he would say so too. I may forgive you for not re-membering my birthday if you do not send any more bad news. You can at least promise me that!

Your loving sister, Linda

That is Linda's news. I fold it and put the letter away. I am taken aback by her comments. I reach back into my pocket and reread the letter. It's absurd that I am now treated as the culprit for their problems resulting from their decision to send me to boarding school. I will not reply immediately while I am upset. I drift down to the sports field. Musso is just finishing his training. We walk back to the dormitory.

"Why don't you write about your trip to Bombay with your uncle? Don't mention the school at all," Musso says.

"I suppose so. Maybe I'll wait till Saturday's game. That'll be good news."

Our school is playing against St. Britto's, and we are worried because they have a very strong team, but we will all be cheering for ours, which is stronger. I'm sure we will win.

Arpora, 25 January 1951

Dear Linda, Mom, and Dad,

I received Linda's letter, and because I am loaded with homework, I am writing one letter to you all with all my good news. We won Saturday's football game against St. Britto's! It was two goals each at half time and then nothing until the last minute, with only seconds to go for the last whistle. Then bam! St. Joseph's sent St. Britto's to hell with a sharp corner kick. I was hoarse cheering our team. You probably heard me even in Nairobi.

My trip to Bombay over the Christmas holidays with Uncle Dominic was great fun, as he is so knowledgeable. Did you know that kings and queens have arranged marriages just like the Goans? Uncle told me that in 1534 the Portuguese attacked Bombay and conquered the seven islands from the Muslim rulers, and the area came under Portuguese rule. According to Uncle, about 130 years later, in 1662, the Protestant King Charles II of England was told by the advisors to the royal court to fall in love immediately with the Portuguese princess, Catarina de Braganza, who was a Catholic like us. This was so that England could trade in ports where the Portuguese had control or influence.

King Charles's father did not take part in the discussions, since he'd been beheaded earlier by Oliver Cromwell. Catarina's father, King John IV, liked the idea.

He persuaded the princess that she should marry Charles II, and in return England would defend Portugal against Spain. In fact, King John was so happy about it that he gave all seven islands of Bombay and the city of Tangiers to the English king as a dowry. Uncle said it was rumoured that the princess wasn't very excited about the marriage, as she already had a secret boyfriend, so she did not attend the ceremony but was represented by a proxy (like my friend Musso's

Braz Menezes

father was represented by somebody else at his mother's wedding in Bombay). That is how Bombay fell into British hands. This knowledge will come in useful for me, as we will study British history next year. It is very late, so I must finish now. I will write again soon. Please spread my love to all.

The ever-loving Lando

It is difficult to be unhappy in Goa in February. The weather is perfect. The fragrance of cashew and other fruit blossoms is in the air. I remember the happy moments Linda and I had discovering Goa barely a year ago—it seems ages, as so much has happened since then. Meanwhile, three of our Matata Four have become camp followers wherever our fourth member, Musso, plays. This week St. Joseph's school once again beat Loyola School in Margao at football in the junior league. That makes us champions again. Father Mendonça seems very pleased. He was especially nice to Musso and me last week; perhaps he had heard we scored high marks in scripture class. Another letter arrives from Linda. It is not as thick as the last one.

Nairobi, 25 February 1951

Dear Lando,

That story about Princess Catarina and King Charles II and the dowry is so funny. Do you remember our safari when we were looking across the Rift Valley at Mt. Kilimanjaro? Dad told us that when England and Germany were dividing up East Africa in the late nineteenth century, Queen Victoria gave Mt. Kilimanjaro to her grandson, Kaiser Wilhelm, for a birthday present. The queen had said she already had Mt. Kenya and didn't need two mountains. Do you remember how Ahmad became angry and said, "These kaisers and queens and popes think they can replace God and do anything they like"? And then you saw those Kaburu men on horseback that you thought were cowboys?

Not much news here. Fatima has moved up to Class 3 in January and seems very happy. She's very serious about school and guards her stuff like a lioness. You wouldn't be able to steal her crayons as you did mine. Joachim will start in kindergarten in March. That's all for now. Please send us more happy stories. We love you.

Your loving big sister, Linda

I realize happy stories bring back happy letters. I reply immediately.

Arpora, 15 March 1951

Dear Linda,

That Rift Valley trip with all of us seems years ago. I feel happier now in Goa, especially after returning from my trip with Uncle. He took me to see the Colaba area of Bombay, where wealthy people live, and to the Gateway of India, where we sat on the steps and watched the movement in the harbour for some time. A notice on the wall explained that when India became independent in 1947, the last British ships left from that dock. Almost next door is the very posh Taj Palace Hotel, but we only walked into the lobby and through a corridor full of shops. Uncle said we couldn't afford to eat or drink anything there, so we went behind to the Green Hotel and had tea and pakoras. Later we walked through the gardens of the Prince of Wales Museum. We visited the actual luggage store where Uncle Orlando bought the black tin trunk that he gave to Dad. It is near the beautiful Victoria Terminus, which Uncle said is the biggest train station in India. We travelled around the city by bus, and twice in a horse-drawn carriage. That night we went to see Marine Drive, which is called the Queen's Necklace, for when the street lights come on the lamps look like a string of diamonds. We saw other areas that were very dark and dirty, with narrow streets full of garbage. These areas smelt very bad because they have open drains and no latrines. Worse, some people even keep buffaloes between the houses, and poor people have to drink the milk from the buffaloes kept in these squalid conditions. After this visit to Bombay, I realize how clean Goa is by comparison. It really was a very nice holiday. Please share this news. Tell Mom I will write soon with more happy news.

Your loving brother, Lando

I think my worst time is over. I am beginning to enjoy boarding school. We had a class outing to Calangute Beach last weekend. It was a long walk of two and a half hours, and we came back very tired. It is a beautiful beach, but in one area there were many people who came only to have sea leeches suck their blood to reduce their blood pressure. I could not bear to watch anything involving blood!

A week later Musso, Peter, Ben, and I are having supper one night when an older boy brings notes addressed only to Musso and me. Some other boys at adjacent tables also receive notes. I wonder what it can be, since it is the last week of March and soon we will break for two months. I open my handwritten note. I am invited on my return from holidays to "Tea on Sunday, 25 June, at the Residence (the Jesuit House) to explore ideas for the future. We will discuss, among other things, the subject of vocations." This is more good news I can send home.

Arpora, 27 March 1951

Dear Mom and Dad,

First some not so good news. You remember about the bedbug infestation? During the Christmas holidays, the school tried to clean up the dormitories. Now only two months later, the bugs have returned and brought their friends. They live between the planks and in the joints of the bed frame. At night these bugs will crawl out and suck the blood that is left in our skinny bodies. I can hear them burst, as their bellies are full of blood, and they get squished when we roll over in our sleep. In the morning there are intricate patterns in dried blood on the sheets. Maybe the school will do something about the bugs again during the coming holidays.

I also have some really good news. Musso and I have been chosen to attend the Fathers' residence in the first week after our return from Easter holidays to discuss vacations. I will tell you about it later when it happens. Do you know Dik-dik will be a year old in two months? I have saved some nuts for him, although I have been tempted to eat them myself, as I think my body is growing faster these days and I am always hungry. Did you know Dr. Salazar does not like the Goans who have moved to Bombay? We hear some of them have been meeting secretly and are talking of independence for Goa. The Indian government says it will close the borders with Goa. If the borders are shut, some boys are afraid they will not be able to return to their parents. Next week I will go to Avozinha's for our two-month-long summer holidays. We were together last year at this time. It seems such a long time ago. Please send me news of Mwangi and Simba, and please ask Linda to write again. I love you all.

     Your loving son, Lando

After dropping the letter in the postbox by the office, I return to the dormitory and organize my Peak Frean filing cabinet. It has filled up somewhat this year.

———•◆•———

31: On the Road to Perdition

A week later I'm back in Loutolim for the school holidays, travelling on the bus with a colleague returning to Raia, the village next door. I am looking forward to the slower pace of life than in school. However, as I arrive at the door, Avozinha is upset. From overhearing bits of the conversation on the balcão, I gather that misunderstandings between the mandukar, the foreman, and the labourers over harvesting fruit have become a full-blown conflict. The labourers will not take his instructions. April and May are the really busy months when the fruit harvest has to be collected, sorted, and distributed, so this work slowdown is very disruptive.

"Welcome back, Lando," my grandma says, giving me a distracted hug.

Moments later, she comes into my room, still looking upset. I have just put all my things away. "We need your help for tomorrow. Lando, will you please help your uncle Armando?"

"Of course, Avozinha," I say. Just that willingness to help makes her happy. I have no idea what is in store for me as Uncle Armando walks into the room, minutes later. He is now quite different from what he was when he scared us with ghost stories on our first night in Goa. He is a year older, and I am now an old-timer in Goa. I notice he has recently shaved the rough stubble on his face and has even had a haircut. I wonder what it is all about; perhaps he is looking to attract a girlfriend, but I am scared to ask.

"We will start very early tomorrow," he says, "but now we must go to Benaulim. You can come."

"Really? Are we going to the beach? I hear it is the best beach in Goa."

"Yes, come quickly or we'll be late. We'll go on the bike."

I skip down the steps and leap over the last two. However, within minutes, my excitement turns into near terror. Uncle leads me to the side of the house. Well hidden from view of the balcão is an almost new Royal Enfield 300 cc motorcycle. Uncle has had it for a day. He tells me tonight he has to decide if he will buy it.

"So are you going to, Uncle?"

"I cannot find the money," he says, "and Avozinha will not give me a loan, so this will be our first and last ride."

I do not like the emphasis on "last ride," but I climb onto the passenger seat and am soon clinging on for dear life. The hot air whooshes past as Uncle zooms on and off the concrete strips on the Loutolim-Margao road past Raia. He seems drunk with speed.

"Please slow down, Uncle!" I yell.

"Does Antonio ride faster than me?" he shouts above the noise of the engine and road bumps.

"You're the fastest I've been with," I shout back. I realize he is jealous of his older brother in Kenya. But Uncle Antonio would not risk our lives with such crazy driving.

Past Margao, road conditions change. He slows somewhat to take in all the sharp turns and bumps in the often-narrow roadway while I struggle to hold on and at the same time wipe off an accumulated layer of sandy dust from my face. Fortunately, without any goggles I have to keep my eyes shut, so I don't have to watch him taking those sharp, winding turns at breakneck speed. I can feel my heart thumping out its last beats as we turn off into a sandy lane through a coconut grove. Uncle has arranged to meet his friends at a beach shack.

The beach at Benaulim is the colour of sugar and so bright that to look at it in the late afternoon sunlight is almost painful. The noonday sun has left the sand hot. I kick off my shoes, skipping and running into the Arabian Sea. I splash water over my face and head, and then soak my feet while trying to regain my normal heart rate. I wonder what sort of deal will be made and what alternatives I have for getting home. For almost thirty minutes I sit at the water's edge watching the waves break along the shore and sweep back into the sea. The tide is running out. The beach is almost always completely deserted except for this popular shack, where liquor and freshly cooked meals are served well into the night. I wonder how my Uncle Armando's negotiations are going. He signals me to join them.

Jorge's Taverna is made of vertical poles dug deep into the sand, with horizontal rails and cross braces lashed together with rope. A light frame supports a roof and sides of palm fronds. At the back is a small bar counter, some shelves on the rear wall, and an opening into a partially enclosed kitchen, although most of the cooking is done in the open air on a brazier. Jorge, the owner, serves feni and other spirits, beer, and carbonated sodas.

Uncle Armando is with his friends. They seem happy, although I cannot tell if it is because a deal has been struck. I am afraid to ask. Uncle asks me if I am thirsty or hungry.

I would like to say, "I'm very frightened about whether we will get home alive." Instead I reply, "Both." His friends laugh. I slink to a vacant seat by his chair.

Uncle orders three grilled recheados—mackerel stuffed with a spicy sweet-and-sour masala mix of red chilies, garlic, ginger, and vinegar—a soda for me, and "another round of the same" for his friends.

A short while later come three platters of the grilled whole fish, lightly sprinkled with oil, and served with tomatoes and lettuce. My ample portion is cooked to perfection. For only a few minutes, it seems a new calm has arrived, for the only sound I hear is surf beating against shore; the men must be famished. Nearby I hear the distinct accent of East African Goans talking at the next table. They must be on their home leave.

"Would you like to try some feni?" Uncle Armando asks me. I am horrified. I had promised Mom never to touch alcohol.

"I must go to the toilet," I say to avoid an answer. Jorge points to a lone cubicle about thirty feet away, tucked among the coconut palms. The facility is no more than a hole in the ground, screened with mats of woven palm fronds on three sides, and a hand-painted board that reads, PUBLIC LATRINE. A palm mat screen covers the doorway. As I walk back, I notice the water supply is temporary and there is no piped service. Instead there's a big recycled forty-gallon oil drum to store water, raised on stilts with a tap on the side.

"Try this," Uncle says in a voice of authority, pushing a glass of feni toward me. "The Jesuits taught us Goans how to distill liquor more than four hundred years ago, so it can't be bad."

I look at the colourless liquid, not sure how to react; perhaps he is just entertaining his friends at my expense and it is only water. Uncle continues. "Tomorrow you will be my chief helper. We are responsible for all the cashew harvest. We must also supervise the preparation of feni. You should know what you are supervising."

Blood rushes to my face before I have even touched the glass: it is not the alcohol but the guilt that is causing the flush. Do I go against my better instincts and disobey Mom? Or do I openly disobey Uncle and shame him in front of his friends, who appear to be equally intoxicated? Either way I will be committing a sin, probably worth the same penance in Hail Marys doled out at Confession.

"Don't drink it all," Uncle says seriously. "Just smell it and taste only a bit, so you know what you are supervising."

I have this horrible feeling that maybe my uncle has had too much, and we still have to ride home together in the dark. He looks at his watch. "Avozinha will be angry that there will be nobody home for the rosary tonight."

Maybe he is not drunk after all. I remind myself we still have a nightmare motorcycle journey ahead. If I refuse and he gets angry and creates a scene, he might be tempted to terrorize me on the ride back.

I take the feni to my lips and sniff it. The fumes shoot to the top of my nose and clear my nasal passages, just like Vicks VapoRub, only much stronger. It reminds me of my brief stay a year ago at the Royal Portuguese Hospital in Ribander, a small town on the banks of the Mandovi River, halfway between Panjim and the abandoned city of Old Goa. It was almost the week before my parents returned to Kenya. I had my tonsils removed under an anaesthetic called chloroform. It was about 9:00 a.m. One moment I was inhaling deeply, but within seconds it was nightfall. When I woke up, Mom and Dad were still there, but my tonsils were gone.

I take a tiny sip. I have not tasted spirits before, so I cannot even compare it to anything. In seconds the blood rushes again to my face. A burning sensation grips my throat and the inside of my mouth. It is as though a deep groove is being etched in the inner lining of my throat. I can smell the feni again deep inside my nose; the fumes are rising from the inside. I am certain I am on the road to hell, just as Mom had warned me. I should never have been tempted to taste alcohol. I reach for a glass of water and flush my mouth, over and over, but the smell lingers on.

"Eat these. It'll take away the smell." One of Uncle's friends pushes a plate of crisply fried dry salt fish toward me, but it just superimposes a worse smell. I feel suddenly alone. All these people are enjoying seeing me slide down a slippery slope.

"Lando, you are like us now," one of Uncle's friends jokes. Uncle Armando stands up. He seems steady on his feet. I had heard that when you drink, your knees go weak and your head spins. In fact, I had seen a man stand up and fall after drinking at the beach shack.

I stand up cautiously, holding on to the edge of the table…so far so good…I take a step forward without holding on to anything. I take another step. Everything seems normal…I think. Perhaps I am exaggerating. I am okay. Suddenly, Uncle grabs my arm. I am so surprised, I nearly lose my balance but manage to steady myself.

"Thank you, Lando," Uncle Armando says. "I may have to lean on you. Shouldn't have had that last one."

From the corner of my eye, I can see the Enfield bike parked exactly where it was on our arrival.

"Shall we take a taxi home?" I ask, hoping that he won't remember that we rode in on a bike. It will be certain death riding home in the dark with no streetlights and him in that intoxicated condition.

"Yes, let's do that," he says.

The two men who were previously at the table with Uncle Armando are walking behind us. They are talking loudly in Portuguese and Konkani. They call out to Uncle. We stop and they embrace him as if they are old friends greeting each other warmly. They are happy too.

"Sorry it didn't work out," one says to Uncle. They embrace each other again. I feel such relief that the motorcycle deal fell through. I will have a chance to live another day.

As we approach the main road, a man shouts to us. The caminhao is approaching. We run. It will take us to Margao, where we will take another to Loutolim. I cannot relax. I wonder what Avozinha will say about the time. I know she will be very angry that we are back so late. God only knows how she will react if she smells the feni that still seems to hover around me. I certainly will not tell her anything about this evening.

All is quiet when we arrive home, except for the dogs, who bark madly at our safe return. We creep about by the light of the oil lamps and crawl into our beds. I include a couple of extra Hail Marys in my night prayers for the gift of an extended life.

I fall asleep, dreaming that I am gripping the handlebars of the motorbike tightly, towing my Uncle Armando, who is peacefully asleep in an ornate gold-trimmed over-sized bassinet lined with deep maroon velvet. We are drifting through puffs of cloud pulled by flocks of white paddy herons. Below us the greens of rice fields and fruit orchards form a quilt. Thousands of lights in red, orange, purple, yellow, and green flicker like distant Christmas lights. I steer closer and study them, careful not to wake Uncle up. They are not lights, but abundant fruit ready for harvesting.

32: The Cashew Harvest

In March and April, everyone is in a hurry to finish their chores before the monsoon rains begin so they can focus their energy on the harvest. As the daily temperatures start to soar higher and higher, the cashew trees compete with each other to see which one will bear the most fruit, and so be the first to be plucked by the fruit pickers. Up on the hillside behind Avozinha's home, and in small plots of land dotted among those of other landowners, fruit trees await the harvesting, each variety with its own timetable.

Today is a cashew harvest day for me.

"You will be in charge of this group," Uncle Armando tells me as we arrive at a collection point next to a simple distillery where the cashew apples will be turned into Avozinha's homemade feni.

He introduces me to the foreman's assistant. "Caetano will work with you. He understands Portuguese and some English, even if he doesn't respond. I'll be looking after two other areas. Remember, these are the things you must write down: the time, the names, and how many basketfuls they brought."

"And if I have questions?"

"Ask Caetano," Uncle says. "But even better, sort out the problem yourself, and later you can explain it to Avozinha." He hurries away.

Caetano shuffles around, organizing space to receive the brightly coloured cashew fruit on swollen deep brown stalks. From the busy chirping and warbles, I know we, in turn, are being supervised by bulbuls, wagtails, and other birds hidden in the trees that surround us. I keep a lookout for snakes and tread carefully. A paradise flycatcher almost runs into my face as it announces that the first batch of fruit has arrived. The foreman has assigned separate spots to the men and women now arriving in a constant stream. The basketfuls of ripe cashews are dumped on a cement slab.

Women separate the nuts from the fruit, which is then squeezed. It is mid-afternoon when Uncle Armando returns with the foreman. I hand him my notes. He checks with the foreman, and Caetano makes a quick calculation, pulls out a wad of banknotes from a cloth bag, and hands these to the foreman. The labourers line up and receive their wages.

"What happens to these nuts?" I point to the two large bamboo baskets packed to the brim with grey kidney-shaped seeds. At a signal from Uncle, Caetano lights a small fire with twigs, and drops a handful of nuts into the flames, which quickly flare up. A few minutes later, he pulls out the seeds and cracks them open, and a handful of roasted cashew nuts emerge. Caetano gives me some to taste. We all pop a few into our mouths.

"The quality has been good this year," Uncle says as he scribbles a note to Avozinha and hands it to the foreman. Two labourers lift a basket of nuts each, balance it on a small cloth pad on their heads, and march off down the hillside behind the foreman, who will report to my grandmother on the day's production.

I walk over to where the fruit is being processed.

"Drink." Caetano offers me a beaker of freshly squeezed sweet, tangy juice, which runs along the cement slab and drains into clay containers. "This fresh juice is called neero." As Caetano explains, it is an instant energy booster, so a little is kept to drink immediately. The rest is stored in large earthenware containers, where it ferments before it is distilled into urrack, the mildest of different grades of feni.

Uncle leaves Caetano in charge of the distilling, and we wander down another path. He has to pick up a bicycle wheel from a repairman in the village.

"When will the feni be ready for drinking?" I ask.

"You haven't become an alcoholic already, have you?" he asks seriously, but I realize he is joking. "Each batch will take two or three days. The urrack is boiled over and over; each boiling makes a stronger alcohol." Uncle smiles to himself.

"That sample I drank for the first time? Was it the strongest?"

"Nearly," he replies. "The strongest grade can light up a fire like gasoline."

"Is this where the Khunbis live?" I ask, referring to the aboriginal peoples. We are approaching a cluster of mud and stone huts in a clearing. I am happy to change the topic from feni. A group of children run toward us, shouting greetings in Konkani and laughing. They remind me of the little totos I saw playing by the clusters of huts as we travelled on safari to Nakuru, near Nairobi. Uncle Armando greets one of the women, who has just returned from picking cashews. She seems happy with her day's labour and is busy preparing the evening meal. I assume it is to feed some of those kids who greeted us. Another group of children from nearby huts come running to join the first group. Most kids have only vests or tops on, and some have a traditional string tied around their protruding bellies. We say goodbye and move on, with the kids following us and giggling happily.

"They mainly do the agricultural labourers jobs that we all depend on," Uncle says, "such as fruit picking and tilling the paddy fields."

I can't help thinking that at least here the landowners are not using prisoners as they do at the tea plantation in Kenya.

On my third week at Avozinha's, Uncle Dominic surprises us with an overnight visit from Panjim, where he works. He seems to be preoccupied with something and insists on spending almost all his time with me. We walk to the bank of the Zuari because Uncle says he wants to buy some freshly harvested oysters.

"Avozinha says you are a great help, Lando," he tells me. "I have seen the baskets of cashew nuts in the storeroom. It's been a good crop this year."

"It's fun, but what will happen to the nuts now?"

"Avozinha will sell them to a man from Margao, who'll pick them up. He will sell them to a large trader, who will take them to a factory where they will roast them, shell them, and pack them in metal cans for export to the rest of India and the world."

"I know those metal cans. We call them debbes in Kenya," I say. "You mean they might eat Avozinha's cashews in Nairobi?" I laugh. What a strangely thrilling idea!

But Uncle Dominic changes the subject abruptly, and lowers his voice. "I hear Armando has introduced you to feni."

I am startled. "Does Avozinha know?" I ask. If Uncle Dominic and my grandmother have already heard, how soon will it be before the news gets to Mom and Dad in Nairobi?

"No one knows besides Armando and me," he says. "Armando blurted it out by mistake, and when I questioned him he explained what happened."

"You won't write to Mom and Dad?" I plead.

"No. I just want you to be very careful," he says. "Armando can sometimes be very stupid. You are too young to start drinking alcohol."

After lunch, as Avozinha leaves for her siesta, Uncle Dominic asks me abruptly, "You are not going on vacation again, are you?"

"No. This is my vacation." I am puzzled by his question.

"Have the priests invited you to go on a vacation?" he asks.

"No. But some other boys and I have been invited to talk of vocations."

"Good. All is okay then." He departs for Panjim at once, leaving me even more intrigued about the purpose of his trip, and especially the question about my taking another vacation. The riddle is only resolved three weeks later on the eve of my return to St. Joseph's, when another long letter arrives from Linda.

Nairobi, 25 May 1951

My dear brother Lando,
Your letter of March 27 has driven everyone crazy. When your envelope arrived, Mom snatched it from Dad, ignoring his gift of chocolates. She read the letter quickly, dashed away to discuss it with Dona Maria, and angrily rushed back ten minutes later. Fortunately, Dad had discreetly left for his card-playing evening

at the club. Mom was convinced that you had suffered a nervous breakdown, and Dona Maria agreed with her. Your letter jumped from one topic to another: first you talked about your holiday with Uncle Dominic in Bombay, then about how the Jesuits invited you and your friend Musso to discuss vacations. You switched to General Salazar being angry with Goans plotting for independence from Portugal, and then you jumped back to your pet squirrel. Mom was convinced that you sound tired, and that St. Joseph's is proving to be too much for you. She kept muttering that what with your loneliness, your chronic hunger, being eaten alive by bedbugs, the sleepless nights, and your dear parents a continent away…how much more could anyone take?

It was Dona Maria's suggestion that Mom telegraph Uncle Dominic to ask about you. The next day Mom and I went down to the GPO, the general post office on Delamere Avenue. After many attempts, the Indian clerk in the telegraph office managed to send the telegram. Mom and I waited nervously for days to hear from Uncle Dominic. Finally, five and a half days later, Uncle's reply came. It simply said, "Lando is okay. Word is vocation. Repeat, vocation. Not vacation. Love. Dominic." Can you imagine how stupid we all felt, just because you carelessly used the word "vacation" instead of "vocation"? But seriously, Lando, I have this suspicion that you really may not be well and Uncle Dominic is hiding some information from us. So please be honest—have you gone crazy, or is the rest of our family slowly going mad? Please reply soon.

You loving sister (but not for long at this rate), Linda

I read and reread Linda's letter. How can I ask Uncle Armando if he thinks I'm crazy when I know he is almost a lunatic himself? I wish Mom wouldn't worry so much. Surely she could have known it was a spelling mistake, and instead of "vacation" I meant to write "vocation". If I knew what that was, I could try and explain it to them. I ask Uncle Armando.

"It's about what you do with your life, like if you become a doctor, a musician, or a baker, but as far as I know the Fathers generally push young boys to join the priesthood."

Not much use to me. I go to my room. I may just choose to stay forever in Goa and help Avozinha as my vocation. I like this life in Loutolim. Sossegade! What a welcome change from the frenzied pace at boarding school. No matata at all. But for now my holidays have run out. I will return to St. Joseph's in three days' time.

33: Three Fathers and Food

One Sunday in June, on a beautiful and unseasonably sunny afternoon, Musso and I walk the short distance from our dormitory to the priests' residence, located just outside the school grounds. Along with a few other students, we have been invited to share a meal with them, and we wonder what awaits us. An older boy told us over lunch that a discussion about vocation was something the priests did over food twice a year. We assumed he was joking about our state of perpetual hunger.

"It's about shaping your destiny," he said. "In any case, it's worth going, just for the food."

The house has a long veranda in front. A giant monstera plant, with its glossy large heart-shaped leaves, stands guard in a large clay pot at the top of the stairs, where a beaming Father Benedito greets us.

Some other boys arrive at the same time. As we are ushered into the dining room, Musso nudges me and points to a stern portrait of St. Ignatius Loyola, founder of the Society of Jesus, frowning down on us. Two long wooden benches, which once may have been pews salvaged from a church, line the long table; a solid armchair has been placed at each end.

I feel my eyes almost pop out of their sockets at the feast that has been laid out for us. Musso and I look at each other, then back at the table, and then again at each other. Here are traditional Goan homemade delicacies, reminding me of Christmas back home: they include *neureos*, *dodol*, mangoes, and papayas, as well as slices of fresh coconut and two platters of roasted cashews nuts, which have been placed on another table by the side. A brightly coloured sweet soda is served for a drink.

Father Benedito has placed himself at the head of the table. At the other end, Father Jacinto signals to us to move. Father Carlito has seated himself strategically in the centre of one of the benches. Father Benedito says a short prayer, and asks us to be seated. There are seven of us present, and like any well-trained Catholic school-boys, we almost cartwheel into place one after the other like a row of synchronized gymnasts, each of us swinging first one leg and then the other over the benches. Musso and I sit opposite each other.

We are encouraged by the three priests to "partake to the full of God's blessings." We instinctively interpret this as licence to gorge ourselves, as gluttony, it seems, is not a sin on this occasion. There is just the briefest hesitation as we calculate the order in which we will attack the delectable items of the banquet. Some food has to be consumed immediately. The homemade cakes and puddings will go fast, and in any case are difficult to carry away. Fruit and hard biscuits can be discreetly tucked away in one's shirt for eating later. We had got advice and tips from older boys, conditional on our showing appreciation for their coaching by sharing our smug-gled goodies when we return.

I catch Father Benedito glance at Father Jacinto and Father Carlito; a silent accord is reached, and the proceedings can com-mence. Across the table, Musso, seated on Father Carlito's right, has already packed something into his shirt, impressive as ever in his level of efficiency at everything he does; I think his dad's employer, Tanganyika Packers, will one day be proud of the next generation if Musso joins the company.

"Boys," Father Benedito says, "it is a special pleasure to have you here today to share in God's bounty with Father Jacinto, Father Carlito, and me." I see uniform panic on my colleagues' faces. We have only just started to do justice to the feast—surely the party is not coming to an end with speeches so soon?

Father Benedito continues. "You have each been selected because of the respect you have earned among your peers and your teachers. Your excellent performance in religious studies, coupled with your exemplary attendance record and assistance with chapel services, has not gone unnoticed."

I follow his glance around the room. Most boys keep eating, but he appears to have their partial attention. Father Carlito glances around the table, smiles, and interrupts.

"Please do not stop eating, but listen carefully, as some of you may have to respond to questions that Father Benedito and Father Jacinto and I wish to ask you." He looks directly at me. "Lando, are you happy at St. Joseph's?"

"Me?" I start to choke. I know this must be a trick question. Fortunately, Father Jacinto comes to my rescue. He reaches out and lightly taps my back. I had just stuffed a crunchy neuri, the size of a large samosa into my mouth, and for good measure a handful of fresh-roasted cashew nuts, like a load of ballast to help the neuri on its way to my overstuffed gullet.

"Aaahh…yeah…yeah…yes…Father," I start to answer.

Father Benedito interrupts with another comment. "Musso, Father Carlito tells me that you have been achieving the highest marks in your class for religious studies. Congratulations. Have you thought of devoting your life to the service of God?"

Confused and nervous, Musso turns his head to one side, expertly disgorging the contents of his mouth into his right palm while preserving the ejected sweets intact so they can be savoured later without wasting a single morsel. I wonder if this random questioning is just a way of reducing our gluttony by keeping us busy conversing on a range of topics between bites, chews, and swallows.

Even though Musso does not respond immediately, the ice

has been broken. Very quickly, the discussion is opened to all. It focuses on the issue of having a "vocation." This is the first time some of us have discussed vocations. We ask questions. Each priest contributes an insight, sometimes anecdotally but always objectively. Simply put, the purpose of the feast is to bring us together; the priests are interested to know if any of us have felt an "inner calling" to join the priesthood.

"You will know it when it happens," Father Benedito reassures us. "It will be a direct message from God to your inner soul. You do not have to discuss it in public, as it is a very personal decision for each one of us when it happens." He looks at each of us. "We have a special program supported by the Holy See in Rome to make sure that those selected to continue the work of God will receive all the financial assistance and benefits necessary so they can reach their academic goals without placing any undue burden on their families. Those blessed by God at such a young age can be transferred immediately to the seminary either at Rachol or Pilar to complete their secondary school."

A thought crosses my mind. Do the priests place pressure on us boys by depriving us of the simple necessities of life like food so we will be attracted to the seminary? A boy puts his hand up.

"Father, will our school records be transferred?"

"Yes, of course," Father Benedito replies. "In all cases you have already shown academic prowess of a high standard. We will arrange to transfer your individual records so that nothing is lost and your life undergoes the minimum of disruption."

Father Benedito seems satisfied that the message has been delivered. I have been watching him intently. From the types of questions asked, I have made a rough guess that a boy called Xavier (from the class above me), Musso, and I are being targeted as likely candidates for transfer to a seminary. Another thought crosses my mind. Perhaps Musso and I are more vulnerable. We are sufficiently helpless and isolated from our biological parents because of the great distance. Psychologically, we are already somewhat alienated and isolated, perhaps we are ready for adoption by another family, albeit a spiritual one—what is more, a family that eats very well.

Father Benedito glances at Father Jacinto and nods ever so slightly, indicating it is time to finish. We leave with bellies and shirts stuffed and with the added comfort of knowing that gluttony was openly aided and abetted by our confessors.

Musso and I veer away from the rest of the group, who are taking a shortcut to the dormitories. As we cross the veranda, I notice from the corner of my eye that a beaming Father Benedito is now standing away from the window in the living room, observing it all. He seems to have concluded that this has been a successful meeting.

Musso and I walk in silence along a raised paddy field embankment, across a coconut grove, and over to the fallen coconut palm, the favourite meeting spot for the Matata Four.

I break the silence. "What do you think, Musso? I know they want you. I was watching and listening to Father Carlito next to you. He knows you're homesick for Dar-es-Salaam."

"Funny! I could swear from your questions that you are definitely going to join the seminary," he says.

"Why?"

"Everybody knows you are determined to escape from St. Joseph's." He has already worked out the implications if we don't move. "I was thinking that if you move, then I would join you. That way we can do things together."

"Look at it another way," I say. "If we stay at St. Joseph's, then we have at least six more years; that is, if we manage to pass our exams every year. We are both eleven. Six more years means spending more than half our lifetime in this place."

"We might die here earlier from dysentery, malaria, or bedbugs."

"Malaria! You remember I told you about my uncle who died of malaria trekking across Africa on his way to Brazil?" I say. "What I was thinking is, I could join the seminary like he did, get trained, and then head off to Brazil. It is a Catholic country. They will have plenty of jobs. You may wish to come too."

"If we switch to the priesthood, we will still have to work hard to pass exams," Musso says. "I think the Jesuits are doing God's work, and they do a lot of good."

"You know, Musso, I've just remembered something," I say. "Mom had whispered to me before leaving Goa that I should not join the priesthood without asking her and Dad. So I will have to tell them first anyway."

"You're right. Me too. Our parents sent us here," Musso says. "We have to tell them we want a change. We'll just tell them we want to become priests and that's that. At least we will have their blessing."

"I don't know how my folks in Nairobi will react to my joining the priesthood, only to go off to Brazil."

"Let's face it. Even if we join the seminary without our parents' blessing, at least we'll never be hungry again," Musso says as he rubs his bloated belly. "The priests eat well, don't they? I've eaten enough for four days."

"But by tomorrow, my dear Musso, we'll be hungry again."

"Hey, Lando. We've forgotten something—have you felt anything yet? A calling? I know I have sometimes felt extra holy in chapel and pray for people whose names I remember from back home in Dar, but I'm not sure that counts." Musso is always the one to worry about the details.

"Mainly I have felt hungry for months," I say. "But also my dad wants me to decide on my future soon, so he will be happy if I make a decision. I do not want to be a doctor or lawyer, so this should do it for him. At least he'll stop worrying about me the whole time I'm away at school."

The next evening Musso and I meet and write almost identical letters to our families in Kenya and Tanganyika. He has decided that he too will go to Brazil after seminary.

Arpora, 28 June 1951

Dear Mom and Dad,

It happened yesterday. Musso and I were invited to a special after-noon with food, soda, and some prayers at the priests' residence. In the discussion they helped me understand special feelings that some of us have been experiencing recently. Before this meeting there was no explanation for these feelings. Even Musso has felt something like I have. Some other boys did too. I am convinced I have a vocation and must join the seminary immediately. God has selected me to become a priest and live well and look after poor people, and to stop them from committing sins and to pray for them when they do. And for those who don't improve, I must give them heavy penance until they learn to behave themselves.

After I am ordained I will be travelling to Brazil to complete Uncle Orlando's journey. The priests say that they will help us make all the transfers with the minimum of trouble to you and the other par-ents, but we need to get your blessing first. I know this decision will make you both very happy indeed, especially Dad. Reply soon, as this matter of transferring to the seminary at Rachol is now very urgent.

I love you all, and thank you for helping me finally discover my destiny.

> *Your loving son, Lando*

Musso and I make sure that our letters go out with the next post. We have no idea if they will change the course of history for us.

34: Adeus Goa

Musso and I sneak a glance from the dormitory as the khaki-clad postman walks away carrying our precious letters in a canvas satchel. Until this moment, transferring to the seminary felt as though God had intervened to take charge of our immediate future. But the devil has entered our heads and is not about to let go that easily; both Musso and I are struggling with guilt, anxiety, and fear. With the postman barely out of sight, we leave for the sports field, taking a shortcut through the main building.

"Musso, do you think we have made the right choice?" I ask. "I feel as if just by leaving St. Joseph's we are denying all the school has done for us this past year."

"Me too. I am suddenly feeling anxious about everything."

"I am scared of something going wrong now. What if the postman stops at a taverna and misses the mail connection? What if he misplaces his mailbag?"

"I was thinking that," Musso replies. "But are you sure we are betraying the school?"

"Of course we are betraying St. Joseph's and our friends by transferring to a seminary. Father Mendonça and the staff here are only carrying out their vocation—'transforming us rocks into polished diamonds,' as Dad used to say."

"Maybe we would have felt differently if we weren't always so hungry," Musso says. "Maybe if they had supervised the kitchen better, they'd know we boarders are perpetually starving. We would not have been driven to take desperate steps like joining the seminary if we weren't driven mad with constant hunger pangs."

My eye catches sight of the school's motto over the entrance. I grab Musso's sleeve to stop. "When my dad told me what our motto means, I didn't think anything. Now I think it is cruel: Cibaria Necessaria Sumite Et Abite—Take the necessary food and depart. Yet we are hungry most of the time, so how can we possibly be getting what is necessary to survive?"

"Ha, ha. It means here." Musso points to his head. "Feed your mind, Lando. Mind!"

We wait weeks for a reply from our parents. Nothing. The anxiety gives way to fear: fear of unknown, unintended consequences. Musso looks for someone to blame.

"Lando, none of this would have happened if the priests hadn't started it with that decadent high tea," he grumbles. "Now we are totally at the mercy of the Fathers, who can make whatever decision they like."

I have a different thought. "Musso, maybe Father Benedict, Father Jacinto, and Father Carlito were only interested in recruits for the seminary. Father Mendonça might prefer to have us stay at the school. They might start a big fight among themselves over what happens to us, and a decision will never be made. We'll be in limbo."

"You know the Swahili saying," Musso says. "'When elephants fight, it is the grass that suffers!' We are grass, Lando. Just grass!"

Another two weeks go by.

"Musso, could our letters have gone astray? Worse still, what if the office routinely intercepts letters sent to overseas parents?"

The stress is unbearable, even as we try to calm each other down. Another three weeks pass with no replies from Nairobi and Dar. Worse still, nobody at the school says anything about our selection. Meanwhile, Musso has started behaving strangely. He has become a recluse; he even avoids me. "Lando, I don't know what is happening. You remember how I broke down one day and admitted to you that I used to wet my bed in the early days?"

"But you have adjusted to the school by now, no?"

"Yes, Lando. But the bedwetting has returned."

"So what do you do?"

"What is there to do? I place my bath towel on the bed every night to soak the piss. It doesn't happen every night, though."

The next week Musso and I see even less of each other. Ben is now openly saying that he too has noticed that Musso is behaving oddly, and Peter says he thinks our Matata Four are disintegrating, but I cannot tell them what is worrying us. I focus instead on preparing plans for my escape from St. Joseph's, in case Dad says no to my idea of transferring to the seminary. Musso and I will go to Brazil, even if it means skipping school and seminary altogether. We will stow away on board a steamer at Bombay and find our way to Brazil from there. But I must plan the timing of my escape well, and we must first figure out how to get to Bombay.

Musso may have his own ideas, but I figure for me the ideal time will be on return from the next holiday break. A suitcase Consu has packed with my freshly cleaned and pressed laundry, and Avozinha's snacks for sustenance should be enough for a few days. I must convince Uncle Dominic that I can travel back to the school alone from the bus station in Panjim. I will argue that if I can supervise the production of feni, I can surely take the bus. I can then switch buses and head off to Murmugoa for Bombay— and then, freedom. By the time anybody in Kenya hears of it, I will be in Brazil with a new name and a disguise, maybe a beard and a handlebar moustache (as soon as I start to grow some hair on my face, that is). Of course, I will have to find a home for Dik-dik. I will share my plans with Musso and see what he says. My nights are increasingly sleepless.

A letter arrives from Nairobi; I immediately call Musso. He has received nothing yet. We go to our favourite meeting spot by the fallen coconut tree. I open the letter. My heart sinks. It is from Mom. It gives some news of Plums Lane and replies to an earlier letter. She says they haven't heard from me for a long time.

Another few days pass with no reply. I wake up, drag myself to class, and retire to bed, exhausted. Musso tells me he, too, is tired all the time. The sports master notices my already mediocre sports ability has reached a new low, and now I am feeling alone, rejected, abandoned, and completely isolated. Musso has also not heard from his folks at all for almost eight weeks. We speculate that perhaps a Japanese submarine or a German U-boat has sunk the Royal Mail steamer. But if another war had started, surely we would have heard about it, even in our backwater village of Arpora?

Every night I refine my plan of escape, but I am torn with indecision. How can I just run away without at least receiving one last letter from home and sending them one final reply to say farewell? I must explain to my parents why I chose to run away to a new life in Brazil, why I am determined and will complete the journey that my Uncle Orlando started many decades ago. I am still not sure who will adopt Dik-dik.

It is about 11:30 a.m. Saturday morning, so I am in my dormitory. We routinely clean the area around our bunk beds, sort out laundry, clean and polish shoes, and prepare for next week's classes. Everything is going badly today. Musso fainted at breakfast and had to be carried by two older boys to the sickroom. We will only know later if he is allowed visitors. I hope he doesn't snitch on me under the influence of fever, pain, or drugs; even if the authorities are upset and try to extract a confession from him, I hope he doesn't break down and reveal my plans.

The teakwood wall clock with the black Roman numerals chimes the half hour. I look up, as there is a commotion at the door and Peter bursts in, rushing toward me. He had been away at his grandfather's village, recovering from some unknown illness and has only been back about a month. He is out of breath, nervous, pale, and almost speechless. I grab him by the shoulders and guide him to the edge of my bed.

"Peter, sit here. Are you okay? Is something wrong?"

"Faff...Fath...Father Mendonça...he wants you now...in his office...right away," he stammers. "I mean immediately...now!"

I hold Peter's trembling hand to steady it; it feels clammy. My hand begins trembling in unison. It is my turn to feel the jitters. The worst of my fears has come true. I must be in deep trouble, as a lesser priest normally deals with misdemeanours at Saint Joseph's, with punishment always accompanied by a visit to the confessional for good measure. But it is Father Mendonça, the high priest among priests, who demands my presence in his study. Peter seems to have broken into a sweat and fainted, so I call to others in the dormitory to look after him, then rush to Father Mendonça.

I make the sign of the cross, grab my shoes, and straighten my shirt and shorts. Musso's pissing in bed is nothing compared to what I might do at any moment!

My mind is racing. Is my plan of escape now out in the open? Is Father Mendonça angry about another recent disturbance involving Dik-dik and some of his furry colleagues? Could the Vatican be requesting Musso's and my immediate transfer to Rome to study directly under the archbishop, having seen confidential copies of the padres' glowing evaluations of our catechumenal prowess?

From the anteroom to his office, I catch a glimpse of Father Mendonça sitting and chatting with Uncle Dominic. Oh my God! My heart sinks. I am to be expelled. Uncle sees me and walks out to greet me.

"Lando, aren't you ready yet?" He looks somewhat perturbed.

"Ready for what?"

He gestures for me to go into the office. "Come, Father Mendonça has been waiting for you."

Father Mendonça greets me with a warm smile and a handshake, without the slightest hint of the strict disciplinarian lurking within that body, and invites us to sit. The tension is unbearable; I can hear my heart pounding and wonder if he can hear it too. He moves the letter tray on his desk a couple of inches to the left, looks up, and launches into a little speech.

"Lando, your uncle has brought me a letter from your parents explaining that for family reasons you must return to Kenya immediately. This is sad news for us. I know your colleagues, the staff, and I will miss you. I have been informed often during this past year what an exemplary student you have been, and I know how St. Joseph's will be lessened by your absence."

I glance sideways at Uncle, who is proudly absorbing these words. I know of some hiccups in my academic work, but this is not the right moment to ruin a good story with the facts.

"Lando, as you know," Father Mendonça continues, "Father Benedict has selected you and your good friend Musso as two of our best candidates so far, destined for greater things."

Uncle Dominic is beaming, though I can't imagine what he is thinking. I glance quickly around the room. The framed portraits on three of four walls, His Holiness Pope Pius XII, President Antonio Salazar, and founder Robert Lyons, seem to agree with Father Mendonça's comments—probably the only time they agreed on anything.

"Your uncle tells me," Father Mendonça continues, "that you have been writing home often to say how happy you have been here at St. Joseph's this past year. For us that is the best way to attract new students—by word of mouth. I thank you and wish you all the best in your future. Please visit us often when you are again in Goa. Now you must go and collect your things and say goodbye to your friends, as I believe you will soon be on a steamer sailing back to Africa. Remember as you proceed on life's journey: God has a special plan for each one of us."

Father Mendonça stands up, walks over, and shakes hands, first with Uncle Dominic and then with me. "Lando, may God's blessings always be with you."

Within two hours I have my meagre belongings packed and I tidy the crumpled bedclothes where Peter had lain earlier. I hear Peter has been interned in the sickroom with a suspected inflamed appendix and is not allowed visitors. Meanwhile, Musso has been discharged by the matron and is helping round up our mutual friends to wish me goodbye.

"Please, Lando, let me adopt Dik-dik," Ben pleads, but I know that Ben is sometimes absentminded and will forget to feed him. Uncle Dominic, sensing my plight and not wanting to hurt Ben's feelings, loudly says that Avozinha is expecting Dik-dik. As Uncle

Dominic helps the driver lash my small metal trunk to a rather precarious roof rack, Musso comes running toward us and pulls me to one side. He is bursting with excitement.

"Lando! It worked!" He is clutching a blue airmail letter, and his eyes are moist. "My parents say they love me very much and can't wait to have me back. They are making arrangements for me to return to Dar-es-Salaam by September. I can't believe it!"

We hug. "Musso, please say goodbye to Peter," I say. "Please tell him to get well soon. We will come back and take him back to Africa, now that we are soon to be free!"

As we drive out of the school grounds, I feel my eyes welling with tears as the white marble bust of Robert Lyons stares resolutely ahead. "Thank you," I imagine myself saying to him. "Thank you for your vision, and now goodbye. Goodbye, Father Mendonça and all you wonderful teachers. More than anything, you have made me want to grow up faster and become independent. I have tried so hard to escape, and yet now it feels as if I am leaving my second home. Thank you."

Uncle Dominic chats to the driver in Konkani as we drive out of the school grounds. I am alone with my thoughts. Dik-dik is sitting on my shoulder taking in the sights. He has been in a car before when he accompanied me home during vacations. As I glance at the school one last time, I can't help wondering if I will ever see it again.

Uncle Dominic breaks into my thoughts. "So did you not hear directly from your parents before today?"

"Nothing," I reply. He hands me a crumpled air letter form to read, just like the one Musso had shown me. It is clear. Dad asks Uncle Dominic to immediately pay all outstanding bills to the school and take me home to Loutolim. Within a week I will board a steamer bound for Mombasa in the custody of Mr. Alberto Pinto, a senior civil servant in the Kenya Colonial Service, and his beloved Dona Pulquera, née Costa, whom I recall as an accomplished jitterbug dancer at the only New Year's Eve dance I ever attended. They are both on holiday in Goa. Their contact address is included. There is nothing that will give me a clue about what happened to my letter.

"I have already met the Pintos at the Hotel Mandovi in Panjim," Uncle says. "They seem like a very nice couple. You should enjoy the trip back to Kenya."

35: The Tree of Life

The taxi arrives at Avozinha's house at about 4:00 p.m. to a loud reception of barking dogs, which brings Consu out to investigate. Moments later Avozinha emerges on the balcão, obviously disturbed from her siesta.

"Lando, why are you back? Is something wrong?" She looks startled. Dik-dik jumps onto her shoulder, as she had fed him lovingly on previous vacations; he sniffs her face, seeming to kiss her on the cheek. Meanwhile, my hastily packed bag is freed from the ropes and rubber straps that kept it in place on the bumpy ride from Panjim. The driver will take Uncle Dominic back to the city tonight.

"Consu," Uncle Dominic says, "please can you give the driver something to eat?"

Uncle Armando and a priest come out onto the sunlit balcão. Uncle Armando seems surprised by my presence. He introduces the priest.

"This is Father Jerome. He is a friend of Father Thomaz and will be staying here until the renovations are complete at the priests' residence in Margao."

"I know St. Joseph's well," Father Jerome says. Since it is midterm, he seems to sense that something is afoot.

Uncle Dominic explains that he had not had the time to inform anyone of our plans. I can see Avozinha is upset at the news of my imminent departure for Kenya. She sends Uncle Armando to Margao to inform Avozinho and summon him to a farewell family lunch four days from now, on Sunday, the eve of my embarkation. Uncle Dominic soon leaves for Panjim. The normal evening routine of rosary, early dinner, and chat on the balcony goes on as usual. Uncle Armando reports on his return that my granddad is also shocked at my sudden change of plans.

"Lando, tomorrow we will be out all day," Avozinha says. "I must go with Uncle Armando to Verna at six in the morning. You want to come with me and walk along the hills?"

I hesitate. I remember it is an arduous walk. Father Jerome, seeing the dismay on my face, invites me to join him on his house visits. "But you must wear an altar boy's vestments and remain silent when we are with a parishioner."

"Thank you. That will be interesting," I say. I am excited at the prospect of seeing what priests do beyond saying Mass. At least I'll know what kind of a future Musso and I may have had awaiting us had we joined a seminary.

It is the evening of the second day of accompanying Father Jerome on his home visits. We are sitting on the balcão. It will be at least two hours before we expect to be summoned by Avozinha to rosary, and I sense that Father Jerome is relaxed and easy to talk to, judging by the way he patiently listened to and spoke with all of his parishioners. When he speaks, it is with the art of a professional storyteller. I think he may know the answer to something that has been bothering me.

"Father Jerome," I say. "These visits were very interesting. Those families that we visited yesterday and today all seemed so different from one another. Are all of them from a different caste, or are they all in the same caste as us?"

"You know about the caste system?" he asks, surprised.

"Not much, but I know two of my classmates at the Goan school in Nairobi had some problems as a result of caste. Because of their caste, they said their fathers could not join our club, and my dad would not be allowed in their club."

"Do you remember your Latin?" "Only what I learnt this year."

"The word casta is derived from castus. 'Caste' was first used by the Portuguese in the sixteenth century to describe the social system in India: the separation of people by their family occupation. It is a complex thing to explain. But you must remember we Catholics believe all persons are equal in the eyes of God."

"That's what Mom and Dad said. But Uncle Armando told me Catholic Goans have the same caste system as Hindus."

"Yes, he's partly right," Father Jerome replies. "Hindus have had four original castes and subdivisions of castes for thousands of years. If you were born into one caste, you could never move into another in this lifetime. The definitions were based on occupations and lineage and became part of the Hindu religion.

"It was the Hindu priestly class, called Brahmins, who wrote the rules for the others. The next made up of warrior chiefs, rulers, soldiers, and their families, were called Kshatrias; they were followed in order of rank by Vaisyas, who were traders, merchants, and farmers, and finally by the Sudras, or labourers. Right at the very, very bottom and far below all the other castes were the Dalits, or 'untouchables.' They did the dirtiest jobs, such as slaughtering animals, cleaning latrines, and so forth."

"But that was the Hindu system," I say. "How did we Catholics become part of it? Didn't our priests write our own rules just for us?"

"Not really. First there were the mass conversions by villages, led by the gaonkars, landowners from the communidade, who were afraid of losing their benefits. They influenced the rules and came mainly from the Brahmin class," Father Jerome explains. "In the early years of our Portuguese colonization, almost all of the priests came from Spain and Portugal. Later other religious orders came out to Goa, and more Europeans eventually came here too.

"With mass conversions and demand for more priests, the Church decided to add Goan priests but recruited only the converted Brahmin caste. To encourage them to come forward, Pope Gregory XV gave dispensation that allowed Brahmin converts to keep some of their traditional customs and to retain their Hindu social structure. The Church really had little option but to adapt and the converts wanted to hang on to their privileges. After that it was natural that a modified caste system remained, especially after the end of the Inquisition, and that's how we ended up with three main castes in Goa: the previous Hindu Brahmins are called the Bamons. The Kshatrias and the Vaisayas merged over time and are called Chardos, and the Sudras became known as Sudirs."

"That's very complicated."

"You asked me about caste." Father Jerome laughs. "Anyway, these days among Catholic Goans, caste issues are discussed mainly when marriages between families are likely. Sometimes land issues emerge, but that is becoming more rare."

"If this caste system is an evil thing, why is it not a mortal sin?"

"That's a good question. When Goan priests were first ordained, they were not accepted into the Catholic religious orders. Later when priests were recruited among the Chardos, these priests could not serve in village parishes dominated by the so-called upper classes like Saligao or Loutolim, as they would not have the respect of the Brahmin goankars. So there was even a caste system within the priesthood. It is a well-known fact that the Jesuits only recruited within the Brahmin class. It is difficult to see how the Church could have declared it a mortal sin while they were upholding their own caste system within the priesthood. It is bad, but it has proved quite difficult to root out for so many complex reasons—"

Consu suddenly appears at the door. I am relieved, as Father Jerome seems about to explain something even more complex. He holds his hand up to signal he still has something to say.

"Lando, our culture will evolve, and one day no one will have to think about caste anymore. Our culture has been shaped by forces beyond our control—by historical events, themselves shaped by the decisions leaders make. This reshaping of cultures I prefer to call 'the tree of life.' Just as when two families join and create another generation, we can trace their family tree, we can trace our tree of life when cultures fuse together." He looks toward Consu, smiling.

"Please come now. Avozinha is waiting to start the rosary," Consu says.

"Come, Lando." Father Jerome puts his arms around my shoulders. "I am glad you have developed such an interest in Goan history. If you stay long in Africa, it too will change and influence your Goan culture."

We stand up. Nightfall will be here soon. In the half-light of dusk, I see bats swirl into the grove of areca nut palms across from the house as we go in for our rosary, then supper and bed.

Sleep is slow coming, and the crickets and tree frogs seem extra loud tonight. My mind races with more than four hundred years of history compressed into two hours.

That night I have a dream. An armada of Portuguese caravels with big red crosses emblazoned on their square sails is sailing up the Mandovi River. Father Jerome, looking remarkably like St. Francis Xavier with a full beard, his short hair curling up the sides and a small circle shaved on top of his skull, is standing up proudly on the bow of the leading ship. His face, flushed from the wind, is glowing with a fervour such as I have not seen before. His rough brown cassock is blowing in the westerly breeze coming off the Arabian Sea. A heavy beaded rosary is strung around his neck, the cross low on his chest. In his right hand he holds a crucifix up high, and in his left a Bible. He is telling stories of his voyage to the Orient.

The next day is Sunday, and we are approaching the Igreja do Salvador do Mundo, the Saviour of the World Church in Loutolim. Avozinha insists that this is a special occasion since I am returning to Kenya, and all special occasions must be celebrated at the church instead of in her chapel. Father Jerome has joined us. He wants me to look at the architecture carefully. I had told him of my visit to Bombay with Uncle Dominic and of the interesting buildings there.

The Loutolim church entrance is set back, off a paved patio enclosed by whitewashed short stone piers separated by ornamental metal railings.

"Look at that magnificent façade," he says, pointing to the three-storey, ornate whitewashed front, "with the arched central doorway that we'll be going through."

"It is beautiful," I say. "But why are so many people using the side doors instead of going through the front doors of the church?"

"Those people come from families who have been using those side doors for generations." He smiles. "Did you forget my story about caste and creed and the tree of life?"

We enter through the main doorway, dip our fingertips into the holy water font, and follow Avozinha to one of the rows that's been reserved for our family over several generations. I notice the congregation seems to be in crowded clusters, yet with empty rows separating them from each other. We take our pew. Father Jerome answers my unasked question.

"Yes, sadly the caste system is still in place here," he whispers. "But one day we will finally do away with it, with the grace of God. Lando, please remember what I told you—we Catholics believe all persons are equal in the eyes of God."

During Mass I am distracted by memories of Kenya. We are not equal in a world run by humans. I think of our church reserving the front rows for white Catholics. I think of how the government has separated us by colour and race, how each one of us has been labelled and classified into groups and subgroups like the reptiles, zebras, and other animals on display in Dr. Leakey's Coryndon Museum. I feel guilty and confused. I don't know which is worse, the caste system or the colour bar and racial segregation.

Avozinha has prepared a grand farewell lunch for seven: two

grandparents, three uncles, Father Jerome, and me. Even Dik-dik will join us. He will nibble some nuts on the wide windowsill. Father Jerome says a prayer of thanksgiving, and lunch begins.

Avozinho looks at me over his thin-rimmed glasses. His eyes have a mischievous sparkle as Consu brings in a shallow platter of freshly shucked oysters.

"Just watch," he says. Uncle Armando leans over, picks up a bottle of Macieira brandy, and passes it over to Avozinho, who sprinkles it sparingly over the oysters, and carefully sets it alight. The blue-and-orange flames dance up off the platter, then die in a few seconds. He smiles proudly at the magic he has just performed and says, "Lando, have you tasted oysters cooked this way?"

"Brandy." Uncle Armando nudges me slyly with his elbow.

"Goans eat what they can grow or fish," Avozinho says to me. "The Jesuits brought us our religion, our printing presses, and taught us to make feni; the Portuguese brought us brandy and wine."

"And we taught ourselves how to eat well and to drink, and we taught all of them how to dance," Uncle Armando adds. Fortunately, Consu enters with another dish and saves me the need to comment.

Father Jerome keeps us chuckling with his stories and one-liners, while Avozinha plays the role of stage manager to Fermina and Consu, keeping them busy ferrying dishes and plates to and from the kitchen.

Avozinho monopolizes me. From that cold kids-must-be-seen-and-not-heard impression of eighteen months earlier, he has transformed himself into a kind, gentle, and affectionate figure.

"Tinto?" he asks, offering me a glass of red wine. I don't know where to look or turn. My uncles sit smugly. Father Jerome watches with an inscrutable expression.

"No thank you, Avozinho," I reply. "I haven't started drinking."

"Good! That's what I wanted to hear," he says. "A man must have strong discipline to know right from wrong. Don't be like this uncle of yours." He looks toward Uncle Armando, who seems unperturbed.

More food arrives. I am served curried frog legs that I think taste like chicken and many other delicacies that Avozinha wants me to taste so I remember Goan food. I find it ironic that I was driven to desperation to leave boarding school over near-famine conditions when I could have swallowed my pride and blurted out my problems to my Goan family earlier. We are about two-thirds of the way through lunch when Avozinho coughs discreetly. The uncles and Father Jerome go quiet, as if the chair has called the meeting to order.

"Each of you must now offer Lando advice to guide him in life in Africa," Avozinho says.

"Study hard for university," Uncle Dominic says. "Study medicine or science."

"Work hard and live well," Uncle Rafael joins in, turning to Uncle Armando.

"Become a businessman in Nairobi," Uncle Armando tells me. "There must be many Goans living there. I want to export feni from Goa." Everyone laughs.

"This boy of mine will ruin his life with alcohol," Avozinho says. I sense he feels very sad about Uncle Armando. "Your turn, Father Jerome."

Father Jerome looks at me. I notice his deep black eyes have turned serious. "Lando, I have known you for only a week, and I know you will do what you want to do with your life, but I have seen too many boys your age lose their direction in life when they are very young. Do not rush into anything, but take your time to weigh the consequences of your decisions carefully, and then be the best you can at whatever you choose to do."

He pauses; I don't know where he is going next with this homily and whether I will have to reply.

"Remember, St. Francis Xavier gave his life to improve the lives of the poor. God will have a plan for you too. The tree of life that nurtured you has been transplanted in a new land. Each sapling will send out its own roots and adapt in order to survive as it must. God bless you."

Father Jerome sits down. I can tell his comments are too philosophical for my uncles. They look to my grandma to provide some relief.

"I have patiently waited my turn," Avozinha says. "Lando, we don't know when and if you will return to Goa. This is your home and you are a Goan, so remember that always. Marry a good girl, have many children, and bring them back here to paradise."

"Thank you, Avo…Avozinha…Avozinho…and all of you for looking after me so well and teaching me so much in such a short time…" I feel my throat go dry, but in boarding school I learned not to show emotion, so I remain tight-lipped. "Thank you…and you, Father Jerome. You taught me so much and answered so many of my questions about the history of our Goan people in just a few days. I will carry the lessons I have learned from all of you with me for the rest of my life. Thank you."

Avozinho stands up. There is a scraping of chairs. Everyone retires for a siesta. I stretch my arm, and Dik-dik leaps onto it. I go into my room to do some last-minute packing, and I find it hard. I realize that I am part of this family as much as they are part of me. If events hadn't turned out the way they did, perhaps I could easily have settled here in Goa for the rest of my life.

I wonder whether Musso is okay and if Peter has been discharged from the sickroom. I open my case and remove the packing I have already done. I will reorganize everything. I pick up the letters from home that I had filed by date order, every one of which, on rereading, was so special. I miss my family in Kenya. I can't wait to see everyone again…and Simba, Jeep, Ahmad, Abdul, and Hardev. I wonder whether Saboti is still at the school near Thika, and if she will remember me.

———— • ————

Braz Menezes

36: Return to Kenya

The next day Father Jerome and my three uncles go with me to the Mormugao docks, where we meet Alberto Pinto and Dona Pulquera.

"Call me Alberto," he says, shaking my hand. He talks to me as an adult, and I warm up to him immediately. I can tell he was brought up with boarding school discipline. Dona Pulquera, on the other hand, pinches both my cheeks and tries to hug me, her eyes moist with affection. I instinctively step back. I am not yet ready for that sort of emotional relationship with a stranger. It was hard enough saying goodbye to Avozinha and Avozinho without letting my emotions get the better of me. And poor Dik-dik—just one more goodbye.

Two hours later, after choking goodbyes to my uncles, I walk aboard with Alberto and Dona Pulquera. The ship sounds its siren, the mooring ropes are released, the anchor is winched up, and we are sailing out of the harbour. I am bursting with so many thoughts, emotions, and memories of my months in Goa that I cannot separate one from the other. For now, I pretend they don't exist. Maybe tomorrow I will have time to reflect on my experiences calmly, but right now I am too happy and excited to be returning to the land of my birth.

The British India steamer SS *Amra* is a much newer ship than the one that brought me to Goa. My sensitive nose tells me immediately that there are no live goats or sheep onboard, but something else smells different. On the second day, Alberto and I join one of the regular small groups to tour the ship. The guide tells us that the ship has been converted to run on oil instead of coal, and the smell comes from the sulphur that's released when the oil is burned. But I am more interested in what's going on with the deck-class passengers; I wonder how many thousands are travelling on just bedrolls on the floor. When our group finally gets to visit the deck class, I find a different world from the one I visited briefly on the outward journey. They have bunk beds now, just like we had in boarding school, and private lockers. Behind the kitchen there is now refrigeration for the supplies, "including separate refrigeration compartments for halal meat for the Muslim passengers," the guide says.

I cannot believe the leap forward. Thoughts are racing through my mind. Yesterday, I lived in a world of four-hundred-year-old churches, prayers, feasts, and fasting; a world of pressure lamps, outrigger fishing boats, legends, and ghost stories. Suddenly, I am slicing through the Indian Ocean at ten or twelve knots per hour, with electric lights and all the modern comforts on board.

What is it that makes Dad yearn for the day he can retire back in Goa? How could he possibly go backwards and give up all this progress? Could I ever really live in Goa at that incredibly slow pace of life? Where do I belong, anyway?

Within twenty-four hours on board, the novelty and adventure of a trip on a modern steamer has gone. Now even the flying fish fail to hold my attention. I sense that familiar feeling of unrest returning. I am just eager to get back to Plums Lane to my family, Jeep, Simba, and the life I knew before I was sent away. Another thing is different on this journey. For the first time, I am treated as an adult; Dad has paid a full fare. No more kiddies' early supper for me. I join Alberto and Dona Pulquera's table of eight, with Walter, Luis, and Paulino, all civil servants, the latter two accompanied by their wives, who do not interrupt when the men are talking. I listen too. I am the fly on the wall trying to understand the adult world.

Every night the four men (who, one wife tells me, are sworn to secrecy about their jobs) discuss the day's harvest of rumours and gossip collected from fellow travellers. Topics range from civil service appointments, office politics, and the personal lives of Goan colleagues working in remote outposts of Kenya. Every night's menu includes anecdotes on the intrigues within the civil service appointments board. The most troubling is the rumour that many new prisons are going to be built in Kenya, and that old ones will be expanded. My mind goes back to those prisoners being used as cheap labour on the tea plantations in Kericho; I wonder if there is a labour shortage on white farms. I ask Alberto about it.

"There's a great deal of trouble," he says. "Strange things are happening on European farms. The Africans are creating serious matata for the Colonial Office." He drops his voice to a whisper. "I cannot talk about it here. Even these walls have ears."

When the wine flows, the men discuss all sorts of topics, some of which make Dona Pulquera's eyelids flutter, and the two wives blush profusely. I see eyelids fluttering and faces blushing all around the table now: the men are discussing whether the flesh of the coco de mer is an aphro— something, and whether it was the aroma of the ripe cashew or the Indian women that drove early Portuguese sailors and soldiers to insanity and intermarriage in Brazil, and why they imported the cashew tree to Goa.

37: Welcome Back, Karibu

Dawn is breaking as the SS Amra steers past the entrance into Mombasa's dhow harbour in Old Town, tucked away behind Fort Jesus. Our ship heads south around Mombasa Island and enters the Likoni Channel for the Port of Kilindini. My heart skips a beat; I am nearly home. A small boat aptly named Saint Christopher is waiting to greet us midstream. A pilot climbs aboard; he will guide us safely to our berthing dock. I can't wait to be on Kenyan soil again. The channel must have increased in length since I last sailed it—otherwise why is it taking so long to get there?

The sun is now fully up and ready to fry us for another day while we fret on deck watching and waiting. The ship approaches the dock cautiously. Crowds of people—well-wishers, merchants, and porters—wait to welcome loved ones and business associates. So many emotions well up inside me; I am frustrated that after ten days on this ship, I have to embark on yet another journey, travelling by train from here to Nairobi. I just want to get home quickly.

"Look over there, Lando!" Dona Pulquera says with a giggle. "Look at that man waving with both hands. He's so funny." I look.

"Landoo! Here, Lando!" Dad has come to meet me! My throat tightens; I feel my eyes tearing up. I am overcome with surprise and joy. I can't believe he has come all this way just to welcome me home. I fleetingly remember Father Jerome's words: "The tree of life that nurtured you has been transplanted in a new land and sent out roots. Each sapling must seek ways to adapt in order to survive."

Dona Pulquera tells me we'll have to go through customs and immigration before I can run to Dad. We descend the gangplank and walk the short distance to the customs shed. Everything at first seems so different from the dock in Goa, especially the sounds. Seagulls gracefully swirling overhead replace the thousands of crows frenetically cawing as they greeted us upon our arrival in Goa. People yelling, and the clanging of overhead cranes unloading cargo from the hold, replace the horns of cars and buses and the bicycle bells. Soon these sounds fade into background noise.

"Karibu. Welcome back," the immigration official greets us.

There are no problems with customs.

Dad is waiting. Never known for displays of emotion, he gives me a big long hug, the kind that reassures me he is happy—perhaps even relieved—that I am back. I imagine Mom has made his life unbearable for sending me away. I have done some thinking on the ship; I will not be easily manipulated again.

We say goodbye to the Pintos. Alberto extends a warm handshake. Dona Pulquera, in an unguarded moment, sweeps me into her ample bosom and plants a big lipstick-laden kiss on my cheek. I push away in horror, convinced I have been scarred for life, like those cattle I saw on the way to Kericho with brands burned into their hide.

We are booked into a small hotel near the Catholic cathedral and the Goan Institute, but Dad does not go to the GI that night. We just spend time walking around and talking. I want to hear about Nairobi and the rest of the family and my friends, but Dad wants to hear everything I did in Goa—it's as if he is jealous that I went to boarding school. I think that perhaps he should have gone instead of me, but of course I do not say anything. I am careful to omit any mention of my first encounter with feni on Benaulim Beach with Uncle Armando. I fall asleep that night, convinced that Dad's dream is still to retire to Goa as soon as he can, but I do not know what Mom will do if the rest of us do not want to return there. The anxiety does not prevent a deep sleep from overtaking me.

The next day we board the train for Nairobi, and suddenly I am reminded of the colour bar. In all the time spent in Goa, I was not aware of people living in neighbourhoods strictly based on the colour of their skin, or their religion. Catholics, Hindus, and Muslims lived happily together. Come to think of it, I do not remember seeing many Africans, except those in military uniform.

Dad and I take our places in the second class four-berth compartment, which we are sharing with Sokhi and Jeet, two Sikhs in their thirties. I feel happy at seeing Sikhs again. There were very few in Goa.

As the train pulls out of the station, a magnificent sunset casts a warm glow over the creek below as we rattle and rumble over the Makupa Causeway. I skip between the cabin and the corridor, unable to decide which view is more stupendous: the one across Tudor Creek with glimpses of the dhow harbour and its steep coral pink cliffs, or the changing one overlooking Kilindini Port and the oil storage farms and warehouses against the backdrop of a silvery-gold Likoni Creek.

"My grandfather helped to build this railway," Jeet says to me, pointing to Sokhi. "His father also. We both come from Jalandhar.

You know Punjab?"

"No. Just Goa."

"Goans are good sportsmen. Next month, the Goan Institute hockey team will compete against the Nairobi Sikh Union. Sokhi and I are on the team. Do you play hockey?" Jeet says.

"Not yet." I am ashamed to admit that my club is hopeless at sports compared to the Goan Institute, and that members of one club are restricted from joining the other club; the two clubs are such rivals that they can't even compete against each other in games.

About an hour later, Jeet, Sokhi, and I are standing in the corridor as the train pulls to a stop at Mazeras Station to take on water. A few Giriama tribesmen sit on the station platform, smoking, and watching the activity passing by. Young women, wearing very short white bulging skirts made of many layers of cotton strips, and others in a kitenge wrap, walk up and down the length of the train, offering baskets of fresh fruit for sale. Some sell *mandazis*, a bread popular on the coast. It is not totally dark yet, but when the girls with their large beaded necklaces and bracelets walk under the lampposts, I notice they are naked above the waist. They are beautiful with bright smiles and flashing teeth; their sweaty faces, shoulders, and naked breasts are like wet chocolate. I have not seen women's breasts before, and I don't know what to do or where to look. I look at Dad. He appears to be smiling but is looking away from the platform toward the compartment door. Sokhi and Jeet wave at the girls and call out greetings, so I do the same.

"Jambo." They giggle and wave back.

Soon the whistle sounds, and we are on our way again. I am a bit worried, since I have not forgotten the story of the man-eating lions of Tsavo. We pass in between stations: Mariakani, and Maji ya Chumbi, which Dad tells me means salt water in Swahili. I can't wait for the train to pass safely through Tsavo. The darkness comes quickly, raising my anxiety about those man-eating lions, and we are just talking about it when there is a knock on the door. I jump up, and Sokhi and Jeet burst out laughing.

"The lions don't knock before coming in," Jeet says. Dad smiles. The bedroll cabin attendant looks amused too. He lays out the four mattresses. I am very tired, but I'm determined to do a night watch for marauding lions, so I prop my pillow upright. As the night unfolds, I count the stops along the way. It is like counting sheep: Mackinnon Road…Voi…Manyani.

Jeet and Sokhi are talking. I hear them first, and when I open my eyes I see them. It is not a dream.

"Good morning," I say. "What time is it? Have we passed Tsavo?"

"Tsavo? It's about 4:30 a.m.," Jeet replies. "Yes, yes. Tsavo was many miles ago. Only four hours more before we arrive in Nairobi."

"Where are we?" I ask.

"Makindu. Here is the holy place for Sikhs. My grandfather built the *gurdwara*—our temple—the house for our holy book. You know Guru Granth Sahib?"

"No."

"It is our holy book," Jeet says. "I have seen your Catholic church, full of statues, pictures, and candles. In our gurdwara we have only the holy book."

"Here, all Sikhs and many Indian people will go to pray and return to the train shortly. You come with us?"

I look at Dad, who is asleep. I would have liked to go. "No thank you," I reply. "I won't wake Dad."

They leave the train. I see others passengers leave as well; the stationmaster, an Indian, is chatting to some of them on the platform. About ten minutes later, the train is on its way again.

I am excited about returning home and stand in the passageway waiting for daybreak. Outside, the grey landscape turns colour slowly, first to a pink and then rapidly to a vivid orange, as if a giant spray has dyed everything uniformly. A lighter sky emerges. Herds of zebra, giraffe, and other game barely look up as our train clatters and hisses across the Athi Plains. They stand still as if in a thanksgiving prayer. Another day has arrived, and like me they have escaped an attack by lions through the dark night.

My nose picks up the faint whiff of an abattoir and moments later, its foul smells. I know for certain we are almost home. We are approaching Athi River. I shut the compartment door for a few minutes while the train gets past this stretch before I come out again to breathe the fresh, crisp morning air of the grassland.

Nairobi is just ahead.

On the outskirts the rows of tiny houses for African employees of Kenya-Uganda Railways are neatly laid out, but the open spaces between the units are neglected. Putrid smells of open drains and decaying rubbish fill the air. The sight and the stench make me angry. I remember Goa was so clean, even where poor people lived.

Outside, totos run excitedly along the length of the train, waving and laughing. I wave back. I can see they are poor, but does nobody in the government see this? Maybe no one cares about the poor here also. I remember the trip with Uncle Dominic to Bombay. We were crossing a neighbourhood of shacks with open drains and the stench of sewage when he grew angry.

"Nobody cares about the poor," he said to me then. "Maybe now, with the British gone from India, there'll be nobody else to blame and the politicians will have to start improving the lives of these people. Thank God our streets in Goa are clean." I remember on my return to Goa that he was right.

Dad has come out into the corridor too. "This is going to be the future industrial area." He points to a vast area of flat open land. "Many of these old workshops, sheds, and stores belong to the railways. They'll all be torn down soon."

"How do you know, Dad?"

"Since you went away, Nairobi has become a city," Dad says, but I am too excited to listen to the rest of the explanation. We have arrived at the railway station!

The two first class cars, reserved exclusively for Europeans, are almost opposite the main entrance when the train finally pulls to a stop. Ahmad is waiting on the platform, his face brimming with happiness. He hugs me. "My wife Serena is here," he tells me glee-fully. "Her visa finally arrived, and she's just arrived from Karachi. Come, we must get your baggage."

Ahmad organizes everything. Soon we are in his taxi heading down Government Road. "I want to show Lando a surprise." We make a quick diversion into Delamere Avenue. Ahmad points to a new ten-storey building—Nairobi's highest.

"What you think, Lando?" Ahmad asks, excited.

"It's different from the other buildings. The windows are large," I say. "Nairobi seems small after the bustling city of Bombay, but there seem to be more people here on the streets now."

"Nowadays many African people are coming to the city to look for work," Ahmad says. "I speak with them every day at my taxi stand—you remember at Hardinge Street bus station? Kikuyus say the muzungus are planning to take more land for the new city council. In Limuru and Kiambu, they are preparing to fight for their land. There will be trouble soon."

We drive along Government Road, past the Norfolk Hotel on the right and the Kenya Police Headquarters on the left, and then, over Ainsworth Bridge and past the Coryndon Museum and the Goan Gymkhana. Ahmad makes a left turn into Kikuyu Road. The sign is still up at the Parklands Sports Club: Europeans Only. Not much has changed after all. We turn into Plums Lane. I feel I am looking through a wet windscreen, but it is not raining outside. Tears are streaming down from my eyes.

A big welcome awaits me. Mom is in tears.

Linda, Fatima, Joachim, Dona Maria, Anita, Hardev, and Abdul are all there. Mwangi Macharia and his young son Stephen stand to one side, waiting their turn to welcome me. We exchange big hugs and kisses. Simba's tail is wagging so furiously, I'm afraid it might even drop off. He welcomes me with sustained wet licks. He has put on weight without regular exercise.

We go indoors. Mom hands me a shawl-wrapped bundle, saying, "This is Niven, your new brother!" I am taken by surprise. The beautiful plump four-month-old gurgles, looks at me, turns away, takes another look at me, and tries to wriggle out of my arms. Fortunately, Mom is standing nearby and quickly scoops him into her arms.

"Brother? I…I didn't know about a baby brother," I mumble.

"I was surprised you never showed any curiosity after I wrote to you," Mom says.

"I don't remember. I—"

"Yes, she did," Linda says. "Mom thought you didn't write back about him on purpose because you thought maybe the baby was going to replace you. We were never sure what was happening to you, and if you were even coming back."

"The news was in the letter I wrote after we heard about the tea with the priests," Mom says.

"I'm sorry, Mom." That letter never arrived.

"Never mind now," Mom says. "Niven is here and so are you, and I am very happy." She hands the baby to the ayah.

"Was boarding school really like you described in your letters home?" Linda asks. "Bedbugs and all that?"

"My letters described my real life," I say. I look around. "Where's Jeep? Didn't he know I was returning home today?"

"Jeep's family has moved to America," Dad says. "We waited to tell you until after you got back. About three weeks ago, Jeep's father Marco announced that a US entry visa had come through, and his new employers wanted him immediately. They left a week later. They will be based for at least two years in Delaware at the insurance company's headquarters."

"Did he know I was coming back?"

"We told him as soon as we decided to bring you back," Dad says, "but we couldn't give you your specific arrival date until we secured your return passage. Sorry Jeep couldn't be here to welcome you. Thank God that Alberto and Dona Pulquera agreed to have you accompany them so you wouldn't have to make that long journey by yourself."

I instinctively wipe the lipstick off my cheek again at the mention of Dona Pulquera, though of course it is long gone. I had scrubbed my face clean as soon as I got a chance.

"Can I write to Jeep?" I ask.

"Yes. I'm sure he cannot wait to hear from you," Dad says. "He must be missing you very much too."

"Wait a few days. Settle down," Mom says. "You have your own room now."

Jeep's departure is one of several changes. One family of sub-lessees has already moved out. Dona Maria and her family will also move to company housing near Thika in a month. Dad and Mom have decided that with Niven's arrival and the other children growing fast, the family will occupy the entire house, even if it involves a financial sacrifice. I go to inspect my new room. At least I will have my own space and independence for once. I see a wire hanging out of the ceiling where the antenna sucked BBC News from out of the dark skies and fed my crystal set. Oh my God! I had offered that to Jeep as a gift when I thought I might die in boarding school.

"Dad, Mom, Linda! Did Jeep take the crystal radio after all?"

"No. It's still in the Bata shoebox where you left it." Mom replies.

Within days the euphoria that marks my homecoming evaporates. The realities of everyday life do not match my expectations of what I thought I was returning to. Dad has been given bigger responsibilities at work and is busier than ever, while Mom struggles bravely with household chores and the baby's demands despite having very little help at home, and even less money to cover the expenses of our growing family. We can hear Niven crying for Mom. It's nice to be sitting out on the veranda at Plums Lane again, chatting with Linda.

"That Niven can really yell when he's hungry otherwise he's so sweet," she says.

"Niven is not a saint's name," I say. "How can he behave like one? Whatever happened to the Goan tradition of naming babies after saints or wealthy relatives?"

"Times are changing. Hollywood is closer than Heaven. Dad took Mom to the cinema to see David Niven, and that's where they got his name."

We talk about other things. Linda tells me she has transferred to the newly constructed St. Theresa's High School by Eastleigh Aerodrome. The Dr. Ribeiro Goan School has been having big problems.

"I don't know what they are going to do about a school for you. I know Mom and Dad are worried, but Mom was convinced the seminary was not for you. She made life hell for Dad, and that's why you're back here." Linda leaves me to fetch something just as Mwangi walks in with fresh lemons from the garden.

"Bwana Lando, you are very thin," he says. "Have you not been eating food there?"

I laugh. If only he knew! "Mwangi, that place was like a prison. I worked all the time, but with very little food. How is your family? Stephen must be in school now?"

"Stephen is four years old now, but life is not good in our village, Bwana Lando. Bad men make problems for everyone—" He stops abruptly, as if remembering something, and goes into the kitchen.

I go to over to Simba, who has been tugging at his chain in the garden and yelping incessantly for attention. I rub his neck to calm him down. Now almost six years old and much heavier from lack of exercise, he is happy to restart our daily walks around the neighbourhood. Back from our outing a half hour later, I go to the peach tree by Jolly's grave. Jeep should have been here with me at this moment; I miss him so much, it hurts. Abdul and Hardev cannot fill that void. They are busier now with their families' businesses. In any case, I never really had the same rapport with them I had with Jeep. I feel lost and more alone than ever, surrounded by my family. The trip to Goa has expanded my world, but my world at Plums Lane has shrunk, and now a familiar but new restlessness grips me.

Perhaps I should have followed my instincts and joined the seminary. Eventually I would have found my way to Brazil so that I could complete Uncle Orlando's journey as I had planned to do before leaving for East Africa. Perhaps I should have stayed back in Goa until I could figure out a way to take Musso with me so that we could see the world together. It feels as though I have used up a whole lifetime already by following my dad's wishes. I thought doing what my parents wanted would make me happy too, but I just feel more alone than ever.

I nudge Simba, sprawled at my feet. "Up. I've got to go and sort out my life."

In my room I flop onto my bed. Then I sit up and fiddle with the radio. Nothing there, just whistles and scratches. I will try again at midnight when the signals are clear. The BBC will tell me what is happening in the world outside.

———•◆•———

Author's Note

Beyond the Cape—Connecting the dots of History

On an overcast day in 1487, crowds of well-wishers packed Belem—the docks of Lisbon—and lined the banks of the Tagus River to see Diaz set out to sea. The three-ship expedition followed the known and tested routes dictated by prevailing winds: sailing toward the Cape Verde islands, then south, periodically docking at small slave and gold-trading ports of the mainland in Mauritania, Guinea, the Gold Coast (Ghana), and on to the Kingdom of Kongo (mostly now in Angola) and the Golfo de Conceicão (now Walvis Bay), Namibia.

Prior to the fifteenth century, trade between Europe and Asia was primarily in the hands of Muslim merchants who monopolized the overland routes to the Mediterranean rim cities of North Africa, Spain, and Italy. Powerful Europeans sought to break this stranglehold and looked for alternative routes to the Orient—the source of spices, gold, gemstones, china, silks, and satins.

On February 3, 1488, the ships inadvertently landed in a wide bay now known as Mossel Bay. Diaz and his men were ecstatic. They had managed to cross the southernmost tip of the African continent. For them it must have been equivalent to the moon landing in 1969.

Ten years after Diaz's voyage, in 1497, Portugal's King John sent out another expedition to India, led by Vasco da Gama, which landed at Mossel Bay. A misunderstanding with the local inhabitants caused the short-tempered da Gama and crew to blast a few cannons—their preferred calling card—at their hosts and sail north, hugging the east coast of Africa. They arrived off Durban on Christmas Day and named the coast Natal (Portuguese for Christmas).

Da Gama was welcomed in the Maputo area (formally Lourenço Marques) but encountered trouble on Mozambique Island. The Portuguese were amazed to discover almost every port on the East African coast under the control of Arabs—sheiks and sultans with roots in the Arabian Gulf.

The coastal people were mainly Swahili of the Muslim faith, while the interior was inhabited by several competing and expanding African kingdoms, whose warring led to domestic slavery and the selling of subjugated peoples as slaves to the Arab, Persian, and Swahili merchants. Dhows crowded the small ports; trade in slaves, ivory, wood, and gold was brisk. Additionally, Indian and Arab traders brought goods and merchandise from India.

After a confrontation with the sultan of Mombasa on the Kenyan coast, da Gama found a receptive sultan in Malindi a few miles north. He negotiated the services of an expert sailor and navigator who guided the Portuguese to Calicut on the Malabar Coast in India. But the Hindu ruler, or *Zamorin*, was suspicious of Christians, and a fierce battle ensued, driving da Gama's ships out to sea. Nevertheless, the expedition finally made its way back to Malindi and eventually arrived in Portugal to a hero's welcome and royal acclaim.

Europe had found an alternative route to India! The discovery of a sea route around the southernmost point of the African continent would soon lead to forceful capture of foreign lands and the establishment of the first European colonies in India and East Asia.

The Portuguese king, hearing of the various confrontations and the lucrative trade on the East African coast, decided to act immediately. In 1500, he dispatched a large armada commanded by Admiral Alvaro Cabral. Cabral's specific mission was to sail around the Cape, occupy a strategic location at Sofala (a major gold-trading port on the east coast of Africa), and build an armed fortress to ensure a secure port of call for future Portuguese merchant ships. Diaz and a small squadron formed part of this fleet.

Cabral, however, had a hunch there might be a quicker way to the Indies. Exiting the estuary of the Tagus River, he decided to navigate in a southwesterly direction across the Atlantic, changing direction at Cape Verde. The armada eventually reached the hump of Brazil, where the crews went ashore. The local inhabitants were extremely generous, offering the seamen unrestrained hospitality: an abundance of fish, fowl, and fruits, and—it is said—the unabashed attentions of nubile, friendly women. Brazil's legendary reputation for hospitality was born.

Although the men were reluctant to leave, weather conditions in the South Atlantic required an urgent departure. They erected a simple chapel on the beach and said Mass. At noon the fleet set sail, heading toward the Cape of Good Hope, but within days a fierce cyclone had engulfed the expedition and many ships were lost, including Diaz's. His body was never recovered.

Cabral and his men managed temporary repairs in Mossel Bay and struggled across the Indian Ocean with what remained of the storm-ravaged fleet, eventually reaching Cochin. There he undertook urgent repairs, concluded trade deals with local rulers, loaded his remaining ships with spices, and sailed home. The Portugal–India trade route was finally established.

Da Gama's enthusiastic tales of his journey had the Portuguese throne salivating at the potential wealth that lay within reach. He returned to India on a second expedition in 1502 with a fleet of twenty-five ships and thousands of men, and a mega-load of cannons to facilitate negotiations. Their mission was to explore permanent arrangements with local rulers for access to ports and trade along the spice route of the continent's west coast, which linked to Ceylon (Sri Lanka) and Indonesia's "spice islands."

Da Gama's euphoric stories convinced the king that the fortune awaiting Portugal was beyond their wildest dreams. He spoke with awe about a city called Goa.

The king was aware that the likely forceful attack and plunder would go against the teachings of the Catholic Church. To placate the pope, he built a church and monastery in Lisbon in 1501 (now known as the Jerónimos Monastery). The monks offered confessions and even medical attention to the returning sailors as they came off their ships. They entered the confessionals from the outside, and only then were they free to enter the church and join their families. For the next century, this project would expand with massive donations from the profits of the spice trade and trade in ivory, gold, and slaves in Africa.

When the Portuguese arrived in India, the pepper ports of Kerala and the cotton ports of Gujarat were of prime importance, followed by Goa. Muslim rulers and traders occupied the trading port of Goa. Moneylenders greased the wheels of business. Turkish, Egyptian, Persian, and Arab dealers transported the finest horses, carpets, pearls, and other supplies to the Mughal emperors, maharajas, and other rulers of India through Goa. They took back spices, Oriental silks, and gemstones (especially diamonds) to Europe. Da Gama advised the throne that invading and occupying Goa would be the best option, but this would require money and a contingent of fighting men permanently stationed there. He had negotiated a deal with an exiled Hindu chieftain from Goa named Thimayya, and together they could oust Yusuf Adil Shah, the Muslim ruler of Bijapur and Goa.

The Portuguese admiral Afonso de Albuquerque led this mission in 1510, but Adil Shah was prepared. A fierce battle ensued, and Albuquerque and his fleet were chased out to sea, where they awaited naval reinforcements. In late November, Albuquerque attacked Goa again—this time with land support of about three hundred fighting men supplied by Thimayya. Adil Shah was dead. All Muslim males over the age of twelve who had not fled were slaughtered. Portuguese rule was established over the captured territory, and European saints were introduced to the Hindus and surviving female Muslim inhabitants.

In the name of the Portuguese king, exiled Hindus were permitted back into Goa, provided they obeyed the new laws and respected the Catholic religion. Traders were welcome. Taxes and fees were introduced. Almost overnight, Portugal dominated trade with India and the East. In fact, by 1542 the first Portuguese traders had already reached Japan. Goa became the epicentre of this trade. Travellers were euphoric in their accounts of its civic splendour and architectural heritage, which they claimed rivalled Lisbon in its beauty. "Whoever has seen Goa need not see Lisbon," they said.

In 1542, a young and zealous Jesuit, Francis Xavier, was sent to Goa to preach. He became totally shocked and disillusioned with aspects of Goan society. The Portuguese viceroy of Goa enjoyed absolute power, and Goa was too far away to be overseen by Lisbon. With the immense concentration of wealth from trade and commerce, and the incestuous, mutually beneficial relationship between the Church and the military, corruption was inevitable. Both institutions colluded with hand-picked Christian, Hindu, and Jewish brokers and operators. Corruption, extortion, and debauchery—all manner of sinful, anti-social behaviour—became the norm.

Three years later, Francis Xavier wrote to the king and asked for the Portuguese Inquisition to be extended to Goa. Almost twenty years later, the request was approved. It was formally instituted in 1561, lasting for more than two hundred years (until 1812). The Inquisition drastically transformed Goan society, forcefully ensuring Hindus and Muslims newly converted to Catholicism did not secretly revert to their original faiths.

Portuguese was decreed the official language. Mass conversions occurred, and a ban was placed on reading holy books from other religions. Temples and mosques were demolished, and traditional marriage rules and cultural practices (such as *sati*) and land rights were modified. Traditional music instruments were banned.

Ritual public hangings, burnings at the stake, and public shaming occurred, as well as personal torture and arbitrary imprisonment. Land transfers from wealthy landowners to the Church and officials of the Inquisition were commonplace and carried out without a proper legal basis or procedures.

For Goan converts to the Catholic faith, there were many positive outcomes. In 1556, the first printing press was introduced to India in Goa, facilitating the dissemination of European ideas in Goa and vice versa. Almost everyone learned to read Western music through singing hymns. Local composers and musicians rewrote their own songs and played Western music on Western instruments. The Goa Medical College, built in the late sixteenth century, was the first European hospital for Western medicine. The Jesuits even taught Goans to refine their homemade fermented brews into higher quality alcohol. Not surprisingly, Francis Xavier was canonized by Pope Gregory XV in 1622 and remains the patron saint of Goa to this day.

The "Christian Indian" that Catholic Goans now represented did not escape the attention of the British East India Company. This was a private trading company incorporated in London in 1600 and given a monopoly of trade with India. It offered jobs preferentially to Goans in its shipping and manufacturing as the industrial empire spread its tentacles across India and the Orient. The Dutch French and Danes also incorporated powerful trading companies throughout the East.

Portugal enjoyed a trading monopoly in Goa for almost a century, but its fortunes and Goa's took an abrupt turn for the worse when Portugal came under Spanish rule, and other northwestern European countries competed for the same routes and trading ports, or factories. The large trading corporations contracted pirates, brigands, and fighting mercenaries to protect their operations (an early form of outsourcing). The respective national navies were put at the disposal of the corporations when necessary to protect commercial interests.

During the Napoleonic Wars, Britain, which had already firmly established the Raj in India, temporarily occupied Goa from 1799 to 1817. The British believed that the Portuguese were too weak to prevent France from taking over their trading ports in India.

Convinced the Catholic Goans were lacking something, the British introduced the game of cricket.

After the Berlin Conference of 1884, Portugal's African territories were further curtailed. Their dream of a Portuguese Africa that stretched from Angola to Mozambique was sabotaged by Britain's dream, which aspired to spread its influence on all the territories from the Cape to Cairo. The seven European countries each awarded a piece of the African pie, embarked on colonizing their respective possessions. As Britain had already succeeded in legally stopping the slave trade in 1833 (though it continued in the United States and elsewhere for decades), some countries, notably Portugal, Germany, and South Africa, continued the use of forced labour. Others resorted to indentured labour, in which workers were contracted for a fee and predetermined period, to support colonization. For just such a purpose, Britain took thousands of Indians to East Africa to build the Kenya-Uganda railway in the 1890s.

By the twentieth century, both the Portuguese in Mozambique and Angola and the British in East Africa turned to Goa for their human resources needs. The Goans flocked to Africa. Like Portugal's size relative to Europe's, Goa is a tiny speck on the west coast of India. But the Goans always 'boxed above their weight' and left a proud legacy wherever they went.

In 1961 Portugal was driven out of Goa, after a rule that lasted four hundred and fifty years. All of British East Africa was independent by 1963.

In *More Matata-Love After the Mau Mau* – the second book of the Matata Trilogy, Lando takes readers through his adolescent years as he and the nation approach Kenya Independence in 1963. It is already available in print form and e-book formats.

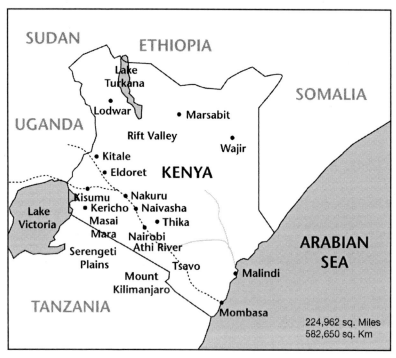

SUDAN

ETHIOPIA

Lake
Turkana

SOMALIA

Lodwar

Marsabit

UGANDA

Rift Valley

Wajir

Kitale

Eldoret

KENYA

Kisumu

Nakuru

Kericho

Naivasha

Lake
Victoria

Masai
Mara

Thika

Nairobi
Athi River

ARABIAN
SEA

Serengeti
Plains

Tsavo

Mount
Kilimanjaro

Malindi

TANZANIA

Mombasa

224,962 sq. Miles
582,650 sq. Km

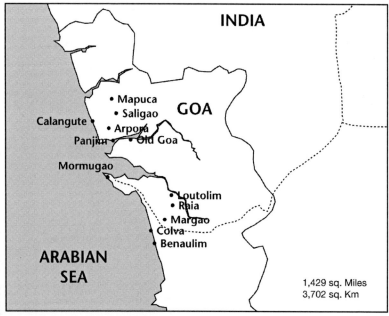

INDIA

Mapuca

Saligao

GOA

Calangute

Arpora

Panjim

Old Goa

Mormugao

Loutolim

Raia

Margao

Colva

Benaulim

ARABIAN
SEA

1,429 sq. Miles
3,702 sq. Km

Acknowledgement

I am deeply indebted to a number of people who helped me bring out *Beyond the Cape*, in a relatively short time, not least a couple of persons who named in this novel, although they wish to continue as fictional characters.

I must thank particularly Clifford Pereira, Historian, who made sure my impressionist sketch connecting four hundred years is factually accurate; and my Editor, Caroline Kaiser, who diligently plowed through the original 'colonial lingo' to bring the stories to an acceptable Canadian and USA standard of perfection. I am grateful also to my special ex-Kenyan residents and 'authentication' experts: Ann Barnes (Australia) and Dancy Mills (USA) who suggested which 'Kenyan-isms' should be put back in the text; and finally Yvonne Robertson (constantly flitting between ON and BC) who seemed to have edited everyone in sight, including me. However none of the above named must be held responsible for my shortcomings.

In turning this manuscript into a book I am particularly grateful to Jim Bisakowski (Book Interior Design), and Rudi Rodrigues (Design and art direction, Avatar Inc. Toronto).

During a period of solitary confinement, it was my partner, Norma Starkie, who supplied me with food rations and water - a thankless task!

And finally thank you my readers for your support in buying this book. Your comments will always be welcome at: beyondthecape@gmail.com

Braz Menezes, Toronto

Glossary

Swahili Words

Askari (s)	watchman, watchmen, policeman
Bwana	Sir
Dhow	Sailing vessel
duka	shop
dukawalla	(Indian) shopkeeper
Goan	person from Goa (Portuguese India) usually Roman Catholic
Kaburu	person, White Afrikaans (South African) Settler
Karibu	Welcome
Matata	Trouble
Mbwa Kali	Savage dog (warning sign)
Muzungu	White person, European
Ndio Bwana	Yes Sir
Parsee	person of Zoroastrian religious sect
toto	child, young boy, teenager
toto mkufa	child is dead

Change of Names
Countries and Cities

Abyssinia	Ethiopia
Bombay	Mumbai, India
Margao	Margaon, Goa
Panjim	Panaji, Goa
Lorenco Marques	Maputo, Mozambique

Street Names (Nairobi)

Ainsworth Bridge

Blenheim Road

Delamere Avenue

Government Road

Kikuyu Road

Whitehouse Road

Museum Hill Bridge

Muthithi Road

Kenyatta Avenue

Moi Avenue

Ojijo Road

Haille Selassie Avenue

The Coryndon Memorial Museum is now The Nairobi National Museum

About the Author

Braz Menezes was born in the British colony of Kenya to immigrant parents from Goa (Portuguese India). He attended racially-segregated schools to the age of seventeen, during which he also spent two years in a Jesuit-run boarding school in Goa. After receiving his degree in architecture, he travelled to Liverpool on a Royal Commonwealth Scholarship to study urban planning. He returned to Kenya in 1966. However, within a decade, deteriorating political conditions forced him to bring his family to Canada in 1976, from where he was recruited by the World Bank to continue his obsession--addressing urban development and poverty alleviation in metropolitan cities. Since returning to Canada he has been active on various causes to help make Canada and the world a better place.

His journey into the literary world did not start until after his return to Canada in 2004. He studied creative writing at George Brown College and later attended the mentorship program at Humber College.

His debut novel, Just Matata-Sin, Saints and Settlers (2011), and More Matata-Love after the Mau Mau (2013), were both published by Matata Books, Toronto. Menezes is currently working on the third book of the Matata Trilogy. His work has appeared previously in various anthologies since 2010.

The books* are available in both print and digital formats. So far they have attracted readers in the US, Canada, Britain, India, Kenya, France, Brazil, Australia, Sweden, and Greece, among others.

Just Matata - Sin, Saints and Settlers*
CAN ISBN: 978-0-9877963-0-1
USA ISBN-13: 978-1466360938 (CreateSpace-Assigned)

More Matata – Love After the Mau Mau*
CAN ISBN: 978-0-9877963-2-5
USA ISBN-13: 978-1480086339 (CreateSpace-Assigned)

What readers have said about Just Matata

The Bulletin—Toronto, ON *"The charm and strength of this book are the detailed descriptions of the rough-and-tumble world of Nairobi under British colonial rule, observed with a keen sense of humour.... Menezes is a sensitive writer with a great memory."*

Gerhard Fuerst—USA *"What in my estimation makes the historical novels of author Braz Menezes so fascinating is his lively and exciting narrative style, which entices the reader to follow him wherever he guides, lures, and leads you, often with a very delightful sense of* **self-deprecating humour."**

Jenny Sohst — Greece *"The story is told with tremendous empathy and understanding but still reveals the cruel divisions caused by race and economy.... Definitely a "must" even if you are not a Kenyan, Goan or otherwise."*

David Grant—Hong Kong *"I bought Braz Menezes' first book, Just Matata, on a whim, having been brought up in pre- and post-colonial Kenya. I was captivated by Braz's style of writing and his vivid portrayal of places and incidents seen through the eyes of a young Goan boy, born and living in Kenya . . . This book should resonate with anyone who was brought up in colonial Africa."*

John Auburn—Toronto, ON *"Braz Menezes, already a recognized writer, emerges here as an adept and highly skilled long-form storyteller as well... His true-to-life characters live it in their day-to-day activities. The circumstances of life in Goa and Kenya, and the realities of the times, the struggles in Africa between the disparate colonizers and native peoples and immigrant groups and developments in Europe . . . all unfold naturally as they touch the Goan community and the lives of the characters."*

Henriette Schalekamp-Roux – South Africa "*Matata did not only touch my emotions, but also my curiosity. Although I have a huge interest in world history my whole life, never knew about Portuguese Goa … I was touched so deeply by Menezes' book and could hardly believe it was his debut. Will take me quite some time to get back to reality. This story must be told and retold. The facts about segregation and unfairness towards humans hit me hard.*"

**What have you to say about
Beyond The Cape –Sin, Saints, Slaves, and Settlers?**